O9-BTI-939

ALSO BY STEPHEN HUNTER

Sniper's Honor

The Third Bullet

Soft Target

Dead Zero

I, Sniper

Night of Thunder

The 47th Samurai

American Gunfight (with John Bainbridge, Jr.)

Now Playing at the Valencia

Havana

Pale Horse Coming

Hot Springs

Time to Hunt

Black Light

Violent Screen: A Critic's 13 Years on the Front Lines of Movie Criticism

Dirty White Boys

Point of Impact

The Day Before Midnight

Target

The Spanish Gambit (Tapestry of Spies)

The Second Saladin

The Master Sniper

I,
RIPPER

A NOVEL

STEPHEN
HUNTER

SIMON & SCHUSTER
NEW YORK   LONDON   TORONTO   SYDNEY   NEW DELHI

Simon & Schuster
1230 Avenue of the Americas
New York, NY 10020

First Simon & Schuster hardcover edition May 2015

SIMON & SCHUSTER and colophon are registered trademarks of Simon & Schuster, Inc.

For information about special discounts for bulk purchases, please contact Simon & Schuster Special Sales at 1-866-506-1949 or business@simonandschuster.com.

The Simon & Schuster Speakers Bureau can bring authors to your live event. For more information or to book an event, contact the Simon & Schuster Speakers Bureau at 1-866-248-3049 or visit our website at www.simonspeakers.com.

Interior design by Claudia Martinez

Manufactured in the United States of America

10 9 8 7 6 5 4 3 2 1

Library of Congress Cataloging-in-Publication Data

Hunter, Stephen.
  I, Ripper : a novel / Stephen Hunter. — First Simon & Schuster hardcover edition.
    pages ; cm
  I. Title.
  PS3558.U494I2 2015
  813'.54—dc23

                                  2014043671

ISBN 978-1-4767-6485-6
ISBN 978-1-4767-6487-0 (ebook)

For the late Jay Carr

Wish you were with me on this one, buddy

Did he who made the lamb,
Make thee?

—WILLIAM BLAKE

1

TIGER, TIGER

CHAPTER ONE

The Diary

August 31, 1888

When I cut the woman's throat, her eyes betrayed not pain, not fear, but utter confusion. Truly, no creature can understand its own obliteration. Our expectation of death is real but highly theoretical until the moment is upon us and so it was with her.

She knew me but she didn't know me. I was of a type, and having survived on the streets for years, she'd cultivated the gift of reading for threat or profit, deciding in a second and then acting accordingly. I knew in an instant I'd passed beyond the adjudication and represented, in her narrow rat brain of what once was a mind, the profit, not the threat. She watched me approach, along a dark street that had subtended from a larger thoroughfare, with a kind of expectant resignation. She had no reason to fear, not because violence was rare here in Whitechapel (it was not), but because it was almost always affiliated with robbery, as strong-armed gang members from the Bessarabians or the Hoxton High Rips struck a woman down, yanked her purse free, and dashed away. Crime, for the working population of the streets, meant a snatch-purse with a cosh, and he would be some kind of brute, a sailor most likely, or a large Jew, German, or Irish Paddy with a face like squashed potato. I had none of these defining characteristics but appeared to be some member of a higher order, to suggest service in a household or some low retail position. I even had a smile, so composed was I, and she returned that smile in the dimness of a crescent moon and a far-off gaslight.

I know exactly what she expected; it was a transaction as ancient as the stones of Jerusalem, conducted not merely in quid but drachmas, kopeks, pesos, yen, francs, marks, gold pieces, silver pieces, even chunks of salt, pieces of meat, arrowheads.

"Want a tup, guv'nor?" she'd say.

"I do indeed, madam."

"It's a thruppence for what's below, a fourpenny for me mouth, darling. My, ain't you a handsome bloke."

"Jenny in Angel Alley offers her lips for a thruppence flat," I would dicker.

"Then off to Jenny in Angel Alley and her fine lips, and don't be bothering me."

"All right, we'll rut front to back. A thruppence."

"In advance."

"Suppose you run?"

"Ask 'em all, Sweetie don't run. She does what she's signed for, fair and square."

"So be it." And with that the coin would be granted, a niche against the wall found, the position assumed, the skirts lifted, and I was expected to position myself suchways and angled so as to achieve fast entry. The system was not designed to accommodate finesse. Of foreplay, naught. The act itself would resolve into some sliding, some bucking, some in-out–in-out in the wet suction of the woman's notch, and I'd have a small but reinvigorating event. I'd feel momentary bliss and step back.

"Thank you kindly, sir," she'd say, "and now Sweetie's off."

That would be that—except not this night.

If she had words to speak, she never spoke them, and that half-smile, in memory of a woman's comeliness, died on her lips.

With my left hand a blur, I clamped hard on her throat, seeing her pupils dilate like exploding suns—that to steady her for the next, which was contained in the strength and power of my stronger right hand. At full whip, I hit her hard with the belly of the blade, the speed, not any press or guidance on my own part, driving the keen edge perfectly and carrying it deep into her, sundering that which lay beneath, then curling around, following the flow of her neck. I hit my target, which Dr. Gray has labeled the inner carotid, shallowly approximated in the outer muscle of the neck, not even an inch deep. It was good Sheffield steel, full flat-ground to the butcher's preference, my thumb hooked under and hard against the bolster for stability. There was no noise.

She meant to step back and had more or less begun to sway in that direction when I hit her again, the same stroke driven by full muscle, with all the strength in my limb against it, and opened the second wound near perfect upon the first.

Blood does not appear immediately. It seems as if it takes the body a few seconds to realize it has been slain and that it has obligations to the laws of death. She stepped back, and I gripped her shoulder as if we were to waltz, and eased her down, as if she'd just fainted or grown a bit dizzy from too much punch before the spin upon the floor among the lads and lasses.

Meanwhile, the two streaks that marked my work reddened by degrees, but not much, until they each looked like a kind of unartful application of a cosmetic nature, some blur of powder or rouge or lipstick. Then a drip, then a drop, then a rivulet, each snaking slowly from the lip of the cut, leaving a track as it rushed down the tired old neck.

Sweetie—or whatever, I didn't know—was attempting to say something, but her larynx, though undamaged by the anatomical placement of my strikes, would not cooperate. Only low murmuring sounds came out, and her eyes locked all billiard-ball on infinity, though I do not believe she was yet medically dead, as she had not lost enough blood from her brain as yet.

That issue resolved itself in the next second. The severed artery realized what its interruption required and at that point, at last, begin to spurt massively. Torrent to gush to tidal wave, the blood erupted from the full length of each cut and obeyed gravity in its search for earth in which to lose itself. I laid her down, careful not to let the surge flow upon my hands, even though, like all gentlemen, I wore gloves. In the moonlight—there was a quarter moon above, not much but perhaps just a bit—the liquid was dead black. It had no red at all to it and was quite warm and had a kind of brass-penny stench, metallic, as it rose to meet my nostrils.

She lay supine, and her eyes finally rotated up into their sockets. If there was a moment of passing or an actual rattle, as the silly books claim, I missed it clean. She slid easily enough into a stillness so extreme it could not but be death.

CHAPTER TWO

Jeb's Memoir

This is a most peculiar volume. It consists largely of two manuscripts which I have entwined along a chronological axis. Each manuscript presents a certain point of view on a horrific series of incidents in the London of fall 1888. That is, twenty-four years ago. I have edited them against each other, so to speak, so that they form a continuous vantage on the material from its opposite sides, an inside story and an outside story. I do so for the sake of clarity, but also for the sake of story effect, and the conviction that everything I write must entertain.

The first narrative—you have just tasted a sample—is that of a figure known to the world as "Jack the Ripper." This individual famously murdered at least five women in the Whitechapel section of the East End of London between August 31 and November 9 of that year. The deaths were not pretty. Simple arterial cutting did not appease Jack. He gave vent to a beast inside of him and made a butcher's festival of the carcasses he had just created. I believe somewhere in police files are photographs of his handiwork; only those of steel stomach should look upon them. His descriptions in prose match the photos.

I have let Jack's words stand as he wrote them, and if he defied the laws of the Bible, civilization, the bar, and good taste, you can be certain that as a writer he has no inhibitions. Thus I warn the casual: Make peace now with descriptions of a horrific nature or pass elsewhere.

If you persevere, I promise you shall know all that is to be known about Jack. Who he was, how he selected, operated, and escaped the largest dragnet the Metropolitan Police have ever constructed, and defied the best detectives England has ever produced. Moreover, you will believe in the authenticity of these words, as I will demonstrate how I came to have possession of Jack's pages, which he kept religiously. Finally, I shall illuminate the most mysterious element of the entire affair, that of motive.

If this portends grimness, I also promise as a counterweight that most romantic of conceits, a hero. There is one, indeed, although not I. Far from it, alas. A fellow does appear (eventually) to apply intellect in understanding Jack, ingenuity in tracking him, resilience in resisting him, and courage in confronting him. It is worth the wait to encounter this stalwart individual and learn that such men exist outside the pages of penny dreadfuls.

I have also included four letters written by a young Welsh woman who walked the streets of Whitechapel as an "unfortunate" and was, as were so many, subject to fear of the monster Jack. They offer a perspective on events otherwise lacking from the two prime narratives, which are filled with masculine ideas and concepts. Since this was a campaign directed entirely at women, it is appropriate that a female voice should be added. You will see, in the narrative, how I came to obtain these items.

Why have I waited twenty-four years to put this construction together? That is a fair question. It deserves a fair answer. To begin, the issue of maturity—my own—must be addressed. I was unaware of how callow I was. Lacking experience and discrimination, I was easily fooled, easily led, prey to attributes that turned out to be shallow themselves, such as wit, beauty, some undefinable electricity of personality. This force may be as ephemeral as the random set of a jaw or shade of eye; it may be found in the words of a man to whom words come easily; it may or may not be linked to deeper intelligence simply by the random fall of inherited traits, which, after all, left us with both a nobility and a royalty, and we've seen how well that has worked out!

So I was ill prepared to deal with that which befell me, and I lurched along brokenly and blindly. That I survived my one meeting with Jack was high fortune, believe me, and had nothing to do with heroism, as I am not a heroic man in either my own comportment or my dreams of an ideal. I do not worship the soldier, the wrestler, the cavalryman (this Churchill is a bounder, up to no good, believe me), or even this new thing, an aviator, who serves only to proclaim the stupidity of mankind and the lethality of gravity. I didn't know what I was then, which means I was nothing; now I know, and it is from this promontory that I at last can survey these events.

So: I was shallow, industrious, grotesquely charming, smart on politics (ignorant, I must add, of women, whom I then didn't and still don't understand), indefatigable, and hungry for the fame and success that I thought were mine by inheritance of a superior being. The fellow Galton, Darwin's cousin, has written at length about those of us of "superior" being and orientation, and even if I hadn't read him yet, I intuitively grasped his meaning. There is a German chap as well, whose name I could never hope to spell, who also had a formal belief in the superman. On top of that, I had an incredibly fertile motivation: I had to escape my loathsome mother, on whose stipend I lived, under whose gables I dwelt, and whose disgust and disappointment I felt on a daily basis, even as I did my best to repay the wicked old lady in kind.

There is another issue beyond my simple gaining of wisdom. It is my current ambition. I have in mind a certain project, which I believe to be of extraordinary value to my career. I cannot deny its allure. I am too vain and weak for such. But it draws upon the Jack business and what I know of it. It uses characters, situations, incidents, all manner of those behaviors deemed "realistic," which I must arrange, soothe, disguise, and cogitate.

Since so many cruel deaths were involved, I must ask myself: Do I have the right? And to answer that question, I must face again the Autumn of the Knife and reimagine it as exactly and honestly as I can. Thus this volume, as a part of the process to prepare and examine myself for the next step in my ambition.

But as I say, I will get to that when I get to that. As did I, you must earn that knowledge the hard way. It will be a fraught voyage. As the old maps used to say: Beware. There be monsters here.

CHAPTER THREE
The Diary

August 31, 1888 (cont'd)

———————

My work was not done. I could not halt myself any more at that moment than I could at any moment.

I pulled up her dress, not the whole thing but rather a section of it. I did not hack or flail. I was not indiscriminate or promiscuous in my movement. I had thought too long about this, and I meant to do it as I had planned, savor it for the pleasures it offered, and at the same time not attract attention by flamboyant action.

I quickly cut a gap in the twisted white cotton of whatever undergarment with which she shielded her body, finding it thinly milled, easily yielding to the press of blade, and the bare flesh itself was exposed. So sad, that flesh. Flaccid, undisciplined by musculature beneath, perhaps stretched by passage of a child or nine. It seemed to have fissures or signs of collapse already upon it, and was dead cold to touch. I placed the tip of my fine piece of Sheffield steel into it, put some muscle behind it, felt resistance, pushed harder, and finally skin and muscles and subcutaneous tissue yielded and the tip punctured, then slid in an inch or two. The sound of entry had a liquid tonality.

Now having the purchase and the angle, I pulled hard toward me, again using the belly of the blade against the woman, and felt it cut. The shaft of the knife produced exquisite sensations. I could actually imagine the subtle alteration in rhythm as the edge engaged differing resistance while at the same time each region of blade had a differing response to what lay before it. Thus the progress, with these two factors playing against each other, ran from the slippery, gristly, unstable coil of the small intestine, all loose and slobbery-like, the thinnest part of the blade more sensitive to the instability, until it became firm and meaty, as the cutwork descended to the stouter and lower end of the blade, stabilized by my pressure against the bolster, this last sensation as it interrupted the outer raiments of the body, the skin, the muscled underneath.

The blade made its pilgrim's progress through Sweetie's abdomen toward her notch, which I had no need to observe and left for other women on other nights. For now it was enough to watch as, in the blade's wake, a jagged, blackened crevice lay revealed to me as the two edges of the wound separated, yielding the structures below. There was no blood. She had already bled out; her heart, starved of fuel, had already ceased to beat, and so no pressure propelled internal fluids outward. It was just a raw wound, a hideous rent in the flesh that would have caused oceans of pain had anyone been home to notice them. It was a fine piece of handiwork, that. I felt some pride, for I had been curious about the yield of flesh to blade postmortem. Not neat, not a bit of it, just ripped and mangled—mutilated, one might say.

I put another one into her to pursue the strange delight it gave me and was equally pleased with the knife's work and my own skill and attention to detail. At this point the odors of elemental reality and extinction had produced sensual epistles. It was a mad stench of the metallic, from the copper-penny musk of the blood, to ordure from food alchemized until it became shit for expulsion at the further end of the coils, and finally to piss, which somehow, some way, had slopped across everything, as if I'd nicked a tube in one of my awkward strokes. I inhaled it greedily. Delicious, almost ambrosial. A cloud of dizziness filled my head, and I had half a sensation of swoon come across me.

Then some mad infant within commanded me to further desecration. I needed to puncture her more. Why? God in heaven knows. It was the music of the kill, commanding me to make the exquisite sensation of triumph and transcendence last a bit longer. Like a playful child, I pierced her seven or eight or more times, down until the pubic bone beneath the matted fur took the pleasure out of it, across, around the navel, which was settled in soft folds of flesh, over toward the far hip bone, whose hardness again diminished the fun of it all. Again, no blood from these ragged punctures, just a puffiness of abraded red skin where the flesh recoiled against the violation as the knife's point struck through it, then swelled into a kind of tiny little knot.

I wiped my blade on her clothes, feeling it come clean, and slipped it inside my frock coat, sliding it between my belt and my trousers, secured out of sight. I rose, rubbed my feet hard against the cobblestones, again to remove excess blood so that no hound could track me by footprint back to my lair. Then I looked upon the poor woman a last time.

She was neither beautiful nor ugly, just dead. Her pale face was serene in the snatch of moonglow, her eyes open but blank, as the pupils had disappeared. I wondered how common this might be and resolved to check for it the next time out and about. Her mouth was sloppy, her grim little teeth swaddled in a captured puddle of saliva. No dignity in the lady's sense attended Judy that night, not that the world would ever recognize, but to me she had a kind of beauty. She would meet the world soon and it would make of her what it would make, noticing or not depending on its whimsy, but it seemed as if right now, having pleased this customer fabulously, she was resting up for the next ordeal.

CHAPTER FOUR

Jeb's Memoir

I had advanced in my career to the point of being the intermittent substitute music critic for Mr. O'Connor's ambitious *Star*, an aggressive afternoon paper among the more than fifty that were trying to prevail in the incredibly competitive London newspaper market. It was a four-page broadsheet that was published six times a week. I liked its politics, which were liberal if much softer than my own, in that they favored the mugs of the lower classes over the prisses of the upper, and cast a snide eye on Queen Vicky's propensity to have a Tommy stick a bayonet in the guts of every yellow, brown, or black heathen who defied her. Thomas Power O'Connor, besides being Irish to the soles of his shoes, was a visionary, to be sure, wiring his building up to the telegraph for the absolute latest from any place in the empire, including far-off, desolate, forgotten Whitechapel, as we were about to see. He also had gotten us wired for the new-to-London telephone system, which connected the paper by instantaneous vocal transmission to its reporters in the press rooms of such places as Parliament, the Foreign Office, the Home Office, and most important, the Metropolitan Police HQ at Scotland Yard. He made war with the *Pall Mall Gazette*, the *Globe*, the *Evening Mail*, the *Evening Post*, and the *Evening News*. He seemed to be winning, too, leading them all in circulation with 125,000. His product was full of innovation—he ran maps and charts before anybody and broke up the dread long, dark columns of type with all kinds of space-creating devices, loved illustrations (and had a stable of quick-draw artists who could turn the news into an image in minutes), and embraced the power of the gigantic headline. He had converted from uncertain penmanship to the absolutism of the American Sholes & Glidden typewriters more vigorously than some of the sleepier rags, like the *Times*.

It happened that on that night, August 31, 1888, I had returned to the offices of the *Star* to hack out a two-hundred-word piece on that night's performance of a Beethoven sonata (No. 9 in A Minor, the "Kreutzer") by a pianist and violinist at the Adelphi named Miss Alice Turnbull and Rodney de Lyon Burrows. They are forgotten now by all but me.

I can even remember my leader: IT TAKES NERVE, I wrote in the all-caps face of the Sholes & Glidden typewriter, TO PLAY "SONATA FOR VIOLIN AND PIANO NO. 9 IN A MINOR" IN MODERATE TEMPO BECAUSE ALL OF THE MISSED NOTES AND HALF-KEYS STAND OUT LIKE A CARBUNCLE ON A COUNTESS'S PALE WHITE CHEEK-BONE.

It went on in that vein for a bit, pointing out that Miss Turnbull was forty but looked seventy and Mr. de Lyon Burrows was sixty-two but looked like a twenty-five-year-old—alas, one who had died and been embalmed by an apprentice, and so forth and so on for a few hundred prickly words.

I took my three flimsies to Mr. Massingale, the music and drama editor, who read them, hooked the grafs with his pencil, underlined for the linotype operators (notoriously literal of mind) all the caps that should be capitalized, crossed out three adjectives ("white"), and turned one intransitive verb transitive (with a snooty little sniff, I might add), then yelled "Copy down" and some youngster came by to grab the sheets, paste them together, then roll them up for insertion into a tube that would be inserted into the *Star*'s latest modernism, a pneumatic system that blasted the tubes down to Composing, two floors below, via air power in a trice.

"All right, Horn," he said, using a nickname derived from my nom de *Star*, as my own moniker would have impressed no one, "fine and dandy, as usual." He thought I was better than our number one fellow, as did everyone, but since I was not first in the queue, that was that.

"I'd like to hang by and read proof, do you mind, sir?"

"Suit yourself."

I went down to the tearoom, had a pot, read the *Times* and the new issue of *Blake's Compendium* (interesting piece on the coming collision between America and what remained of the old Spanish empire in the Caribbean), then returned to the city room. It was a huge space, well lit by coke gas, but as usual a chaotic mess covering a genius system. At various desks editors pored over flimsies, tightening, correcting, rewriting. Meanwhile, at others, reporters bent over their S&Gs, unleashing a steady clatter. Meanwhile, smoke drifted this way and that, for nearly everyone in the room had some sort of tobacco burning, and the lamps themselves seemed to produce a kind of vapor that coagulated all that ciggy smoke into a glutinous presence in the atmosphere.

I picked my way across the room, weaving in and out of alleys of desks and tornadoes of smoke, stepping around knots of gossiping reporters, all in coats and ties, for such was the tradition in those days, and approached the Music and Drama Desk. Massingale saw me and looked up from his work. Under his green eyeshade, his eyes expressed nothing as he pointed to a nest of galleys speared into place on a spike.

"Thank you, sir," I said.

"Hurry up; they're wanting us to close early tonight. Something's frying."

"Yes, sir," I said.

I pulled my galley proof off the spike, read, caught a few typographical errors, wondered again why my brilliant prose had yet to make me a household name, then turned the long sheet back to Massingale. But he wasn't paying attention. He was suddenly jacked to attention by the presence of a large man at his shoulder. This fellow had a beard that put the stingy ginger fur clinging to my jaw to shame, and the glow of a major general on a battlefield. He was surrounded by a committee of aides-de-camp, assistants, and errand boys, a whole retinue in obsequious quietude to his greatness. It took me a second to pull in the entire scene.

"Horn, is that it?"

"Yes, sir."

"Well, Mr. Horn," the powerful figure said, fixing me square in his glaring eyes, "you've left the hyphen out of de Lyon Burrows's name." He was holding my original flimsy.

"There is no hyphen in de Lyon Burrows's name," I said, "even if all the other papers in town put one in. They're idiots. I'm not."

He considered, then said, "You're right. I met the fellow at a party recently, and all he did was complain about that damned hyphen."

"You see, Mr. O'Connor," said Massingale, "he doesn't make mistakes."

"So you're persnickity about fact, eh?"

"I like to get fact right so that my overlords don't confuse me with the Irish, from whom I am but of whom I am not." I was always at labor to point out to all that I was Protestant, not Catholic, had no snout in the Irish republicanism trough, and considered myself English to the bone, in both education and politics.

It was intemperate, given O'Connor's heritage, but I never enjoyed playing mute in the presence of power. Still don't, in fact.

"Chip on the shoulder, eh? Good, that'll keep you going full-bang when another man might take a rest. And fast?"

"I wrote it in Pitman on the hansom back," I said. "It was merely a process of copying."

"He's very good with his Pitman. Maybe the best here," said Mr. Massingale. "Pitman" was the system of shorthand I had taught myself one recent summer in an attempt to improve myself.

"So, Horn, you're a bit frivolous, aren't you? The odd book review, mostly music, silly nonsense like that, eh?"

"I feel comfortable in that world."

"But you're comfortable on streets, in pubs, among coppers, thugs, and Judys? You're not some fey poof who falls apart outside Lady Dinkham's drawing room."

"I've studied boxing with Ned Corrigan and have a straight left that could knock a barn down, and you'll note me nose ain't broke yet," I said, adding a touch of brogue for emphasis. It was true, as all Irish-born learn the manly art at an early age or spend their lives among the girls.

"Fine. All right, 'Horn,' whatever your real name might be, I'm in a fix.

My night crime star, that damned Harry Dam, is cobbing with a floozy in a far beach town this week, and we just got a call from our fellow at Scotland Yard with news of a nice juicy murder in Whitechapel. Someone downed a Judy, with a butcher's knife, no less. I smell the blood of an English tart, fee-fi-fo-fart. So I want you to take a hansom, get out there before they move the body, snatch a look at it, find out who the unlucky gal is, and let me know if it's as much the meat-cutter's work as the fellow says. See what the coppers say. The Bobbies will talk; the detectives will play hard to get. Take it all down in your Pitman, then get back and hammer out a report. Henry Bright here, our news editor, will talk you through it. Can you do this?"

"It doesn't sound too terribly difficult."

The hansom dropped me there at about four-forty-five A.M., and I told the fellow it was worth half a quid if he'd wait, since I didn't want to have to look for another at that ungodly hour in a neighborhood known for coshes and Judys. My noggin was too delicate to enjoy a gnashing by a Russky sailor or some such.

Buck's Row was a kind of subshoot of White's Row, which was bigger and brighter, but just before the rail bridge over the tracks into Whitechapel Station, it divided into Buck's Row and Winthrop Street, both tiny and dark. I could see the coppers clustered around something down Buck's Row, itself a nondescript cobblestone thoroughfare of brick walls fronting warehouses, grim, shabby lines of cottages for the workingman, gates that locked off yards where, in daylight hours, I supposed wagoners would load goods of some sort or another—I really couldn't imagine what—for delivery. It was but twenty or so feet wide.

A bit of a crowd, maybe ten to twenty pilgrims in black hats and shapeless jackets, Jews, sailors, maybe a worker or two, maybe some Germans, stood around the cluster of coppers, and so, caution never being my nature, I blazed ahead. I pushed my way through the crowd and encountered a constable, who put up a broad hand to halt my progress. "Whoa, laddy. Not your business. Stay back."

"Press," I announced airily, expecting magic. "Horn, *Star*."

"*Star*! Now, what's a posh rag like that interested in a dead Judy?"

"We hear it's amusing. Come now, Constable, let me pass if you will."

"I hear Irish in the voice. I could lock you up on suspicion of being full of blarney and whiskey."

"I'm a teetote, if it matters. Let me see the inspector."

"Which inspector would that be, now?"

"Any inspector."

He laughed. "Good luck getting an inspector to talk to you, friend. All right, off you go, stand there with the other penny-a-liners."

I should have made a squawk at being linked to the freelance hyenas who alit on every crime in London and then sold notes to the various papers, but I didn't. Instead, I pushed by and joined a gaggle of disreputable-looking chaps who'd been channeled to the side and yet were closer to the action than the citizens. "So what's the rub, mates?" I asked.

Fiercely competitive, they scowled at me, looked me up and down, noted my brown tweed suit and felt slouch hat and country walking shoes, and decided in a second they didn't like me.

"You ain't one of us, guv'nor," a fellow finally said, "so why'n't you use use your fancy airs to talk to an inspector."

The holy grail of the whole frenzy seemed to be acknowledgment by an inspector, which would represent something akin to a papal audience.

"It would be beneath His Lordship," I said. "Besides, the common copper knows more and sees more."

Perhaps they enjoyed my banter with them. I have always been blessed at banter, and in bad circumstances a clear mind for the fast riposte does a fellow no end of good.

"You'll know when we know, Lord Irish of Dublin's Best Brothel."

"I do like Sally O'Hara in that one," I said, drawing laughter, even if I'd never been brothelized in my life.

"Sell you my notes, chum," a fellow did say finally. He was from the Central News Agency, a service that specialized in servicing second- and third-tier publications with information they hadn't the staff to report themselves.

"Agh, you lout. I don't want the notes, just the information. I'll take me own notes."

We bargained and settled on a few shillings, probably more than he would have gotten from *Tittle-Tattle*.

"About forty, a Judy, no name, no papers, discovered by a worker named Charlie Cross, C-R-O-S-S, who lives just down the row, at three-forty A.M., lying where you see her."

And I did. She lay, tiny, wasted bird, under some kind of police shroud, while around her detectives and constables looked for "clues," or imagined themselves to be doing so by light of not-very-efficient gas lanterns.

"They've got boys out asking for parishioners to come by and identify the unfortunate deceased, but so far, no takers."

"Cut up badly, is she?"

"First constable says so."

"Why so little blood?" It was true. I had expected red sloppage everywhere, scarlet in the lamplight. Melodramatic imagination!

"I'm guessing soaked into her clothes. All that crinoline sops up anything liquid, blood, jizz, beer, wine, vomit—"

"Enough," I said. "Anything else?"

"Now you know what we know."

"Excellent. Will the coppers let us see the body?"

"We'll see."

I stood there another few minutes, until a two-wheeled mortuary cart was brought close to her, and two constables bent to lift her. They would transport her—now technically an *it*—to the Old Montague Street Mortuary, which was not far away.

"I say," I said to the nearest uniform, "I'm from the *Star*. I'm not part of this jackal mob but an authentic journalist. It would help if I could see a bit, old man."

He turned and looked at me as if I were the lad in the Dickens story who had the gall to ask for more.

"The *Star*," I repeated as if I hadn't noted his scowl and astonishment. "Maybe mention you, get you a promotion."

I was naturally corrupt. I understood immediately without instruction that a little limelight does any man's career a bit of good, and having access to it, which the penny-a-liners never did, was a distinct advantage.

"Come on, then," he said, and although it wasn't expressed, I could sense the outrage and indignation of the peasants behind me and rather enjoyed it. He pulled me to the mortuary cart, and as the fellows struggled to shove the poor lady into her carriage, he halted them, so that she was held at equipoise between worlds, as it were, and pulled back the tarpaulin.

I expected more from my first corpse. And if the boys thought I'd puke my guts up, I disappointed them. It turned out that, like so much else in this world, death was overrated.

She lay, little bunny, in repose. Broad of face, blank of stare, doughy of construction, stiller than any stillness I'd ever seen. There seemed to be the purpling of a bruise on the right side of that serene face, but someone had otherwise composed her features so that I was spared tongue, teeth, saliva, whatever is salubrious about the bottom part of face. Her jaw did not hang agape but was pressed firmly shut, her mouth a straight jot. I wish I could say her eyes haunted me, but in fact they bore the world no malice and radiated no fear. She was beyond fear or malice. Her eyes were calm, not intense, and bereft of human feeling. They were just the eyes of a dead person.

I looked at the neck, where the dress had been pulled down so the coppers could have their look-see at the death wounds. I look-saw two deep if now bloodless slices, almost atop each other, crisscrossing from under left ear to center of throat.

"He knew what he was doing, that one," said the sergeant who was sponsoring my expedition. "Deep into the throat, no mucking about, got all the rivers of blood on the first one, the second was purely ornamental."

"Surgeon?" I asked. "Or a butcher, a rabbi, a pig farmer?"

"Let the doc tell you when he makes up his mind. But the fellow knew his knife."

With that, one of the coppers threw the tarpaulin over her again, and her face vanished from the world.

"There's more, I'm told," I said. "I have to see it. Spare me her notch if you can, let the poor dear have a little dignity, but I have to see what else the man did."

The three officers held a conversation with their eyes among themselves, and then one flipped up the material at midsection and carefully burrowed into her nest of clothing, exposing just the wound and nothing of delicacy.

"That, too, took some strength, I'd judge," said the sergeant.

Indeed. It was an ugly excavation running imprecisely down her left side, say ten inches to the left of the navel (which I never saw), curving at her hip bone, cutting inward toward the centerline of her body. It, too, was bled out; it, too, left flaky blood debris in its wake; but it was somehow rawer than the throat cuts, and I could see where the blood had congealed into a kind of black (in that light) gruel or even pudding.

"Show him the punctures," said the sergeant.

Another adjustment was made, and I saw where the knife's point had been lightly "danced," almost gaily, across her abdomen. A smudge of pubis hair was exposed in this exploration, but none of us mentioned it, as such things, even among men, were unmentionable twenty-four years ago.

THE BODY OF A WOMAN WAS DISCOVERED LAST NIGHT—

"No, no," said Henry Bright. "We're selling news, not informing the ladies of the tea party. Get the blood up front."

Henry was hovering over my shoulder as I assailed the Sholes & Glidden, moving my Pitman notes into English prose. I had just returned from Buck's Row, paying the hansom driver extra to force his way through the dawn and its increase in traffic, and seated myself directly at the machine. Henry was on me like a crazy man. Maybe he was the murderer!

A WOMAN WAS BUTCHERED LAST NIGHT IN WHITECHAPEL BY PERSON OR PERSONS UNKNOWN.

"Yes," said Henry. "Yes, yes, that's it."

THE BODY WAS DISCOVERED—

"No, no, save that for the jump. Get to the wounds, the blood. Get a copper assessment up there, too, to give it some spice."

HER THROAT WAS SLASHED—

"Brutally," offered Henry.

—BY TWO PENETRATING BLADE STROKES WHICH CAUSED VIOLENT EXSANGUIN—

"No, no. Are we at Oxford? Are we chatting with Professor Prissbottom about the latest in pre-Renaissance decadence?"

—BLOOD LOSS. SHE EXPIRED IN SECONDS.

THEN THE MAN—

THEN THE BEAST—

"Yes, that's it," said Henry.

—THE BEAST RAISED HER SKIRTS AND USED HIS KNIFE TO MUTILATE HER ABDOMEN, OPENING ANOTHER LONG, DEEP, AND THIS TIME JAGGED CUT.

"New graf," said Henry.

FINALLY, HE FINISHED HIS GRISLY NIGHT'S WORK WITH A SERIES OF RANDOM STAB WOUNDS ACROSS HER BELLY—

"Can I say 'belly?'" I asked. "It's rather graphic."

"Leave it for now. I'll check with T.P. It's right on the line. The gals don't have bellies or tits or arses in the *Star*. Maybe the *Express*, not the *Star*. But times are changing."

—AND HIPS.

POLICE SAY THE BODY WAS DISCOVERED AT 3:40 A.M. BY CHARLES CROSS ON HIS WAY TO WORK AS HE WALKED DOWN BUCK'S ROW, WHERE HIS HOME—

"'is 'ome," joshed Henry, playing on the cockney aversion to H's, and evincing the universal newspaper stricture that all reporters and editors are superior to the poor sots they quote or write for.

—IS LOCATED.

"IT TOOK SOME STRENGTH AND SKILL TO DO THIS TERRIBLE THING," SAID METROPOLITAN POLICE SERGEANT JAMES ROSS.

POLICE REMOVED THE BODY TO THE OLD MONTAGUE STREET MORTUARY, WHERE A SURGEON WILL FURTHER EXAMINE IT FOR CLUES. MEANWHILE, A PHOTOGRAPH OF THE WOMAN'S FACE WILL BE TAKEN FOR CIRCULATION IN HOPES OF IDENTIFICATION.

There was a last bit of business. Since my pseudonym, Horn, was affiliated with music, it occurred to Henry Bright that I should write crime under my own name. Gad, I didn't want that, as I had aspirations of mingling with the quality and wanted no whiff of blood floating about my presence. So he said, "All right, then, lad, come up with something else. Dickens called himself Boz; certainly you can do better than that."

"I can," I said, and reached into my past to something only my sister, Lucy, had called me, as her child's tongue could not manage my initials and they had eroded into a single syllable. "Call me Jeb."

Sept. 5, 1888

Dear Mum,

I know how you worry, so I thought I'd write and tell you that all is fine here, even if you never answer me, even if I never send it. I know how disappointed you are in me, at the low way I turned out, and I wish it had been different, but it ain't, and there you have it.

Anyhow, I didn't know the girl that got cut. There's a lot of us down here and our friends are usually in the same area, a block or so, and poor Polly was out east, near a mile. Never laid an eye on the poor thing. We're all talking about it, and we all feel pretty safe down here. We're always together, and as I gets it from the newspapers, poor Polly was all alone on a dark road and the fellow that done her just did it for her purse and the thrill it gave him, and now he's gone and won't be back again. They've increased the coppers everywhere because the newspapers have made such a big skunk about it, so all of us believe he's long gone and won't be coming back, and if he does, it won't be this year or even the next.

Other than the fright it give me at first, I am fine. I have so many things to say to you, I wish I talked and wrote better to get them all out. I know what upsets you and Da the most is the s-x. Really, that's the smallest thing in my life. You get used to it early, and it comes to not mean nothing. It just happens, it's over in a second, and you go on, it's all forgotten.

As for the blokes, you'd think I'd be down on them, but I'm not. Most seem like gentlemen. I've never been cuffed about, nor coshed, nor robbed. Nobody has ever forced himself onto me against my will. Even the coppers, at least the ones in uniform, are nice enough to us gals. They have no interest in hurting us or "punishing" us, we're just something they get used to fast down here, and they don't want no bother from us, only to get through the day like we do, and go on home to the missus.

My problem ain't never been the blokes, or the s-x they wants. Don't all men want that? They're going to get it one way or the other, is how I sees it. No, what my problem has been, ever since I were a little girl, is the demon gin. I do like my gin. I like my gin so much. All the girls down here drink it for the way it makes them feel and the happiness it brings. You and Da and Johnto never had no idea how young I was when I started it and how it explained all the trouble that I got into and why no matter how the nuns and priests talked to me and Da smacked me and you squashed me with that look you get when you're disappointed—do I know that look!—it was always the gin that was behind it, and here I am all these years later, sometimes down and out, having lost everything, even a bed to sleep in, and all I think about is the gin.

I call it my disease. I can't do nothing without thinking about it, and when I have it, I am happy. My happiness comes out in my singing, which I love, which is my way of telling the world that don't otherwise notice I exist. Sometimes, too, I know, I can get pretty uppity on gin. I won't let nobody tell me what to do when I am fortified up, because it don't seem nobody knows any better than me, that's how strong and good I feel.

I will tell you, Mum, they'll never take the gin away. If reformers close the shops and burn down the gin factories, someone'll figure out how to do it under the tracks or in a cellar nobody don't know about, and it'll be back on the streets in a day and I'll be first in line.

Mum, I know you don't want to hear that, but I have to tell it anyway, because it's the truth. Mum, I miss you so much and remember such good times and how tender you always was with me before the sickness. I remember Johnto and Paul and the others and how happy we all was. I wished it had never changed, but it did and we went where we did and done what we done.

I love you, Mum.

Your daughter
Mairsian

CHAPTER FIVE

The Diary

September 5, 1888

As I had anticipated, the excess butchery of my method, satisfying though it might be to mind and soul in and of itself, had an electric effect on London journalism. It was the new rag, the *Star*, that took up the clarion most energetically. It is run, so it is said, by an Irishman; therefore all is understandable by virtue of the cruder Irish temperament, their propensity for the bottle, their impulsiveness and natural tendencies to violence, all of which are manifest in the *Star*.

MAD BUTCHER SLAYS WOMAN, it announced in a headline smeared across leader boards all throughout London. The newsboys bustled about, screeching, "Mad butcher, mad butcher, mad butcher!" You could not escape these tribes of annoying urchins, noses all runny, pouty faces red, the glee of greed in their beaming little rat eyes. I'm betting the dim, dull shopkeeps and salesclerks of the town couldn't resist such titillation. More deliciously yet, an artist had provided a detailed drawing of the poor woman's major wounds, by my memory quite accurately evoked. There, in all their glory, were the two fatal cuts, deep and profound, that settled the issue.

And, flirting with the very limits of propriety, there was the abdominal excursion, with its sloppy jag halfway down as it veered to center.

A debate soon developed in the rags as the week wore on. This is excellent. Now, five days after the event, they have yet to put this bone down. It seems to be breaking along evening and morning lines. The *Star* and the *Pall Mall Gazette*, our leading afternoon exponents, are purveyors of the single-killer theory. Can you see why? It's obvious. Unlike their morning brethren, whose product arrives by discreet carrier, the unruly afternoon boyos must sell their wares to walkers-by, people headed to the train stations or coming off shift from some coal-powered hellhouse or waiting to get aboard the horse trams or looking to amuse and edify themselves as they are trotted crosstown in a cabriolet. Thus, the fare offered them will be more salacious, more provocative, more tainted with the odor of sex, blood, and ruin. Their baser natures must be appeased. At the same time, at the end of their journey home, the dirty rag itself, sucked dry of the lubricious, can be stuffed in a refuse can, and our hero may enter his home under the fraud of being morally sacrosanct, ready to speak the blessing before the dinner of meat and potatoes that his spouse has so dutifully and lovingly prepared.

The morning papers, by contrast, do go into the home, to be devoured along with breakfast. They are limited in the extent of the gore and nastiness they can allow; it is of significantly lesser denomination than among their opponents. No filth can be allowed to besmirch the purity of the hearthside and the little nippers frolicking there before being shipped off at age seven to a decade of buggery and horsewhipping, plus proficiency in Greek. The same rags are also more likely read by women, whose delicacy in most cases cannot stand exposure to the rawness of life and death.

The morning fellows—the *Times*, the *Mail*, the *Sun*, the *Standard*, all the others—backed the gang theory. It held, quite absurdly, that possibly the lady, in her peregrinations for customers, had bumbled into a robbery by a set of hooligans and, as a witness, had to be silenced. Had the poor girl failed to pay up or witnessed a robbery? Was it part of some initiation rite by which a novice proved himself manly enough? The gang theory was meekly buttressed by the lack of blood along the street, held to be evidence that she had been killed elsewhere and deposited along Buck's Row. Obviously, the authors of this nonsense had not looked at the soppage in her knickers, which had absorbed all those pints of the vital life fluid.

The *Star* led the pack, and the *Gazette* was not far behind in pursuing the mad-butcher thematic. It was a newsstand natural. It played brilliantly on primordial fears of lurkers with knives, and what evil simmered and boiled down dark city alleys or in precincts where whores sold their bodies to the night. There was probably a sense of divine punishment, unstated because there was no need to state it. The victim was beyond the pale of Queen Victoria's formal, dark-garbed, earnest empire of rectitude, where the strength of conformity was just as strong on the home island as a bayonet's steel in the outer rings of our Christian conquest of the world.

You could see that pattern play out in the fate of the poor woman whose fate it was to encounter the butcher's Sheffield. It turned out, courtesy of someone named Jeb on the *Star* who was running this story as if his life depended on it, that the poor dear's name was Mary Ann Nichols, called Polly by all who knew and used her. She was exactly as expected, the dreg of a system that had no place for her, except to spread and pump her cunny in an alley, drop off a thruppence, and forget all about it in the next few seconds.

She is exactly what our system must necessarily produce. A disposable woman. If she does not have the sponsorship of a male, there is nothing for her except the meanest of charity interspersed with the whore's plight. Darwin's absolutism becomes the ruling principle of her existence: She develops cunning, deceit, cleverness as her only means of survival, her only goal the thruppence that will get her the day's glass of gin. She becomes horrid and disgusting, blackened by the streets, rimmed with grime, her teeth rotting, her hair a scabrous mess, her body flaccid and fallen, her language and discourse degraded, and thus we are able to dismiss her from our view without qualm. She is sewage. She exists only for those randy men in the grip of sex fever, and when they have spent their pence and jizz, off they go. Any sane system would spare provision for the wretched creature and possibly save her from her wretchedness. Possibly men will invent it someday—but I doubt it.

The *Star* brought this tragic nonentity to banal life. No one read of it with more fascination than I. The method of identity: The police noted a laundry marker on one of her underclothes and, in a bit of time, found the laundry, displayed the morgue picture, and identified her. So Jeb, with that advantage, was able to track her last day's odyssey toward a pool of blood in Buck's Row. She was forty-three, he tells us, mother of five children. Her character flaw, for which God above and I below exacted our justice, was alcohol. It destroyed her life and, I suppose, killed her. After twenty-four years of marriage to a locksmith, as Jeb told the tale, her husband, finding her frequently inebriated, kicked her out. A divorce followed. There was no place to go but down and no place to land but the bottom. Her shabby last few years were mainly about raising enough money per diem for that glass of blissful gin or several, plus a grim bed in a doss house, of the many that festered in Whitechapel for her and others of the ilk.

Jeb constructed a template of her last hours. The details the plucky bastard unearthed were quite interesting. At twelve thirty A.M. she left a public house called the Frying Pan (who could make up such!) and shortly thereafter returned to her lodging house, where it turned out she hadn't the cash to spend the night. Out she went. She met a friend and they had a nice chat, even if Polly was quite drunk, and Polly told the friend that she'd had her doss money three times that day but always drank it through, but she claimed that she'd get it again and everything would be all right. Then Polly walked on down Whitechapel Road and, when she saw a potential tryster following her, diverted to the far darker Buck's Row to earn that doss fee. We know what happened next, don't we?

Jeb's account was also notable for the narrative it gave of police movement, and it contained a warning that I took seriously. It seemed that minutes before the dispatch of Polly, two constables on their patrol entered and coursed Buck's Row from opposite directions. I saw neither; obviously, neither saw me. Yet it is in the record, Constable Thain being the first in one direction, then Sergeant Kerby in the other. Within minutes of my departure, first along came Cross, then a Constable Neill who made the second discovery (after Cross) and signaled to Thain, turning up again like a bad penny. Finally, a Constable Mizen arrived, he being the copper Cross alerted.

Good Lord, it was like Victoria Station when the express from Manchester arrives! All those men on that black, bleak little street in the space of twenty minutes or so, during which a dastardly deed was done unseen. How close I came! How lucky I was! How the whimsies favored my enterprise!

It taught me an important lesson. Luck would not always be my companion, so I must plan more carefully. I must choose the spot, not the woman, henceforth, based on the patrol patterns of the constables, thereby decreasing the chances of discovery in flagrante. I must examine the spot for escape routes so that I would not hesitate in disarray if noted, but could vanish abruptly. I also must locate less well-traveled areas of Whitechapel than the one I had so foolishly chosen, that close to a main thoroughfare lit brightly by gas illumination and the glare of grog houses and constable's lanterns.

This was good to know, as certain auspicious signs suggested that I must strike again, soon.

CHAPTER SIX

Jeb's Memoir

Success is a narcotic. Experienced once, it must be had again and again. Pity the man who has it young and can never regain it. His must be a parched, bitter life. As for me, the week of September 1 through 7 was the best I'd ever had, and it strengthened my resolve to never, ever return to being the nonentity I had been my first thirty-two years.

I owe it all to Jack, though the name would not be affixed into eternity for another month or so. It's terrible, but as truth is the guideline here, I must nevertheless confess it. Jack's depredations made Jeb's successes possible, and fixed Jeb on the course his life would take, giving him the sense of importance that he would never again cease to maneuver in search of.

Brilliance followed brilliance. I grabbed a nap in the *Star* office and watched with utter satisfaction as the MAD BUTCHER SLAYS WOMAN editions sold out, went back to what O'Connor said was "replate" seven times, and effectively not only invented but drove the story onward.

Such energy and determination. Such tirelessness. Jeb was the hero of the day, the ace reporter who had found and amplified the case for the millions of shopkeeps and -girls who comprised the London population. I was their thrill machine, I was their fear of darkness and sharp instruments, I suppose I was the swollen penis or the wetted cunny that they could never admit to having had. Jeb brought all this to them. It was a shame, then, that I had no idea what I was doing.

"Get yourself to the London Hall of Records," Henry Bright instructed. "Find an amiable clerk to look up the name of the lady. Her official records should have leads—if she has children, an address, a husband, real or common-law. Go to them, not wasting a ha'penny's worth of time, and chat them up. Stop off here first, pick up an artist, he will accompany you to sketch the faces. We need to put their faces in the newspaper."

"He's right. Readers need to attach a human identity to whoever's doing the talking. It makes the thing have a complete sense to it," said Mr. O'Connor.

"If you get the name, you'll be way ahead. Also, cultivate that copper. The bastard detectives will play awesome, as if they're university men among the pig farmers, but they probably don't know half as much as the sharp-eyed street constable. Maybe your friend has resentments against them from slights delivered with which you can pry information out of him. Envy is the juice in which the world bubbles, with dashes of malice tossed in to bring the human stew to a delicious boil."

I did all of that, napping at the paper. It worked out surprisingly well. Indeed, Sergeant Ross gave me the name out of thanks for the light the *Star*'s original story had shone on him, more than the poor man had ever got in his life, after years of dedicated work. Most important to him, it turned out, was how his mention had buzzed off the gentlemen from the Metropolitan Police Bethel Green J Division, CID, who had been handed the investigation.

Via the Records Department, I got to poor Polly's husband first, and even broke the news to him. If I'd had a shred of human mercy left, I might have allowed the fellow a moment of repose after hearing that the woman he once loved, the woman who gave him five children, made his food, and gave him her body for twenty-six years before she lost her soul to demon gin, was now dead horribly in the gutter, all cut and minced. Quite the opposite: Knowing him to be vulnerable, I pressed him and got good details. My ambition was as fully sized as any addiction to opium by now. It had been a bit of time since he'd seen her, but through his eyes, I was at least able to give the poor old girl some humanity. That's the rub of the newspaper game, I realized. It helps me, it does indeed, but it helps you, too, in the long run, though the gain may be a bit late to play out.

Then I went to the Frying Pan, a disagreeable enough place, and there found two souls—the barkeep and Emma Lownes, no fixed address other than the odd week or two in the Lambeth Workhouse, and for the thruppence it took to secure Emma a nice glass of gin that I doubt was distilled by Boodle's, she evoked the decency of her late friend, her own fear of a man who stabbed and slashed by night, and her extremely limited prospects. In the end I gave her another thruppence, meant to go for a quiet night at a doss house, but I'm sure it went through her gullet and was pissed out by seven that evening.

Finally, having evoked the victim in vivid colors, I went on to the sorry state of the police investigation, Sergeant Ross being once again my confidential source. We met furtively, like spies, in a Whitechapel public house called the Alma, after the great victory in the Crimean War nearly half a century before. By day, it was a dark and low place, with no energy nor fire to it and only dissolute beer fiends and lonely Judys wasting their doss money on gin.

"You can't use me name on this one," he said. "Old Warren"—he meant Sir George Warren, embattled head of the Metropolitans—"has set a policy of reticence. You won't be hearing much on this case, and anything gets out, they'll be swift after the talker."

"I will protect you. But in stories to come, you'll emerge as the true hero of the case. To hell with the CID. They only exist to take bribes anyhow."

"Appreciated, guv'nor. So this is where we seem to be at"—he paused for the effect—"and that's nowhere."

I nodded, having suspected as much. It would be a hard case to crack.

DESPITE INTENSE EFFORTS, POLICE PROGRESS IN THE CASE OF THE SLAUGHTERED WHITECHAPEL UNFORTUNATE, I would write that night, HAVE YET TO YIELD A SUBSTANTIAL CLUE.

AN EARLY ARREST IS RULED OUT, POLICE TELL THE STAR, AND THERE'S

LITTLE THAT CAN BE DONE EXCEPT WAIT FOR THE DEMON TO STRIKE AGAIN
AND HOPE HE LEAVES A CLEARER TRAIL.

Ross had confirmed what everyone with half a brain knew already, which was that the Metropolitan Police were dependent on the old methods. Though they knew of fingerprints in theory, they had no base or file of them to deploy and, unless left in blood on a knife blade or painted wall, were hard to record from other surfaces. They had only primitive chemistry and medical help, estimating time of death by lividity or temperature of body, a chancy method at best. Their techniques were as old as the Middle Ages: protection and examination of the crime scene, autopsy findings, questioning of suspects, local intelligence, interviews with witnesses, increase in patrolling in the crime area, and finally, reward. However, those techniques worked best when applied to a fellow who was part of an organized criminal underworld, worked for a gang like the High Rips, had mates and a boss and all the appurtenances of the aboveground world only perverted into criminality. He also would have competitors or enemies, neutral observers who would sell him out as a favor for someone else. There was a whole barter system—negotiation, feint, bluff, reward, and punishment—that really underlay the Metropolitan Police's attempt to control the underworld, even as half successful as that was. Our boy, the mad butcher, was vulnerable to none of it, except by a chance that hadn't happened or hadn't evinced itself yet.

You could tick off the mistakes already made one by one: Not realizing how big the case would get, the coppers had been very sloppy on Buck's Row, even allowing Jeb to track across the murder ground to look at the body as it was fitted into the cart; and the two constables had already mucked up the soil where they'd squirmed to find the leverage to lift poor Polly. The autopsy might yield something, but unless he left a calling card, it would reveal only that a knife was used, which was obvious even to Charlie Cross on his way to work.

As for suspects, presumably the coppers had an index with names of boys in the area who'd taken a hand or even a blade to whores in the past, but this crime was so out of scale with what had come before—and was being blown up even further by the industry of Jeb—that it was unlikely one of these lads had done the deed. All of us, copper, reporter, and reader alike, understood that some threshold had been achieved, some new level had been reached, and like it or not, we had entered a modern age. So the records would be of little use. Maybe the whores knew something, but by nature they weren't the sort to chatter to CID swells, though the constabulary who shared the streets with them might fare a bit better.

Would extra patrols help? That alone bore some promise, if only to act as a deterrent to the killer's mad impulses. Maybe, knowing that more constables were about, he'd decide his one triumph was enough to savor in old age. But that was unlikely. There was something unformed, even callow, about the taking of poor Polly's life. It was like an expeditionary force, not an occupation; he wanted to see if he could get away with it, what it felt like, what could be learned from it, and might regard the increased patrolling as more of a challenge to his intellect.

After all, for all his boldness, he'd been very lucky, barely missing the blue bottles both coming and going. That would annoy him; he had expected so much more to be on his side than pure dumb luck. This time, having mastered the basics, he'd be sharper.

I left the Alma with my Pitman notepad chuck-full, looking for a hansom cab to get me to the office so I could amaze London tomorrow with yet more new revelations. But the traffic on Commercial Street was so heavy, a hansom would do me no good. So I decided to walk a few blocks up till it crossed Whitechapel, and if that broadway were clearer, I'd find the cab there. It was now about eight o'clock by my pocket watch, and up the street I hastened.

It struck me that in my several times here in Whitechapel, I'd never really looked at the place in full clarity. Now, at last, I had space and time and opportunity to behold the hell den where the killer lurked, the ladies walked, the gentlemen searched, and sex and death were in the air.

What you saw, on Commercial Street, at least, was a great bazaar of humanity, a sort of gathering of tribes for sustenance of all sorts (all sorts were available) amid clamor, dust, the smell of horse ordure and human excrement, various foodstuffs, including meat and fruit and candy offered from the abundant stalls clotting the sidewalks, the eau de toilette the ladies presumably splashed about between commercial transactions, and the ever present London tang of coal-oil smoke from all the burners at the hearth, which I am told sometimes combined with the evil sea dew to create the city's cottony billows of fog. But mostly, you felt the hubbub, the bustle, the clamor, the circus-midway urgency of people unconsciously living out their lives without much thought or hope or worry.

It was a festival of hattery, as none in those days went uncapped. The men beneath, most in heavy frock coats or tweedy Norfolks, all with dark ties cinched about their necks, and most obscured by beard, were unknow-able and mysterious as they drifted this way and that. Not all were hunting for Judys, but I think it fair to say that all were hunting for something, be it a beer in a public house, an oyster in a stall, a piece of meat on a stick, a glowing globe of fruit, a new trinket or toy, a bonnet for a lover, an office for a lawyer, a freak with no nose, conjoined twins, magic shows, minstrels true Negro or just paint, or what have you, and I do not know what you have. Some were just slumming, as coming in from the sober City to see the show was quite the habit.

Meanwhile, those of lower origin and destiny fought for space amid the costers' stalls, coal heavers and dock laborers, dolly mops and magsmen, cabinetmakers and seamstresses, bug hunters and mudlarks, and "enter-tainers" of various type, ballad singers and oratorical beggars and running patterers and the street-fire king, who devoured and disgorged great scuts of flame for a penny a pyre.

Dust rose from the streets as the cabs and wagons and tram buses coursed slowly up or down, the horses pausing now and again to beshit themselves and the cobblestones, all of it creating a mad din that, heard once, would ring forever in your ears (I hear it now, in a quiet study, twenty-four years later). God was not entirely absent: At street corners the anointed addressed small flocks of believers or want-to-believes and threw scripture hard and loud at them. Commerce of a thousand kinds transpired. But Babylon demanded its obeisance as well: Down side streets were the penny gaffs, wherein, or so it was claimed, scantily clad young maidens cavorted to bad music. Gambling went on everyplace, and if you looked sex-wanting but frightened of a real Judy, a scurvy-looking fellow might approach and offer you French postcards from underneath his coat, these being glimpses of carnal entanglements that took some deciphering. Rat killing seemed an enjoyable sport for certain Johnnies, while others turned to dog fighting, all forms of barbarism offered to the top hats without a blush of shame.

So much frenzy, so much throbbing, so much shove and slip and shuffle, everywhere, everywhere. Chanters, second-edition sellers, boardwalkers, strawers, mountebanks, clowns, jugglers, conjurors, grease removers, nostrum vendors, fortune-tellers, French polishers, turnpike sailors, various classes of lurkers and peepers, stenographic-card sellers, racetrack-card sellers. It was all illuminated by naphtha lamps atop high poles but also by swaths of glare from the public houses, of which there appeared to be one every thirty or forty feet. Besides the Alma, I passed the Ten Bells, the Queen's Head, the Britannia, the Horn of Plenty, the King's Share, and the Princess Alice. Each was full packed, in full swing, in full glug, for I should add that liquor was the fuel that kept the human fires of Whitechapel ablaze, which meant that it slowed speech, slurred and slowed and misguided decisions, stuttered steps, and slewed behavior this way and that. A man fully drunk is not fully human: He pisses and shits without remorse, he speaks without thought (the truth, usually, God help us), and he's quick to fist or blade or bullet. So that, too, that distance from normal discourse, hung over everything like a cloud, a pall, garish in the grotesque play of the light on the puddles in the street or the windows across the way or the shine of the beaver in the hats. No wonder the slummers came to watch.

And the women, of course. By law they could not stop. If they stopped, the coppers could nick them, and it was off to the tank for a night, a night without the comforts of gin, and the quick blast of jizz to pay for it, and finally, hard earned, the lice-infested bed at a doss house. So walk the poor dearies did, in a great circle, up Commercial to Whitechapel, down Whitechapel to Brick Lane, then Brick Lane to Hanbury, which led them back to Commercial. It was said by the Metropolitans that there were at least fifteen hundred Judys on the streets and, in the dark avenues off the lighted concourses, sixty-six brothels, perhaps for a higher class of girl and a higher class of customer. The street girls, however, were the permanent feature of the Whitechapel experience.

Which brings me to the core of the issue: the presence of all those streets and alleys. That was what made the whole thing go, that was what turned Whitechapel into a square-mile outdoor brothel where the grunts and squeals and gasps of the sex dance were never far from the ear, and if you turned as you walked by a dark passageway off the boulevard, you could often make out the shadowy figures of those seeking oblivion in the final spurt of the act.

Whitechapel was so fully laced with dark roads off the main stem, which functioned as "rooms" in the imaginary brothel of which I speak, that you could almost smell the jizz and cunny in the air. The stage design of the immense show was structured along elemental lines: It was simply dark vs. light, each being intensified by the presence of the other, and perhaps many came simply to appreciate the sharpness of the divide between those two worlds. I know I found it fascinating and could not stop turning it over in my mind, believing it had to mean something more than it did.

The light was commerce, family, order, civilization; the dark was raw sex, violence, and by implication the end to civilization. I took as premise that our fellow, our mad butcher, our fiend with a knife, was a creature of the dark, and as such had a kind of mythical significance few could articulate but all could appreciate, for it quivered the marrow of the human bone.

He was what we left behind when we moved indoors, he was the beast of the heart, he was a creature of pure will without interest in, much less an obedience to, all those rules we agreed upon when we put ourselves under roof. Mercy? Pity? Cooperation? Civility? Brotherhood? The hallowed temple of the soul? Bah, he pushed them aside with a single brutish swipe. He was out of the Cimmerian darkness, mangy, hairy, quick to slash and cut and exult in the spillage of blood. He cried havoc, he let slip the dogs of depravity and murder, but even more loudly he cried, *Not so fast. With your modern age, your railways, your steel ships and machines of war and deep penetrations under the earth for a fuel to drive it all—not so fast, you blighters. Here is the message I deliver for you to contemplate. I am anarchy. I am fear. I am carnage, slaughter, destruction for its own sake. I will remind you: It is your vanity to believe you have come so far and left me behind. You will never leave me behind. Don't you see it yet? I am you.*

That, really, is why I knew he'd strike again.

And he did.

CHAPTER SEVEN
The Diary

September 7–8, 1888

——————

I left my dwelling at nine P.M. and took a hansom to city center, and had a repast in a public house, aware that I had my Sheffield in my belt at my hip, under the shirt and the frock coat I chose to wear on these expeditions. It gave me a nice shiver of bliss to be sitting there amid men of business and journalism or whatever, serious men, being seemingly one of them, and them not knowing what lay beneath my coat, them not noticing me at all or if so only in passing, them never guessing in a million years that eight inches of just-sharpened steel held tight in a grip of fine English maplewood pressed against my flesh, rather uncomfortably but not without its own measure of pleasure. A man with a good knife feels king of the world, that's for certain!

I ambled about, taking pleasure in the city at night. It was such a mad, delirious carnival, and because the weather was superior, most seemed to be temporarily jolly and taking pleasure in the fact that life had put so much on their table. In this way I passed the hours, partaking, enjoying, meandering, observing, and, one supposes, gathering. Everywhere the lights were magnificent and in them showed the red, pleased faces of common men, pleased again to be common and to be men. By midnight I had made my way to Whitechapel by avoiding the Underground railway and its steam-engined efficiency and shoulder-to-shoulder crowds entirely. The flesh parade was in full operation. Again I ambled, even took a stroll down Buck's Row to see the spot of my previous action. There, flowers and candles and various memento mori had been placed on the street just beyond the bridge over the East London Railway tracks, exactly where I had felled poor Polly. A few others stood by, trying to absorb what had happened there, standing, pointing, hoping perhaps to find in the dark a clue the police had missed in full daylight. I suppose some thought that the murderer always returns to the site of his crime, and though in this case it turned out to be true, it happened not out of will or even vague plan but just because at the time the whimsy took me.

I returned to Whitechapel High Street, ambled down it, found a crowded public house—the Horn of Plenty—and had a stout. It wasn't for nerves, for mine were steady on without a problem; it was to kill time. But I had wanted plenty of time, and to make my way on foot in a moseying fashion, so that no hansom cabman or horse-tram driver could remember, no matter how small a chance that might be. One couldn't be too careful, except in the act of commission, where one had momentarily to be bold as a pirate, to strike and go to red carnage, and then obsequiously depart under cover of darkness and unprepossesion of being.

Sometime after two, I slipped out; the crowd was thinning, and again I was worried about standing out. Now my course took me down Whitechapel, where the crowds were more or less thick, and I began my wend through smaller streets until I found myself at Hanbury and Brick Lane, another thoroughfare known as a Judy broadway. It was well lit, and though the crowds were thinner, the business—which, after all, is based on the eternal fires of lustful loins and the eternal availability of opened thighs—still produced a human density. I glanced at my watch, saw that it was nearly three, and instead of continuing down Hanbury, took a right to eat up some more time and wait for the crowds to thin further. I stopped for another stout, finding a seat at the bar where I could keep an eye on the street, and there watched for constables and, at a certain time when the street seemed devoid of them, wandered out upon it.

I spotted her right away. This one was short and thick but obviously a Judy on patrol, trolling for her thruppence. She wore two rings on her left hand, middle finger; I had already conjured a use for such a clue. It fit neatly into the overall plan animating my campaign. I approached her, moving a bit faster than she, until I was just behind her left shoulder, where I adjusted my pace to hers and made certain to violate the commonly understood social principles of space, coming far too close, so that my intention was clear. She turned, but not fully to face me, and I saw her doughy profile at the quarter-angle, the broad nose, the painted-on brightness of inexpensive coloring. I could smell her eau d'toilette. She flashed a sliver of a smile, enough for me to see amazingly strong teeth, and more or less whispered, "What's it, then, dearie? Bit of sport for the gentleman?"

"I am indeed hoping for just such, my dear," I said. I had timed it perfectly, intercepting her before and making the connection exactly at the Hanbury Street junction.

"We'll find a lovely private spot, then," she said, and led me to the right, into the darkness, down Hanbury.

We drifted slowly, my love and I, along the dark block, lost in a canyon of dark brick, illuminated here and there by a late reader's light. Ahead, another block away, we could see the brightness that was Commercial Street, and see the traffic upon it, the drift of the gals and beaus and visitors and innocents. As a twosome, we were too close, not quite a couple but not strangers, either. Ghostlike apparitions drifted by us now and then, a Judy, a John, an early-rising workman, who could tell?

Near the end of the block, as I had anticipated—for I had probed the area for possibility a few days earlier—she indicated a rightward turn with her head and put her weight against a door, and it opened to reveal the dark passage that was the throughway to the backyard of 29 Hanbury. We slipped along a dark corridor, passing a mute stairway at the left, and came to nestle near the way out.

"Got a present for Annie, your lordship?" she asked. She had a rheumy, wet slough to her voice, as if her lungs were full of death, and seemed a little blurry, not drunk as a sailor but in that zone of vagueness that the gin confers before it hammers one into full-bang disorientation.

I pressed the coin into her hand, and she took it greedily, sliding it into some hidden pocket of her voluminous dark dress. I said, "Come, let's move a bit, into more privacy." I had a fear that this place was too vulnerable, that noise would rise through the house or that another Judy and her companion of the minute might enter 29, not knowing it was occupied.

And here is where what happened began to deviate from the ideal. I had imagined a hundred times since picking the site how we'd end up in the backyard, and how I'd cut her hard, and how fast she'd die, and how I'd do what must be done, and how smoothly it would all go. But no plan survives contact with the world beyond the mind.

"Sweetie, here's fine, come on, then, let me pull up me petticoats and we can—"

As if it had a will of its own, my left hand shot out like a snake and bit hard at her throat. Recalling now, I realize that I was not prepared to be defied, I was certainly not willing to argue, and my threshold of frustration was dangerously low, though I had been unaware, thinking myself blissfully composed and utterly in control of both self and lady. It was not so. My hand clamped at her larynx and began to squeeze with the full force of my musculature and my will behind it. Even in the dark, I saw the surprise light her face as the oxygen was pressed off, and though so cinched she could not cry out, her throat's machinery began to manufacture unintelligible noises of despair, dry clicks and hitches, half-grunts, spitless, noiseless screams, the sound of inner structures rubbing frictively against each other, words that no letters exist to approximate, a whole product line of constricted-throat expectorations, and one hand feebly came to beat against my pinioning arm. I knew this would not do, not here, not indoors, where at any moment we could be interrupted, and so with my right hand, I grabbed her fleshy biceps and put force behind, bumping her along, if you will, shoving her with my chest, guiding her with one hand to arm, one to throat, all the while strangling. It was as weird a dance as has ever been danced, an uncoordinated shuffle of bodies set against each other with the ultimate progress to the way out ten feet, then seven, then four away.

Three, two, one, and we were out the rear door. Still almost carrying her—she was not light, but the intensity of the struggle released strange fluxes of strength through my limbs—I took her down three steps, pivoted to the left, and braced her hard against the wooden fence there, well constructed, as I have said, and able to sustain the force of my thrusting her body against it.

In a flash, I let go of her arm and reached back to withdraw the Sheffield from my belt, aware the whole time that the episode had completely veered south from perfection and become a graceless, cruel thing. Whether she was dead or not—her tongue seemed to protrude from her lips, and her eyes were shut—I could not tell, but if so, just so, and if not, almost so. I struck her neck hard with the knife, blade belly sinking into the softness, and drew it strong around, letting my left hand slip off her throat at last.

That was a moment. She was propped against the fence, unsupported by me, her throat ripped but not yet producing blood, utterly still, quite vulnerable. I struck her again, again felt bite of knife's belly, again drew down and, pivoting myself, around until my natural length of arm ran out and the blade broke free of its cutting stroke. Now came the blood. As before, a progression, first the droplet, then a few crooked tracks tracing the geography of her neck where it merged into shoulder, an area as full of subtle hollows and ridges as a landscape, then a black stream, then a torrent, then a deluge. She slid to the left as the blood continued to gush, and came to rest with her head next to the three steps down which we had come, parallel to the fence.

Again, there was no death rattle; no sound marked her passing from this world to the next. I controlled my breathing—exertions so intense always stir the heart, it is a natural rule of the body, found universally in biology among all mammalian creatures—and reacquired the focus I needed. First the rings. I pulled her dead hand up, laid the knife upon her chest, and yanked the two brass circles off her pudgy digit. I may have done some harm, not that she noticed, for the finger fought me and I had to yank and twist quite aggressively. I deposited them in my pocket. Next up was her pitiful estate, as looted from her pocketbook. I took some care in arranging its meager contents neatly next to her feet: two small hair combs, one in a paper sheath of some sort, and a piece of coarse muslin whose function was utter mystery to me. An envelope didn't fit into the line by her feet, so I placed it daintily next to her head. That neatness stood in contrast to what came next, and I was not unaware of the effect.

I reacquired the knife, pulled her petticoats up, saw—oh, comic detail, too pretty to be true but true nonetheless—striped bloomers. I pulled them down until I'd exposed her slack gut, a large dish of pudding, creased and gelid and wrinkly, with a kind of substrata that looked, even in the quarter-moon, like curdled milk.

I cut a deep stroke, left to right, across her lower belly, but unlike with Polly, did not stop there. More work was to be done. My cut was longer, deeper, more workmanlike. I opened a flap into her bowels, pulling it back as one would pull back a canvas, and they lay before me, almost an abstraction. In the moon's faint blush, they were like a sausage stew, all interconnected in twisty, labyrinthine ways. Perhaps I hesitated, perhaps I didn't. There was blood, but, the heart that drove it being quieted, no pressure, and so it simply ran downhill to disappear in her swaddles of clothing.

I had seen beasts gutted and felt no remorse, for I was applying myself merely to a sack that now had no spiritual dimension, no sentience, memory, individuality, hope, or fear. I slipped the knife behind the tubes to find the way out—that is, the large one leading to the anus—and cut through it, finding it slippery to penetrate but yielding once the knife edge had found purchase and made its argument persuasively. The whole bloody pile was open for play. I grabbed, my gloves turning black in the moonlight where they would have been scarlet in the sun, and extracted one slippery clottage and tossed it over her shoulder, where it did not quite fly away but rather unraveled, as the flight through air took out its kinks.

That foray into the cavity took most of her from her stomach, but at least a quarter of the tubing remained, and so I repeated the act, removing all but remnants of what remained, and flung them over the same shoulder. Again the phenomenon of unraveling, as the yards of curled loop became, under the process of being flung, a long and stringy ribbon.

Thus was she excavated. Now, pièce de résistance. Dr. Gray was my guide, Sheffield's legendary sharpness my facilitator, but will to complete the task was the true coal that made my furnace rage. I dipped into the crater I had created, searched downward through wreckage and liquifaction, and even though my gloves cut off the subtle sensations to my fingers, found what I desired. I thought of them as the woman's biscuits. Once found, I quickly removed, by suppleness of hand, the two trophies I will leave to the reporters to identify, if they dare.

I stood, after cleaning my blade on her dress, and restored it to its place. I deposited my trophies in an inner pocket, where, after wiping and wringing them, I was certain they would not be moist enough to stain through the heavy wool. I peeled the gloves from my hand and put each in a different pocket, gave my suit a quick examination so that I was confident its darkness and the darkness of the quarter-moon night would camouflage it well. I clutched the two rings in my pocket to make sure I had them both, and departed through the same door by which I had come.

On Hanbury I took a right but didn't bother with either Brick Lane or Commercial Street, as both, I feared, would be too well lit to conceal the moisture from the dear lady's insides if it sneaked through the wool. Instead I turned down Wilkes Street and continued to more or less track my way helter-skelter through the dark warren of Whitechapel. I saw only the occasional ghost and once or twice heard a gentle call—"Sir, is the gentleman seeking something?"—but shook my head firmly and continued on my way at a medium, somewhat relaxed pace. I looked at my watch in the farthest light of a gaslamp I encountered, and saw that it was not yet four-thirty A.M.

CHAPTER EIGHT

Jeb's Memoir

It was about six-twenty A.M.—I could tell by the clock on the spire of the Black Eagle Brewery just down the street—when I arrived, in pale, moist dawn, a ha'penny's worth of moon above the western horizon. At 29 Hanbury, there was no cordon of coppers, no wagons drawn up, no sense of municipal officialdom. Rather, I saw something between a group and a crowd of citizens already formed; it lacked the crowd's anger and purpose, being not packed, angry, clamoring to all get somewhere at once. Too, it was more than a group, for it had purpose and focus, not random togetherness, as its organizational principle. I suppose it was something oxymoronic, like a "crowd of individuals," that is to say, each of the men—mostly workers—was there but not bonded with any other particular person. They were there because of the fascination of death, fate, slaughter, crime, murder, all those Big Things that have an eternal pull on heart and mind. I was the same, except that I had a mission, not just a fascination.

Thus I slid through them easily, and no one felt pressured to block the way or forbid me passage. It turned out they were clustered at an open door, and I could see that it revealed a passage through past No. 29 to what was presumably a yard in back. I entered the tunnel, again found no resistance, and moved along the shabby walls, the peeling paint, the unvarnished wood, all of it screaming its message of messy squalor, Whitechapel style.

I reached the doorway, took a quick peek out, and saw nothing to impede my progress. Only a single man was there, and he was kneeling over what I knew to be the body, to my immediate left at the foot of the steps, next to the fence, though in the still-dim light, from my angle, I could make no sense of the corpse: It appeared to be some kind of spilled, opened suitcase, as I saw mostly disheveled clothes and could make out no identifiable features. I did what no other would do; I stepped into the yard.

The man looked up, his face grave and his demeanor stilled by trauma. "Dr. Phillips— Say, you're not the surgeon."

"No, Inspector," I said. "Jeb, of the *Star*."

"Bloke, Old Man Warren doesn't like you press fellows mucking about."

"I'm fine with that, but since I'm here first, I'm a responsible writer and not a screaming lying hack, and I can get your name in the largest newspaper in the kingdom, you won't mind if I peek about a bit, will you then, Inspector . . . ?"

"Chandler."

"First name, rank?" How quickly I made him a conspirator!

"Inspector Joseph Chandler."

"Thank you."

"All right, but don't dawdle, and I'll show you the particulars."

That's how I met the lady who turned out—by eleven-thirty that morning, another Jeb scoop—to be Annie Chapman. I met her; she did not meet me. All she did was lie there, her guts spread to the sun, moon, and stars.

"God," I said.

"Ever seen an animal gutted?"

I lied. "Many a time, hunting red Irish stag."

"Don't know if our boy is a hunter, but he does like the knife."

I immediately noted, as I bent over her, the difference between her and her sister in martyrdom, Polly Nichols, and that was her tongue. It was bloated like a hideous sausage, so wide an impediment that her lips were distended about it.

"Seen anything like that, Inspector Chandler?"

"Unfortunately. It happens as a consequence of strangulation. He crushed her throat before—"

He pointed. As before, the two deep eviscerations in the left quarter of the throat, leading around to the front before petering out. As before, clear of blood, as it had all slobbered out, sinking into her clothes and the ground and leaving spatters on the fence, where she had been cut. The dawn rendered it more as to coloration but not as to truth; in the pale light it was a kind of purple or lavender. I had yet to see the mythic red.

"Look here," said Chandler, "this, too, is extraordinary." He pointed to her possessions, which had been neatly arrayed, as if for an inspection, next to her roughly shod feet, between them and the base of the fence. I wrote down what I saw: a few combs broken and whole, another piece of raw muslin that I thought the ladies secured as a handkerchief for wiping up the fluids generated by their profession. A crumpled envelope lay next to her head.

"Quite tidy," I said.

"Maybe he's something of a perfectionist."

"He certainly did the perfect job on her middle parts."

"Aye, that he did."

Yes, no doubt. I will here spare the reader and myself another recitation (vide, the diary, previous chapter) of the destruction.

"Quite nasty," I said. "Obviously mad as a hatter."

"You wouldn't want to meet him in the dark. Not without a Webley, that is."

Suddenly a third man joined us.

"Dr. Phillips, sir?" asked Chandler.

"Yes, yes. Oh, God, look at that." He was brought back by the carnage inflicted, as would all men be.

George Bagster Phillips, the surgeon of the Met's Whitechapel H Division, which would take over the murder cases, slid by me, drinking in the detail. He seemed to assume I was another plainclothes copper, and Chandler was so nonplussed by the arrival of the higher rank that he never introduced me. Meanwhile, other cops were drifting in, taking a look at the body. They stomped about in their heavy black shoes, flattening all upon which they trod, trying to be efficient but, as per expectation, doing damage to the scene far more than uncovering any clues. They were like penned hogs fighting to get to the trough. A supervisor was trying to impose some semblance of order. "Now, now, fellows, let's be thorough, let's be organized, let's not rush through the scene. We need clues."

"Here's a dandy," said Chandler. He had bent and turned the envelope, which said "Sussex Regiment" on it. That seemed to be the first break! And I was there to witness it.

"Good work, Chandler," the supervisor said. "Now you others, you do the same."

Well, I knew that it took no great genius to notice an envelope on the ground, but Chandler seemed so pleased with the nod, he again forgot to explain who I was and what I was doing there.

At about this time, Dr. Phillips arose from the body, scribbling notes to himself on a notepad.

"Sir," I said, "have we a time of death?"

"She's cold except where her body was in contact with the ground, and so I'd put time of death at about four-thirty A.M. Rigor is beginning to set in."

"Any interesting tidbits?"

"I noted bruises on one finger. It wasn't broken, but all blotchy blue, as if roughly treated. I saw the indentations of rings, so he clearly helped himself to her jewelry. It can't have been much, given her circumstances, but I do wonder why."

"Did the killer remove any parts of her?" She seemed not merely destroyed but looted as well.

"I'll know when I get her back to the mortuary. It's quite a shambles in there now."

"Any man stains on her, indicating an attack of a salubrious nature?"

He turned and looked me full in the face. "I say, who are you?"

Well, the jig was up. Two constables quickly escorted me to the street. My time in the yard at 29 Hanbury was finished.

It was about now that genius of O'Connor came into full play. I did not race back to Fleet Street by hansom, eating up the minutes in traffic, stuck behind horse trams and delivery wagons and other hansoms. No indeed. Instead I went to the Aldgate East Underground station, which had just opened at seven, and found a telephone cabinet. I picked up the instrument, waited until one of the girls at the Telephone Exchange came on the line, and in five seconds, I was talking with Henry Bright.

"Woman in backyard, 29 Hanbury, Whitechapel. Tongue swollen as if strangled, two deep cuts to neck, as at Buck's Row. Henry, this next part is nauseating."

"Spit it out, young fellow."

"He pulled out her guts and flung them over her shoulder. They quite unraveled. It looked like spaghetti, purpled spaghetti."

"Superb," said Henry. "Oh, excellent."

I went on with details, putting Dr. Phillips there, confirmed the lack of identity of the victim, and told him I'd be headed next to the mortuary.

"Splendid, lad. Bang-on splendid."

So the *Star* was again first with the worst. I don't know how they did it, but Henry Bright turned my notes into serviceable prose, as abutted by official responses garnered by someone at Scotland Yard, mostly piffle, and the story was on the street by eleven A.M., beating all the other afternoon boys by a good thirty minutes. In O'Connor's world, that was a mighty triumph.

But the true depth of Henry's greatness was expressed on the front page. It bore one word:

FIEND!

Who in passing could not pick that up for a shilling and lose him- or herself inside, where "'Jeb' on the scene at Whitechapel, and Henry Bright at the *Star*" had all the nasty details?

FURTHER MUTILATIONS
INTESTINES TOSSED
POLICE FIND CLUE
WARREN: NO COMMENT

And now on to my greatest triumph. It was so simple I hesitate to give it away. But it made me a legend, it earned me a ten-pound cash bonus, it went to six replates, and it impressed even Harry Dam, though I had yet to meet him. I went on a certain day back to Whitechapel, looking for a gal who knew Annie. I found her on station, as it were, in a slow patrol down Wentworth, looking haggard and ill used, which was clear indication that she was haggard and ill used.

"Madam, Jeb of the *Star*; I saw you at the occasion of Annie's death."

"You," she said. "Reporter, news fella type. You wrote nice about poor Annie, everybody read it and remembered the poor gal."

"May I buy you a gin? Perhaps we could discuss her some more."

"I likes me gin, sure," she said, and we shortly were arranged at a table at the Ten Bells, a watering and ginning hole to the trade.

The chat was general and pleasant and sad for a bit, and like all of the unfortunates I would meet, she turned out, once one was by her defenses, to be an all right sort, brought low by her love of the fiery blur she held in the glass before her, but she didn't produce anything I could use for the longest time, and I began to wonder how to pass her off without buying her another thruppence of bliss, when she said in response to nothing I had been clever enough to ask, "Wonder what the bloke done with 'er rings?"

"I say, what rings?" And then I remembered Bagster Phillips remarking on her bruised finger and surmising the absence of the rings.

"Annie had them two brass rings. Nothing to 'em, but they was dear to 'er. They was wedding rings, she said. 'E cuts 'er guts out plain, and 'e takes them rings. 'E's off 'is chum, that one."

I nodded.

And thus the next day's *Star* front page, consisting entirely of:

ANNIE'S RINGS
FIEND STOLE VICTIM'S BELOVED WEDDING BANDS
POLICE HAVE NO EXPLANATION FOR BIZARRE THEFT

That moved the story hard for a few days, being the sort of homey, horrifying detail the shopkeeps and shopgirls and clerks and barristers' assistants could get an emotional fix on. Where were Annie's rings? If the fiend was one of my readers, he'd be wise to chuck them in the Thames and think no more. But I thought I detected a whiff of vanity in him; he just might be arrogant enough to keep them. Be interesting, I thought, if it was the evidence of the rings that sent him to the gallows.

Many other issues drifted in and out of focus over the next weeks, all of them ultimately meaningless and not worth recording here, one of them being what time it was the poor girl expired, as several highly dubious witnesses reported hearing, seeing, and not seeing things at conflicting times during the morning. The coppers believed them and dismissed their own surgeon's learned opinion. What utter foolishness!

But in the end, only one thing lingered: a business of the Jews. I suspect the large influx of them excited anger, fear that they would bring alien ways to old Albion, undercutting the labor market and driving good Englishmen out of work. Of the seventy-six thousand occupants of Whitechapel, thirty to forty thousand were Jewish, while of that same total population 40 percent were below the poverty level. Thus, in many minds, Jews equaled unemployment. So there was no love for them to begin with when the murders started.

This anger began to coagulate at their commission. We of Fleet Street were no help at all. One of our reporters—not the famous Jeb but the Yank calling himself Harry Dam, whom I didn't know except by name, as, recall, his absence "with a floozy" had gotten me into this game in the first place—had reported even the week before Annie's death that a fellow named "Leather Apron" was a suspect. That was, by the way, what many called Jewish butchers. That a leather apron was found soaking in a tub in the yard of 29 Hanbury (yes, I had missed it, as had the clomping coppers for quite some time) didn't help matters, even if it was soon proved to have nothing to do with the case. Still, the Leather Apron whisper would not go away.

Harry played up the Jewish characteristics of this beast Leather Apron, intimating mystical use for the blood and certain body parts of poor Polly. And the killer hadn't even taken any body parts! One day Mr. O'Connor, who knew a replate story if ever there was one, ran the headline LEATHER APRON: ONLY NAME LINKED TO WHITECHAPEL MURDERS. I suppose I didn't approve, but I was hoping to be taken on permanent-like, so who was I to go against the great man's judgment?

Then the *Manchester Guardian* wrote, "It is believed that (Scotland Yard) attention is directed to a notorious character named 'Leather Apron.' . . . all are united in the belief that (the killer) is a Jew or of Jewish parentage, his face being of a marked Jewish type."

You could feel a fever building. I was part of it but had no tool by which to stop it. I also had no will to, being largely agnostic on the issue and knowing no Jews and feeling a little suspicious of them myself. That indifference, plus my customary greed and ambition, got the best of my low character; I had signed on to ride the train as far as it would take me, and damnation to all crushed beneath its progress. I had no idea how far that would be.

The mobs responded to this campaign as mobs do: violently. Crews of young toughs roamed Whitechapel and roughed up individual Jews. The coppers seemed to pick up anybody with a Jewish name and bring him in for hard questioning: among the arrestees, Jacob Isenschmid and Friedrich Shumacher.

Finally, a Jewish slipper maker, actually nicknamed Leather Apron, was arrested and interrogated. It turned out he had knocked a Judy or two about, but that was all, and he was in no way affiliated with knives or the sort of carnage our fellow had made twice. He had well-proven alibis and was let go.

But the Jewish fear grew. On several occasions, mobs formed outside the Spitalfields police station where this Leather Apron (John Pizer, by name) was incarcerated. Anti-Jewish graffiti began to appear mysteriously on tenement walls and storefronts. A very uncomfortable tension, palpable and unsettling, began to course through the lower orders—I love them in principle, but I was to learn on this adventure that they can be reprehensible louts in ungoverned mobs and need stern leadership to harness their rage—and violence was in the air. If our killer was a Jew, killing on some kind of twisted religious grounds, I had no idea what mischief might be released. For that and that alone, I began to hope that early suspicions of a doctor or a surgeon played out, for if it were an upper-class nob, it's unlikely that a mob would head into Kensington with torches and pitchforks. For one thing, the Queen's Royal Horse Guards would stop them with Gatling guns before they got across the street, just like the black-skinned ugga-buggas, and that would be a bloody day for old London.

Among all these voices, one was not heard from. The killer's. His weekly schedule was not kept, and he did not strike again for two weeks after Annie. What was he doing?

September 10, 1888

Dear Mum,
I never heard from you after the last letter, but maybe that's because I didn't send it. Ha-ha! Maybe when they catch this fellow, I'll send it and this one and you and Da can have a good laugh about how your bad daughter survived what all about is calling "the autumn of the knife."

You know the fellow is back and he cut up another girl. He even stole her wedding rings! It's been in all the papers, so I know you heard about it, and you'll be worrying because this time it's so close by me. Well, I am writing to tell you don't be worried! Nothing's going to happen to me. I have a guardian angel now!

I have a fellow, a nice man, he doesn't beat me or try and shove me about to be a certain way. He lets me be, and what more can a girl ask, plus he brings in a good penny as he works as a porter at the Billingsgate fish market, where there's a lot of packing and loading and ice chipping to do, so when he gets home, he's a tired fellow and we'll have a glass of beer at the pub. He wants me to stop with what I do bringing in the money, and maybe that's in the cards, who can read the future? But I'll tell you, he won't let no other fellow on to me, well, on to me to hurt me. As I said, see, it's different down here, all of us are so close to going under that it's more forgiving of certain things. There's no high and mighty. Nobody's high, nobody's mighty, you do what you has to, and you helps out them what needs it and in turn, when you're down, they'll help you back. The girls is all so nice, not like some I've known.

The other thing is that poor Annie, that's what the newspapers say was her name, she was again a lone gal on a dark street, with nobody about to see or stop nothing. He fooled her into taking him into a backyard where it was even darker than the street, and that's where he ripped her up, and you must have heard, as I have, it's in all the papers, this time he did a job on the ripping.

I don't know what makes a fellow want to do that. We girls never hurt nobody, and only a few of us gets involved in any bully game, and then only when a boyfriend threatens with a whipping or worse. But mostly we get along with each other, with the blue bottles, as we call coppers, and with the boyos who come down here for their bit of dirty.

See, Mum, I'm always with other girls, and we'll be walking round and round and keeping an eye out for each other. And we'll only go with a gentleman if he's nicely dressed and polite and don't smell too bad. It's said this fellow is a Jew called Leather Apron, as all the Jew butchers seem to wear such a thing. One of our better coppers, called Johnny Upright for his good and fair ways, done arrested him, and for a time, it seemed there'd be no more cutting. Johnny Upright got his man! Too bad, ain't it so, that this Leather Apron wasn't the true bad bloke, only someone the papers said was bad. They had to let him go. But Johnny Upright's still on the case and you can bet on that one.

Sometimes you do see the Jews down here, but usually they stick to their own section, which ain't far, but almost always they're doing some business, they're always buying for three and somehow turning it about to sell for four, so I'm not one who thinks it is a Jewish fellow. They're too busy counting their gold, ha-ha! More like a sailor or a soldier, they can be brutes and want what they want. I don't like soldiers; hurting is what they does.

But as I say, even after the job he done on poor Annie and the ripping they say was horrible, and even though it was but a few blocks down, I know it'll be all swell. Johnny Upright will save us, and then my man's always on guard and won't let nobody touch me. Well, ha-ha, "touch" me. Now I know I won't send this letter to you, Mum, because you wouldn't find it so funny ha-ha at all.

But still it makes me feel so close to you and to all that I miss so bad. I keep hoping that someday I'll wake up and the thirst will be gone and I can go back to having a nice life like everybody else. I hope that so bad and I love you so much.

Your loving daughter
Mairsian

CHAPTER NINE

The Diary

September 24, 1888

———————

To quote my many Cockney friends, it only hurts when I larf. And there is much about which to larf. I cannot help the larfter, for example, when I contemplate the accounts of the bumbling clowns better known as the Metropolitan Police, Scotland Yard, the coppers, the Bobbies. Make that Boobies. What a show of idiocy.

Forget the idiocy of competing, distracting witnesses, the crushing of the crime scene until, if it wasn't clueless to begin with, it was quickly rendered thereup, forget that one thing, they dismiss their own surgeon, according to the *Star*, who correctly placed the time of Annie's journey at four-thirty A.M.

No, the issue here is Lieutenant Colonel Sir Charles Warren, the soldier fellow who runs the coppers in his dotage, a gift, one supposes, from the monstrous dowager Vicky as reward for having sent so many heathens to heathen heaven, so our merchants could move in and rob the survivors blind. Note how a certain pattern holds true: The more honorifics before a man's name and the more initials after them, the bigger an idiot he is likely to be. Thus, he is at his worst when his best is most demanded by the situation. How our empire managed to crush all those wogs under such fools is a mystery, the answer, I suspect, having to do with a superior mechanical imagination as to machines than its poor victims as opposed to any genius among its leaders. We had got the Gatling, and they had not. Sir Charles is so pressured by my predations that he has lost all ability to discriminate. What is needed is the sharp intelligence of a single man who has the wisdom to penetrate the obvious nonsense and press hoo-hah and understand exactly how it happened and from that deduce who did it. Alas, such a man only exists in the fancies of a fellow named Conan Doyle, and his portrait is an ideal, not an actuality. I would tremble in my boots if Sherlock Holmes were after me, but dear Sherlock exists only in the vapors of the Conan Doyle mind, not on the cobblestones of Whitechapel! Ha, and double ha.

But idiocy doesn't stop there. Even Dr. Phillips, whose expertise, if ignored, specified the deed's time, is not immune. Upon discovering some sweetbreads gone from Annie, who needed them no longer, he expostulated that I—that is, a theoretical "I"—had sold them to medical schools. Indeed, yes, another ha. And how would a fellow go about doing such, I wonder, without giving up the jig? A far more judicious interpretation, even if equally untrue, would be that "I" am a researcher of some sort, an MD or a Doctor of Science in chemistry or some arcane element of body knowledge, and needed the U and the V for experimentation. From that supposition, all kinds of worthy enterprises could be hatched: One could go to medical faculties and inquire about "unbalanced" graduates with an interest in the areas inferred by these sweetbreads; one could inquire of pharmaceutical companies, who would know such things, what drugs had been and were still being or were possibly being implemented to affect these areas of the woman body. One could also take inquiries into a much lower realm, for example, and examine the nonoccidental element for magic uses of these two biscuits in preparing such products sexual as aphrodisiacs, pregnancy terminators, love potions, and the whole panoply of imaginative folkloric usage. All would be wrong, but all would nevertheless be intelligent deductions from the material at hand.

The only sensible man alive appears to be this Jeb of the *Star*, who quite helpfully noted and played all ruffles and flourishes with the missing rings. ANNIE'S WEDDING RINGS! The fiend even took poor Annie's rings. If only she'd have had a cat to murder, that would have blown the keg full to heaven. But the rings thing was perfect calculation on my part and perfect application on Jeb's; his mission is to sell newspapers, at which he no doubt succeeded, and though I have a different product in mind, his enthusiasm at his "scoop" is a first stop on the way to my triumph. It pleases.

Yet in all the mirth, a certain melancholy cannot be denied. First, poor Annie has been lost in all this. It seems that I, her slayer, her strangler, her vivisectionist, am the only being on earth who laments her passing, doomed enough by corrupted lung as the poor lass was, testimony of Dr. Phillips proving the point. I could solipsistically argue that my intercession spared the poor lady much in the way of pain and dissolution, in exchange merely for time, a year's worth. But I will not. Each man's death and et cetera diminishes even me. It was my agency and I am the bloke all are on the prowl to bring down and see floating beneath the gallows arm, suspended by a stout piece of hemp. I am guilty, guv'nor, at least by your laws.

Like that of Polly before her, Annie's character flaw appeared to be alcoholism, perhaps brought about by the wretched and crushing fates of two of her three children, one an early death, the other a cripple who had to go into a state ward. As before, there was no net to capture the falling Annie, and she landed in Whitechapel's most wretched slum, the Wicked Quarter Mile, as it has been called, selling notch and lip for enough bad gin to drown the pain. There is little else to tell; the most remarkable thing about her was the encounter with me and, I suppose, her surprisingly strong, straight teeth, so unusual that even Phillips remarked on them in his report. If anyone of celestial royalty is listening—as an atheist, I doubt it, but one must abide by the ceremony—I hereby apologize for the botch I made of the passing. The business of the left hand and the constriction of the throat happened, as it were, spontaneously, but nevertheless, it speaks as an expression of and extension of my will which would not be denied, so

I will not deny responsibility. The knife at least takes these angels quickly and sends them painlessly to their god and his heaven, if that is where they in fact go, or possibly just into a painless forever of dreamless sleep. The strangulation business is ugly, to say nothing of difficult to manage and slow to take effect. My apology and my pledge to all who come before me never to repeat the sacrilege.

On the other hand, another of my plans is working splendidly, beyond ANNIE'S WEDDING RINGS. That is this business of the Jews. It is something I had foreseen, as it seems to be a universal. Wherever they go, these people inflame malice, envy, anger, suspicion, and violence. Yet Mr. Disraeli was a Jew, was he not? The great banking family Rothschild, which has financed many of the glorious buildings of Paris and other cities, is Jewish. Many great philosophers are Jewish, as are scientists, mathematicians, scholars, and doctors. I suspect the hatred that always accompanies their presence has to do with the fact that some of them have a gift for numbers and are able to figure in extreme speed the advantage of this rate over that rate in the long term versus the short term, and they have a way of offering deals that sound good to the taker, except that in time he learns the terms were not in his favor.

An ugly current has been loosened, egged on by reprehensible newspapering, as led by the noxious Mr. Harry Dam of the *Star*. He was, for a time, obsessed with some apparition called Leather Apron, a mystical Jew butcher-beast, and as a consequence, Whitechapel became unsafe for the many poor Jews who live there. About that reality, neither Dam nor the *Star* appears to care a jot! In any event, Leather Apron was soon rounded up and found completely innocent, as were several other Jews and marginal wretches who bumbled into Warren's crude dragnet. But even as these cases are revealed to be without foundation, nobody is listening and the temperature is rising. Soon lynchings may occur, followed by pogroms, neighborhood burnings, the death of innocents. It will be a return to the Middle Ages.

It is the most perfect screen for my next and most ingenious move. My mind is clever, and if I plot carefully, reconnoiter adroitly, and am bold, I will triumph in the end. This stroke of genius has an added advantage: I have enough blood on my hands and will happily greet Old Scratch when he leads me to hell's tenth circle, but I do not need to add that of a thousand Jewish babies. I will be cleansed of that sin. Egad, have I accidentally done something moral? How appalling!

CHAPTER TEN

Jeb's Memoir

I opened the envelope—finding it first of all to be on the heavy cream stock of higher taste, familiar somehow—removed the missive inside, unfolded it, half recognized the penmanship, and then fully recognized it fully: *Charlie!*

That is, Charles Harrison Hilliard, editor of *Contemporary Review*, a lively and often bawdy arts journal that I contributed to quite regularly for some years before falling into the *Star*'s orbit, therefore aligning myself with Big Boring Press and cutting loose from Small Impudent Press. Charlie came from department store people in some far provincial town, but he, having none of it, was quite content to spend their hard-earned money on a quarterly of sublime physical beauty that was notably full of irreverence, immaturity passing as wit, radical politics, the need to shock for its own sake, and the occasional truly well-conceived essay by someone whose name was not yet big enough to get him published in the *Atheneum*. That was me. The *Atheneum* crowd, very Oxbridgy and, for all their liberal airs, quite nose-up when it came to rube Irish geniuses in brown suits with the look of a pig farmer's right-hand man, had yet to notice me and perhaps never would. Very well, I snorted to myself many a time, I shall live quite happily without the *Atheneum*, and I paid them back the insult of not noticing me by not noticing them, which they never noticed.

So here was Charlie, after a few years' absence from my life.

It's been too long. We had so many good laughs but now you've disappeared, even from O'Connor's horrid Star. You were the best critic in London, which meant you had to be punished for your temerity in so regularly humiliating the bigger fishes. Hope you're writing a novel or a play or something. Can't wait to hear.

In any event, do please come to a soiree I am holding tomorrow night at eight, full of interesting chaps, all of whom hate Atheneum, having not been noticed yet by them, either. Rather a chatty lot, you'll fit right in. Gals, too, artist and poet types, perhaps shady in certain aspects if you wish that game upon yourself. Teetote if you want, but the punch will be spiked with rum and the fizzy in the bottle will knock a jack-tar on his arse!

Best,

Charlie

It arrived at the perfect time. I'd worked myself to exhaustion on the murders, much to O'Connor's satisfaction, but even he could see I was running ragged. He instructed me to take some days off, which I spent mostly sleeping, to avoid my mother. Now, just as I was feeling revived, Charlie's invite arrived and it seemed a perfect anodyne to dead whores in alleys and yards.

I had a bang-up time. I didn't dominate, no, but neither did I withdraw into recessiveness, and I came up with as many clever lines and swift retorts as any of them. It was a fast crowd, they drank and smoked too much, they fancied themselves "outlaws" (but of the safest sort), and the alcohol liberated them to pretend to be who they wished to be. As for me, I pretended to be a more widely published writer, or a writer rather than a subspecies called "journalist" or "critic." I wore the brown wool suit, having no choice in the matter, with a blue cotton shirt, and looked like a cross between a barroom poet and an IRA gunman, as I had wanted. Some may have thought me dangerous, which I rather liked, not knowing that lump in my pocket was an extra handkerchief instead of a Webley, and I enjoyed the mystery I seemed to carry about, the sense of knowing more than I did. As a veteran observer of life and death, I thought myself superior to all of them, for their bohemianism, social nonchalance, and contempt for convention was mostly affectation. I'd seen gutted lasses and knew in fact, not merely in theory, how short, nasty, and brutish life could be.

I'm not sure when I noticed him. It was subtle. He was just there. No, I am not about to confess some homosexualist secret, like the one that doomed poor Wilde to Reading Gaol a few years later, and I have no pressing desire to touch the flesh of a being of the same sex. But I am wooable by wit, dynamism, worldliness, good taste, and as I pretended to myself, the certain knowingness that bespeaks a fellow who has seen and tasted much.

"You're the music critic, no?" he asked me when the drifting of people and the vagaries of alcoholic imbibing brought us together on the flow of the currents. He was tall, and his tweed, I noted, was of fine quality. The tailoring was superb, a three-piece suit of very modern cut, with red four-in-hand instead of a black fluffy bow tie, and the whole effect was of a fellow who paid close attention to his clothes until he put them on.

"I was for a time," I said.

"Hope you closed down all the concert halls," he said. "Such puerile jibber-jabber. When are they going to have the guts to change one single thing about the classical canon? It's mostly Wagner done poorly, since we treacle-slopping Brits don't have the coldness of soul to do Wagner as he should be done, all savage and scary. We do him like Dion Boucicault doing Dumas with kettledrums and trombones. Not a damned thing for anybody with a brain, or at least the aspirations to thought. Music as social instrument is an alien concept to them."

"I must say," I said, "you speak like a critic yourself, sir. That's a thought I've had many a time. Meanwhile, in Europe there's some interesting work. The Russian Anton Rubinstein is using the baton to do something other than slop treacle for the pigs."

"'Treacle for the pigs,'" he said. "I like that. My name's Dare."

I told him mine.

"Of course," he said. "I pretended I didn't know you, but I've read your pieces in Charlie's little rag. You were a boy worth watching, I thought. I watched, I watched, I watched. Where on earth did you go?"

"I wrote music under a nom de guerre for a year for the *Star* and then had an opportunity to try my hand at another part of the journo game. It's been interesting, though without much glory."

"Well, you had the divine spark. Don't lose it in some larger outfit that wants to regulate all voices to the same modulation. But I have tenure, so I'm great with career advice, not having to worry about such things as food, board, and money."

"You teach?"

"I yell at them. They pretend to listen. I grade the papers by throwing them down the steps and determining which land on the ninety step, which the eighty step, which the seventy. No one seems to care much, and I can never get in trouble with the department, since I'm also the department head. The corruption is blissfully total."

I found this line very amusing, almost irresistible. I love it when those safely in the bosom of a comforting institution trash it savagely, pointing out its follies, brutal politics, bad behaviors, and utter tomfoolery, but with such good cheer and equanimity as to suggest that all they say will be so relentlessly honest.

"You have a dramatic way about you, sir," I said. "I'm sure you entrance the students."

"I'd like to entrance some of the girls into bed, I would. The beastly boys, I'd entrance them off to Afghanistan or the Crimea—say, are we still in the Crimea?"

"I believe we've moved onward in our Christian crusade."

"Well, wherever there are too many wogs, the darker the better, all fuzzy and wuzzy at once. Every good English boy should spend a few years Gatling-gunning nig-nogs for queen, country, and the interests of the Birmingham steel lords. And to keep the price of silk for Charlie's pater's department stores down."

Speaking of Charlie, he suddenly bore down upon us, holding a champagne bottle in each hand. He'd been pouring his way through his guests.

"I see you two have found each other," he said. "I knew you would, as you've much the same temperament and scabrous insight. Tom does phonetics at the University of London."

Good God, I thought. *The* Professor Thomas Dare!

"I was telling our young friend here the sad truth of academics today," said Professor Dare. He had round black spectacles, wavy blond hair, and one of those aquiline profiles that seemed to make him the grandson of the Iron Duke. But his irony had no Wellington in it. "At least my lackadaisical approach to duty leaves me with enough time for my experiments, which are the real thrust of my life. I can tell you, if you want, why a tribe in Africa called the Xhosa speaks with a peculiar popping sound, like a short, dry belch; they literally communicate by burps."

I laughed. Amusing fellow.

"And then there are the Germans. Do you know, they form words by just sticking them together, so that their word for 'Gatling gun' literally translates into 'mechanicaldeviceshootingwithoutcockingrifle?' The words get longer still. No word is too long for a German because it's quite impossible to bore a German. You cannot entertain a Norwegian, you cannot bore a German, and you cannot educate an American or a chimpanzee."

I laughed again, then sought to turn him on another course. "What experiments have you done?"

"Too many by half," he said.

I had read of him and thought I knew the background. Renegade intellectual, too bold for Oxford or Cambridge, too radical for any provincial place, always going off exploring, had theories of language as it related to society, and had invented—yes, that was it—a universal alphabet.

He wanted to do away with tribalism, nationalism, paternalism, capitalism, communism, militarism, vegetarianism, colonialism, ismism, anything that could take -ism as a tail end. Any thought, belief system, article of faith, uniqueness of dress, or size of boot heel. His methodology consisted of converting the world to one language that all would speak without accent, or indication of geography, class, or origin. Each man, each woman, each child would be a tabula rosa, so to speak, and come at the world without prejudice or hostility applied before he even got a chance to show what he or she could do.

Naturally, Dare was laughed off the front pages and hadn't been heard from in some time. For one thing: Who would pay for it? For another: Who would teach it? For still another: Who would enforce it?

"I do remember your piece in the *Times,* Professor Dare," I said. "A nice stir it caused, as I remember."

"Dare's Dare. What piffle. All gone, best forgotten. I was a fool, believed in the educability of the species and that humanity was capable of acting on its own behalf. But people are born with such deep ideas and grow so attached to them that it's like trying to argue them out of a limb. If I said to you, 'Say, your life would be better without that damned leg,' what would you say?"

"Why, you're a madman."

"Indeed, and that is what they said to me. Anyhow, enough of this chit-chat about my squalid past. I will leave you and mingle. I think there's someone here who could help my reputation whom I haven't yet insulted tonight. Possibly it will come to fisticuffs, which would be the ideal outcome."

And he was swept away.

"Interesting fellow," I said to Charlie.

"Tom's a charmer. Brilliant but won't back down. Perhaps a ruinous fault. You could call it a personality flaw, but you could also call it a heroic attribute. Socrates had it, too. So he gets destroyed and the mediocre continue to clump along to domination, producing universal stultification. Perhaps in a hundred years he will get his due. Champagne, my friend?"

I turned Charlie down, and he drifted away to fill more glasses. The party waxed and waned like a moon, and it seemed little eddies of energy were forever breaking out wherever I wasn't, and when I turned to the laughter, I always saw Professor Dare at the center of it, and yet when they seemed to have him pinned down for serious conversation, he'd somehow peel off and take his magic elsewhere.

At last the party seemed to be breaking up, and by my pocket watch, I knew it was time to say thanks to Charlie and depart from this leafy street in Bloomsbury. I assumed finding a hansom wouldn't be much of a problem. But a crowd had backed up around Charlie at the doorway, so I backed off and, seeking relief from the closeness of the room, stepped out on the terrace. Ah, the sweetness of the clean air, the drift of some sweet flower's perfume, the clear night above. I drew it all in, enjoying, and then who should I find hunched against the balustrade but Professor Dare, enjoying a cheroot.

"Oh, hullo," I said. "I enjoyed your company. You see the world much as I do myself."

"I hope not. I detest it and everything in it. I once believed in everything, now I believe in nothing. You're much too young for such cynicism. You have bruising and scarring left to do. You must earn the purity of your contempt, else it's a pose meant to attract attention."

"Well, you hide your disillusion brilliantly by the boldness of your wit."

"Could always crack a line, I'll say that for myself. But we do have something in common, I might add, now that I think of it."

"And that would be?"

"Why, Jeb, we both detest Sir Charles Warren and understand that he is entirely too stupid in his thinking to catch this fellow you chaps call the Whitechapel Murderer."

It was quite a moment. Not a word had been said about the murders the whole night, and I had presumed no one there had any idea I wrote under Jeb for the *Star* and had seen the wrecked and bleeding bodies steaming and leaking in the cool night air.

"I say," I said, which is what people say when they have nothing to say, "I say, you have the advantage over me. I know not—"

"Oh, come now. I've particularly enjoyed the pieces on Warren's folly. Your analysis of the broken system that underlies his Scotland Yard is spot-on, but even if they become more efficient and get more boots to the street faster, I don't think the killer will fall to dragnet. If he were that careless, his luck would have run out, given his need to commit his deeds in heavily patrolled areas, just missing the blue bottles by a hair each time out."

"Professor Dare, I shan't lie, because I am indeed professionally Jeb, but how on earth, sir, did you know? Did some kind of spy—"

"No, no. Language. Phonetics. One of my many theories is that we speak two Englishes, a shallow English and a deep English. The second is the language of structure, organization; I call it the Beneath. It lurks, prehistoric and brutal, under the gibbets of grammar, words, punctuation, and neatness in penmanship. It is a reflection of the manner in which we solve problems, it expresses how we think, it expresses our true self. It is, in the end, our truth. I believe I've trained myself to read for the tracks of this Beneath, and when I read Jeb in the *Star* over the past few weeks, I saw those tracks. The music was extremely familiar. Some of the words, too, some of the effects—though now you're drawn through the sieve of newspaper editing, with some dilution occurring. But I recognized it. You have much to write, much to learn, but if you give it your life, you might at one time accomplish something of note."

"I've actually written five novels. Unpublished, the lot."

"Write five more."

"Perhaps I shall. But may I ask, to return to first causes, why you despise Warren at my level of intensity? It seems to be my job, and that explains my occasional interceptions of his vector, but you, sir, a professor at university, I cannot—"

"The murderer. The fiend, of course."

"The murderer?"

"I adore him. He is so real, he is so fascinating, I cannot get enough. And unlike anything in years, he provokes me. That is why I pore over the accounts; that is why, when time has cooled off the curious mobs, I visit each murder site and look hither and yon for whatever the coppers may have missed. Haven't found a thing yet. And the most demanding question of all: Where is he? Do you have theories?"

"I don't believe, no matter what the *Star* publishes, that he's a Jew. What little I know of Jews convinces me they are not of killing ilk. No, he's one of us, and his contempt for the poor degraded Judys is really a critique on our system. But perhaps I impose my politics. Sir, do you have theories?"

"In formation. Unsuited for expression at this time."

"I would love to hear them."

"Perhaps, then, when they jell into aspic, I shall invite you to the club for a chat. Does that suit?"

"Fabulously," I said.

CHAPTER ELEVEN

The Diary

September 25, 1888

I had planned very carefully this time, and reconnoitered skillfully, examining against the triple indices of privacy, escape possibilities, and constable patrols. I had found a perfect spot, for this one had to be perfect, and for it to be perfect I had to have privacy with the body for more than a few minutes. I had this night an important agenda. Too bad a poor missy would have to pay for my higher purpose, but then that is the way of our wicked world, is it not?

This time I marked the area south of Whitechapel Road as my hunting ground, while my two previous expeditions had been well north of it. Where Commercial crossed it, then bent toward the east—Whitechapel's layout is a mess, by the way, having been invented a thousand years ago by wandering cows, chiefly—it pursued an admirable straight course for quite a ways, and the fourth intersection it afforded was with the nondescript Berner Street. This byway yielded a low no-man's-land of grimy brick and chimney, and being close to Commercial, where the Judys still were ample, it offered darkness for many a secluded rut. I reasoned it would be easy enough to engineer a tête-à-tête with one, and she would turn off Commercial and lead me down Berner. That such a spot was but a few blocks from the police station did not particularly perturb me, for in my observation, the constables did not favor Berner with their attentions.

Perhaps they had been warned off by Sir Charles, because halfway down the first block was a queer institution known as the Anarchists' Club, where I'd once heard William Morris hold forth on a new aesthetic for modern times to an indifferent audience. He preferred wallpaper to revolution, not a popular position in those precincts. It was full nearly every night with radicals of various Slavic, Jewish, and Russian origins, singing and chanting and conspiring the night away. The coppers would fancy that so much energy would keep any mad killer away, when the exact opposite was true. I knew that such men as were drawn to the club were of a species known as zealots, which would mean that though their eyes were open, what they were really seeing would be dreams of a society where they, and not the pale, lily-livered millionaires of the Kensington Club set, were the masters. The anarchists would hang anybody who belonged to a club, and it was the image of those well-shod feet dangling eight inches above the ground that occupied their imaginations. Then, of course, they would found their own clubs. Such it is with all grand dreamers, of this ilk or that.

I spent this evening rooting around the club. Since radicals believe (happily) that property is crime, they find the notion of locked doors abhorrent. Anyone radical or pretending to be radical may enter and wander the club, which sits next to one of those improvised spaces in chockablock Whitechapel called Dutfield's Yard. It's not a yard and there's no Dutfield anywhere, save painted long ago on the gate. I observed that Judy would frequently open a door in the closed gate for a quick stand-up assignation in the darkness and quietude of the yard, then leave, always pulling the door shut behind her. Thus for my purposes, it was perfect.

But I had to know what species of experience the club offered, so I found myself one of a hundred or so throaty rip-roarers purporting to represent the masses as they—none more enthusiastically than myself—bellowed forth the sacred hymn of all those who believed we had to tear down before we could build up. I came a bit late, so it wasn't until the fifth stanza that I made my contribution.

> *The kings made us drunk with fumes,*
> *Peace among us, war to the tyrants!*
> *Let the armies go on strike.*
> *Stocks in the air, and break ranks.*
> *If they insist, these cannibals*
> *On making heroes of us,*
> *They will know soon that our bullets*
> *Are for our own generals!*

Lovely sentiment, but try singing it in the mess of the 44th Argyle Foot and you'll end up swinging from a tree overlooking the parade ground. Were they planning this year's uprising or celebrating last year's? Was it to be Mittleuropa or some unpronounceable republic in the far Balkans? Or maybe they were planning to go against the Great Bear herself, which meant that of the two hundred comrades the building held, at least a hundred and fifty of them were tsarist secret policemen, but they would have no interest in what happened in the yard outside their windows, only in far-off dungeons and torture rooms. However, I shared my doubts with nobody and presented to the company the very image of a happy mansion arsonist and execution squad commander. The louder I was, the more invisible I became.

After group sing, there was much hugging and babbling in a number of languages alien to my ear, but the universal thematic of the room was brotherhood, as accelerated by the effects of vodka. Everyone glowed in the pink of either revolutionary fervor or rotting capillaries. When the bottle came to me, I took a swig, finding it to be liquid fire, more appropriate for battle than society, but who was I to disagree with the masses. I hugged, I kissed, I shook hands, I raised fists, I shouted, I carried on essentially like a bad imitation of a drunken bear. However, there was no penalty for overacting on these boards.

In time, after the minutes had been discussed and accepted in several different tongues and certain policy issues debated rather too fiercely (suggesting that the participants loved debate over revolution) and the next picnic/mass action planned, postponed, and ultimately canceled, the meeting atomized, and various cliques and factions withdrew to their own counsel, and all the lone wolves too anarchistic to join were free to mosey about. I fit that category, in shabby clothes with a derby pulled low, and it was via this process that I was able to make a secret examination of the building in public, without rousing suspicion. They were too busy contemplating dreams of Thermidor and who would run the Midlands Electrification Program to pay attention to any particular individual. To their imaginations, it was the mass, not the man, that mattered. I would soon set them straight on that matter.

At any rate, the building was what one might expect of such a place, the second-floor meeting hall rather like the vaulted cathedral of the religion, all sorts of ancillary rooms off or below it, including a printing shop at the rear to crank out the necessary broadsides, a crude kitchen for brewing soup by the gallon, a reading room that collected the latest in revolutionary news from all over the world, a cellar that seemed like cellars anywhere, even under the Houses of Parliament. All in all, quite banal.

That is, unless one knew where to look.

CHAPTER TWELVE

Jeb's Memoir

Indeed, where was he? The party finished with a vague invitation to drop in on Professor Dare "sometime," and it was back to the murder grind. The monster missed his weekly assignment, and then he missed his second. Was he planning some extra-special extravaganza? Had he gone on the slack? Was he bored? It was hop-picking time, so maybe he'd gone to the country to earn a few quid filling sacks for our brewers. If rich, perhaps he was even now luxuriating at Cap d'Antibes, eating snails and other Frenchy things, his knife forgotten for a bit.

Whatever the reason, O'Connor could see the consequences playing out in newsstand sales, upon which we depended for our circulation of 125,000, "Largest Circulation of Any Evening Newspaper in the Kingdom." I tried my best, and the rings push was of some help, but after the ludicrousness of the Polly and Annie inquests, the multiplicity of absurd clues, such civic vanities as a vigilante committee forming to offer the reward that Warren had so far refused to authorize (as if this fellow were part of a network of criminals and could be ratted out like a common cracksman or swindler), and many heated speeches against the Jews for this, that, and the other thing, some other detective blowhards who opined that the High Rips or the Green Gaters were the culprits, and finally some high copper muckety-muck's much promulgated idea of a husky Russky, it seemed both pointless and hopeless. I wrote a nicely vicious piece on the inefficiencies of the police, which attracted very little attention, Harry Dam reheated shabby notions of Jewish ceremony, which until now required only Christian babes for blood with which to make matzos, but henceforth he claimed that the blood of whores was some part of some ritual in the cabala that I suppose was to make Baron Rothschild the richest man in the world again twice over. As far as progress in the investigation, practical steps to deal with the issue, shrewd analysis of the evidence, none of that. Nothing was happening.

An idle mind is indeed the devil's plaything, so we entered full scoundrel time, and who but I would enter history as the biggest of all scoundrels. That is, at the urging of the damned Harry Dam.

I was transforming some Pitman into typing, some nonsense that would go on page 4 under an advertisement for Du Barry's Revelenta, the flatulence and heartburn cure, when a lad approached and said, "Sir, Mr. O'Connor needs to see you."

"Eh?"

"Now, sir. I gather it's urgent."

"All right, then." I rose, put on the old brown, and followed the boy across the room and down a hall, where he knocked, and we heard a gruff Irish rasp respond, "Come in, then."

O'Connor put no store in majesty. I imagined the office of the editor of the *Times* to be a bookish chamber with a fireplace, a stag on the wall, and a globe, where cigars and port were often enjoyed. That of the *Star* was half a compass in another direction. Shabby is as shabby does, or perhaps the word would be "utilitarian," for it was simply a larger room with a desk, a table, and a few books. On the desk were several spikes, and on each spike were dozens of galleys of the stories that would comprise that afternoon's *Star*. At the table, I could see mock-ups of the front page, with nothing so dynamic as FIEND across the front, but rather, the usual gabble of unimpressive notices, such as 13 DIE IN AFGHAN SLAUGHTER (theirs or ours, I wondered), REWARD FOR WHITECHAPEL MURDERER DOUBLED, BISHOP PLEADS FOR CALM, and WHITECHAPEL LIGHTING BILL TURNED DOWN.

O'Connor sat at the desk, and next to him, almost invisible because he was backlit against a window that occluded his details, another man. They had been chatting warmly, I judged from the postures, the odor of cigars (one, still lit, sat in an ashtray and leaked a trail of vapor into the atmosphere), and the fact that before each was a glass.

"Sit," O'Connor commanded, "and possibly a spot of the old Irish?" His glass had a dram's worth of amber fluid left inside, whether a normal routine or the product of emergency, I didn't yet know.

"I'm a teetote, sir," I said. "My drunken father, this day sleeping under Dublin soil, drank more than enough for not only my own life but the lifetimes of any sons I might have."

"Suit yourself. Have you met Harry? You two fellows ever cross each other in the newsroom? Though Harry is no newsroom rat, I know."

"Hiya, pal," said Harry, rising, putting out a big American hand. It must have been his straw boater's hat on O'Connor's desk, for only an American would wear a boating hat where there were no boats to be found. He had a big, raw-boned face and a winning smile under a droopy red mustache, which displayed spadelike, rather gigantic teeth. He was wearing an Eton rowing blazer edged in white, a white shirt, a deep blue cross-hatched waistcoat, a tie of color (red), trousers of white with dark blue stripes, and white shoes and socks. Was there a regatta? Was he going picnicking with a lady on the Thames, or perhaps coxswaining a boat in the big tilt against Balliol's eight? I put it all on loathsome American crudity; as a people, they seem to lack any sense of tradition and are utterly incapable of reading the cues and learning from what they see. They're entirely bent on results or, rather, money. What they like they take and make their own, regardless.

"Nice coat," he said as we shook. "Can I get the name of your tailor?"

"Alas," I said, "a German madman."

"Too bad," he said. "I like the sort of belted, harnessed look that thing has. Is it for some kind of fishing?"

"Hunting jacket," I said. "Vented shoulders, gives one more flexibility on the turning shots. It's said the coloration dumbfounds the grouse, but even if their brains are the size of a pea, they cannot be that dim."

"You never know. Good shooting?"

I had no idea. I'd never done it, would never do it. "Quite jolly," I said.

"Now, fellows," said O'Connor, "glad to have us together for our little chat. Jeb, as I've been telling Harry, I'm proud of what you fellows have done. You've lit this place up and set the pace for the whole town. We're driving the story, and all the other rags are following us. And I know, if anything breaks fast and sudden-like, whichever of you is here will get it first, hard and straight. And we'll continue to drive, which means we'll continue to sell, which means my investors will shut up and leave me in peace."

Neither Harry nor I said a thing.

"However," said O'Connor, "I don't mind telling you, we have a problem."

He paused. We waited. He took up and sucked on his cheroot, and its glow inflamed as he drew air through it, then exhaled a giant puff of smoke.

"The problem is: Where is he?"

"In hell, hopefully," I said.

"Good for the world, bad for the *Star*. These greedy investors I have, they're like opium addicts. They get a whiff of the profits when something this bloody-wizard big happens, they want that to be the norm. So they put the squeeze on. You have no idea what I go through."

It occurred to me that it was quite wrong to hope for the killer to strike again as an aid toward boosting sales, but that was the reality of the business; O'Connor had no moral problem stating it so baldly, and the American wasn't about to make a speech, so I kept my own mouth sealed tightly.

"Boss, do you want me to go out and slice up a dolly?" said Harry, and we all three laughed, for it somewhat ameliorated the anguish in the room.

"No, indeed," said O'Connor. "The lawyers would never approve. But I want us to put our heads together and come up with an angle that we can push to heat things up again. The rings gag was a start, but there's more we can do. That's what this meet is about."

It never occurred to me. Covering the killer was enough; the idea of generating news, presumably of some sort of fabricated nonsense, struck me as appalling. Yet again, because I am who I am and lack certain moral strengths, and because I had gotten so much out of the killer's campaign against Whitechapel's Judys, I said nothing.

Dam mentioned something about a special edition that put the pictures of the two victims on the front page, to be run in black borders, with comments from the various children.

"Not going to do it, I'm afraid," said O'Connor. "Our readers don't want maudlin, they want mayhem. They want the red stuff sticky on their hands."

We batted it around for a bit, nice and easy-like, and I popped up with a few absurdities—what would the day's leading intellectuals, such as Mr. Hardy, Mr. Darwin, Mr. Galton, think, for example.

But the chat ran down sadly, and gloom filled the room. And then— hark, the herald angels sing!

"I got it," said Harry. "Yes, I do. Okay, what's this missing? It's even missing here in this room, and we're talking around it."

Silence, not of the golden sort.

"It's a story," said Harry finally. "It needs a villain."

"Well, it's got a villain," I said. "We just have no idea who it is."

"But he's not a character. He's an idea, a phantom, a theory, an unknown. Sometimes he's 'the fiend' and sometimes 'the murderer,' but he has no personality, no image. We can't get a fix on him. It's not enough that he's an Ikey, even if the folks do hate their Ikeys. He's still blurry, indistinct."

"I don't—" I started to say.

"He needs a name."

It was so absurdly simple, it brought conversation to a halt.

O'Connor sucked the cigar, Harry tossed down more brown and looked up, smiling. I sat there, feeling like a conspirator against Caesar, but then remembered I hated Caesar, so it would be all right. I also hated Harry for coming up with such a great idea. He was not without ability.

He was so positive. It's an American trait. Doubt is not in their vocabulary, nor half-speed ahead, nor anything that smacks of consideration, context, contemplation. They leave that for the poofs. For them it's always Dam the torpedoes!

Harry went on. "It can't just be any name, like Tom, Dick, or Harry. It needs to be special, clever, the sort of catchy thing you remember and that sticks in your mind. It's got to have that ring to it. I thought of 'Ike the Kike,' but that's too ridiculous."

"And suppose he turns out to be a High Church Anglican bishop," I said. "How embarrassing."

"Good point," said Harry. "That's why it has to be a good name. We need a genius to figure it out."

"I'll drop in on Darwin," I said, "and if he's not busy, I'm sure he'll pitch in. If not he, perhaps Cousin Galton will join our campaign." Sarcasm: last redoubt of the utterly defeated.

"I don't know those guys, but I get your point. We need something thought up by someone who's got a big talent."

"Harry," said O'Connor, "do go on. I like this, even if I can't yet see where it's going. And I'm confused how to make it happen."

"Okay," said Harry. "Here's how I see it. We come up with a letter from the guy, and he signs it with a name that will ring bang-on through the ages. No advert can top it, it's so perfect. Now, we can't run it ourselves, because everyone would sniff a phony. So the letter goes to the Central News Agency. You know, they're such hacks, they won't think twice about spreading it throughout the town. And now he's got a name, he's hot again. It bridges the gap until he strikes."

"Suppose it makes him strike again," I said.

"Come now, man," said O'Connor. "You saw the wounds. This darling rips them up so bad, he's obviously mad as a March hare. Nothing we do is going to influence that degree of insanity a whit."

I did see the wisdom in this. After all, I had seen the gutting of Annie Chapman, and I believed no sane man could do such a thing. It was hard for a sane man to even look upon it.

"Since it's your idea, Harry, perhaps you should write it," said O'Connor.

"Wish I could, boss," said Harry. "But I'm not what you call a poet. Words come out of me like little tiny rabbit turds. Grunting, oofing, and pushing. I'm a reporter, not a writer."

Again silence, but this time it was accompanied by stares, which came in a bit to rest on me. They both bored into me. It dawned on me where this was going, and I had to suspect it had been set up this way to make it seem spontaneous.

"Jeb's the best I've ever read. He can't put a sentence together that doesn't sound like music. He's the poet we need," Harry proclaimed.

"Ah—" I started to object, but being hopelessly addicted to praise, I didn't object too violently, for I wanted a few more gallons to come slopping down the chute onto my head.

"I wish I had his talent," continued Harry. "My energy, his talent, his, uh, genius, no telling how far we'd go."

"I think you're right," said O'Connor.

These fellows obviously thought it was something that could be turned on like a spigot. All I had to do was crank my genius faucet fully to the right and out would gush words for the ages. They had no idea that the faucet was rusty and temperamental, and the more you twisted it, the more you fretted and forced, the less likely it was to arrive on schedule. In fact, there was no schedule. It happened when it happened, and sometimes that was never.

"Now, listen here, Jeb," said O'Connor. "Let's think this through carefully. Indeed, yes, it's built around a name, a name that clangs like a fire bell. But it's also a tone. You've got to find something new. It has to play with words in an uncommon way, strike a chord that hasn't been heard, affect an attitude new to the world. It has to be coldly ironic, for a start."

"I don't get ironic," said Harry. "Never have. Iron, the ore? It has to have iron in it?"

"No, no, Harry, not the ore. It's got to have a deft way of saying something A, so absurd and preposterous, that it decodes to something B, the exact opposite. When you asked Jeb about the shooting, he said, 'Quite jolly.' Lacking much sense of how we speak over here, you thought he meant 'Quite jolly.' But in his voice was that elusive tone of which I speak, nuanced, coded, subtle, a series of inflections meshed perfectly with little facial expressions such as slightly lifted left brow, slightly snarled upper lip, and a kind of trailing, dissipating rhythm, by which he communicated to me and far more to himself that he considers such action as blowing little birdies out of the sky with twelve-dram blasts, so that there's nothing left but feathers and gristle, positively ghastly. *That's* irony. *That's* what this letter needs. *That* will make it last."

Harry took an excellent lesson from this. "He doesn't like hunting?" he asked incredulously.

We ignored him. He'd never get it, even if the initial impulse had been his.

"I'm not sure I'm up to this," I said.

"Jeb, you're halfway to a fine future. I'll play you big in recompense, and in a bit you'll be able to jump to a posh rag like the *Times*, where your gifts will make your fame, and they'll send you all over the world and all the publishers will be beating down your door for a manuscript."

I knew I was doomed. He had me cold. I was the birdie in the sights of his four-dram. The man was a genius.

And so, my first masterpiece. Like any piece of great writing, it has no autobiography. You cannot segmentize it and say, This came from there, and then I figured out that, and then from somewhere else that arrived, and there it was. No, no, not like that at all. It is more a process not of writing, I suppose, even less of willing, but somehow of becoming. You become what you must become.

Still, as I sat at what had become my desk in the newsroom, later that night after all the editions had been put to bed and most of the boyos had gone home or to the beer shop, I do remember odd notes coming together to form a melody, almost as if I were merely the conduit and something, some force (not God, as I don't believe in Him and if I did, surely this is not the sort of enterprise He would willingly join), were dictating to me. For some strange reason, the word "boss" was in my mind, as Harry had used it to O'Connor, and it was not a common Britishism but more a bit of American slang, not the word, per se, but using it as a term of address. We call no one "boss," we call the boss "sir." Universally. So it amused me that whoever our fellow was, he'd address the world, via the Central News Agency, as "Dear Boss." He wasn't writing the coppers, you see, but in some sense the public, his true supervisor, as if putting on the whole show for their edification. I was conscious also of O'Connor's dictate of irony, and I knew instinctively he was right. Our writer couldn't be a foamer, a threatener, a bloviator, a loudmouth on a crate in Hyde Park haranguing the proletariat on its meat-eating habits. You couldn't feel the sting of a volley of saliva when he talked. No, he'd been much too dry for that, so I used my own line from the meeting, "down on whores," which understated by a thousand percent the carnage that he had released upon them. The word "shan't" quite naturally appeared to me next, as I had never heard it spoken except on the lips of genteel vicars at the occasional ecumenical tea I had attended; I needed something harsh to play off the softness of "shan't," so I tried "cutting," "slashing," "whacking," "sawing," "hacking," all of which did not, to my ear, work.

Then from somewhere—God's mouth to my ear, or the devil's lips to my brain—I came across "ripping," which was perfect euphonically, even if wrong technically. He hadn't ripped them, he'd cut them. But ripping had the right sound and connoted a savagery that the world would adore, even if, bent in the quarter-moon over his felled carcass, the man would in no way resemble a wild ripper, since his movements had to be focused, concentrated, driven by considerable application of disciplined force, all of it done with the knife's sharp edge, none of it "ripped" as if by a crazy man's churning hands, fingers all tightened to clamp strength as they tore asunder gobbets of flesh and flung them wildly. Whatever he was, he was no ripper, and perhaps the man could not have called himself a ripper, but the delicious sound of the word "ripper" trumped all those considerations. There is a poetic truth higher than fact.

After that, it seemed to come. I had to work in the word "jolly" some place, and I did, and I left it poetically adangle, in a form I'd never seen or heard. "Just for jolly," I said. I avoided, out of fastidious liberal grounds, any mention of Jews, as one of my secret impulses was to absolve them in my fiction. I wanted no pogroms and no Peelers acting as Cossacks on my conscience, as full as that organ already was. That I was proud of, that I took some moral pleasure in.

And finally, the name. Well, "Ripper" was already achurn in my mind, and I was so pleased with the phrase "shan't quit ripping" that I didn't want to let it go, although I knew I had to alter it to a noun form from the verb, both to prevent repetition of an uncommon sound and to continue a kind of word melody playing with that sound. "Ripper" presented itself to me. So if "Ripper" is more or less the anchor, one needs something without an R in it, to avoid singsong or alliteration. "Robert the Ripper" or "Roger the Ripper" just sounded silly. Indeed, you needed counteriteration, a name bereft of R's and P's, yet also, to place it firmly in British tradition, a stout, sturdy Anglo-Saxon blurt of a name. "Tom" came to me, and I almost went with that, as "John" was too soft and "Will" hard to say because it need a fricative stop in order to slide easily into the sibilance of the R's and P's, and then I remembered the flag, like some common shopkeep or mill hand, and the patriotic treacle of it provoked my radical sensibility profoundly, amused me.

Here was Irony, capital I, in bold italic. *Irony*! something that O'Connor would grasp and poor Harry Dam nevermore. A smile came to my face. Union Jack, waving atop some battlefield atangle with drifting rifle smoke where the stench of cordite and blood intermingled in the air, and the Gatling guns had piled up heaps of wogs outside the wire, and the officer classes had broken out the beer ration, and all the lads in red had turned and raised a glass to the Union Jack. Yes, Jack, Jack, Jack, as our Lord and Savior Kipling would have it, and I knew I had my name. It was exactly what my masters had demanded: a perfect name, resonant, memorable, easy on the tongue, solidly British, conjuring up the dark warrens of Whitechapel and the idea of a sharp steel knife against the alabaster of Judy's throat and at the same time containing the faintest echo of the stripe-spangled banner waving o'er our green fields and sanctimonious pieties. I had given the world Jack the Ripper.

II

BURNING BRIGHT

CHAPTER THIRTEEN
The Diary

September 30, 1888

———

Good Christ, what a day! I almost ran my luck, my escapes were equal to any hero's at Maiwand, I felt the incredible agitations of the spirit and soul, to say nothing of abject fear turning my stomach to an ingot of pure lead. I had to improvise desperately, change courses, take risks, and cling when all else was gone to the mandate of boldness. And yet at a certain point I ran from a child. I now reach for a fine glass of port to settle myself enough to record the events of the last few hours.

And it began so well.

I did not connect on Commercial at all, as the pickings seemed slim thereupon. I took the turn onto Berner on my lonesome, meaning, I suppose, to take it to the next right, take that, then the next, and in that way circle the block, coming up for another run down Commercial. But ahead of me, bustling by, was a young man in one of those absurd deerstalker hats, package in hand, looking somewhat flustered, as if he'd just engineered a disaster. He sped by me without a look, and that was when I saw what catastrophe he was fleeing. It was a she, clearly a working lass, short of carriage, standing on the sidewalk a half-block ahead in what appeared to be a disappointed posture. Whatever discontent had passed between them, I did not know, but I put my eyes square to her, and she felt them and looked to me, not moving a bit. I sidled up, as was my fashion, the well-turned-out gentleman gone for a rogue encounter with change to burn in his pocket, and when she flashed me a smile, I merely nodded sagely, my face fully commanded by my will and lit with a kind of sexual glow from within. Actually, it was a glow for murder, but this one didn't know that yet.

She was a short one, tonight's. I must say, she was an improvement, gal-wise, over Polly and Annie. Any normal fellow would fetch a tup with this one on looks alone. Her near beauty almost exempted her from my attention; alas for her, it was not to be, as she alone was issuing the kind of signal that implies availability. All in black, she was, as if in mourning for herself already, and saving all the trouble by choosing sackcloth for her wardrobe.

"You're a compact one, my dear," I said.

"My legs is good for a wraparound, sir," she said, "as they've a lot of muscle to them."

I noted a trace of foreignness in her voice, not sure which part of the world to ascribe it, even as I replied, "That's the spirit a bloke wants."

We were in a canyon of darkness, as darkness was general all over Whitechapel, the city elders being ungenerous with gaslights for their poorest district. There seemed to be a little action across the street; I saw lighted windows at the Anarchists' Club, where I'd visited on my scout. We drifted across Berner, passed by the club's front under the sign International Men's Educational Club, Yiddish translation in smaller letters below. We were out of the glare of those second-story windows because we were too close to be emblazoned. From above, I could hear indications of great rambunction and knew that throaty, endless choruses of "The Internationale" could not be far away.

We passed, the hubbub of politics not quite dying out but subsiding to a low murmur. We reached a gap in the building fronts that held, a few feet back, a double gate in darkness, scribbled with indecipherable lettering in white. Because I had scouted well, I knew what it contained: a few houses immediately across from the south wall of the club, and the "yard" where a cart manufacturer and a sack manufacturer had set up shop; next to that an abandoned building that once contained a forge and then a stable but now housed only rats.

This would be my lovely's destination. The gates were not locked, and we slid through, opening them, and entered a channel between the club building and some kind of tenement housing not fifteen feet apart, where, off the street just a bit, it was dark as Erebus. We were swallowed and my darling took my arm—I was careful not to let her feel the knife in my hand—and pulled me closer as she glided to the wall just inside the arc of the hinged gate. Her breath was close and she pretended excitement, good actress she, playing the part till the end, and I smelled a bit of cachous on her breath, a little spice the gals would nibble to sweeten their mouths for whatever duties lay ahead.

Her face was pale before me, an apparition out of a painting by one of the pre-Raphaelite brotherhood, perhaps Ophelia lambent in her drowning pool—Elizabeth Siddal in her most famous pose for Mr. Millais—so natural and so ghostly at once, beautiful yet not quite knowable, shielding her mysteries well and radiating no pain, no fear, no dread, only the countenance of relaxed content. I made the traces of a smile upon that face, not forced but real, for she knew that the coin I would give her would earn her a room in a doss house for the night, to begin tomorrow's struggle refreshed, or a glass of gin, to forget today's struggle temporarily, the poor dear.

I believe this was my best stroke yet. I am indeed improving. I hit her hard with the belly of the blade, and it sank deep, an inch, maybe more, and I felt the tremble of impact ride my bones up to the elbow. I drew, rather artistically, almost like a Spanish fencer, the blade around the half-circumference of her neck, pivoting as I opened her. Then an odd thing happened. She died. She simply died. Well, yes, I had cut her throat, but somehow in the power of my stroke, I had launched a bomb into her arterial system, and it hit home in seconds, exploding her heart. That, at least, was what my instincts told me, for she went into the instant repose of death and her heart's energy failed, so there was no propulsion to the system to drive, as before, the first trickle zigzagging across the neck's lovely contours, then the gush, the tide, the wave. Not at all—no pump, no evacuation. She lay in a small puddle, as if I'd spilled a glass or two of cabernet on the pavement.

She was more or less resting against the wall, the better to receive my entry and offer friction amid the lubrication in right proportions, and had no idea it was a blade that would enter her, not a penis, and yet her face never bore distress, much less fear or pain. It was as if—or possibly I flatter myself—she wanted to die at my hand. I would at least make her famous, maybe not such a bad bargain, given her day-to-day.

Of the ones so far, hers was the easiest; there was no mess with the choke hold, no crush of clamping hand, no shove or push. With my other hand I grabbed her shoulder, to keep her from thudding or falling forward, and guided her down to earth, she rotating downward until she came to rest next to and exactly parallel to the building. I knelt to her, put my hand to her heart to feel its absence of beat, looked to her soft, relaxed face and gently closed eyes, and knew that she was gone.

My next task was her chemise, for I had use of a garment, and as I slithered down her still body just a bit to reach under her skirts for my trophy, that was where my luck both soared and crashed at the same time.

It soared in that, moving and dipping, I lowered my profile deeper into the dark, so that a man standing but ten feet away could not see me.

It crashed in that a man did stand but ten feet away.

What alerted me was the sudden bluster of a beast, and I looked up to see not three feet from me the face of a pony who knew that I was there, his animal senses being sharper than any human's. He clomped twice, foot heavy against the cobblestone of Dutfield's accursed yard, but locked his legs in refusal to move, for he was as scared of me as I was of him. He was in harness, and behind him, barely identifiably by outline, he pulled what appeared to be a cart of some sort, and over his rear haunch, I could see the profile of a man standing in the cockpit of the vehicle.

He snapped his buggy whip at the animal's flank; the animal tossed his head, shivered, flinging mane into commotion, but resolutely stayed where he was, all the while his big eyeballs lancing directly into mine. He snorted and I felt the cascade of warm, slightly moist air from his lungs wash across me, with an odd musk of grass woven into it. He breathed heavily, wheezily, now and again shivering, and when he shivered, his tack rattled and jingled. I could not crouch any lower over Ophelia in her small ruby pond, but I did have knife in hand, and my first thought was to plan an attack. If the fellow got out of the cart and came snooping, he would come upon me, and I would rise like the devil reborn and plunge blade into throat, aiming for a spot a whisker off the larynx (thank you, Dr. Gray), and rip through that structure so that no cry would accompany its owner's exsanguination. Then I would bolt the yard and disappear.

He climbed down and stood in the narrow space between the wagon and the wall, my only escape route.

"Vas ist? Gott verdammt! Vas ist?" I heard him ask of the pony, about whose welfare he was clearly not sentimental. The pony was equally unsentimental, as he remained in his place, his joints having alchemized into steel fixtures by suspicion of whatever life-form he smelled (he would have smelled her blood as well) and whatever life-form he made out with those huge billiard-ball eyes.

A match flared in the darkness, and its circle of illumination reached my fingertips but no farther; I was out of the zone of visibility by a hair's width. The man held it tremblingly, unperturbed as it burned toward his fingers, and began to rotate to see what its light revealed. As he turned his shoulders to the right, he drew the cone of light with him, and my love's dark clothes were revealed, as were her shoulder, and then her pale, serene, beautiful face, and next to it, crimson as the blood of the Lamb spilled off that Golgotha cross, the satiny pool of her own life's fluid. It was so red. I'd never seen their blood in full light before, only by the quarter-moon's low-power beam.

"Mein Gott!" I heard him expel. He seemed to shiver in confusion up there on his contrivance, as he tried to make a decision, and then he made it.

I gripped the knife hard, collected my muscularity as I slipped into a raider's crouch, ready to spring and bring the man down hard and dead, and indeed, he nearly plunged through to his death at my hands. In the last second he pivoted not forward, toward me, but backward, toward the gate.

He slipped through and dashed hard left, and I heard him bang hard on the Berner Street door of the Anarchists' Club. I recognized the sound as he remembered the door wasn't locked and pulled it open.

I was trapped. It was too late to dash in my own fashion to the gate, for the damned pony still blocked it, and if I squeezed by in time, the street would in the next instant be flooded with excitable Russian revolutionaries and vegetarian socialists who would draw Peelers from every nook and cranny, and there was nothing behind me in the yard that would permit escape, only locked shops and homes and a small deserted building.

There was nowhere to go.

CHAPTER FOURTEEN
Jeb's Memoir

I was not in the newsroom when news of the slaughter at Dutfield's Yard came, although since Jack, as I now thought of him, struck near or on the weekends and late, I had rearranged my schedule to night hours so that I was present and ready to fly when it seemed most propitious that he would pay another visit. But Harry had adopted the same schedule (as had Mr. O'Connor and Henry Bright and several others, a flying squad of Jack boys, if you will), and so he was the one to race out there, leaving me and my bitter tea down in the tearoom, where I was sulking.

Here's the irony: My sulking stood me in very good stead. Not being at the Anarchists' Club where the one called Long Liz was found that night freed me up for the evening's second act, of which more anon.

It is relevant as to why I was sulking. Of course it had to do with that damned letter. I had labored over it until achieving what I thought was perfection, then I'd given it to Mr. O' Connor. I thought he'd be pleased, but a full day passed before his boy came and got me—much too long, I feared, and that was where my confidence, always a frail vase in a typhoon, began to spring cracks. I went to the office, and there, wearing an eyeshade, was O'Connor, and in shirtsleeves next to him was Harry Dam, damned Harry. I did not hate Harry, you must understand; I actually had some respect for his reckless energy and cagey way with all the tricks of the trade, but I did fear him a bit, as I knew his ambition was as outsize as mine and that he was capable of nearly anything to advance it. Moreover, his contempt for the Jews was a signal that something inside was not right.

"Ah, there you are!" said O'Connor, and I read him anxiously for signs of love but could tell that he was focused totally on task. "Come in, come in. This letter you've written, it's quite good. I believe we're almost there."

Almost there! Those are not words any writer pines to hear. Much more preferable is "masterpiece" or "timeless brilliance" or "it shall live forever." But such accolades were not to be.

Harry said, again damning with praise so faint it was almost inaudible, "Wow, it's a great first pass. I can't begin to tell you how glad I am we got you to do this. I could not come even close to such a brilliant thing." In his voice I could hear a contrapuntal going in another direction; it suggested that he and he alone knew how to fix it, not that I could ever accept that it needed any sort of fixing.

"Drink? Oh, that's right, you're a teetote," said O'Connor. "Well and good, I should be myself, maybe me nose would stop glowing in the dark"— a little attempt at levity that got profoundly insincere smiles from Dam and me. He took a draught of whatever is brown, is served in small glasses a third full, burns and yet calms on the way down; he accepted a tear at the corner of each eye from its impact, then said, "I think it needs a bit more."

"Do you want me to take it through another draft, sir?" I asked with perhaps more tremble in my voice than I cared to acknowledge.

"No, no, the words are great. 'Jack the Ripper,' by God, a name to conjure with, absolutely magnificent, it will rattle the city to its cellars and sell a million papers, no doubt. No, that's not it. It needs one more touch. An amplification, as it were."

"I see," I said, though I didn't.

"Harry has a very fine idea, I think. Go ahead, Harry, tell him."

"Better, I'll show him!" He ran to his Eton rowing blazer, reached into it, and pulled something from the pocket. "The piece of resistance," he said, meaning, of course, "pièce de résistance," "yep, you're gonna love this." He paused, letting his little presentation acquire the drama that a pause provides, and then held aloft his treasure. *"Red ink!"*

Good God, I thought. Can he be serious?

"Red," he said proudly, "as in blood."

"Isn't it a little melodramatic?" I asked. "Perhaps overstated."

"Hmm. Can a guy overstate murder?" Harry asked.

"As a practical matter, I believe you can," I said. "You can make it so bombastic that no man in his right mind would believe in it. 'Jack the Ripper' would be a joke and not a symbol of chill aspect, meant to frighten for a thousand years."

"Your pride is commendable," said O'Connor. "Which demonstrates that it's a writer you are, sir, without doubt. But can I suggest what goeth before the fall? Knowing that, I ask you to listen to what Harry proposes."

"It's not much," said Harry. "It's hardly anything. It's still ninety percent yours, maybe ninety-five percent. It's not as if there will be royalties, you know."

"I hate to see my efforts trifled with," I sniffed. "Maybe bring in Henry Bright for an opinion. He's a sound man."

"No, no," said O'Connor. "Henry knows nothing about this, nor does anyone else, and that's how it should remain. Jeb, just listen to Harry."

"Here's my concoction," said Harry. "Flat-bang-out, no palaver or jerky chewing."

I had no idea what he was talking about except that he was about to pitch his "improved" version.

"Red ink is just the start," he said. "And really, that's more the package than the content. But a sentence is added. Jack says something like 'I was going to use whore's blood, but it turned all sticky, like gooseberry jam. Now I've got this damned ink on my hands.'"

"Does it in fact turn all sticky?"

"So I hear," Harry said. "Not having scalped a whore lately, I'm not sure. But see, it's the cold detail that nails it. He is so insane that he thinks nothing about using a dead gal's blood for his little note, and maybe he adds a 'ha ha' or something like that. The red ink makes it jump as a package, it's like the wrapper on the Black Jack gum pack, and bang-on, nobody can ignore it."

I could not think of a response to a Black Jack gum allusion; who could? After all, what on God's earth *was* a Black Jack gum pack?

"Then," said Harry, "we need one gory detail. I mean, he's the *Ripper*, right, not the Kisser or anything. So let's add a line, say, in which he tells us he's going to chop off an ear and ship it to the coppers."

It was horrifying. It was perfect.

"One last thing," he said. "More packaging, that's all, it's still the great Jeb who came up with Jack the Ripper, but let's mangle the punctuation. I was never good on apostrophes anyhow. Can't seem to keep the rules in mind. Whoever thought that one up? Anyhow, I'll dump the curlicue things—"

"But," I said, "that would give it the diction and vocabulary of an educated man, yet the form of an uneducated one. I do not see how that advances the cause."

"It makes it scary," said Harry. "The final nail in the coffin is, I copy it over in my hand. The reason for that is, unlike you boys, I only have one posh thing going. It's my handwriting, and I can still feel the smart where Sister Mary Patricia hit my wrist a dozen times with a steel ruler. That girl packed a wallop. So believe me, I learned a fair hand. It just makes the whole thing, I don't know, mysterious. It's got a lot of this-ways but also a lot of that-ways."

"I must say, it's a dandy idea," said O'Connor. "Deftly employed, it will sell thousands more papers and elevate Jeb's Jack into the bogeyman of the nineteenth century. Maybe the twentieth as well."

Who was I to protest such imbecility? I had no moral standing to argue it the other way, so I just nodded grimly and sat down. In for a penny, in for a pound.

"Great," said Harry, and with relish he set to work, clearing space on the makeup table. O'Connor and I watched as, in his surprisingly adroit hand, he copied my words on a piece of foolscap, so the whole thing did come to resemble a missive from the devil himself, had that old boy been educated by nuns, and come to think of it, he probably was!

When Harry was done, he pinched it by the corner, waved it about to dry, then folded it and crammed it into an envelope. "I'll go hire a kid and make sure he drops it in the right slot at the Central News Agency," he said. "By God, it'll shake the old town up when they run it. And we'll be ready to jump on the horse before anyone."

"Excellent, Harry, positively brilliant. Jeb, you agree?"

"I suppose," I said poutily, having lost on all rounds; I had written a document without integrity, then gotten all prideful over my effort, as if it were a noble calling, and now, absurdly, I felt degraded by further breaches of its integrity inflicted by others. Suddenly, I wanted to vomit.

"All right, then, boys," said O'Connor, "let's get back to business."

Harry threw on his hat and coat and smiled as if he'd eaten the Christmas goose.

"Off you go, then," said O'Connor, and Harry departed. O'Connor turned to me. "No long faces, Jeb. It's just business. It's how we operate, always have, always will. Now mind your P's and Q's, and wait for this to stir the pot."

But I was far too much a baby to let a nice period of self-pity and victimization go wasted, so I took it upon myself to spend more rather than less time in the tearoom. And that was why I was playing the injured party, even several days later, and only Henry Bright noticed, if circumspectly.

So it was that when I came back to the newsroom after my dawdling, I was late to learn that Jack had done his bad trick a third time, at a place I'd never heard of called Dutfield's Yard, and that Harry was shortly to be, if not already, on the scene.

"There you are, old man," said Henry Bright. "I'll be in makeup. We've got to redesign for tomorrow. Harry will call in with details and you—"

Someone came running over, and to this day, I cannot remember who, for the news was so overwhelming.

"My God," whoever it was said, "the bastard's done it again. Two in one night! This one at a place called Mitre Square a mile away. Two in one hour! And she's really chopped up!"

"All right, Jeb," said Henry Bright. "Get on your horse. It looks like it'll be a long evening of fun."

CHAPTER FIFTEEN

The Diary

September 30, 1888 (cont'd)

I now pass to the second event of the evening. As to my disappearance from Dutfield's Yard and the Anarchists' Club, I record nothing, as I am exhausted (you will see why), and though it might be of interest to readers, I anticipate no readers and thus airily mean to skip that which I find tedious.

I found myself 1,570 paces to the west, on Aldgate, that being the same concourse as Whitechapel High Street, but having moved from London to the City of London, it had acquired a new name, as well as a new municipal government and police force. It was well after one A.M., and on the street I found myself, no rumble of the momentous events transpiring some blocks behind me evident. It was as if I had magically migrated to another planet, another atmosphere, another range of life-forms. I was disconsolate, as I had extremely well-laid plans for the evening and goals to be achieved, and I had failed utterly. It was my first such failure, and I had left the thing unfinished by a far part at Dutfield's Yard, where my cursed luck had produced that Yiddish oaf on a pony cart, with his wonder horse, Boobsie, to muck everything up. Gad, I was angered. I am, as it turns out, not the type to go all jabberwocky and expectorate in rage; rather, my fury is entirely inward and takes the form of a fiery furnace in my chest, blazing madly in the chill air. I would have to start again, and damn thee to hell. Dutfield's, carefully selected, had been so perfect for my plan. I wondered if ever I would find such a spot again.

And yet, as if Satan himself had become my sponsor, what should I spy as I moseyed drearily up Aldgate past the pump, past Houndsditch, but a lady herself. Judy or no? Difficult to tell, as she was in dark and the streets were not well lit, as all the newspapers continued to point out, but in an instant my mood transfigured from the blackest of black to the sudden blast of high engagement. I watched her meandering along, as if a bit unsteady, and noted that outside her skirts she wore an apron, a wide white expanse of milled cotton that marked off her whole front. It was most useful for my purposes, and seeing it, I decided her fate in an instant.

It took no speed or athleticism to catch up to her, and when she sensed my heat as I placed myself at her left shoulder, I in turn sensed her drunkenness, or should I say, her recent close acquaintanceship with liquor, for she fairly reeked, poor lass, of the devil's favored beverage. But not then or consequently did she seem impaired as regarded her faculties.

Her first response was quite sensible, that being fear, but when she saw how fair of face I was, how kind of countenance, how much a gentleman stroller out for a bit of rogue notch and nothing else, she forced a smile to her worn and plain face. She was no beauty, as had been the last unfortunate to cross my path, and one would not notice her in any crowd except those more interested in notch than face. She was a short one, too, even shorter than the first, and rather square of face, a solid block of a gal.

"Good evening, madam," I said.

"Just put off a drunken sailor," she said. "All over me, that one was. You're not that sort, is you, guv'nor?"

"My dear," I said, "I'm a gentleman, I assure you, I only do that which is allowed, when it is allowed, where it is allowed, and I pay generously, not the usual thruppence for a night's favor but a full fourpenny, good for both a gin and a night in a doss house."

"No more gin for me, as I taxed my limits earlier. But a soft bed is worth a little putting out for such a fine man as yourself, sir."

"Then lead on, and I'll give you a swag you'll not forget."

She even giggled. "They all say that, they do."

She led me another half block up Aldgate, and though it was late of hour, that avenue was still lit and bore some traffic. As was the way in the larger polity, no one paid us a bit of mind, since gentleman-and-Judy was such a common sight.

We reached a corner that led off to darkness, and not knowing what it could be, I glanced at the sign, learning that it was Mitre Street.

"A nice quiet square down this way for our business," sang the nightingale. "Come on, then, don't be shy."

She lead me down this Mitre Street, and indeed there lay another passage, off to the right, between what appeared to be commercial buildings, maybe a dwelling or two, though I could not tell, as it was so dark. We followed the passage but a short bit, and it led us into a square, bulked up on either side by larger buildings that appeared to be of commercial nature. It was a tiny oasis in so vast a metropolitan desert, being barely if at all twenty-five yards on a side. I could make out in the dim light—our parsimonious city fathers allowed only two gas lamps for the entire square—some white lettering of the kind that usually heralds an owner's name, but it was so dark and far that I could resolve no meaning for it. Besides, we were not to tarry. She took a direct right once within the square and led me, again not far, into its darkest corner. No light from the two wan lamps reached us, yet there was enough ambient illumination from our vantage point to see that the square was empty. I had no idea how long it would so remain, for I had not reconnoitered it and was not entirely sure where I was or how I would get out if danger appeared. But the opportunity was here, and fortune, it is said, always favors the bold, and I am by nature bold, and so I went ahead.

We stopped in the corner against a wooden fence that seemed to cut off some more room, perhaps forming a yard within a square. I had no idea why it was there or what its function was. There was no illumination from the usual quarter-moon, as clouds covered and produced a fine mist, near to but not quite a drizzle. She halted, pivoted to face me, and upped her skirts.

"There now," she whispered—we were so close—"let's get it done, Old Cock, and be on our ways, you a fourpenny lighter, meself the same heavier."

Of the stroke I will not say much. It was better than some and worse than others, being a passing middling effort. It was not nearly so poetic as the Spanish duelist's thing of beauty back against the Anarchists' Club wall forty-odd minutes ago, but it was solid, straight on, dead to target. She stepped back, seemed to lose balance, coughed delicately, looked at me with beseeching eyes, which in eight seconds' time, as the blood emptied from her brain, ceased to beseech and commenced to lock hard on a far-away nothing. I did not strike her a second time because I felt that the first had been so solid, going deeper than most, and there was no need of the redundancy. Down she went, quiet as a mouse, me nursing her to earth. And there she lay on her back, her sightless eyes open and not a trace of pain nor fear on her square face. She could have been asleep as easily as freshly murdered.

I had much to accomplish and no idea how much time I had. It was better, I knew, to assume little and discover much, rather than the other way around. The first business was her apron. With my knife, I opened a cut at the bottom, then ripped upward, almost halving the thing, and when, near her waist, I encountered a seam, I nicked another bit to change the direction of the rip, and continued to pull it apart. I daresay the noise of the cloth ripping was greater than the noise of the woman dying.

Once I got the rather large segment free, leaving the missing piece so obvious that even the most obtuse copper idiot would be sure to notice, I wetted it with blood, then wadded it into my pocket. Now to the night's real work.

I situated myself at her middle, perpendicular to the body's length, and rolled up her garments to lay bare that which was indecent. She was a scrawny thing, ribs all slatlike against her skin, breasts like shrunken cook-ies. These poor girls are rarely heavy because their access to food is so inconsistent. I put the knife into her and cut her good, straight down the middle, and laid open her guts. I had need to make a show, as my mad plan required an increase in frenzy at each stop along the way. Gloves on, of course, I reached in and disconnected the guts. It was slippery and squirmy in there, and nothing seemed stable at all; organs squirted from my fingers as if unwilling to be cut. But cut I did, sawing through tubes whenever I came upon them, and when I adjudged my efforts enough, I set down the knife and reached both hands into the slithery mess, took a heaping hand-ful in both left and right, and pulled them out, dripping, and flung them over her shoulder, where they made a kind of a wet plop against the stones when they hit. The smell of feculent matter reached my nose, as did the tang of urine, and I realized that a nick somewhere had let those unpleasant reminders of the biological reality of our species out to play. Where once it had thrilled me in its perfervid illicitness, I was by now so old-salt at this business that it meant nothing. I looked and a long tangle remained, evi-dently untouched in my butchery, so I sliced it through at one end and laid it like a dead snake between her body and her arm.

I needed a trophy, something that would get them talking, as they had after Annie Chapman's sweetbreads turned up missing. (Deposited, if you must know, in the River Thames, never to be heard from again.) I reached in and, owing to my study of Dr. Gray's epic work, took hold of something, then, securing it with one hand, cut it free with the other. I pulled it out, whatever it was—spleen, kidney, maybe displaced heart, uterus, some other womb part, whatever—and slid it into a pocket. And then I looked up, and across the square, holding a lantern, was a copper.

I froze instantly, though I doubted his eyes could have penetrated the darkness that cloaked me. He stood at the head of what looked to be a sort of passageway between buildings of whose existence I'd had no suspicion. His circle of light seemed to capture with great precision the texture of the brickwork that was his backdrop. It was a moment of high dread. If he advanced, in a very few feet the limit of his lantern's illumination would reveal me, red of hand, crouched over opened body, viscera everywhere like the remains of a gaudy party. Then he would instantly go to whistle, his shrill blasts filling the night air and bringing aid from all quarters. More distressingly, he was too far away for me to bring down fast, as I had planned to do with the man on the pony cart. Plus, in physical affray, he would indubitably prove a wilier opponent than a man who drives a pony cart for a living. He would know tricks, blows, holds, be well versed in pugilism and knockabout play. He would net me sure. Thus did the angel of death's wings flap o'er me, so vividly I felt the noose tightening and sensed the crowd's ardor as I stood on the trembly platform of the Newgate Gaol gallows.

It seemed like an eternity. He stood there, peering about, but did not take one step closer. The odor of my lovely's shit must not have reached him yet, nor the penny-bitter smell of her blood.

He turned, he retreated, and soon even his light was not in evidence as he departed by that narrow passageway.

I felt the rush of air from my lungs, as I had just had another escape so near it was disorienting. Disaster that close, so close you can hear the whisper of the ax, is an unsettling thing.

And perhaps that is why my next reaction, unbidden, unexpected, was rage. It was as if I had my guts clenched in a giant fist, and when whoever held it tight let me go, what rushed in was anger, the urge to hurt, to smash, to kill that which had been killed. Someone in science should make a study of what secret fluids race to a man's brain in extreme moments. Whatever they were, they did not leave me calm and collected, capable of wit or irony. Instead they turned me—perhaps this would surprise a reader if ever, by chance, this volume should come to light—insane. Insaner, this theoretical reader might say, but I reply, No, no, I was perfectly sane through it all, except this one moment. Forgive me, unknown unfortunate, it was not you upon whom I was spending my wrath, but *it*—the universe, the empire, the system, the nearness of my own destruction, the whimsies of fate and chance, in short, all those permanent entities that no man may affect— upon which I felt the need to rain destruction. Alas, your freshly murdered body was the only vessel available.

I destroyed that which had been heretofore sacrosanct. I took the dear lady's face from her. It took but a minute, a sharp knife being an instrument of great utility when properly applied. I had been until then a cutter, but now I sank another grade deeper into human depravity and became a stabber. I stabbed her face, feeling the blade puncture and slide off the hard mass of skull below, then slide through the flesh, ripping and tearing and removing immense pie-shaped units of skin with each drive. I could not stop myself and was almost sobbing in hysteria. I cut her eyes, even, driving the blade through the lidded orbs, feeling what lay beneath go all slippery and slidey, like grapes in a bed of mechanic's grease.

And I chopped, another new thing. I chopped strong against her nose, cutting through the cartilage that gives that organ shape, and before I could stop myself, I slightly rotated the blade, yanked hard, and the whole damned thing came off. I went for her ear, sawing like a laborer, and was not rewarded with so smooth a response as from the helpful nose. The ear fought me hard, and I never got it off cleanly, leaving it hanging on a gristly ribbon of cartilage.

I brought my focus down and, in childish tantrum, began to stab at various massifs left in her innards, a kind of mechanical up-down of arm, fist, and knife point, and I could feel the thing bucking into various and sundry structures left aboard. Then my rage exited the excavation proper and moved to skin unopened and unflayed on abdomen and pubis; I stabbed, I stabbed, I stabbed, again feeling point overcome the tensile elasticity of the skin and give way to the subcutaneous tissue beneath, and I further felt that human aspic split and sunder to my enraged energies. Suddenly, I was spent.

I looked at what I had wrought. The face was ruined, a seething mass of dappled black in the lightlessness of the square. It required color to express its truest, purest horror, but it would be the coppers who got the benefit of that display, not me. I would not let myself view the body. I was not squeamish. How could a squeamish man author such an atrocity? I suppose I was still in shock and suddenly, as well, became aware of the passage of time, and knew I had other appointments to keep. I rose, secured the blade in my belt, peeled off my sodden gloves and pocketed them, made sure the apron—so important—was still in my frock coat pocket and Judy's sweet-breads in the other, rose, and pivoted without a sound.

I crossed the square, clinging to shadow. I didn't want to leave the same way I had entered, by the opening to Mitre Street, because that copper might have circled on his beat and been headed down Mitre Street even now, and I'd hate to run into him as I exited the square. I turned in to the blackness where I'd seen him, finding it a narrow brick lane between two buildings, and rushed down it. I heard the harsh, overpropelled pitch of the police whistle and realized that constable or another had just discovered the body. Another close-run thing! I continued unabated until the passage delivered me to a dark street leading on the right to Aldgate, on the left to more darkness. This had to be Duke, from which I had seen my thrush emerging a few minutes ago. I took the darker option and came shortly thereupon—insane!—another Duke Street. I was therefore at the corner of Duke and Duke, and despite the bloody business of the evening, I could not suppress a grin at the absurdity of such a thing and the centuries of confusion it must have engendered. Soon I was beyond Houndsditch and moving at a comfortable pace toward the next duty of the evening. As for what was going on in that little chunk of London I had left behind, I neither knew nor cared.

CHAPTER SIXTEEN

Jeb's Memoir

It was all different. For one thing, the Peelers weren't the embittered lack-eys in a class war between constables and detectives, and for another, there was no looming figure of mad authority like Sir Charles Warren to impress fear and confusion and other idiocies of his ill-trained, overused crew.

All this is ascribable to the higher level of proficiency of the City of London Police over their much more intellectually impoverished brethren of the Met's H Division. They ran a far cleaner crime scene: no crazed wandering this way or that in rogue hope of encountering something even they would recognize as a "clue," such as a note saying, "I am the murderer and I reside at 15 Cutthroat Terrace, W3." Whichever executive was calling the directives gave each man a zone that was his and his alone, and the man crawled it, touching, feeling, looking. They brought in, first thing, a large supply of bull's-eye lamps, as all the constables carried, and dim as they were, lighting and placing them about brightened the scene considerably. The Met's rozzers never would had thought of such a thing. Most aston-ishing of all was how they treated we Johnnies of the press.

"I'm Jeb, the *Star*," I'd said to the first constable I'd encountered as I arrived on-site and slipped through the crowd gathered at the Mitre Street entrance to the square.

"Yes, sir," said the constable. "Now, if the gentleman will follow me, I'll lead him to the gallery where we're asking reporters to collect until we've throughly examined the scene. It shan't be a long wait, and Inspector Collard will speak with you directly as soon as his duties allow him. Our police surgeon, Dr. Brown—"

"Full name?"

"Yes, sir, Dr. Frederick Gordon Brown, will arrive shortly and supervise the removal of the body to the mortuary."

"May we see it?"

"Inspector Collard will make that decision, sir, but our policy has been to cooperate with you lads in order to get the best information out to the public."

"If you know my reputation, Constable, you'll know I don't make mistakes."

"Yes, sir, as you say, sir."

I followed him to a roped-off area in the center, where I learned that I was the first of the real reporters on-site—the others were penny-a-liners—and took a few seconds to look about. The square was quite small, particularly in scale to the larger industrial buildings enclosing it, mainly vast, mute warehouses of sheer brick, two owned by Kearley and Tongue, one by Horner and Sons. Beyond, over the hulk of Horner's building, I saw an even larger behemoth that I knew to be the back wall of the Great Synagogue where the Jews gathered each Saturday for their worship. I thought that made it less likely, rather than more, that a Jew was involved, for a Jew would be careful to absolve his own heritage group by distance if nothing else.

All the activity was centered in the southeast corner of the space, where a wooden fence seemed to mark off a yard behind it; another house was hard by it, maybe a few feet away. Certainly someone in that house had heard something! Meantime, a doctor—he was in a white medical coat—stood by, not doing much (I was later to learn he was a local, the earliest to the scene, who had pronounced the poor girl dead, and he had not touched the body save to determine how warm it was, and infer from that a time of death. She was too much in disarray for him to get any closer.) The others were detectives or detective constables, some of them sketching, some of them looking at goods on the ground that must have been the victim's, perhaps to make a catalog.

I kept waiting for the others to show up—where was Cavanagh of the *Times* or Renssalaer of the *Daily Mail* or any of the boys I'd run into at these damnable sites? No sign. I guessed they were still tethered to the Berner situation, looking at Jack's last crime, and couldn't get over here, though it was under a mile. The *Star* was lucky again, as was I; having a chap in the building when the call came got him to the place first and fastest, while the other rags had to round up a late-night second-stringer, their fancier boys having been sent to Berner.

In time, a large fellow with a walrus moustache, a derby, and an overcoat that could have concealed an army rifle came over to our little crowd, looked at us, and singled me out with his inspector-intense vision. "You're Jeb of the *Star,* is that it?"

"That I am," I said.

"You other fellows, I'm taking Mr. Jeb for a look-see on the poor gal. You'll have to hold here because I can't have you all mucking up the crime scene. He'll tell you what he sees, won't you, sir?"

"I will, they can be sure of it," I said.

If there was discontent, the large officer didn't care, and his bulk and seriousness of mien stood firm enough to close out any objections. I dipped beneath the rope and made to accompany him step by step to the body.

We made it to her but halted a few feet out, so the details were not exact yet. I could see general derangement, mussed clothes, implications of disorder, but it was somehow so abstract at this distance, I could make little sense of it.

He said, "By the way, I'm Collard. My first name is 'Inspector.' Dr. Brown, our surgeon, will be along in a bit, as will, I'm sure, Commissioner Smith." Smith was the high sheriff of the City of London Police, the rough equivalent of the Yard's Sir George Warren.

"Yes, sir."

"Jeb? First name or last?"

"Last. My first is 'Reporter.'"

"Very good, then. Some spirit. I like that. As for the particulars, we have called in all our officers and are mounting one of the biggest dragnets, if not the biggest, the City of London has ever seen. We have detectives everywhere, canvassing for witnesses. If anything's to be found, if this mad brute left anything behind, we'll find it, I assure you."

I took this down in Pitman while answering, "As a reporter and citizen, I am grateful."

"Now, as to the body, I must warn you to steel yourself."

"I have seen all the other bodies, except for the concurrent one on Berner Street."

"I hear it's not too bad."

"I hear that as well."

"Well, this one is very bad. From your accounts, I suspect it's the worse by several degrees. As I say, time to be all manly and stiff-upper-lip, all that brave-Englishman rubbish you journos preach."

"I will try and buck up and play the game."

"So has said many a rookie to murder, only to end up vomiting fish and chips in the gutter. You have been warned." He led me to her.

Must I describe this? I suppose I must. I will not censor, but I will go hazy on the details, for myself as well as readers.

She lay on her back, her palms outward and up, one leg bent over the other. Her dress and petticoats had been scrunched up to her shoulders, with no concession to Victorian modesty. She lay bare from collarbone to pubis, showing things that are never seen, much less acknowledged, though I cannot conceive a fellow getting an illicit masturbatory thrill off the spectacle. If so, he'd be as guilty as Jack.

After that, the thing that struck me was new to Jack's crimes, the redness of the blood. I realized I was noting this for the first time because the City of London coppers had put so many more lanterns in place, so the degrees of illumination, color, and detail were amplified. This being the first time I'd encountered it in the raw, I was almost knocked flat by the visceral power of the color. It touched so many primal, mythic chords. It seemed to spring not merely from the girl's body but from the slaughter in the last act of *Hamlet,* the quartering of William Wallace, the beheading of Mary Stuart and Anne Boleyn, the many mythological tales in which beings were sundered for dubious reasons, like the death of Oedipus's father or the sack of Troy, our sense of the suspicious lack of it in Richard Caton Woodville's glorious-seeming battle paintings. When cut, we bleed. And bleed. And bleed. The kindness of night's dark had shielded me from this base epiphany until now.

Near upon that was the face. Or, should I say, was not the face. There was no face. He had taken it. What animal hatred could propel a man, supposedly in some fashion civilized, to do such a desecration? He had removed her nose, he had jabbed her eyes, he had flayed the lower half of her visage until it resembled some hideous slop of thick red jelly upon a sleeping woman.

"Good Christ," I blurted.

"I hope you have plenty of adjectives in your little pouch, Reporter Jeb," said Inspector Collard. "You'll need every last one of them."

Though normally I enjoy badinage and consider myself more than adequate at the quick riposte, I did not have enough oxygen left to consider such a thing. The air seemed thick, and the more I inhaled, the more reluctant it was to inflate my lungs.

"But the face is for show. It's really the gut that's remarkable," said Collard coolly. "Had a bit of the fray in earlier days in Africa and saw enough of this kind of butcher's work done on the wogs we loosed our Gatlings upon to last me forever. This poor daisy looks like someone blew off a threepounder in her stomach."

The allusion to explosion was apposite. Indeed, not a bomb but a human stick of dynamite called Jack the Ripper had blown up her belly, pulling, yanking, flinging, cutting out this, that, and the other thing, and when finished, as one could tell from close by, he'd stabbed. And here I go to mute. You can imagine. Actually, you cannot.

But it was now that head cheese Smith and a small retinue showed, and in seconds a tall chap of scientific imperturbability whom I took to be

Dr. Brown arrived. He went straight to the body, touched it full-handed, shaking his head, looked up at the man who had to be the first doctor, and nodded.

"I'm guessing not an hour dead," Brown said. "Maybe not half. She's still warm as a biscuit. Do you agree, Doctor?"

"Absolutely, though I thought of a bun, not a biscuit. I did no poking about, leaving that for a man who knows his forensics."

"You did well, Doctor. The crown thanks you. Time of death"—he pulled out his pocket watch—"one-forty A.M."

"Does it accord, Collard?" asked Smith.

"Perfectly, sir. Constable Watkins found the body at one-forty-four A.M. and whistled; a watchman at Kearley came out, and he puts that notification at one-forty-five. A.M."

"He killed another bloody woman at one A.M. at Berner Street, or so says the Yard," said Smith. "You can say this for the bastard, he's got a fine work habit."

I was writing that down in the dizzying blur of Pitman when Smith noted me. "Reporter pukka wallah?" he asked me.

"I am," I said. "Jeb, the *Star*."

"Well, favor me by not using the juicy quote I just uttered. It sounds casual, but Peelers see enough of this raw hacking so they usually joke about it on-site. It doesn't play well with the public."

"'Commissioner Smith solemnly told the *Star* that this new murder demanded the utmost in professionalism from all authorities, and pledged to provide it,' that sort of thing, sir?"

"This man will go a long way. All right, Jeb, stay close, don't make us look bad, and make no mistakes."

"He never makes mistakes, sir," said Collard.

"Yes, the fellow who uncovered the Mystery of Annie's Rings. How poignant that was. How many extra papers, I wonder, did it sell?"

"My job, sir. That's all."

"May I interrupt to point something out that might be a clue?" said the surgeon.

"Good God, a clue! How novel! If you please," said Smith.

"I note raw hem in the bunched cotton at her neck. May I unbunch it?"

"Why would you not?"

The doctor's fingers probed the rolled lineaments and glibly separated one sheaf. He unspooled it, being sure to keep it off the body itself, so as not to contaminate it with blood or other fluids. It turned out to be apron or, rather, half an apron. A rather large segment had gone missing.

"A trophy, I wonder?" said Collard.

"Possibly. More like a missing piece of a puzzle," said Smith. "We could not miss such a thing, nor the shape of what's missing. Planted somewhere else, it would link sites for some mad reason that only this fellow understands. He likes that we wait, we wonder, and he explains when and if it pleases him. But it is something new; it is a communication. He has a message to put out. That's why you're here, Jeb. You explain it to us."

"Perhaps it's for himself," I said. "He has taken organs before but has learned they are perishable. Or he's eaten them already, with a fine claret and field beans from the South of France. He wishes to have something to cling to, to clutch tight to bosom, to look upon and remember his moment of glory. Something more meaningful than Annie's famous rings, perhaps, which would carry no texture, no odor, no absorbency."

"Mad as a monkey," said Smith. "But in a highly organized way. This is no hot-blooded maniac. It's something I've never encountered. A cold-blooded maniac. I believe he's got a plan behind all of this."

It proceeded then at a slow pace. I felt no pressure myself, for it was Sunday early, and the *Star* didn't publish on Sunday, which meant my deadline wasn't until seven A.M. tomorrow, Monday, over twenty-four hours away—so I knew that we had to be thorough, steady, fair, and well organized. The rush to deadline would not be an excuse, although I had yet to make a mistake.

I meandered about Mitre Square. The coppers had let more and more people in, including some of those aforementioned daily reporters. I shared what I had with them—you don't want your peers hating your guts if it's not necessary, now, do you?—and they appreciated Jeb's cooperative nature. I saw that Constable Watkins was freed up and chatted with him, getting good quotations. Sometimes the directness of the nonliterary can be a refreshment. He said she'd been "ripped up like a pig in a market." Good line, that.

Just when I thought I was done and could get back home, grab some sleep, curse out my mother again, then return to the office refreshed for a long session at the Sholes machine, what should enter the yard but a copper who raced to Smith in alarm.

I could see the jolt of electricity it supplied to the worn-down crew of police executives. Smith seemed especially to pop to life and began shouting orders. I moseyed to Inspector Collard, who seemed in a rush to leave. "I say, what's it all about?"

"They've found the missing apron piece not four blocks off. And the bastard has left us a message."

CHAPTER SEVENTEEN

The Diary

September 30, 1888 (cont'd)

———

I strode through the night, imagining what I'd left behind. It may have been my happiest time in the whole adventure. Again, I had missed apprehension by the width of a hair, so I was feeling invulnerable. I felt my superior intelligence was validated on the grand scale, and in a game against not only my enemies but the entire city of London, from working girls to academic aristocrats. I was on the verge of not merely victory but triumph. I was routing them. They had no idea who and what I was, why I was doing what I was doing, what drove me. The last was important, because without knowledge of it, they assumed I was a chaotic madman and could be caught only by the net of chance, not logic. And all the lists of "suspects"—Jews, Poles, boyfriends, witnesses who lied—published by the newspapers proved that our best minds were hopelessly out of the game.

I eventually reached Goulston Street. It was deserted. By day a buzzing commercial street (the poultry market was thereupon), it was by night closed down, not a beer shop or Judy part of town, and the shuttered costers' sheds along either side of the street were unpatrolled and locked. I could see piles of fruit behind iron gratings, hear the squawk and bustle of crated chickens that hadn't been sold and had therefore earned another day of life in their tiny dung-crusted dungeons, smell the shit from the horses as it formed a steady presence on the dirt road. All the pennants—why are market streets usually festooned like medieval jousting tournaments?—hung limp in the moist though not rainy air. It had the feel of a city abandoned by its citizens, who'd fled to jungle or cave to escape a portended doom. Perhaps I was that doom, or at least its harbinger.

I eased down Goulston between the shuttered stalls and the blank wall of this or that apartment building, looking for a nook where I could do my business without observation. I was alongside something calling itself the Wentworth Model Dwellings, a grim brick fortress against the night for those fortunate enough to afford the tariff, when I espied an archway that contained a door to whatever squalor and degradation lay on the several floors above. It was perfect.

I nipped into it, and first thing, I pulled the damned lump of apron from my pocket and dumped it. It did not fall right—I wanted the blood to show conspicuously so not even the thickest of the thick could miss its implications. Some fluffing was required to achieve the proper show.

That done, I fetched a piece of chalk from my trousers, where it had been secured for just this purpose. I had thought carefully about the message for almost a month, parsed it as lovingly as any poet does his poem, for it had to carry certain messages and certain implications but nothing more. I found a suitable emptiness of wall and began to inscribe my message, large enough to be seen as language, not scrawl, taking my time. I had thought it out as a visual expression, lines perfectly symmetrical, a quatrain of long, short, long, short, a few brisk syllables, perfectly clear as to meaning and intent and—

Good Christ!

I nearly leaped out of my boots.

As I labored in intense concentration and was nearly through the third line, something—someone—had poked me in the small of the back.

I turned, aghast, my heart hammering like a steam engine gone berserk and near exploding, reached back for the Sheffield, and turned to confront the enemy I must slay.

It was a child.

She was about six, frail and pale with a raw burlap makeshift sack on, her grubby feet bare, her hair blond and stringy, flowing down her face over huge and radiant eyes, skin like pearl yet here and there smeared with dirt.

"Would the gentleman care to buy a flower?" she said. She held out a single wilted rose.

Was this a scene from Old Man Dickens? Perhaps Mrs. Ward, who produced her share of the lachrymose treacle for genteel, tea-sucking lady readers, or even the humorless Hardy? They'd both killed off lads and lasses every fifty pages or so to make a dime or so off their penny dreadfuls. But this was not literature, it was real, this thin-shouldered beauty standing for all the dispossessed, the impoverished, and the slowly starving, cowering under their bridges and by the railway tracks in the cruel London night, aware that even crueller temperatures lay a month anon.

"What on earth are you doing out by yourself, child?" I said.

"Wasn't no room in the doss ternight, so me mum took me under the bridge. I think she's dead, though. She's been coughing up blood awful bad. I could not wake her. I been walking an hour. Found a rose, thought I might sell it to a gentleman. Please, sir. It would mean so much."

"You cannot be out here alone. It's a dangerous time and place. Have you no people but your poor mother?"

"No, sir. We moved in from the country some months ago, for work, but Dad could find none. He went away some time ago, don't know where to. Been alone with Mum ever since."

"All right," I said, "I shall find you a place to be."

"Sir, just a penny for the rose is all I needs."

"No, no, that will not do. The rose is worthless, you are without price. You come with me now, child."

And so, the message unfinished and forgotten, I wrapped the child in my coat and lofted her to my torso, where she soon fell asleep across my shoulder. I headed up Goulston. At a certain point I looked back at what I had abandoned, wondered if I could get back to finish once I had attended to the girl, but instead saw, a block behind and approaching the nook where I'd paused for labor, the bull's-eye lantern of a copper, swinging to and fro, at the end of the fellow's long blue arm as he bumbled along, searching for rapers, robbers, bunco artists, pickpockets, and even the odd whore murderer such as myself.

Good Lord, I thought. Had this small girl not interrupted me, I'd be there still, finishing up my task. But no, she came along, I forgot that which had brought me there, and I abandoned my post. So once again my escape was too narrow to calculate, my luck too vast to appreciate. The whole episode seemed divinely plotted, though there was no room for divinity in my thoughts.

I carried the broken, tiny thing with me for several more blocks, past dark and sealed houses on streets that led nowhere, reached another intersection, and saw illumination a long block away. The child was light as a leaf. I thought at one point she perhaps had died, and it occurred to me that if so, I could be arrested and hanged for a crime I had not committed, and that might have been God's way of showing me what an idiot I was to disbelieve in Him. But that was a petty hack's irony, and our Father who art not in heaven or any place clearly saw through such a tinny conceit and stayed far away.

The girl stirred, rearranged herself to increase comfort against my shoulder, and I turned toward the incandescence, and in a bit found myself and my new charge in the gaslight of Commercial Street, perhaps a mile north of its intersection with Whitechapel Road. It was not crowded, but neither was it quite empty; a few public houses were open, spilling good cheer into the night; a few Judys patrolled this way or that; a few costers hawked meat and vegetables and candy to the indifferent after-midnighters.

I passed by several of the working gals and finally came upon one who seemed somehow less desperate than the others. I put up a finger to halt her. She showed no fear of the Whitechapel Murderer, as the street was well lit and I was with a child.

"See here, madam," I said, "I found this poor girl wandering about a few blocks back with no place to go. Could you take her somewhere?"

"It's a shame about the wee child, who reminds me of my own two girls," she said. "But I'm a down-and-outer trying to earn me doss money for the night, guv'nor."

"If I give you money for doss, will you first find a place for the girl, a church, a home, or something? I must be off. No gin, now. You've had your gin for the evening, haven't you?"

She narrowed an eye at me, looked me up and down, and I prayed that whatever violence I had done back in the square or before, in the yard, had not left a scarlet letter on my face or chest.

It had not.

"All right, give me the girlie. There's a home down the way for the wayward kiddies of the workers. Reckon she'll fit right in."

I handed my charge over to her, then pulled out a few quid and crunched them into her fist. Only a Rossetti could capture the soft light for *The Good Whore, the Destitute Child, and the Insane Killer* on a Whitechapel street late Saturday's eve turning to Sunday's morn; too bad he was dead. But then I thought: We are so beyond the artist's ability to record that it nears a sort of black comic spiral of absurdity.

"I see you've a kind face," she said, "as well as a kind heart. God will look after you."

"Doubtful," I said, and walked away.

CHAPTER EIGHTEEN
Jeb's Memoir

By the time I arrived at 108–119 Goulston, the idiot Warren had already ordered the inscription washed off.

"*What?*" I barked at the constable who told me this as I stood in a cluster with the gentlemen of the *Times,* the *Evening Standard* and the *Mail,* the *Pall Mall Gazette,* and others outside the doorway into the tenement. That vast building was known humorously enough as the Wentworth Model Dwellings—yes, they were a model, all right, for how to debase the worker by cramming him and his into a brick cracker box twelve to a room, hot in summer and cold in winter, with the crapper out back so that all who used it were degraded by its squalor.

"He ordered it removed?" seconded Cavanagh of the *Times.* We were astounded, restless, and I suppose quite rude. In other words, we were doing our jobs.

"Sir, he—"

"What's the damned bother with these unruly gents now?" Somebody interrupted the poor constable's excuse-making, and I looked away from the clearly troubled face of the messenger and thus encountered Sir Charles himself as he clomped over like Mrs. Shelley's beast or the golem of Jewish lore, a brutish man, all ancient muscle and large bone and imperturbable glare in his beady eyes. Sir Charles Warren was made to wear a uniform—even as head of the Met's HQ, known as Scotland Yard, he wore his like something you'd wear on the foredeck of HMS *Pinafore;* stuffed into civilian garb, he looked about to take a deep breath, expanding his chest explosively so that shards of black wool were blasted about without mercy. I will give the man this: He had a presence. His was the Gordon-at-Khartoum sort of Englishman, a human fortress of rectitude, self-belief, conviction of superiority, and view of world as only glimpsed down the barrel of a rifle at a running wog. A shame, then, he was so stupid. He was stout, bull-chested, bowler-hatted, waistcoated, and his blunt features were somewhat obscured behind one of those walrus mustaches that certain men of power found appealing, two great triangles of fur that both encircled and camouflaged his mouth. His chin looked as if it was made of British steel, and if you smacked it bang-on with more British steel, sparks might fly, but no damage to either piece of steel would be recorded.

"Sir, it's a clue," I said. "It might lead you to the fellow. One wonders how—"

"Nonsense," he said. "We recorded the words, and Long will give them out. However, the message chalked upon the wall is clearly excitory in intention, meant to focus anger on certain elements. I will not have a riot in this city and need to call the Life Guards to quell it—"

"As upon Bloody Sunday, Sir Charles?" someone asked, alluding to the great man's most famous (heretofore) blunder. I think the person who spoke was me, now that I remember it.

"I'll ignore that crack, sir," he replied. "The larger point is that London needs no blood spilled. Public order is the first order of business, on orders of the Home Office, and all orders will be followed." With that, he turned, then turned back. "You, who are you, sir?"

"Sir, I am Jeb, of the *Star.*"

"Lord of the rings, eh? Do you know the man-hours you cost us checking into reports of strangers with rings? An abomination."

"It's a fair clue, fairly reported," I said.

"You should be advised, sir, that I have sent a letter to your Mr. O'Connor in complaint of your misrepresentations of our efforts."

"Sir, with two more butchered on a single evening, and the case's most important clue having been erased, it seems your efforts have come to nothing. The public has—"

"By God, sir, we at the Yard will do our duty, and intemperate commentary and preposterous, misleading clues in the press only worsen matters. I assure you, the Yard will prevail, good order will be kept, and all will be as it should be. We will catch this nasty boy and see him hanged at Newgate Gaol. But you must do your part, for we are all on the same side, and that part does not include making us look like asses. Good night, gentlemen!"

One perquisite granted a general is that he need not hang around to face the consequences of his decisions, and so it was with Sir Charles, who turned and was immediately surrounded by a flock of aides-de-camp who clucked and cooed around him and nursed him to a carriage, at which point he sped off into what had become the dawn.

Poor Constable Long was left alone to face us, while all the other Bobbies and detectives stood around, perhaps relieved that the big boss hadn't made them perform close-order drill, as was his wont, in some cuckoo effort to instill military discipline on men who were underpaid and undertrained and overmatched.

"So, Long, out with it. You found it; the story, man."

We crowded about poor Long as if we were going to devour him, to discover the red nose and bloodshot eyes of a man who'd soaked the better part of his brain in gin for a dozen years and smelled the same as well.

"I's on me beat, and it's near on three A.M.," he began, and then told a dreary tale of walking down Goulston with his lantern, peeping into nooks and crannies, when his light illuminated a bright splotch of crimson on a crumple of cloth in the corner of a doorway arch that could be but one thing. He picked it up, smelled it to learn that the red was indeed blood and that stains of a certain ugly shade suggested fecal matter. He claimed that he thought it might be evidence of a rape, as he had not received the bad news about Mitre Square and Dutfield's Yard, and then he noticed some words scrawled on the wall. He went straight back to the Commercial Street station and showed them the clue, and a wiser detective sergeant put the picture together, which is how now, at around five in the pale light of dawn, such a scrum had formed in front of the Wentworth Model Dwellings.

"What was on the wall?" Cavanagh demanded, rather harshly, as it was not this poor idiot who'd ordered it erased but Sir Charles himself, who had adjudged it important enough to arrive at the scene posthaste.

Long said in an uncertain voice, "It read, 'The Jews are the men that will not be blamed for nothing.'"

"Jews?"

"Yes, sir, so it did, and here's the odd-like part, even a bloke like me knows 'Jews' to be spelled J-E-W-S, but this fellow must have been off his chum, he spelled it all wrong, it was 'J-U-W-E-S,' it was."

All of our pens took the strangeness down.

"You're sure?"

"Sure as I'm standing here before you."

We all shook our heads. Indeed, the Jews had been a theme in this thing, and my own paper, the *Star*, had not been circumspect in controlling speculation. Jews were, to so many, an alien element, and certain were quick to blame them. It would, for that same some, be quite helpful if the Jews or a Jew were in some way to blame, and the strange opacity of the graffito tended to point to that possibility, if to anything at all.

"Has the piece of bloody rag you found been definitely linked to the dead woman's apron?"

"Sir, you'd have to ask at the mortuary, sir," said Long, and then another copper—this may have been Constable Halse, of the City Police, who would make himself more visible in a few seconds—chimed in with "I can help with that; I'm just from the mortuary, as Commissioner Smith has put many of us out on the street, and yes, indeed, the rag matches by shape, texture, and size exactly the torn apron that was on the poor woman's remains in the square."

That was it, then. He had come this way. But were those his words? It certainly seemed so, for indeed they spoke to the central social issue of the case, and it seemed that he had indeed communicated a thought.

But . . . what thought?

Before we separated, we coagulated a bit on our own, we old boys who'd been on the case since Polly, even the penny-a-liners, treated for once as if they were equal, and we stood there in the pale light as Whitechapel came awake around us, and tried to make sense out of it. I cannot recall who said what, but I do remember the various arguments and now set them down as relevant and, moreover, typical of what transpired regarding this issue not merely in the week and the weeks that followed, but even now, twenty-four years after, is argued vehemently.

Some, I should add, believe poor Long got it wrong. It developed that the aforementioned Constable Halse of City had shown up before the erasure and inscribed in his own notebook a slightly different version. Thus there was no stationary target, which is why the damned thing still floats in the ether so provocatively.

Halse said the words were "The Juwes are not the men that will be blamed for nothing," as opposed to Long's "The Juwes are the men that will not be blamed for nothing."

That damned "not"! It drifts hither and yon like a balloon, untethered, on the zephyrs of the interpreter's bias.

"Double negative," said Cavanagh, university man. "Technically, grammatically, by all the rules, the two negatives cancel each other out, so the true meaning, regardless of the placement of the 'not,' is that the Jews are indeed guilty. It is saying, 'The Jews are the men who will be blamed for something.'"

"That does not impute guilt," said another. "It is neutral, simply stating the Jews will be blamed, and as we all know and have observed, the Jews being this era's prime bogeymen, indeed they will be blamed."

"So he's merely a social critic, like Dr. Arnold?"

There was some laughter at the idea of killer as essayist, but then the subject drifted elsewhere. On and on it went for almost an hour, as the boys tossed various ideas to and fro. Was our nasty chap really mad or only pretending? Did he have a program, or was he random? Was he intelligent, even a genius, or pure savage brute out of the dark forests of the east, full of primal blood lust for arcane religious purposes? Could he even be, after it all, someone similar to Robert Louis Stevenson's Jekyll and Hyde, two separate personalities in one body? Perhaps, as in the Scot's fiction, the one did not know of the other. It was all quite curious—pointless in the end, I suppose—but one remark stood out and colored my reactions to all that was to come.

"Well," someone said, "one thing's for certain, the only man who could solve this one is Sherlock Holmes."

Laughter, but not from me. Now, that was a damned fine idea. I had read Mr. Conan Doyle's "A Study in Scarlet" the previous year in a magazine where it was published, though I understand it has since come out in book form. Sherlock was exactly what we needed: a calm, dispassionate intellect with a gift for deduction, who could master a complex set of clues and make appropriate inferences, and through the swamp of this and that track a steady course that led inevitably to but one culprit. It was to be done, moreover, stylishly, with dry wit, wry observation, and despite a sort of academic diffidence, a true grasp as to how the world actually worked.

Where could we find such a man? Where was our Sherlock Holmes? I was ready to be his Watson.

CHAPTER NINETEEN
The Diary

October 4, 1888

I have been named.

It had to happen. If I am the demon incarnate, sooner or later some fellow will pin a moniker on me, first, to simplify communication of my charisma, and second, in some way, to diminish me by cramming all my nuances, improvisations, heroic acts of sheer will, bravery, and long-term shrewdness into one banal package that at first holds those attributes in high regard but eventually erodes until the name—and I—become commonplace.

25 Sept. 1888

Dear Boss, I keep on hearing the police have caught me but they wont fix me just yet. I have laughed when they look so clever and talk about being on the right track. That joke about Leather Apron gave me real fits. I am down on whores and shant quit ripping them till I do get buckled. Grand work the last job was. I gave the lady no time to squeal. How can they catch me now. I love my work and want to start again. You will soon hear of me with my funny *little games. I saved some of the proper <u>red</u> stuff in a ginger beer bottle over the last job to write with but it went thick like glue and I cant use it. Red ink is fit enough I hope <u>ha ha.</u> The next job I do I shall clip the ladys ears off and send to the police officers just for jolly wouldnt you. Keep this letter back till I do a bit more work, then give it out straight My knife's so nice and sharp I want to get to work right away if I get a chance. Good luck*

Yours truly
Jack the Ripper

Don't mind me giving the trade name.

wasn't good enough to post this before I got all the red ink off my hands curse it. No luck yet. They say I'm a doctor now <u>ha ha</u>

However, I rather like it. Whoever coined it is not without a certain low genius. Jack the Ripper. I, Jack. I, Ripper. It's both violent and short, it combines two commonalities in an unexpected way, it uses the verb "to rip" in an equally unexpected way, as very little of what I've done involves ripping. But Jack the Cutter would not work, because cutting is a term, though accurately employed here, that more usually finds its place in discussions of tailoring. So Jack the Ripper it shall be.

I suspect it's the business of the ear that drove it home. Whichever pusillanimous journo coined "Jack the Ripper" had no way of knowing that in my frenzy in Mitre Square involving what was left of Mrs. Eddowes, I indeed loosed an ear from its mooring on the side of the skull. I had no memory of doing so; that was a period of blur, although rereading my last entry, I see I retained enough recollection to record it immediately postcoitus, if ever so swiftly it vanished under the tidal swell of sleep that overwhelmed me.

But that freak of circumstance gave Jack the Ripper's missive, with its lurid silliness about using blood as ink, a certain kind of instant celebrity. You need a vivid detail to nail something hard and permanent into the public consciousness, and whosoever my benefactor was, he provided that. He should be writing adverts!

Meanwhile, the "double event," as the papers are calling it, seems to be seen as evidence of a particularly malignant higher genius. How I wish it were so! Were I that genius, I might not have had to improvise so desperately and to depend on luck so totally. But nobody seems to have cottoned to the fact that the second event existed purely because the first was so unsatisfactory, just as no one has an inkling as to why JEWS is spelled JUWES in my graffito, or why that sentence seems to make no sense, grammatically or otherwise. I have to laugh at how incompetent are our supposedly great minds. It appears that nobody has the gift of putting these things into their proper pattern and inferring where this campaign is ultimately going. That pleases me no end.

In fact, I am at this time more happy than I have ever been in my life. Those who smote me so deeply and took from me that which I had created and loved, they will meet the knife—of one sort or another—soon. Those who criticized me, those who disdained my work, those who found me shallow and overambitious, I am in the process of proving them all wrong, in thunder. "Ha ha," as Jack has written, and whoever he is, the anonymous scribe got exactly the joy I feel in confounding the world. Sir Charles, the boys of the press, all the mobs who cannot help themselves but for prattling and dreaming of Jack, all of them are miles from the truth, and the only crime is that if I succeed, as I surely feel I will, no one will be wise enough to put it all together.

I have a little left to do. I must be on with it.

October 24, 1888

Dear Mum,

Well, I know you heard the news. He done two up, one real bad. They even have a name for him these days, the newspapers do, they call him "Jack the Ripper" on account of some letter he's said to have written, although if you ask me, it's all a bunch of horseradish, as a fellow who could do what he done to the last one wouldn't make no sense when it comes to writing letters on account of his being all crazy and everything. He's like an orang or something, in human form, some kind of crazy ape with a knife, maybe a Russky or a Pole or a Chinaman, but no Englishman, that I'll tell you.

That's what us girls think. No Englishman could do such horrors and so we still feel safe with our own kind, which seems to be how we're doing things these days.

And we are not alone. You'd think the city might sit back and enjoy this foul brute chopping on unfortunates but it's like everybody is behind us! It's something! Why, just a few weeks back, before the double event, two constables spotted a local hooligan and gave chase to him. People thought it was Jack himself, and they got in on the game, and soon a mob was on this chap's tail, they right near strung him up. Well, he weren't no angel, but he weren't Jack, either. It was a fellow called Squibby, a low common bully. The coppers got there in time to save him a jig under the gallows tree. They even went to the police station and tried to get him for the rope, sure it was Jack, but the coppers held firm.

I know all this scares you and Da, Mum. But don't let it. See, I'm not like those other girls. They all works the street and their jobs take them into alleys. All Jack done, he done in alleys and squares or other dark nooks. Myself, it's all different for me. I'm safe and snug as a bug in a rug in my own little room. My fellow and I are sort of on the outs now, but I see him every day and I know he'll be back soon. Having Joe around is one thing, as he won't let nobody hurt me. Oh, and on top of that, there's a watch dog. Well ha ha ha, there I go again, making jokes. It's not a dog, it's a cat. The lady upstairs, Elizabeth, she keeps a kitten she calls Diddles, but Diddles ain't no ordinary cat. Diddles knows when somebody's about who shouldn't be, and you can be sure Diddles will let out a racket if anyone shows up here who don't belong.

So I know I'm safe. I've got my room, locked hard by automatic spring mechanical system, so even if I ain't paying mind because of my thirst, it's solid shut behind me, and then upstairs there's

Diddles, and he's paying attention if anyone comes poking around, and then there's my fellow Joe who wants me out of my business and comes by every day to talk about it, and believe me, if anyone tries a thing when Joe's here, Joe's going to leave him in the worst shape he's ever been in. Then there's Constable Johnny Upright and there's Constable Walter Dew, who chased after and arrested Squibby, and above 'em all is Detective Abberline, the smartest fellow there ever was, and then there's the big boss himself, Sir Charles, a war hero, so I've got all these important and powerful men to save me from Jack the Ripper.

So Mum, don't worry. I'll be fine. Maybe I'll lose my thirst, maybe I'll marry Joe, maybe we'll leave London if Joe finds work someplace clean, away from all this trash here, and maybe we'll even take Diddles the cat along with us.

Oh Mum, miss you so, wish it had worked out different, but I know it'll be okay. I have nothing but hopes for a bright future and happiness for all.

Your loving girl,
Mairsian

CHAPTER TWENTY

Jeb's Memoir

Since the aftermath of the famous "double event" is so well known, it hardly needs dramatization; summary will suffice. As it turned out, the murder of the two shocked not merely London and the empire that sustained it but the entire world. At the precise point in the hysteria, the name Jack the Ripper arrived out of nowhere (that is, if my fevered imagination can be considered nowhere) and, taken with the coincidence of the chopped ear and the brilliance of the contrivance (ahem!), became instantly accepted by that same world, a globe terrified with Jack and yet desperate for information about him. By midweek the enigma of "Juwes" had emerged, lodged as it was in an opaque sentence, to further excite comment, fear, hysteria, and all sorts of bad behavior. Various suspects were named, their curricula vitae examined, and ultimately, when their regrettable innocence was proved, they were left to fade back into nothingness. We did our best to keep the hubbub hubbing along nicely, as O'Connor insisted on running a letter, a postcard actually, that he knew to be fraudulent, simply because it rehammered the Jack idea and contained the felicitous self-identifier—clearly inspired by my insouciant tone—"Saucy Jacky."

Jack became a virtual industry, as all papers went all Jack, all editions. Replate, replate! (I still hadn't figured out what that meant.) I'm not sure if fear was driving the frenzy or something a little bit more dubious, being some kind of secret, sick fascination with the hideous tragedy of others. As long as Jack limited his slaughter frenzy to whores, he'd have hundreds of thousands of fans among the bourgeois and the intelligentsia, safely fenced from his hunter's dementia as they were. Let him knock off one of those poofs, however, and he'd be less titillating and by far a more palpable threat.

In all this, I was kept incredibly busy. On Sunday the first, Harry Dam and I worked through the night with Henry Bright, who united our two stories into a single seamless piece of reportage that I thought, having read what the *Times* and the *Evening Mail* and the *Gazette* offered, was quite the best. Henry was a talented journalist and an ethical one, and he knitted the stories into a calm tapestry of murder, mystery, mayhem, and official police ineptitude. It can be read today with profit, I say with some pride. It was my best journalism.

I will merely allude to subsequent developments of the next week or so, among them the upping of various rewards, the holding of inquests, funerals, the staging of a bloodhound test at Regent's Park that produced yet more humiliation for Warren (his prize beasts, Barnaby and Burgho, managed to find only a couple copulating in the trees!), who was rapidly becoming the laughingstock of Western civilization. The victims of the double event were quickly identified, and their names became as well known as any West End ingenue's. Poor Elizabeth Stride, who is always short-shrifted, as her murder is so much less interesting, was the lady who met her end at Dutfield's Yard, being a Swedish immigrant, who, despite her nickname Long Liz, was another dumpling, she having just returned from the country where she and her paramour had been hop picking, though without much success. The second was Catherine Eddowes, in Mitre's, where Jack had taken his time to do right by her and left some kind of hideous exhibition on the theme of "her guts for garters" for all to see.

When everything had been reported, we in the journalism business, knowing a good thing, rereported it with embellishments, theories, illustrations, and so forth and so on. Issues emerged: How had Jack miraculously escaped from Dutfield's Yard when the pony wagon clearly trapped him in it? How had he then gotten cross town, near a mile by the shortest street route (shorter by crow, but as far as was known, he was not a crow) to butcher Mrs. Eddowes within forty-five minutes under the very noses of two separate City constables, without a noise being sounded, and then, still more intriguing, how had he escaped from that locked box, surrounded as it was by patrolling coppers, to arrive at Goulston Street and the Wentworth tenements to deposit his obvious clue and leave his opaque, tantalizing inscription? And what could those words mean? What was the secret of "Juwes"? Was it a code, was it a foreign word, was it a willed misspelling, was it a Masonic symbol, was it a tsarist ploy, was it an obscure cockneyism? Many a tea and crumpet were downed over consideration of the Juwe jigsaw.

At exactly this moment, what should arrive but a note from my new friend Professor Thomas Dare. Eager to keep acquaintance with so brilliant a mind and keen a wit, and still hungry for his alluded-to theories of Jack, I tore it open.

"My dear Jeb," it began. "How pleasant to chat with you at Charlie's soiree. You may recall the subject of he who is now called 'The Ripper' came up. Saucy Jacky, what a fellow. He sells your newspapers, he keeps my mind aflutter.

"But nothing has so moved me as this business of 'J-U-W-E-S.' It's on my foredeck. It's language. It's communication. It has a Beneath. Thus I have spent a good part of the last week trying possibilities against the archetype, in hopes of cracking the code.

"I have reached certain conclusions. Being civic-minded when it's not too much trouble, I went to Scotland Yard and waited three hours to reach an inspector, who listened politely, nodded, then said, 'Well and good, sir, noted, now if you don't mind, I've other duties,' and showed me the door. That uninterest I put to Warren, who after all is no policeman, certainly no detective, not even a soldier, but really a kind of engineer. When brick and mortar have to be calculated against the requirements of budget, transport, estimated time of use, repair costs, all for a bridge to be built in Mesopotamia, I suppose he's the fellow you want, but that's how he sees the world, nuance-free, unburdened by a Beneath, ultimately quantifiable and mea-surable. Such silliness won't catch a devil like Jack.

"In any event, I believe I know what 'J-U-W-E-S' is. I'm the only man in London who does, unless I tell you. Would you be interested?

"Yours, Thomas."

CHAPTER TWENTY-ONE
The Diary

October 15, 1888

———

I had to see it, of course. It had been a darkened, even a dream, landscape, in a part of the city I hardly knew. I acted on instinct, boldness, without hesitation, and thus, like Cardigan at Balaclava, my headlong, crazed charge through the enemy phalanxes enabled me to survive for another day's fight.

I waited, I waited, I waited. Today was long enough after, the air was coolish, the sun bright, and it seemed as good a time as any. I wandered out, seeming merely to take a stroll as might any Londoner, and meandered casually this way and that, though trending toward Mitre Square. Being no fool, I would now and then double around to make certain no one was following, though that felt impossible. Indeed, no one was on to me, I was just another citizen, strolling haphazardly block by block, perhaps on the way to an appointment, a meal, an assignation. Nothing about me was remarkable.

Now and then I passed an apothecary's, a tobacconist's, or an out-and-out newstand, where this afternoon's leader boards blazed away with the latest revelations. It was all old milk, reheated ever so slightly for misleading sale. Jack, Jack, Jack. Jack everywhere, Jack nowhere, Jack spotted in the

Thames Tunnel, Jack observed in Hyde Park. Who Jack, where Jack, how Jack, why Jack? When they imagined Jack, I had to laugh. Their Jack was a skulker, a creeper, a lurker who slithered through the fog in a giant topper, with some kind of curving Oriental blade clenched in his fist, held close to his face, which was shielded by the cape he drew tight around his neck with his other hand. His posture was feline, for he moved by cat law, silky, silent, gliding on only toes to ground. Ha and ha again. I was as normal a bloke as you could imagine, nobody but the thrushes saw the blade, which in any case was a straight piece of Sheffield steel, as found in every kitchen in Great Britain. I walked through crowds, shoulders back, head erect, my garb not at all theatricalized along West End variations on cunning evil, and never in my adventures had I glimpsed so much as a wisp of fog. I had a fair, somewhat blocky face, hair of modest attainment, and wouldn't be caught dead in a top hat. Was I going to a ball after my dates with murder, is that what they thought? Perhaps to Buckingham for tea with the queen? Newspapers: What's the point of existing if you're always going to get everything so wrong?

As I got deeper into Whitechapel, the roads clogged up with horse traffic, and the costers' stalls became obstacles on the sidewalk for pedestrians, all of us squeezing around the choke points, careful not to get shit on our boots or to be crushed by horse tram or beer wagon or speeding hansom. There were dollies out, I suppose, for theirs was a twenty-four-hour-a-day business, men needing notch at any odd stolen hour, but they did not dominate as they did during the evening hours, nor was there the sickly glare of the gaslights and beer shops and public houses to give the place its customary demimonde grotesquerie. It was just business as usual among Brits themselves, the low dregs of empire drawn here, more and more Jews, Indiamen, Teutons, Slavs, and Russkies, so much so that English did not prevail in the constant din of shouts and shills. The overwhelming miasma of the horse deposits that no street sweeper, no matter how energetic, could keep up with, occluded both the nose and the eyes (which wept unavoidably, and who could blame them?), as well as the drifting tang of methane, that other more deadly horse product, headache-inducing if sampled too intensively. The shops, the stalls, the pubs, they fled by in no pattern, as did the various appliances that sustained a horse-drawn economy, troughs, hitching rails, gates leading into yards for the unloading of goods, stables here and there, and the constant noise of the brutes themselves, sometimes a neigh or a whinny, sometimes a cloppity-clop as shoed hoof struck pavement, sometimes the general bluster and sigh of the beasts who basically carried the city on their broad backs without a complaint or a speech. All and all, there was no palpable sign of Jack panic, giving the lie to the conceit that the city was clenched in a fist of fear. Newspapers again, telling a tale that wasn't.

I passed the Aldgate pump, then Houndsditch and Duke, and there spied the spot where I'd come upon Mrs. Eddowes and put a proposition to her so she'd lead me into the darkness down Mitre Street. When I reached Mitre Street, I turned, finding myself surrounded on either side by low residences undistinguished by anything except that they were sublimely undistinguished. That led, within half a block, to Mitre Square, and on normal days, a lone man entering its portal might attract some suspicion, for what would his business be, but not today, as it still enjoyed its celebrity from my earlier visit.

I cannot say it was packed cheek by jowl like an exhibit at the Great Exposition, but gawkers were all about, most of them clustered in the right-hand corner, near on the wooden yard fence, where Mrs. Eddowes met her fate. I felt no need to approach it and infiltrate the mob just to see a patch of flagstone no different from any other flagstone; instead I took in the whole of the place, seeing in the sun that which had been shrouded in the shadow.

It was a series of brick structures of no particular style or pedigree surrounding for no reason a small patch of space in the middle of a city wilderness. No care, no thought, no wit, most assuredly no brilliance, had gone into its design, if it had indeed been designed, but far more likely, it just happened, as various structures appeared along slipshod principles around it, and someone finally got the idea to crush the wild grass between them under flagstone. Why was it even called a square? Nothing about it suggested the acute angle.

The murder, however, drew many to this otherwise undistinguished lot, and if you guessed the murderer would return to the scene of his crime, you would have been right, I suppose, but at the same time, if you perused the crowd for just such a man, I, the authentic guilty party, would have been the last upon which your eyes would light. Murder has a peculiar odor, and some are drawn to it despite themselves. Many of the people were singles, men mostly but a few ladies as well, all of them unsure how to act, possibly a bit ashamed, but unable to stay away. They stood around stiffly, trying to remain inconspicuous, as if Major Smith and his blue bottles were likely to sweep them up. Nobody made eye contact or really acknowledged each other; out of deference to the newspaper image of Jack under his topper in his opera cape, nobody wore a topper: It was strictly a bowler or slouch hat locality, the clothes all dark and lumpy, as if Mrs. Eddowes would have been insulted by a splash of color.

I glanced over to the left and saw the church passage from whence I had escaped, and again thanked the God whom I knew did not exist for providing it, copper-free, for that reason alone in His Grand Plan, just as I owed Him for constructing this helpful place so I could improvise brilliantly that night. I meant to leave that way as soon as I got over my disappointment at the prosaic nature of the square and its lack of drama or dynamism in the daylight, but at that point I was discovered.

My guilt was known. It was pointed out. The jig was up. I had returned to the scene and paid the price. All that is true.

It is also true that I was discovered by a dog.

I do not know what higher sensitivities these creatures have, but this one knew. She saw into and through me. She had me, whether by rude particle of blood scent adhering to my flesh (I had meticulously burned all the clothes I wore that night and bathed scrupulously) or some instinctive warning system that highlights predators, or maybe by shrewd analysis of my uninterest in the site of the body for the channel of escape, I know not.

She was a small Scottish West Highland terrier, dead white to proclaim virtue and justice, proving that symbolism of times appears in reality just as readily as it does in fiction, poetry, or art. Her bark was not alarming, but it was insistent; truly heroic, she pulled hard to assault me, plunge her fangs into my flesh, and bring me down.

"Maddy, my goodness, you must stop at once, oh, bad lady, bad *bad* girl," yelped her embarrassed master, a grandmotherly type under a straw bonnet with more than a few ribbons, posies, and bows, another murder gawker embarrassed to be stirred into human contact by her doggie's misbehavior.

But Maddy knew and would not relent. She screamed aloud, "It's he, it's Jack, it's the knifer, the ripper, the killer, oh, you foolish people, if you would but look into this blackguard's soul, you would see his evil and smell the blood he spilled not thirty feet away!" Unfortunately, since she spoke only terrier, the doltish humans about her paid no attention whatsoever and went about their nervous murder-site gawking.

The mistress bent and scooped up Maddy and hugged the squirming thing to her bosom, but Maddy kept trying to alert civilization to the threat it faced, although to no effect.

"Sir, I am so sorry, I cannot fathom what has got into her today, she is usually so polite."

"Madam," I said, "do not be concerned. Dogs, children, and women universally loathe me, but on the other hand, gentlemen do not much care for me, either."

"Well, sir, at least you're not a Mason!" said the lady, a rather game riposte, I thought, and it brought our conversation to a pleasing close, as we had chatted in the enjoyable language of high irony. I bent, bowed, removed my bowler in a sweeping, overmagnanimous gesture to signify theatrical-sized graciousness, and turned smartly to abandon the square.

I walked to the church passage, and it was much narrower by day than I recalled by night, with the brick walls pressing in fiercely but a meter or so apart. As I meant to make egress, I turned and saw that the lady had gone back to her ruminating on the events of the square, but Maddy, ever vigilant, had me fixed in a baleful glare.

CHAPTER TWENTY-TWO

Jeb's Memoir

Was he our Sherlock Holmes? Could the long-hoped-for genius intellect at last be entering the fray? Lord, I did so hope. I also, ambitious wretch, did so hope that I'd be the one to take it all down.

Two days hence I met him at the Reform Club, at Pall Mall next to the Traveler's Club, in the high club land of central London. His tweeds were magnificent, flowing like the land forms of the heather itself, and again he seemed utterly unimpressed by the figure he cut with his wavy blond hair, his aquiline nose, his round specs, and his general air of Porthos amid the corpses of freshly skewered Richelieu swordsmen.

"Do sit down," he said, "and pay no attention to the various Irish revolutionaries about you, as they are not apt to plant a bomb in the only place in London where you can have a good dish of lamb stew."

"As I speak with a wee but insistent Dublin brogue," I said, "I suspect they would not explode until I left the premises, for fear—misplaced, of course—of blasting one of their own."

I knew there were no revolutionaries about, not even many radicals, rather that wan and forlorn tribe of misbegotten and guilt-bearing mere liberals, who wanted change at only a slightly increased pace over the progress of a turtle across the Sahara.

We sat in a corner nook of the great cigar- and pipe-smoked room, amid lustrous mahogany walls lined with books and portraits of various liberals from Anne Boleyn on down, and he offered me a cheroot and a drink, the first of which I took, the second of which I turned down.

"Probably a wise decision," he said. "I have too many times awakened after a night with friend Jack Barley in the arms of a whore whom I promised to marry and thereby render licit. And bourgeois. Believe me, it takes more than phonetics to get out of *that* one with phiz intact."

I laughed, loving again a wit based on shock, which I had not encountered in so pure a form. Perhaps Wilde had it in him, for his was also a sharpness of the knife as applied to moral convention (and how, as it turned out, poor man!). I wondered then, as I do now, if Wilde knew Dare and borrowed from him. I knew I would borrow from Dare. And I certainly have!

"So," he said, "the Irish journalist who's really a music critic wants a solution to the mystery of J-U-W-E, does he?"

"I've read and heard so many, I yearn for a thing I can believe in."

"Not for you, then, satanic or Masonic ritual, ancient cockney slang, the ravings of a ill-educated lout who cannot spell a three-letter word and would, if challenged, produce C-A-E-T for cat? Are there others?"

"Some seem to think it Chinese. Or rather the pronunciation of a Chinese pictogram. Others place its derivation in the steppes, where Russia runs out and tribal Cossack elements begin. Language, most agree, is at the heart of it."

"I do, too. Indeed, it is language."

He reached into a briefcase I had not noticed and pulled out a volume, not a book but more than a newspaper, a kind of heavily bound journal of the sort I would later learn was a part of medical and scientific worlds.

"Here is your answer," he said, "and congratulations on being the second man in London to behold it."

I took it eagerly.

"Pages 132 through 139," he said helpfully.

Alas, they were in German, as was the whole damned thing.

"Sir, I have no German."

"Why, you have been advertised to me as a sort of genius."

"I have taught myself Pitman shorthand and am able to read French, which I taught myself as well. I am known as a wit and have some potential as a writer. But that is where it stops, alas."

"All right, then. The journal you have before you is *Zeitschrift fur vergleichende Augenheilkunde.* Which playfully translates into the 'Journal of Comparative Ophthamology.' On the pages specified, a brilliant German opthamalogist—that is, eye doctor—named Rudolf Berlin has published a study entitled *Eine besondere Art der Worthblindheit (Dyslexie).* Does that clear things up a bit for you?"

He was playing with me as a cat plays with a mouse. But he wasn't meaning to eat me—rather, to enlighten me. To do so, he had to destroy me. Thus is education built.

"You know it hasn't, sir," I said.

"I think rather too much of myself, don't I? I find myself so amusing. Always had that problem. All right, then, Herr Doktor Berlin's title translates as 'A Special Kind of Word Blindness,' and in parentheses he has coined a term for a condition relevant to our inquiry here."

"And that is—"

"This condition posits an interference between what the eye records and what the brain receives. He called it *dyslexie,* or in our more felicitous tongue, dyslexia."

"You're saying—" I was struggling with the concept.

"I am saying Jack has a condition known not as stupidity or insanity or immorality or even cannibalism, but while he may indeed have all those, his condition is scientifically called dyslexia. He is dyslexic."

I nodded, even if my eyes were occluded with confusion.

"Put simply: He looks at the letters J-E-W-S and that is what he sees, but as his eyes send that information brainward, they become, by tangled paths not yet understood, J-U-W-E-S. To him, J-U-W-E-S is objective reality. He has no idea he's 'misspelling,' though assuming that he's mature, he's presumably aware that he has certain spelling and reading problems, but as no diagnosis for his condition existed until last year, he has spent his life quietly devising strategies to get around it. His friends, his family, his society, none of them has any idea he has this condition because he has gotten so damned good at hiding it. But it tells us certain things. For example, he is certain not to have a job in any firm or institution that demands carefully written reports, which lets out most forms of science, medicine being one. There goes the mad-surgeon theory. His infirmity would hold him back, even make him a laughingstock. He must therefore be in some action- or behavior-intensive line of work, such as policeman or soldier, perhaps a surveyor, or an architect. His form of the condition may not at all affect his acuity with numbers or images, so he could be an engineer, a retailer, a manufacturer, what have you. He might be very gifted in verbal expression, and thus a barrister, a sales representative, a stockbroker, a carnival barker.

Berlin says what's fascinating about the condition is that it is in no way limited to idiots or half-idiots. Normally intelligent or even highly intelligent people can suffer from it and—as has our Jack, I suspect—they have found quiet ways to compensate. For example, he will always avoid reading aloud before an audience, as he may encounter a word whose letters will be scrambled and read, say, 'detour' for 'doctor' or 'lofty' for 'laughter,' and produce gibberish. He will have done that a few times, learned from it, and strategized a way around it, do you see?"

"So when he chalked that inscription, he had no idea he was giving up a vital piece of information about himself?"

"Exactly, though now he knows and is probably cursing his own stupidity. Being well versed in the avoidance of such faux pas, he presumably made elaborate plans to prevent the mistake, but something happened that startled him or frightened him, and he reverted unconsciously to form. As near as I can tell, it's the only mistake he's made so far, and it's a mistake only because one man in London, and now two, understand what was going on."

I was impressed. This was the first real insight I had encountered, discounting the mystery of the missing rings, since the Sussex Regiment envelope found at Annie Chapman's side proved to be nothing. "I see what you are saying, and I am impressed. But I must say, Professor Dare, how does that advance the investigation? I mean, practically, one cannot suddenly test all three and a half million male Londoners to see which might have this dyslexia condition. And it seems not to be known how general a condition it would be, and so suppose it's quite common—I recall a large number of bad spellers throughout my rather patchy education—and in the end you might have so many possible suspects that the winnowing didn't winnow near enough."

"That is true," said Dare, "and I suspect that is why the inspector was so unimpressed with my analysis."

"However," I said, seeing some light in it, "as you say, this condition might be associated with certain other behaviors. You inferred an 'action'- or 'behavior'-style career path for such a man, so it seems we could rule out a huge number of suspects."

"I think you're beginning to catch on," said Dare. "The test for dyslexia is so narrow that it would have to be the last, not the first, criterion for identification. My idea, at this point, is that someone gifted in analysis—"

"That would be you, indeed, sir—"

"Don't underestimate yourself, Mr. Jeb. Two minds are better than one, and in the dialectic between them, they might create something better than either could do on his own."

"I agree," I said.

"So what I propose is this: We each take a few days off, not merely from the case but from each other. In solitude, using my distillation of the dyslexia as a guide, we see what we can infer or deduce from the events before us. You would know more than I, having been at most of the murder sites when hot with blood and having discussed the case with many professionals. On the other hand, that might make you too close to the events, and it might also lock your mind in the set of those professionals, who, after all, are wont to pin this on a Russian sailor or a Jew in a leather apron and have a bias against admitting that a homegrown Englishman could do such a thing."

"What is our goal?"

"Our goal is to assemble a portrait of the man by his salient aspects. He has to be thus and so, and he cannot be anything other. The more we think, the more we shrink. As opposed to a dragnet that hopes to catch him in flagrante or post flagrante, we assemble this—well, perhaps 'profile' is a better word than 'portrait'—*profile* of the man, and locate those few suspects who might fit it. Then we—you and I, of course—investigate each of them and see if there are any indications of such deviant behavior."

"The rings," I said with excitement. "Suppose we can ascertain that indeed he has recently acquired two wedding bands, or perhaps those bands might be located in his kit or jewelry drawer."

"Yes, yes, that's it," said Dare. "Suppose we learn, for example, that Mr. X, a dyslexic barrister, was seen to return to his dwelling very early morning on all the days there were murders. Somehow—I'm not a detail type of fellow—but somehow we penetrate his rooms and there locate his rings. That's a clumsy example, but it's the idea. We might locate the fellow who has left other clues, but since no one was looking for them, he went unobserved. We are identifying a pattern. That is my real idea."

I caught fire with it. "Perhaps I should obtain a revolver for the arrest."

"Arrest? Confrontation? Gad, no, I will have nothing of heroism. That is for the lunkheads who stood with Chard against the Zulu at Rorke's Drift intead of sensibly running like flaming bats. They didn't realize that Chard's awesome stupidity was his armor. They, being more fully evolved humans, were so much meat for the blackie spear points. I'm far too intelligent to be brave, thank you very much."

"No confrontations, then. No revolver. But we take our findings to the Yard and let the blue bottles on to it from there. The story and the glory are ours but the danger theirs. I think I could grow friendly with that."

"It's police business, indeed. For me, Jack's transit to hell aboard HMS *Noose* on the Newgate gallows is reward enough."

"Without ignoring the moral implications of such a coup," I said, "do not think ill of me, sir, for admiring the professional implications! Why, man, we'd be glory on two legs."

"Glory's overrated," he said. "You'll see that when you advance in years somewhat."

"You misunderstand. Not glory in and of itself, as a shallow end, but as part of a process. With glory comes influence, and with influence, perhaps the chance to change things. That's the legacy I'm conjuring with. Although as to the shallower glory, I suppose I could use a little of that, too."

"Your idealism will get you killed or, worse, knighted, and you'll spend the rest of your days among fools and MPs. As for me, the chance to refuse an audience with the queen would be exquisite."

CHAPTER TWENTY-THREE
The Diary

October 18, 1888

———

I wanted a pretty. The others had not been pretty, though Liz had gotten near; but this one would be. She would be lean of face, not doughy, like a muffin or a crumpet. Her skin should be smooth, her hair smooth, the color of corn silk. She must be clean, not just in from picking hops or awakened from a night in doss or the gutter; she must be delicate, with elegant fingers, long, thin legs whose coltlike grace would be evident even under the crinoline; an alabaster neck. If the eyes be blue, so much the better, although a lass with blond hair and brown eyes has a fetching quality, whereas the blues tend toward a frostiness that I do not find appealing. She must be young, fresh, innocent to serve as the vessel of my desecration.

It seemed hard to believe that such a creature, more out of a fairy tale or a myth or even a Rossetti painting, would be working the streets of Whitechapel. Whitechapel is the grinder of the flesh; it sustains its girls but at a price almost too steep to pay, for it erodes them swiftly, it takes their singularity, their character, what wit they have, what memories, what hopes, what dreams, and swiftly makes them a crude composite, rimmed with grime, surly and cynical, untouched by melody in carriage or voice, vacant of eye, loose and slack of mouth. Black or broken of teeth. It's the trade, it's the gin, it's the spunk, it's the nightly ritual of finding a posture in which to be penetrated easily, it's the disease, it's the closing of horizons, it's the crush of destiny, it's the immense indifference of society, of civilization, even.

In short, I wanted what I couldn't have.

I went far afield. I perambulated in my slow, easeful way down the Whitechapel High Street, beyond the intersection with Commercial, that hub of the flesh and sperm trade, passing as I went such lesser applicants to Sodom and Gomorrah as the Black Horse, the Black Bull, the Blue Boar, as if any such animals had been seen in the wild here in a thousand years. It was softer beyond Commercial, and the coster-squatters had relented, so no stalls had been spread about like obstacles against normal pedestrianism, and I hoped to find a softer woman. I walked, I walked, I walked. I cut down Angel Alley, I walked the Wicked Quarter Mile, I looked into Itchy Park at Christchurch and thence to the coagulation of flesh outside, within and around the Ten Bells. It was not as late as I prefer, but the quarter-moon stood guard, providing enough but not too much light, and now and then a gaslight flung its bit of glow off a corner, just enough to suggest safety without actually providing it.

I saw several. One, too old by far, turned out not to be in the life, and when I approached, she skittered away with a haughty tut-tut to her carriage to inform me that I had made a mistake, that she was not up for trade, and to chastise me for my impertinence with the suggestion that I return to busier thoroughfares. Another, alas, was too swift; I never caught up with her and lost her in a crowd on one of my peregrinations.

In time, I wore out and found a seat at the bar of the public house called the Three Nuns—not many of them about, either, I'll tell you! In that rowdy place, among the many and anonymous, I refreshed with an ale, then another. Eventually I arose and escaped the clamor, then found that the beer had slowed and dulled me and moved my mood toward the sourly comic, in which everything was amusing and nothing meaningful. I knew I had no patience for the kind of careful stalk I had planned; the evening was well shot. Accepting defeat is sometimes the best way to assure victory, for as I began my desultory walk homeward, I saw her.

I dubbed her, in my mind, Juliet, after Shakespeare's most tragic young lover. She was no thruppence Judy, that was for sure, and you saw them sometimes, for among the twelve hundred who plied their trade to stay alive down here in hell's maw and Jack's feeding ground, now and again a lass of some exquisiteness might appear. She'd be quickly bought up by a rich man for mistress or recruited by a house for the room of highest ceiling and reddest silk, but in this way she got her start and advanced in her trade and, who knew, ultimately made it to the arm of someone already chosen by society as a lucky fellow. The lucky get luckier, that's the rub.

She was tall and thin and painfully young, as if untouched, even *virgo intacticus*, with a doll's delicate translucent face and tendrils of curled blond hair framing it. Her hat was pert, her bodice tight, gathered in satin posies about her swan's neck to emphasize an impossibly adorable bosom, the amenities contained within not heavy to flesh and droop, but all perfect in pouty haughtiness. She would do perfectly for the blasphemy I intended, and by the luck of He Who Does Not Exist, she was exactly where she had to be when she had to be there.

The quality of her clothing gave her away, I saw in a second. She was of a subspecies in the trade called a "dress lodger," meaning, poor girl, that she was employed by a house, lent finer clothes than she could afford on her own and, in return for them, split the fee with the madam who ran the place and was further obligated to steer her client its way when all was done. It was a form of advertising, if you will, in the brothel industry. Whatever, I knew then she was no innocent. Oddly, that inflamed me even more.

I approached, brushed close by her, and smelled her—delicious, ambrosial—then turned to melt my eyes on her, noting a spray of youthful freckles across the bridge of nose, playing out on her cheeks. Our eyes beheld each other for just a second, but it was a long and, for me, a passionate one. As for her, nothing perturbs the calm of beauty, for she believes beauty is her Achilles' potion, shielding her from all harm. Generally, that is a terrible mistake.

"Would the young lady care for an escort?" I inquired, removing my hat and bowing slightly.

"I know your sort," she said. "Start off nice and friendly, all gentle-like, then directly comes the cuff and the fist and finally the kick."

"I would slay any man who would kick, even slap, such a face, whose eyes, I might add, sparkle with intrigue, not the cow's surrender to its fate."

"He talks fancy, then, does this one. Maybe you're Saucy Jacky, the one that rips, and it's something sharp is my destiny, not something sweet."

"Madam, this Jack works a later shift. As well, I invite you to examine my body and see it bereft of blade," I said. "For who could see you and think of such?"

The poor thing. She had no idea with whom she spoke and how close was the Reaper's—the Ripper's, another hidden meaning in whatever hack had so coined the moniker—scythe.

"We'll walk a bit now, and I'll see if you're one that I like enough."

"You among all the birds can pick and choose," I said. "Perhaps my luck is to be the chosen tonight."

We fell into an easy rhythm, and for a second, as we passed along the way, I saw us as a perfect couple, he of property, she of beauty, both of style and wit and grace, and thought how London rewards such worthies, and how at a certain point I was convinced, goddess on arm, that such was my own destiny. Alas, and bitterly, it was not to be, and that outcome carried with it the mallet of melancholy. But this melancholy, like a headache, passed as we approached the structure around which I had planned tonight's infamy, and in time we came under the shadow, had there been a sun or a moon bright and well placed enough, of that large entity.

She stopped as if she had made up her mind. "You smell good," she said. "If it's something you'd be wanting, I could provide, I think, if only for my dying mother."

"I am happy to keep Mum alive another night or so."

"And it's not without considerable cost. I'm told I'm selling something above common, far above common."

"Far, far above common."

"I don't do this all the time, you understand."

"Nor I. It'll be an adventure for both of us. Did I hear a figure mentioned?"

"Five, I think, would put me in the mind."

Five! And it wasn't pence she was talking but shillings. Good Christ, she thought highly of herself. But she'd read my want, my cleanliness, my prosperity, liked my smell since I'd bathed in anticipation, so she'd set the market to the customer. It was pure Bentham.

"That lightens my purse considerably," I said. "But I shall happily meet the tariff on the condition that, for our privacy, it's the building beyond us that contains our assignation. Having *you* in *it* makes it worth the five. In fact, I'll give you six, my dear."

She looked, reading the place up and down. It was a fragile moment, for some would panic at the prospect and others blush. But this Juliet was a bold young woman. "Six, then, for the Church."

I pulled a crown from my pocket and fished the coinage of the rest and pressed it all into her hand. She tucked it in some pouch beneath her petticoats. "Then leave us proceed, sir," she said.

We advanced up the stone walk. The spire of St. Botolph's rose above us. It was not the loveliest church in London, or even Whitechapel, appearing prosaic next to the Methodist adoration of deity that propelled Christchurch to such height and glory, but it was not without its merits. It had been called the prostitute's church, for it was on an island, surrounded on four sides by street or walk, and they could be in constant orbit and impervious to the reach of the rozzers. Its steeple was a pile of size-descending boxes, as a child might assemble from blocks of wood, each with its note of decoration, one being a Roman clock, another a square window, the third an arched window of louvers, and above that a cupola festooned in urns of some sort. Now that I think of it, it wasn't lovely at all, and it was rather close to Mitre Square, which lay a bit down the street that we had just left. Still, I hadn't come for the sightseeing, as there wasn't much of a sight to see. I had come for the blasphemy.

We stood in the shadow of the great thing, though at that hour there was no shadow, and after a second, we rose up the steps and entered, there to be greeted by an Anglican goodbody of minor capacity, who greeted us with a nod, saw that we were of bourgeois and not of street, and let us pass, as would happen in any church, town, city, pub, restaurant, fancy house, factory, or office in Britain, so enamored of the bourgeois was this country.

Did I feel God's presence? Since there is no God, I could not, don't you see? If there were, surely He would send a bolt from the blue to electrify me into bacon grease before letting me enter His house holding in mind what I held in mind. Not being there, He did nothing. We entered the nave and walked down the center aisle, feeling the marble serenity engulf us, hearing our footsteps echo against the polished stone flooring. We could see the crossing ahead under the circular gulf that allowed the steeple, saw the lectern to the right at the epistle side of the holy space, and turned left from the altar—rather prim, I might add, lacking the theatricality of the papist version—and headed into the north transept, where indeed there was privacy. It was dark, the stone carried a bit of the night's chill, and from here the ever burning candles had distilled their light to flickering on the stone wall.

We stopped. We looked. All was quiet; no other churchgoers interrupted our concentration. It was the time. It was the place.

"Forward, or would you be of the backward persuasion, sir?"

"Why, it is your angel's face that I'm paying for, dear girl, as all men and all women are pretty much the same to the anterior. I need to see it as I work and enjoy its passion, for its passion will enable my passion."

"Then I'll arrange meself as you yourself make ready."

She smiled, showing perfect white pearls, and I do believe a trace of anticipation leaked from her large gray eyes. She was not scared, she was not quick, she was not desperate, she smelled of flowers and powdered sugar, her breath was sweet as I neared.

CHAPTER TWENTY-FOUR

Jeb's Memoir

First I had to sell Mr. O'Connor on letting me take a few days off to work on some "ideas."

"Ideas?" he said. "Heaven forfend reporters start having ideas."

"Sir, I have made acquaintance with a brilliant man. I feel he may have insights of some help. I would be remiss if I did not pursue them. And the paper will be to the profit if he is even half correct."

"Gad, professors now. Careful he doesn't try to slip his woodpecker into your bum, though even a homosexualist would be hard pressed to find such a scrawny rat as you worth a tup. Still, they do have odd tastes."

"Sir, I assure you, no such possibility exists."

"Who would this genius be?"

I told him.

"That one? Then it's your sister's bum I'd worry about, give him that much."

"You know Professor Dare?"

"A few years ago, I played the bright London scene, trying to scare up investors for this enterprise. At that time, I saw him quite a bit with a lovely girl on his arm. Handsome couple they were, quite mysterious but also somewhat enjoying their mystery. I do remember a reception at an embassy one night, they were much amused by some Hungarian professor who kept chasing the gal about, so smitten he was. I could see they enjoyed the game, and the little Magyar was hopeless in his romantic silliness. It was like watching a terrier attempt to mount a Great Dane. So no, he is a brilliant man, that I give you, and a charmer, too. I'd just, as principle among them folk, be sure to keep my hand on my wallet."

After receiving that lukewarm blessing, I was off, with the proviso that if I heard of another Jack action, I'd find a telephone cabinet, get the details, and decamp posthaste.

But disappointment lurked ahead. It turned out rather too swiftly that I was no detective. I could make no headway, not with my sister Lucy trilling away in the studio and Mother watching me like a hawk about to pounce upon and devour a mouse. I retreated to my old haunting grounds, the reading room of the British Library, thinking its intellectual solemnity might inspire or provoke me.

Alas, even surrounded by the ghosts of Britain's great writers and thinkers, I was all dried out. I was a pickle absent the brine, a desiccated raisin. No ferment, no bubbles, whatever inappropriate metaphor one could create, they all applied to me. My brain was bereft of electricity. I tried many things: I wrote on a big yellow tablet in Pitman's shorthand "Jack" and then listed at speed all the theories I had heard from both high and low, from copper and reporter, from harlot and poet, and all seemed gibberish. I thought one might inspire something, but it didn't. How did he move, how did he disappear, what were his attributes? Whatever I tried, my dim mind could not find its genius, if it had any; in the end, it merely revealed its fraudulence. My performance suffered from the want of energy and impetus.

I could see areas to check out, lines of inquiry that the coppers, even the purportedly great Inspector Abberline, the Scotland Yard star recently appointed to head the investigation, had not explored. Yet there was no energy in me, or even in the others, coppers, citizens, vigilante committees, the Home Office ministers, any of them. It seemed we were all locked in a box and couldn't get beyond the obvious. We loved the image of Jack as skulker in a topper, gliding through the nonexistent fog on empty streets under gas lamps, caparisoned against the damp, cackling maniacally like a brute in a West End melodrama. Clearly that could not be him, and remaining manacled to the image was harmful to investigative enterprise. There was something pathetic in us that wouldn't let us abandon our earlier conclusions: sailor, Jew, doctor, royal. That not one shred of evidence pointed to these solutions made us hungrier to cling to them. It was as if they formed a known coastline, and we sailors upon the sea of Jack were afraid to sail beyond the horizon, thinking we'd never find our way back.

So it was with both eagerness and trepidation that I called on Professor Dare on the appointed morning three days further along through October to discuss and assess. I hoped he had better luck than I did, and realized that I had in some way come to put too much hope upon the man, who would be, I wanted to believe, our savior in all this. I was a seriously confused and dazed young man.

He lived near the university, 26 Wimpole Street, in a grand house, larger than I expected. It spoke of private income, though he'd never said as much, being, I recognized, somewhat reticent on the topic of his real self. I knocked, feeling the chill of late autumn, as November was fast on, drawing my brown wool drabs about me, and a senior servant lady opened, looked me over with a Scot's eye toward detecting common riffraff, and finally allowed, "Sir, the professor is awaiting you."

I nodded, handing her my mac, and followed her to the study.

He was in a red velvet dressing gown with an ascot over heather trousers and velvet slippers with dragons embossed upon them, very fetching. He looked quite home-from-the-hunt. His pipe jutted furiously from his lean jaws, emitting briar vapor. His wrinkly blond hair was pushed back, his noble temples gleamed, his strong nose cut through the miasma like the scimitar it was, and behind his circular round spectacles, in a kind of dappled maple, his blue orbs took me in quickly.

"I fancy the house," I said. "Well done."

"Evidently my father did something quite remunerative. I meant to ask him about it but never got around to it. I didn't enjoy his company much.

Horrible fellow. However, I do enjoy having the money that I never earned myself. It makes life easy, frees me for my fun, and pays for all of this."

I looked about. The room was like so many of the professorial class I had seen behind London's brick and ivy, all booky and leathery, with brass gas outlets for nighttime illumination so necessary to the soirees that drove their society and furniture heavy enough to crush an elephant's skull and carpets from the Orient that would tell pornographic stories of Scheherazade's actual relations with the Caliph if one but understood the code. What distinguished it from all the other Bloomsbury iterations was a contrapuntal melody that might be called "Throat." It was quite extravagantly decorated in Throat. Was he a Sherlock Holmes of the voice?

That is, it was dedicated to matters pertaining to the vocal cords and their substructures, from charts of that particular organ in profile half-section complete to Latin labels for all the tiny flowerlike leaves and tendrils, charts on the wall that I took to be for eye but revealed themselves to be of the letters we call vowels; then strange devices on a large laboratory table that could be for torture but seemed for measuring breath, both intensity and consistency, including a tiny torchlike thing against whose flame one would speak, I'm guessing, and by that method give visual evidence of the absence or presence of the letter H, whose existence bewildered half the population of our city.

"I say, you take this phonetics business rather seriously, don't you?"

"Voice is communication, communication is civilization," he said. "Without the one, we lose the other, as those festivals of slaughter called wars attest."

"May I write that down? It'll do for an aphorism."

"Go ahead. Claim authorship, if you prefer. As I say, I am beyond glory. I merely want to stop this nasty chap from gutting our tarts. That's enough for me." He bade me sit.

"I have to tell you," I said, "I have not accomplished much. I go forward and back, upward and downward, I enter randomly or by system, and I cannot seem to get beyond what the police know, that a skilled, dedicated individual is, as has been said, 'down on whores,' and butchers them with such grace that he has yet to be caught or even seen."

He drew reflectively on his pipe, the atmosphere he was pulling past the burning tobacco intensifying its burn so that more great roils of vapor tumbled forth. It was like the skyline of Birmingham.

He proceeded to ask questions that showed intimate familiarity with the material. How wide was the passageway Jack had taken Annie down on Hanbury Street? What were the dimensions of the pony wagon at the Anarchists' Club, versus the dimensions of the gate, and how low to ground was that wagon? How many stone was Mr. Diemschutz, the pony-cart man? Over which shoulder were Cate Eddowes's intestines flung? How quickly had the various teams of coppers arrived at Buck's Row? Why did he only cut Polly but not eviscerate her like the others, assuming interruption in the matter of Liz Stride? Why was there no moon her night but quarter-moon the others? What explained the odd irregularity of rhythm between the murders? What was my opinion of the quality of mind of both Sir Charles and the number one detective, Abberline? Did I get a bonus for writing the Dear Boss letter?

"Now, see here," I said, all fuddled up, "that is uncalled for." Particularly since it was true.

"It is quite called for. As I have said, I have a gift for the Beneath of a piece of writing. Beneath 'Dear Boss', not entirely but mostly, lies our friend Jeb, for I recognize the boldness and clearness of his sentences united with his vividness of image. Those are separate talents, by the way, not a single general one for 'writing.' You are lucky to have them both. Anyhow, 'Jack the Ripper' is indeed vivid, if not quite accurate. It certainly echoes and deploys a genius for the exact and the resonant. It may indeed become immortal. I love the melody of 'reaper' in its own Beneath, and I like the 'Jack' for its onomatopoetic evocation of brisk, decisive action, as the snap cutting of a throat. I mention your clear authorship not to embarrass you or flatter you but to point out that the reason so many have tested their brains against the riddles Jack poses and failed is because they now see him as you created him—Jack, demon of mythology, folklore, mischief, a god of mayhem and slaughter—and that will occlude their thinking, cause them to miss what I would consider obvious. So even as I twit you, I do so because I want you to exile this Jack-demon idea from mind and concentrate instead on a human being who is knowable, trackable, and findable. Will you do me that honor, sir?"

"I will," I said.

"Then let us turn this hellhound."

"May I record in Pitman's? This may be historic."

"I doubt that. I hope only that it's coherent."

For the record, then, here is Professor Thomas Dare's interpretation of the phenomenon of Jack the Ripper, as recorded with sublime accuracy by me on that date at that time, October's third week, 1888, in his study at 26 Wimpole Street, London, England, via the Pitman method of shorthand. I have the papers before me as I translate them to English in my study, also London, England, in the year of someone else's Lord 1912. Let me add, I did not bother to record my interruptions, which in any case were few and stupid.

"I begin with the conclusion and will then support it," he began. "Here's my somewhat radical final sum, new, I think, to the field. Our man is military. More, he is army; that is, a soldier."

He paused, reading the look on my face, which was not stunned surprise but at least a minor bit of being taken aback, for this possibility had not been postulated previously. "Now I will track my argument through a series of subarguments, the first being attributes, the second being character, the third being physical, and the final being spiritual."

He cleared his throat, rose, and began to pace back and forth while I sat, scribbling away in the Pitman notation.

"I say 'soldier,' but I mean not merely a soldier; rather, a certain kind of soldier, a type so rare that there are but few of them in London, much less the army as a whole. He is not an artilleryman, he is not a lancer, he is not an infantry lad. He is no engineer; he certainly has nothing to do with quartermastering or the medical ends of the profession of arms.

"His sort of soldiering is so rare it has no name, at least not a proper noun in the folk vocabulary common to newspapers and barroom chatter. Perhaps, as I believe this sort of thing is to become more, not less, utilized in the future, someone will christen him. But for now the closest I can come is 'scout,' or perhaps 'agent,' or perhaps 'raider.'

"I will go with 'raider,' as it's easiest off the tongue. Let's define the attributes. The raider is used to operating alone. He is very well schooled in certain skills: He must be an officer, since he is literate, despite his dyslexia, and in these days few rankers are. Furthermore, like an officer, he plans well, scouts thoroughly, and memorizes routes in and out. He is not averse to killing, obviously, having done and seen much of that work. But for him, killing is not the point; it is part of the job. He's always driven by task, not mere infliction of damage. He has purpose, design, agenda as his Beneath.

"This one, in particular, clearly served in Afghanistan, because the wounds he leaves on the bodies are typical of the sorts of mutilations that the Pathans commit against British troops, alive or dead, quite routinely. The women torture our wounded. They cut them open and pull their guts out while the boys are quite alive, but no one except the mountains can hear the screams. The guts are flung, the point being to attract buzzards, the further point being that relief columns will see the buzzards, find the bodies, and suffer the dislocating shock of the carnage, which must have a terrifying influence on morale. Jack has seen enough of it not to be agitated, either by seeing it or by doing it, but for him, it's part of doing business in a certain methodology. It is restricted, I should add, to the mountains of the Hindu Kush, where so many have died so horribly. The Negroes of Africa are savages, but not so committed to dogma in their desecrations. The Pathan go more toward beheading and dismembering, as part of their primitive faith insists that by disassembling the body of the enemy, it follows that he will not bother you in the afterlife. From their point of view, it makes very good sense, if it is a little monstrous by our standards. We feel that a bundle of bullets out of Gatling, traveling faster than the speed of sound—yes, sound has a measurable speed—so that it shatters bone and shreds muscle is far more civilized.

"Then, our Jack is highly organized, as the neat setting out of Annie

Chapman's goods next to her desecrated body indicates; he seems to think tidiness counts. In fact, his sites are all notable for their concision, economy, succinctness, even. They're very small, never orgiastic or out of control in suggestion. Contained, I suppose, would be the word. It's like a kind of sex fetish, this need he has to do his damage in very small compass, and I can ascribe that only to years in the military trade, which demand of a man few possessions arranged by rigid convention for inspection, until such habits, which pay their premium on campaign for months if not years, are ingrained.

"And the final attribute, which deserves some additional commentary. That is, like all raiders, he is quite bold, almost nerveless. Perhaps he became a raider to harness that which he already knew was within him, the courage for heroic action in extremely mortal, frenzied circumstances. Now, many think of courage as moral, even noble. Not so at all; it is instead neutral and may be applied equally in the service of good or evil. It offends to say of a murderer, an assassin, a spy, an exploder, an agitator that he is courageous; but he is, for he risks life and tests arcane skill, whatever the purpose. Whether it's Jack mincing a tart on Buck's Row or Color Sergeant Archie Cunningham skewering six Fuzzies on his bayonet to inspire his men to stand firm, it's courage nonetheless, in that it features bold action at moral risk in service to some sort of larger idea.

"Jack has courage, undisputedly. It may be twisted savagely by madness, but in the end it's the same stuff that rode the charge of the Light Brigade to the Russian guns at Balaclava or stood up to the Zulu Impis at Rorke's Drift. He's not a man to panic and flee: He gets his mission accomplished."

Dare paused as if to check on my progress and, satisfied, awarded himself another nugget of tobacco, plugged it into his pipe, put it aflame with a large wooden match, sucked, enjoyed satisfaction, exhaled, filled the air with the architecture of castles in clouds, and then set back to task.

"We may also infer certain physical attributes: He is slight. Some say he's strong. I say not necessarily. Despite the purported 'strength' evinced by the savage wounds inflicted, an experienced fellow using a sharp blade and the knowledge of anatomy—as a man who'd been in battles with bladed instruments and field hospitals where such wounds were crudely treated would have—could supply the same result. So he does not have to be a big fellow at all. More important: Jack had to take advantage of those narrow passageways and warrens that afforded him access to and escape from the murder sites. A full-bodied man could not, at least not without some effort.

"Consider, for example, his escape from Dutfield's Yard. It seems to have been forgotten that the pony cart was lodged in the gate, which itself was only nine feet wide. There was little room around, and the cart was low, so little room under. Yet somehow, there being no other way, he slides through. Consider again the pony. We know that it's skittish from Mr. Diemschutz's testimony at the inquest, where he stated, 'My pony is frisky and apt to shy.' He noted also the pony's 'odd, continued reluctance to coming into the yard.' After all, its skittishness has informed Diemschutz of Jack's presence. Now, when Jack rises from the darkness to slip out in the man's rush to the front door of the International Working Men's Educational Club, he must confront the nervous horse. But the horse does not react, does not rise, buck, neigh, whinny, jostle, jingle, shudder, panic and flee, whatever. That is because the horse, while no genius, knows certain things and is able to recognize certain things. It knows, for example, that a large man will beat it, while a small one would be a child and will not. Thus the horse does not frighten or comment upon the sudden appearance of the dark figure; it knows instantly, by reading the size, that the figure is no threat.

"Then, Jack must be invisible. Not in the physical sense but in the social sense: He must be someone whom all could look upon, of high station or low, of fine education or none, and see nothing. This is partly that aforementioned slightness, but it is also his demeanor. Such a demeanor, carefully calibrated, is again exactly the sort of behavior the raider, a scout in mufti among an enemy population, must achieve. He must pass for the banal poor, unremarkable of aspect and unsurprising of presence; he must be part of the wallpaper. But that accounts only for witnesses on the to-or-from. More pertinently, none of the victims screamed or gave evidence of having fled or fought. They identified Jack, from the first time they saw him to his approach to all that passed between them before the incidence of the knife, as being without threat, which is why he was able to close to cutting range on them and finish them so devastatingly.

"Now let us talk of vision. His must be extraordinary, not a mere 20/20, as is normal, but at least the rare but infinitely superior 20/200. He sees farther into the dark and retains more precision from the quarter-moonlight he prefers—"

I could not but interrupt. "Professor, Annie Chapman, the second, was not slain in quarter-moonlight but in full dark."

"Indeed. That was his exception. And why? Because he had already performed reconnaissance, like the good raider, and knew from observation that she would guide him to 29 Hanbury Street, through the passage, and into the yard. He knew there would be illumination from still-lit windows on the backsides of 29 and 27, next door. The moon's light was not a consideration on that one. He made adjustments; he struck outside the range of his vision requirements. That, too, is what a soldier does, or he dies. He must adapt. So he found the generally correct range of illumination, when there's enough to commit but not enough to give one away. He must have been on campaign in these conditions and gotten used to it and feels capable and more than equal to the police in the circumstance. On the other hand, being both resilient and inventive, he is supple enough to violate the dogma when he finds he must do so."

I was writing this all down in the twisted dashes and swoops that formed the Pitman method; at the same time, I was hearing interpretations that fascinated me. He had seen so deeply into it! Was he the world's greatest detective? Or was I the world's greatest boob?

"Let me sum up: He is a very special sort of Britisher. He is comfortable among wild tribes and in desert or jungle wilderness. He loves desolate spaces. He yearns to be free of the filaments and silken bonds of our Victorian society, with its rigid caste system and its terrible hypocrisies, yet he's willing to risk his life for those alone. He can live, even thrive, amid a native element, which means he has a quick ear for language. He is what might be called a pathfinder for empire. He was the first boyo to go beyond the frontier and reach out and open communications. He was a quick study on the intricacies of tribal politics and could play faction off against faction, all while keeping the agenda rolling to the queen's good. He must have been adept, it follows, at the tricks of espionage, such as coding, signaling, assassination, subterfuge, camouflage, gambits of deceit, disguise. He must have a love of adventure and tire quickly of the nonsense that is spoken at balls and soirees and in Whitehall or Parliament or Buckingham. He has friends in intelligence or political circles, so he's a public school man, where he met those he would be serving, and where they learned him to be a good man, reliable, loyal to the throne."

"That plus his dyslexia," I said, so excited I could hardly contain myself, "and by God, sir, we've got him."

"Oh, I left out his most salient aspect," said Professor Dare. He paused, for he was not without theatrical guile.

"What, dammit?" I said.

"As I said, the spiritual."

The man was a sphinx with his mystery, playing me like a fool. And like a fool, I could not resist. "What, Professor? What are you—"

"Why, man, is it not obvious? The man indeed has a faith, and he has expressed it every time he has struck. It is his bedrock, his religion, his God. He is a true believer."

The look on my face must have amused him. He finally took pity. "The man, above all else, is humanitarian."

Humanitarian? A humanitarian throat cutter? At that point, I thought: Farewell, Sherlock Holmes!

CHAPTER TWENTY-FIVE
The Diary

October 18, 1888 (cont'd)

———

I pulled my weapon. It was my cock.

"Here, then," she said, "let Suzie put you to me and make you feel all good and warm, that's what Suzie does, she does."

Her hands upon me were indeed an angel's. I felt each of them against my stout member. As she guided me into her, her fingers were gentle yet firm, kind yet serious, ideal yet sensual. I felt some wiggle as she found opening, acquired proper angle, pushed, pulled, guided, adjusted, corrected, bringing herself to me as much as me to her, and then she had me full in, set, and into her center I plunged. I felt it as satin on silk with some hint of lubricity, the surfaces meshing against a whisper of friction for the thrill of tightness, and we formed perfectly into a dynamo of smoothness, a sense of gliding, gliding, gliding until, in so far I felt I'd die, either she ran out of channel or I ran short on instrument.

"Oh, God," she said, "oh, sir, how wonderful you feel inside of me." Was this malarkey she gave all the boys? Who cared at that point, for my hips took up a natural rhythm and we began the dance, the ritual, the tribal ceremony. I felt her heart, her thin-boned chest against my heavier issue, the damned interference of our clothes, but soon, in the plunging and partial withdrawing to plunge again, there was a magic in her hips, and she found the primal rhythm, she was able to arrange her body and her hips as if on a sustaining armature, and it freed her hips to begin to move as if alone in space, propelled by a reptile brain unacknowledged by higher functions, and that is why it was so magical and that is why men and women in circumstances high and low, mortal or humane, decent or desperate, sell their souls in a trice for its exquisite anarchy.

I lost all sense of clothes at all, two bodies in a church, the church in the city, the city in the nation, the nation on the planet. With my hands I pressed her against me, believing I could feel her shudder, knowing I could feel her hips find and match my speed and urgency. I kissed her hard, and it was a tongue-tongue thing, all thrash and suck and slurp and mash, feeling our breath combine as it poured from engorged nostrils. There remained but the spasm, and it occurred when it should occur, too soon yet too late, which is to say perfection, as there seemed no point of postponement, to say nothing of the will. My release was cataclysmic. I have heard of of a chemical called dynamite that can explode anything, and it was as if I'd been packed with this wonder stuff. The details are banal in the telling, but not in the remembering, and not in the actual.

I pulled back, breathing hard, sucking for God's oxygen to fill my depleted lungs and bring vigor to my exhausted limbs. I felt the great, satisfied emptiness. I saw her in candle flicker, skirts dropped again, smiling almost as if it had been more than a performance, shaking her head to release her fair hair from the tangles that the dampness of her sweat had ensnared it within. She dipped into her purse and pulled out some muffinlike piece with which to powder her face.

"There now," she said, "feeling all better, are we?"

"Indeed, my Juliet. It is the east and you are the sun."

"You talk fancy even after I've yanked me knickers! Now, there's a gentleman."

CHAPTER TWENTY-SIX

Jeb's Memoir

"Jack the Ripper is humanitarian," he said.

"Good heavens, Professor. The man has ripped four women to shreds, pulled their guts out, and lived to laugh about it. How on earth could you apply that term to such bestiality?"

"Indeed, his work is total destruction. Consider it not as we find it, all messy and blood-spattered, with lakes of red about, but as it is experienced. He is, it must and should be noted, not torturing the women. He takes no thrill in their pain. He feels no pleasure in slow, screaming deaths. Quite the contrary, he is well practiced in the art of the immediate and silent kill. Part of this, to be sure, is pure efficiency. It is much easier on him, though a case could be made that chloroform and transfer of the sleeping body to a private nearby spot would clearly not be beyond his powers, and once there, he could amuse himself with torture games for hours and hours. He seems not remotely tempted by such a thing. I suppose another part of it is that selfsame military technique, for part of a raider's skill must be in eliminating sentries before the attack or ambush. One slithers silently through the brush and fells the watcher from behind with a sure stroke. It must be well done or the watcher screams as he dies and alerts the campful of Pathan or Zulu about to go to the slaughter.

"While there's all this, consider that of all ways to kill a human being, the sudden sundering of the carotid artery is among the kindest, assuming consciousness. A bullet to the brain might trump it, as would the immensity of an artillery detonation. Next comes Jack's method, which would be experienced as a blur, an impact, a tingle, an instant fatigue and loss of balance, perhaps a fleeting awareness that the end is upon one, which would be somewhat occluded by the cloud of disbelief, and then the slip-sliding away of consciousness. It's unlikely that much pain would accompany the journey."

"Sir," I said, somewhat arisen, "that hardly counts as humanitarianism."

"By liberal pieties, no, which is one of the things I find so appalling about liberal pieties. You see it in terms of the discomfort it gives *you* in the contemplation, because you lack the imagination to see it in terms of the pain it spares *her* in the occurrence. Think on it, if you would, and put aside all those bromides and homilies that sustain the bourgeoisie in the face of reality, which I believe you are becoming aware of in your forced sojourns into Whitechapel."

"I will hold it in abeyance until further evidence is produced, but my tendency is to discount it and prefer the first two explanations."

"Well enough. I proceed, confident that I am soon to convince you."

More pipe theater as he emptied, tamped, refilled, lit, inhaled, exhaled, enjoyed the mushroom of vapor that billowed before him, then turned.

"I await," I said, pen poised above tablet.

"I deliver," he said, smiling at his riposte. He found himself, it must be said, quite amusing. "Now turn to the incident at Goulston Street."

"The baffling graffito, with J-E-W-S misspelled, on which you have already theorized."

"Put aside that for an instant. Put aside the business of grammar. Turn to punctuation. What is missing, as the reports all agree?"

I thought a bit. I saw it in my mind's eye.

"The Juwes are The men that Will not be Blamed for nothing"

Or was it "The Juwes are not The men that Will be Blamed for nothing," as some had it?

"Hmm, missing? I suppose, other than sense, grammar, somewhat chaotic capitalization, I don't see that anything—oh, yes, wait, well, that is being very persnickity."

"I am a persnickity sort. I am a phoneticist."

"Then one would say the concluding period. None of the three copyists recorded a period at its conclusion. However, that may be because of an error in transmission. The copyists—"

"*All three* forgot a period?"

"Hmm," I said again. "All right, I take your point."

"Do you? The larger point?"

"The larger point?"

"He was interrupted, who knows by what or whom. Possibly that copper coming down the street. But he realized that although he had really engineered the whole thing to pass on this message, he had the discipline—military, that is—to retreat upon threat of discovery and not drive himself on false pride and end up in the bag. He decided not to compromise the completion of the whole mission for this one component of it. Do you see?"

"So there's more?"

"Indeed. What could the next few words be, considering what was going on in London then, his character as we have drawn it, his few but admittedly existent virtues, perhaps even, out of his military past, a sense of duty, moral duty. It must also fit on the wall, which limits the space. Limits it to just a few more words, another line at most."

Was Dare mad? "I have no idea."

"This," he said. "'The Juwes are The men that Will not blamed for nothing . . . was done by them.'"

I looked at him.

"WAS DONE BY THEM! It's in the passive voice of so much military report writing, it restores the grammatical integrity of the educated man—Sandhurst, I'm guessing—to the composition, it is succinct, the space on the wall would permit it, and it could be written by the light of a quarter-moon by a fellow with sharp eyes. But its point is to absolve the Jews, because he could see that fear and hate was building, that beatings had taken place, that the newsrags, including yours—"

That damned Harry Dam again!

"—were fanning the flames to sell yet more papers, that the thugees and druids of the slums were building up energy. He saw all that and could not live with the idea of a thousand Jews dying in the flames of hatred because of his mission. So he took it upon himself to formally absolve them, signing his statement with Mrs. Eddowes's blood and placing it on a police route where it could not be missed."

I was not convinced, although the man's argument had logic to it. "And if so, of what import? I see it leading us nowhere."

"Quite the contrary, it leads us very much somewhere." Dare smiled.

He was a cat toying with a mouse, and I, the great Jeb, did not care a bit to be made mouse of, to have all my arguments dashed upon the stones so insolently by a fellow who was not only smarter but could afford a better tailor and didn't live with a horrid mum and a trilling sister.

"What somewhere, pray tell?"

"Where would he get such ideas? Clearly, he believes that the Jews— bogeymen of the popular press, demons of the working-class imagination, devils of the retail exchange, depraved and violent in folk rumor, despised by the capitalist class because they are so much better at capitalism, de- spised by the revolutionary class because they are so much better at rev- olution, detested for lacking fairness and physical beauty and portrayed everywhere as hook-nosed, yellow-skinned, shawl-wearing, matzoh-ball- eating vermin—he believes them to be human beings, like all of us. Where on God's earth could he have gotten such an idea?"

"I see it," I said.

"Then explain it."

"Those ideas are hardly held anywhere in the world except in certain liberal reform circles, very small but very passionate. Not at all the place where one would find a soldier or intelligence agent of much battle ex- perience. So your point has to be that he has been exposed, somehow, somewhere, sometime, to those ideas, but more important, to people who espouse them, for it is not the sort of inconvenient passion one would absorb merely from reading. You'd have to live it, feel it heavy in the air, indulge in it at length as an assumption, not an argument. And where would we find people of such ideas? I cannot see him gadding about among the better sort of intellectual circles in Bloomsbury, can you?"

"No, I do not see that."

"Only one possibility remains. In the church. Possibly in family, given a rector as father or brother, possibly by marriage to a Quaker woman."

"You have it, sir. Exactly."

"A soldier—raider, rather—experienced in Afghanistan, highly evolved military skills, dyslexic, Sandhurst, yet the son of a pastor or minister of some sort."

"*Ecce* Jack."

I realized then: He had made his sale.

Against his campaign, my little foray into detectivism seemed trivial.

"All right," I said, "it's quite brilliant, so much further along than anything anyone else has said. You have a genius for this sort of analysis, I must admit. I am humbled. Why, it is as if you are Sherlock Holmes himself."

"Who?"

"The detective Sherlock Holmes. The genius who can decode a crime scene brilliantly, sift through clues with ease, point out the plot, its purpose, and its perpetrator. In Conan Doyle's book *A Study in Scarlet*."

"Never heard of it. As I said, let's just stop the gutting of the whores. Now I turn to you for practicality."

"Perhaps I can at last contribute," I said. For even as I had been listening and recording in Pitman, I had been, in a different part of my mind, seeking utility for these new ideas.

"I await patiently," he said. "As you know, I am somewhat bereft of practicality. I am an expert on one thing alone, the voice." So Holmesian!

"My thought," I said, "is that I am, after all, a journalist. While the *Star* is not the best of all papers in London, even if it is one of the loudest, my connection to it secures me entry into the journalists' society. On our paper or on another, there has to be a fellow who has made it his speciality to cover issues of war. He's been to many, he knows the officers and the civilians who supervise them well, and most of all, he already has cultivated a network of private informants. He is well known at Cumberland House, army headquarters. My idea would be to locate this man and somehow entice him to our aid. We would start with the broadest categorization of what you have said. We are looking for someone recently retired from active duty, with connections to intelligence, who is privately known by those who are privy to such things, as a superb operative in mufti, particularly in Afghanistan, who has a gift for languages and a reputation for that which we will call 'efficiency,' it being understood that such a word connotes the willingness to kill if necessary. He has been, further, much exposed to the horrors of battle and mutilation as performed in that hellhole, perhaps his mind subtly addled by it."

"Excellent," said Professor Dare.

"If we can get a list of such, some being more closely matched to the criteria than others, we can our own selves identify them and continue to winnow, by which method we can determine if the other markers are present: the dyslexia, the religious childhood, the superb night vision, the physical aspect of slightness, perhaps even the possession of poor Annie's rings, though that may be too much to be wished. In that way, we can ultimately identify the one man who matches the template with perfection. Police notification would follow, then arrest, and we bathe in glory. I do like the glory part."

"Then you may have it all, sir."

"I am no hog. I will share, I swear."

"And we'd better hurry, Jeb. After all, the quarter-moon fast approaches, on October 28. Our soldier of night will soon pursue another mission."

CHAPTER TWENTY-SEVEN
The Diary

October 26, 1888

———

It would soon be time again, since the campaign had obligations that needed to be met. I went on search, being careful to use what I had learned: I needed crowds—of Johns, citizens, and Judys—into which to melt anonymously. I needed quick access to dark streets. I needed at least one and possibly two escape routes. I needed to be cognizant of the police constables and their patrolling. I had to negotiate all these factors brilliantly, weighing them and finding a perfect balance, and remain aware that the task was made infinitely more difficult because Warren had put so many more blue bottles on the street, thinking the dragnet, the sheer number of uniformed men, plus a nice reward, would do the trick.

He was an idiot. For one thing, it is true of military and of police intelligences and also of engineers—and Warren was all three—that they conspicuously prepare for that which has already happened as opposed to that which has not. In my amblings around Whitechapel, I saw that the coppers were flooding the areas where I had already struck. They thought I was such a slave to habit (and as stupid as they were) that I would do the same.

It took no genius to look at the map and determine that aside from Long Liz Stride's encounter, which had been governed by special rules, all the others had been north of the Whitechapel/Aldgate axis. So that was where the genius Warren deployed most of his troops. You could not go for a stout, or an apple from a coster's stall, along the Whitechapel High Street without bumping into a constable with his ding-dong lantern and his whistle on rope. There were so many, they had naught to observe but themselves!

Meanwhile, as one progressed toward the southeast, the coppers seemed to dissipate, to thin, the spaces between them wider and yet wider again, block by block. At first I thought it might be a trap and that in some cellar along Stepney Way or Clavell Street he might have secreted a hundred men, ready to leap out upon the whistle and begin the hunt along the byways of the district's quadrant, oriented southeast by compass. But he hadn't the wit. Was the man stupid? Maybe he was merely slow and would eventually comprehend his own folly, but he lacked the adaptability and agility that the modern police executive needed. And who should know better than I?

My plans thus moved my area of operation away from the well used, down toward the river. For Jack, the area was virgin.

However, it did seem slightly different in element. Yes, dollies plied their trade down this way, but the road inclined toward the port, where the great ships bearing their Oriental loot tied up, and so the milieu became not only seedier but more infused with the accoutrements of maritime enterprise. The smell of riverine damp, that is, a kind of swollen density of water suspended in the atmosphere, seemed to fall like a curtain on these twisty streets, and the gist of retail somewhat altered, now presenting sailor's dives with names like the Mermaid or the Bosun, or South of Fiji or Pitcairn's Paradise, and as well what had to be Chinese opium dens (the smell outside started one hallucinating!) and places where tattoos could be inked on arms, chests, or, as I saw on one fellow, faces. If one looked during daylight hours down certain streets, or alleys or walkways between the humble buildings, one could see the maze of spars, masts, and rigging, the gathered, roped sails and crow's nests of these behemoth vessels, as they berthed in the Western Docks in Wapping, or even farther out, on that strange near-island of wet creeks, swampland, and riverettes called the Isle of Dog, which offered a meander to the great River Thames and bent it around its own promontory and presented its own endless dockage. It was called Canary Wharf, where the East India Company, that grand circus of larceny and exploitation by armed robbery, unloaded, and where all the spices and silks and fruits and rice and whatnot were removed to be sold to poor Johnny English at sixteen times their cost in rupees or yen, and Johnny considered himself bargaineering in the process. This was the great mountebank's engine that sustained our tight, lovely little land and, other than the dank warrens of Whitechapel and its brethren, kept it all green and happy, its victim-citizens as dim and blissful as mudlarks.

I mention this because it also somewhat changed the nature of the crowds one encountered, again a part of the element. One no longer saw the predominance of the top hat or the derby but, instead, the strange plumage of all the many jack-tars, the endless types of sailor caps the crew jerries wore. They came from all nations under these vagabond coverings, and one saw rounder eyes, bluer eyes, squintier eyes, darker skin, lighter skin, bigger skulls, smaller skulls, hair of blond and black and red and even shaved—the Russkies, I'm guessing, who like to show their skull in contrast to flowing mustachios, meant to frighten, as they were all huskies to boot. Conversely, one saw fewer and fewer of the square, dull symmetrical faces of typical Englishmen. I fancied I could smell foreign spicings in the air, and even the costers offered fruit from different parts of the globe, some strangenesses that I could not identify as being from our very planet. I was quite convinced that I was no longer in England, for the babel of foreign voices.

One was aware that it was different down here and that the customary precautions might not be enough to provide security, and so made a pledge to self to make certain, then doubly certain, then certain a third time, before committing to action. The chaps about here would be burlier and more prone to violence of their own, so it was incumbent upon me not to incite a mob of mariners, as they might turn immediately to rough justice of the sort the Peelers and a stickler like Warren would abjure. I could end my days decorating a yardarm as it steered south by Java Head.

I chose at last and after much consideration a block that might have been in Wapping, in the way that Mitre Square turned out to be beyond Whitechapel, which would bring in a set of detectives from a division other than Whitechapel's H. That would be fine and good, for the new boys would get all mixed in with the old, the communications would be worse, the cabals of influence more diffuse, Inspector Abberline's control might be challenged and in all it would be a merry festival of more mucking up, Sir Charles Warren–style.

I chose a street one could exit either by heading in one of two directions or cutting through to a street just behind and parallel. My plan was to unite with a gal, nudge her down William for the necessary dark, finish her there, and make it the most famous thoroughfare in the Western world for a day or so, while making my usual coolly nonchalant exit back to civilization by morning. I realized the street names meant nothing, nor should they; all were alike, tiny streets of humble brick abodes linked in long ungainly strands, sporting a castellation of chimneys, poorly lit, of course, peopled with the invisible of London living and mostly dying without notice in the great city's most obscure precincts. Wapping? Who had ever heard of such a place? No one on the *Times* or the *Star* or the *Atheneum* or at the British Museum. Ridiculous name, no, Wapping? Is that not what you do to an unruly child, give it a wapping until it shuts its mouth?

Everything was swell, that is, until it wasn't.

I had thought finding a dolly would be the least of my problems, but right off, it became the most of them. It was late, it was dark, it was empty. I think in daytime, when I had scouted, the area was more frequented, but now there was nothing to be found. My first plan perished before it was even tested.

I knew bad things were more likely to happen when I had to improvise, as my lucky escape at Mitre Square proved, and every sensible part of my being argued for a retreat and another foray tomorrow, when the conditions would be more or less as good. But I'm like a rat aroused by the smell of blood sometimes, and against my own better judgment, I kept coursing ahead, thinking one more block closer to the docks, that'll be the ticket, that'll get me what I want.

At last I reached St. George, with hardly any of London left between me and the basin, wherein was moored a fleet of pirate vessels otherwise known as British shipping. I swore I could hear the stretched rope squealing and the stressed wood squeaking. Possibly it was pure imagination. I wandered up St. George, a wide street of extreme maritime atmosphere, and found it crowded in its way with the colorful specimens of the ocean-going brethren, hats and all, and I was aware that my more civilized garb made me stand out a bit, always a mistake in the mad-killer trade.

She was neither older nor younger than the other birds. She was neither prettier nor uglier. She was simply there, a figure out of a socialist painting that might be called *The Eternal Streetwalker,* puffing on a cigarette, resting against a gaslight, one hip provocatively cocked. I could see a bit more of neck and shoulder, as that seemed to be allowed down here. I also thought it was illegal for the girls to stand still, but this brazen Bessie betrayed no fear of the blue bottles. She was eyeing the trade and the trade was eyeing her, particularly her bosom, which men, perhaps out of collective maternal nostalgia, seemed to yearn to bury themselves within. Hers was vast and deep. Fortunately I am not so mentally constructed, so the bosom, present or vanished, is of little interest to me. She looked tough, and as I drew near, her eyes fixed on me and mine on hers, and in a few steps I was at her but not with her. That is, I stood close but conspicuously oriented away from her as crowds of drunks wobbled by, rocking as uncertainly as the big ships at berth a few dozen feet down the black alleys.

"Now, dearie, would you be looking for a spell of fun?" she eventually said.

"I might be, madame," I said. "The mood is presently upon me."

"Come on over so Evelyn can get a look, then."

"That I will," I said, and broke my pose, and made an elaborate charade of orbiting her station so she could inspect my goods.

"You don't look like Saucy Jacky," she said. "These days a gal has to be careful."

"I thought Jack worked up the street a bit," I said.

"Maybe he's come slumming, like you. We don't get many gentleman. This is mostly sailortown."

"I would never characterize my efforts as 'slumming,' my dear. To me, all women are equally beautiful and equally desirable but, alas, not equally available."

"I'm thinking this is a night for availability, then, not beauty nor desire," she said. She was a game one!

"Well said, my dear. A mile that way, the tariff is thruppence. What would it be closer to Mother Thames?"

"Can't give you no discount for your long walk," she said. "Ain't my bother the coppers is all over that street up there. We've got our pride in Wapping, too."

"So a thruppence, then, and both are happy."

"I daresay."

"Proceed. I'll follow upon."

She launched herself from the lamppost, tossed the cigarette, and I saw why she had elected to go permanently at mooring: She had a limp, some mangled business at the hip that probably was something tragic out of a Russian novel that I didn't care to hear of. She made her progress at less than spiffy pace, up one block, up another, and at long last, she turned between two brick buildings a short distance away, whereupon we came to another street, small and darkish, and continued. Just a few more feet and I could see the gently rocking hulls of two great vessels at mooring on the quay.

It fell to darkness, and except for the heaving and cracking of the ships at rest, I could hear nothing and see nothing. We were in a passageway between the walls of two great warehouses, on cobblestones far from the interest of the street traffic. It was perfect.

She turned, exactly as Polly had turned, exactly as Annie had, exactly as Liz had, exactly as Cate had, and in turning offered me her long bare throat, and as my right hand slid inside my coat and I felt the grip of my Sheffield,

I could see the tendons, the muscles, the softness of the skin, and knew exactly where I would drive the edge for maximum carnage.

"Now, guv'nor," she said, "I'll take me coin, if you please."

And at that point, someone hit me hard on the back of the head, and all the stars in heaven exploded behind my eyes.

CHAPTER TWENTY-EIGHT

Jeb's Memoir

I confided to O'Connor what I was up to, omitting key details that I knew would bore a man with the attention span of a gazelle. He was substantially impressed, so he gave Henry Bright the word that I was to be left alone as I continued my individual inquiries; Harry Dam could cover the Yard and keep the fires stoked. O'Connor also set up a meeting with a man of our staff who covered military matters and was on good terms with a more august personage named Robert "Penny" Penningham, who had covered the War Office for decades for the *Times* and had been to more wars than most major generals and, it was said, had ridden unofficially with Cardigan at Balaclava. He knew everything there was to know about issues of war and more war, as waged by Her Majesty's forces from the wedding-cake building at Whitehall called Cumberland House.

I loved Penny straight off. He was a bounder, a cad, a merry fellow full of grand gesture and good heart, and he drank fishlike in a rear room of a Fleet Street pub called the Pen and Parchment, where, it was said, Mr. Boswell had sat inscribing the words of Dr. Johnson. It was quite possible, judging from the ancient air of the place, and I was willing to play Penny's Boswell.

He drank stout out of a monster pewter tankard with "47th (Lancashire) Regiment of Foot" inscribed in gold across it. No doubt there was a tale behind it. In fact, I guessed Penny to be a walking Canterbury's full of tales of life on campaign or in barracks.

"Now, yes, I do know a fellow at the War Office. I made him to be a hero in Africa during the Zulu business, when he was actually a bumbler. I knew his da and couldn't let that old color sergeant down. As per my account, the man was decorated and advanced, and now he occupies one of those key spots in Cumberland House where everything passes across his desk. He pulls strings far in advance of his rank and can ferret out anything. He would fetch this bit in a day or so, for me and me alone, if I asked him. But tell me again, laddy, why it is you're needing it?"

I thought I had explained but evidently I had not, at least not clearly enough, or at least not clearly enough for him, or at least not when he was paying attention. This time he paid that attention, and I reiterated what Dare and I had worked out and what I had sold O'Connor on, which stopped one stop short of our ultimate destination. I told him that a "source" at university had looked at information I had assembled and, without realizing it was the Ripper I was describing, had concluded that the killings all bore the mark of a highly experienced military man of particular heritage, the raider type known to intelligence and reconnaissance. I hoped to locate a few experienced fellows in that subspecialty of the soldier's trade, put it before them, and see if it rang bells; they might steer me in the proper direction. If Penny didn't realize it was those men themselves who were suspect, all shame to him, but he played along just the same.

"It's not a thing the army wants out, you see. It could help the foe, this year's or next year's."

"I do understand that, Penny," I said, although it had just occurred to me, for concerns of empire had never been prominent in my thinking, "and I can assure you that the interest is purely domestic, in re: our Jack. The only nation of concern is the nation of Whitechapel and its civilian population of twelve hundred whoregirls."

"They be citizens, too, even if they pay no taxes, and they deserve the same protection of any major general surrounded by Lancers. Can't say I've never had a bounce in my long gaudy life, so you'll get no moral posturing from me."

"I've seen the bodies, Penny, hacked as if in the cross fire at Balaclava."

"All right, that's a good case you make."

"So you'll assist?"

He considered, quaffing and squinting, quaffing and squinting, and at last said, "All right, if only because I think you've done bang-up work, and I love to see a professional breaking the news. You've given that dumb bugger Warren a few hard, dry shits a long time over the hole. And you'll not be giving my name to nobody, is that understood? I can't give up my fellow, so you can't give me up."

"It's a bargain," I said.

Feeling quite healthy toward myself, I set out to return to the office. My step was light, almost a dance, a waltz, say, full of love, not for women but self-directed, toward me, Jeb, hero of the Jack saga, and I was so in love with myself that I paid no attention to what lay about. In a few days, Penny would give me his list, and with the professor, we would somehow examine the lives of each man on it, and surely if one were Jack, there'd be a manifestation available to plain eye. We'd inform someone we trusted at the Yard—Ross, I was thinking—and he'd go and arrange a meet with the mystical Inspector Abberline, and the trap would be set. A raid would spring it, for surely the knife, bloody clothes, perhaps even, God help us, Annie's wedding rings or, as we referred to them in the *Star,* ANNIE'S WEDDING RINGS would be found, and then the world was ours. I was famous, I had entree everywhere, my good friend Professor Dare would go emeritus at any Oxbridge house he chose, and Saucy Jacky would go for a long walk off a short gallows, to everybody's pleasure. It might even be that his horrors, horrific horrors though they be, would shine light enough on the appalling reality of Whitechapel that some benefit to the population, especially those hard workers of Angel Alley and Fashion Street, might come about.

Yes, I was mighty pleased and—

A hand clapped hard and sudden upon my shoulder. "'Ello, your 'onor, 'ow's about a nice sip with your fine friend 'arry."

I feign the swallowed H's here to convey the comic fraudulence of the attempt at cockney. Harry thought it was funny because it was so grotesquely unfunny in his Yank accent, full of elongated vowels, misunderstood rhythms, and fractured timing; perhaps it was also an indicator of the full strangeness of the American mind. I turned, and yes, it was he, Harry Dam, in full boating regalia, waiting for the coxswain to start beating time so that his eight could beat Magdalen's eight. He came stepping out of an alleyway across from the Pen and Parchment, where he had clearly followed me.

"Harry, where's your megaphone?"

"Eh?"

"To count cadence for the oar strokes."

"Oh, the boating stuff. You guys sure think that's funny! Come on, chum, I'm serious. We need to powwow."

"What on earth does 'pow-wow' mean?"

"You know, chitchat, palaver, yakkity-yak, have a sit-down, that sort of thing. A meeting!"

"Not now. It's late and—"

"It may be later than you think," he said. "Really, this is for your own good, pal. I could be with my girl—let's see, Tuesday, yes, that would be Fran—I could be with Fran, but I'm here looking out for you."

He was so absurd, standing there in his comically inappropriate wardrobe, complete with white suede shoes and straw boater, but nevertheless so beaming confidence and self-adoration that I let him steer me into a place called the Farmer's Pig, and there we found a booth in a dark corner, and he went and got a beer for self and a frothy ginger beer for me.

"This ain't the moment for you to start drinking, friend, believe me," he said, and drained half his glass, then licked the foam from his upper lip. I assumed he was cheesed off because I was on this "secret project" and he was not, and I was off "making inquiries" while he was not. He was planted at the Yard, waiting for something to happen, a hard sit for a go-and-grab-it fellow like him.

"Harry, believe me, nothing is going on, I am not plotting against you, I just—"

"It's not that. If you break the story, makes no dif, because there'll be other stories that I'll break, you can be sure. No, it's this. I'm worried about you, pal. You're overconfident but underexperienced. I'm worried you're getting yourself in way beyond your depth, and it's you we could next find in the gutter."

"Whatever are you talking about?"

"What do you *know* about this Thomas Dare?"

"How do you even know the name?"

"I heard J.P. tell Bright your caper. I'm good at overhearing stuff. It's sort of my trade, you might say. Anyhow, I heard it, and I didn't get a schoolboy crush on him like you did, and I thought he ought to be the one we look at, so I took the liberty."

"He's a brilliant man!"

"How's he know so much?"

"That same brilliance."

"Too brilliant, if you ask me."

"There are such men. Rare, to be sure, but genius is not without documentation. Surely Darwin, his cousin Galton, Matthew Arnold . . ." But I had been so taken by the brilliance of Professor Dare's explanation that I had never questioned its origin. Surely he was a shrewd analyst, but he was so far ahead of the others that it might mean he had some kind of inside information. Inside what?

A far more likely explanation involved Harry, not Dare. Was Harry a more jealous type than I had figured, and was he working now to drive suspicion between me and Dare? That would be a sure way to destroy our partnership, and Harry might benefit, picking up the pieces we'd left on the floor and assembling them. Such deviousness seemed not only beyond Harry but beyond the American mind. Now, were he a Hungarian, one might think it plausible, but a son of the middle prairie, with those broad, flat vowels and that total absence of irony, much less subtle thinking, nuanced calculation, patience, cleverness? Hardly likely, I'd have thought.

"What are you here to tell me?" I said.

"It took some digging, some bribing, some considerable yakkity-yak and palaver, but the second best kept secret in London after Jack's identity is that your Tom Dare has a violent streak in him."

I looked at Harry, searching for signs of jest. I knew irony was well beyond him, but his crude American mind might conceive of a crude practical joke. "What are you talking about?"

"A few years back, he almost went on trial for assaulting a colleague. He and this guy, they got into it over a project they'd been working on, and Tom Dare jumped him, smashed him, shoved him down the steps, and was throttling him, only to be pulled off by cooler heads. This was at the school, you know, the University of London, where he was some mucky-muck-mullah type. You know how discreet your own people are, chum. It was, what's the word, 'hushed up.' Can't have a high-up professor at a high-up school acting like a low hooligan, cracking pals over the head and all. Tut-tut, old chap, we just cannot have it."

"I have never *heard* of such a thing." And I hadn't. No, it was not done. Among "our" class of folk, that is, those of us with higher mental function, exposure to education, mastery of culture, familiarity with the genius canon of Shakespeare, Marlowe, Beethoven, Mozart, Wagner, proficiency in the dead languages, the brightest, the best, the most gifted, it was understood that the laying on of hands was strictly off limits. One did not do such things. That was for Kipling's sort of brutes. If there was to be pugilism, it would be at the gymnasium, under the regulations of the marquis of Queensberry.

"The guy has very strong ideas and, more to the point, a crazy belief in them. He cannot stand to be defied, and when he is, he goes all nuts in the brain. When he and this guy had a falling-out, it got real bad fast."

"Come now, Harry, you must do better than that. Particulars? Names, issue involved, social ramifications? I feel certain that, had such an incident occurred, it would have been the talk of all London, it would have made all the rags, the *Star* especially. 'PROF BEANS CHUM,' as O'Connor would have it, a huge scandal, that sort of thing."

"I don't have that stuff yet. I only know what I know, and I wanted to warn you, tread easy with this guy. You never know what you might jiggle loose."

That tore it. I am not a violent man, I despise and fear confrontations, and too many times I've not stood up to bullies for my own interests, but at that moment something either heroic or insane arose in me, and perhaps they are the same thing.

"All right," I said. "I'll have no more of this. I don't know how they do it in that rustic backwoods you come from, but over here we do not spread ugly rumors and attempt to ruin the reputations of men without foundation. We even have laws against it. Dare could sue you for slander, and if you were found guilty, you could end up in jail. It's happened before, it will happen again, and it's our good insurance against nasty buggers spreading nasty rumors."

He looked at me, shocked-like. "Whoa, there, friend Jeb, I'm not here for my health and to put a bullet in the professor's back. I'm just telling you, this guy is a little nuts. He goes off, loses control, all that crazy—"

"Mr. Dam, I must inform you I am no longer interested in this conversation, whose veracity I entirely doubt. I believe you're trying to sabotage my superior efforts on solving this issue. It's a low-breed stunt that only a Yank could come up with."

"That's right, we shot you guys from behind trees, and it wasn't fair, was it?"

"Mr. Dam. I will leave now. Please do not approach me with any more discussion on this topic. I find it distasteful. Even allowing for your frontiersman's ignorance, I find *you* distasteful. It's not acceptable, and I will not be a party."

With that I rose, feeling I'd broken all relations with Harry permanently. At least I had by English rules. Who knew what an American would do?

I stomped out self-righteously, only to hear him cry, "Friend, if I was you, I'd get a gun."

CHAPTER TWENTY-NINE
The Diary

October 28, 1888 (cont'd)

I went to my knees, down hard but not quite unconscious. The sensations of the blow were unpleasant. It had sounded like a locomotive crashing hard against my ear, all clang and gong, echoing around my brain at a hundred miles an hour. My will vanished in the pain, as did my ability to think clearly. The world went to blur and whiz as I blinked, blinked again, felt the urge to vomit, put my hand to the site of the blow to feel, thankfully, not a laceration spurting blood but the swelling of a knot. I looked up to see him towering over me, blunt fellow in black wool, black cap, black of eyes, and beefy-wide of face. I saw his boot come out, and he didn't kick me but put it square on my back and crushed me to the earth.

"Go on, Rosie, get out of here," I heard him say.

"Don't kill him," she said, then clarified so that her intent wouldn't be taken for mercy, "that'll get the coppers on us like buzzards."

She skittered away, and he bent low and whispered into my ear, "Now, guv'nor, I can cosh you till your brains is scrambled good, or I can let you alone if you promise to be a proper fellow and do as you're told."

This was the bully game. It happened, not a lot, but it happened. A tart made an assignation and drew her John to darkness, and as he was about to hand over the coin, her bully jumped out and gave him a knot on the head. The robbery was clean and usually involved no more violence. The clouted knave would never go to the coppers, as to do so would involve confessing he'd been on the scout among the Judys, so he would just write off the six or eight quid or whatever it cost him, swear off the Judys, and limp home with a headache. This threat was always there, nothing to be done about it, but now I'd walked smack into it, obviously on account of my bad judgment in improvising off-plan and ending up in circumstances I couldn't control. Fool! Idiot!

"Now, sir, you just stay where you is, flat as an empty sack, and reach back there for that wallet, and I'll take all them bills. No fancy tricks or I cosh you again. I am a bloody artist with cosh, I am, and I know a fine gentleman such as yourself don't want no more trouble. I'll even leave you a thruppence for a stout after I'm long gone, that's the kind of mate I am, guv'nor."

"Don't hurt me," I said feebly.

"No need for hurting," he said. "Who you think I am, Jack the Ripper? He'd cut you for the larfs it brung his lips. Me, I just want me pay and I'm off, and you and I are well quit."

"So be it," I said, rolling slightly, pulling myself up.

"Sure, make yourself comfortable, but no fast moves or I'll do what I must. I'm a businessman like you, and I don't want no trouble."

"Yes, sir," I said.

"Garn," he said, a cockneyism that I believe means "Imagine that!" but loaded to brim with cynic's irony, "a guv'nor like 'im calling a blackguard like me 'sir.' Who'd a seen that one coming?"

My servile manner amused him no end. It confirmed all his social prejudices. I knew him in an instant: He believed his own physicality and willingness to go brute made him the superior man, and that it was he who was nature's nobleman by rights, but with the coming of civilization, the "gentlemen" had taken over, being book-smart if muscle-dumb, and had contrived unfair methods to cheat him out of his natural lordship over all things. He was merely seeking compensation for his loss.

"Yes, there now," he said as I withdrew my hand from my coat and handed over what he thought was my wallet. He reached for it and at that moment was monarch of a tiny kingdom, this lost alleyway on the quay. His rectitude blazed outward, his sense of self-righteous justice having been served, his appetite whetted for what pleasures were upcoming and soon. He was feeling generous and magnificent, a "larf" on his merry lips.

Hello, sir, allow me to introduce myself, all proper-like, I'm Jack the Ripper.

It was a wonderful stroke. Well, not a stroke so much as an épée's hit, a darting jab faster than the eye can see, much less track, so swift it cannot be blocked by hand, and I drove the six inches of steel into him hard at a kind of upward angle, through his right side under the arm so that it would glance off ribs if it happened to strike them (it didn't) and cut through his abdomen on the rise toward his thoracic cavity where it pierced the lower left ventricle, opening a wound that would never close, and his blood began to drain into his guts. It lasted only a second, but I felt the bliss of steel in muscle, I felt all the infinitesimal vibratory sensations of the muscle fibers yielding as the point penetrated and opened the pathway wider for the blade to glide through, slicing deep and wide as it went. I even fancy I felt the slightly more gelid obstruction of the heart, where, for an instant too small to be measured, that lump of muscle resisted, then yielded as the point pushed a full inch into it, opening it to drain its contents and cease its throbbing evermore. Then the withdrawal, neat as the closing of scissors; with a sense of zip and snick to it, the blade was out as fast as it had entered, perhaps in his flesh for less than half a second. The peritoneal lining closed over the small wound, so there was no copious outflow as I had observed in my other escapades. All his bleeding would be internal.

He felt little pain, perhaps a sting, and jerked, as if to say "Ouch!" or "Damn!" but his pressure dropped instantly and he sat backward with a smack as his buttocks hit cobblestone, the cosh dropped from hand, and he shook his head. He could not believe, as I have noted before, that this moment, which all must face, was upon him. An instant senility came across him, and his face seemed to melt toward languor, losing all firmness and jut.

"By Christ," he said, "you've killed me."

"By Christ, I have," I said.

"Aw, Jesus."

"He can't help you, friend," I said as I cleaned my blade on his rough workman's sleeve. "He's working elsewhere. You heart will pump dry in less than a minute as you become drowsier and drowsier. Any last words for the monseigneur?"

My little jest flew over his head. Nothing like being murdered to kill a sense of humor!

"Sir," he said, "me boy Jamie is parked at St. Barnaby's Rectory orphanage in Shadwell. I've got a few pounds in me stash, can you see he gets it?"

"Don't be ridiculous," I said. "If I give the money to Jamie, his mates will be jealous and beat him and steal it, and he will curse you into eternity. Instead, I'll give it to the rector for all the boys in your name, and all will benefit. I'll even match it, and you should consider yourself well treated by Jack the Ripper. On top of that, you got to meet a famous man before you died, and how many of your station can say the same? You have no cause for complaint."

"Aw, Christ," he said, eyes opening wide in amazement. "Jack himself! Just my bleedin' luck!"

It was his last sentence.

I looked about and all was silent. Pennington Street, a hundred feet away, showed no sign of commotion. The woman was long gone, no doubt back at the Rookery, waiting for her man to come home so they could go out for a nice glass of gin and then have a bounce among the bedbugs.

I thought the better of leaving him there, so I dragged him to the quayside. He was heavy, but my sense of the pleasure of the kill filled my muscles with magic elixir, so it was not as difficult as it might have been. Before I let him slip, I removed the cache and found four pound eight, which I wadded and stuffed in my pocket. I rolled him, controlling him as he went, almost wrenching my back. But there was no splash as he slipped away, disappearing in seconds in the quarter-moon's light, beneath the arrival of a swell. On either side, two vast merchantmen towered, creaking, rocking, but from them came nothing but silence. I picked up the cosh, a leather pouch filled with lead shot grafted to a short wood grip, and tucked it away for who knew what possibility.

I expect to hear nothing about the fellow. It was as if he never lived, and the lump on my head will go down in two days or so. It will ache a bit longer, but that is the price of the business I am in.

CHAPTER THIRTY

Jeb's Memoir

It all turned on three letters, and the colonel knew where to look for them, and quick as a fox, he provided Penny with the names so designated and specifics of three officers so marked, and just as quick, Penny forwarded them to me.

The three letters of the crucial designation were: "s/ID." That meant "Seconded to the Intelligence Department," which was both the kiss of professional death in the army—once tainted with exposure to the black world of intelligence procedures, the officer had sealed his administrative fate and would never rise to the level of a general officer, as the boys in charge did not trust their own spies—and the ticket to some truly interesting adventures. It was amazing how many brave officers would give up forever their chance at wearing the general's insignia for a few years of scuttling around the hills beyond Kabul with the Pathan. To a certain mind, I could tell, it was someone's idea of jolly fun! Pip, pip, ho, ho, all larky and merry in the Great Game, shan't we have a dashing good time, Geoffrey, and to Hades with those hidebound mummies at headquarters! Perhaps sexual possibility was part of the lure, for the dusky-skinned, sloe-eyed beauties of the brown races were said to have lesser standards of acquiescence than our Victorian ladies behind their crinolines and tight bodices. Because we had so many men with these issues in their brains, we had an empire.

Two majors and a lieutenant colonel. The names meant nothing to me, nor the regiments from which they had sprung, though one fellow, a major, was a double outlier, as he was seconded initially from his "real" regiment to something all woggy called the 3rd Queen's Own Bombay Cavalry. It was in the Bombay Cavalry that he had survived the ruinous defeat at Maiwand, in 1880, as had the other two in their respective regiments or whatever they were (I'll never get the military system of regiment and battalion and brigade straight!). All were shortly thereafter "s/ID"ed, if such a term existed, at which point the archivists of the British army lost track of them, and at intervals of, respectively, eighteen months, two years, and, my God!, five years, they were "r/RHq," meaning "Returned to Regimental Headquarters," which is a way of saying home safe. Who knows how many of the s/ID boys never made it back to r/RHq and had their guts pulled out on some dry knob in the Hindu Kush? Such is the price of empire.

Major R. F. Pullham (Ret.), 8th King's Royal Irish Hussars, (KCB) (DCM)

Major P. M. MacNeese (Ret.), E Battery/B Brigade, Royal Horse Artillery (DSO) (DCM) (CGM)

Lieutenant Colonel H. P. Woodruff (Ret.), 66th Berkshire Regiment of Foot (KCB) (VC)

The fuel of empire is bravery. Whatever it is, wherever it comes from, whatever the mechanics of the thing, these fellows had it, as the bland display of initials compressed between parens behind their "(Ret.)" designation made clear. Knowing full well I was a congenital coward, I could never understand what makes a man brave. Is it strength, stubbornness, intelligence, instinct, possibly even fear of something worse than what awaits him in the ordeal immediately ahead, whether it's a valley with guns to left and right, or the cunning pleasure of a tribal torturer? As I say, one can doubt the wisdom of it, the ethics of it, the sheer criminality of it on the global scale, but one cannot doubt the courage.

At the same time, I took to this development rather wholeheartedly. It provided something to Jack that heretofore was absent, and that absence—a clear frame of reference and possibility—had occluded, I believed, our attempts to understand and thereby locate him.

Clearly, the only men with answers were the listed three, all Afghan vets of great valor, all recently retired, all s/ID at length, all well under six feet. Like a Tantric prayer, I committed the rhythms to memory: MacNeese, Pullham, and Woodruff. One, it seemed, would have a spelling impairment and two purloined wedding bands and that, as they say, would be that!

Penny's knowledgeable colonel had even provided addresses, so that cut one difficulty out of the process. Dare and I charted them on a map of London and learned that Major MacNeese lived on one of the better streets in Whitechapel, while both Major Pullham and the Welsh colonel (H stood for Huw, Welsh spelling) Woodruff were farther out, though all were within an hour's walk of the murder sites, and all were close to public transportation—the Underground or horse-tram lines—that could get them there and back without a bit of trouble.

We agreed to start with MacNeese, on the grounds that the closer he was, the more likely his candidacy seemed. We were aware, too, that time was passing. We had gotten by the quarter-moon phase of late October without a death, for no reason anyone understood. If Professor Dare's theory of quarter-moon-as-optimum-mission time held true, that meant that November 6 or 7 would bring Jack and his knife to the street again. We felt it best to make quick surveys of each man and determine if any was more promising than the others. If one stood out with a special vividness of possibility, he would be the one we focused on exclusively, and when we developed evidence, we would take it to Inspector Abberline. It seemed sound then. It still does, even when I know how it all turned out.

It was about now that the two genius detectives, Mr. Jeb of the *Star* and Professor Dare of the University of London, made an interesting discovery. They hadn't the slightest idea what to do next! The actual detecting part of detective work was utterly beyond them!

We looked at each other, almost daft with disbelief. Did we follow the suspects? Did we hire professional investigators? Did we attempt to burglarize their home quarters? Did we interview their neighbors? Did we hire thugees to knock them down and rifle through their wallets and any other personal papers while they were unconscious? Did we research them at the British Museum? Did we . . . At that point, we more or less ran out of possibilities.

"You're the practical one," said Professor Dare—the site was his study, we were drinking some foul tea his Scots maid had assembled for us from terrier piss, he was smoking, and I was not.

"Sherlock Holmes would hire boys to watch each man," I said. "He is a great believer in the skill of urchins as opposed to coppers in matters of observation."

"That name again! Who the devil is he? Must find out."

"You would find it interesting, as in so many ways you resemble him. As for this here and now, I do believe the more people we involve, the more difficult the thing will be to manage, much less keep secret. For that reason, I would also avoid private inquiry specialists. One cannot control whom others speak to and what gets known generally."

"Well-made point," allowed the professor.

"All right, I would say as follows. In the morning, you station yourself at the MacNeese house, and when he leaves for work, you follow him at a discreet distance. Perhaps you could address your wardrobe accordingly, as such fine tweed so well tailored is rather conspicuous."

"I'm rather a dandy," he said. "I hate to give up on it. Dressing well is its own deep pleasure. But if you insist."

"I shall never insist, only suggest."

"Excellent policy," he said.

"You stay with him, determine what kind of employment he's found, and if it's open to the public, enter and discreetly observe. In the meantime, I shall go to the Hall of Records, find a clerk to run his name through various municipal filings, see what can be learned of his financial situation—I would infer that from taxes paid—and make other determinations, such as police records, birth records, marriage certificates, and so on, all traces of him recorded by the government. Then I shall go home and nap for several hours. You, meanwhile, stay with him through his return home."

"Seems amenable," he said.

"I will rendezvous with you at a spot outside his place at nine P.M. You will then be off and, well rested, I will remain on station until, say, two A.M., following him anywhere he goes."

"Yes, I have it. I will work one long day at the detective's trade; you will work two half long days with a break in between."

"On the following day," I said, "we'll exchange schedules."

"No, no," he said. "Since you're so damned good at fetching records, you might as well return to the municipal seats and do similar searches on the other two. At a certain point, say three days hence, we'll meet and consider next moves. Does that feel efficient? And if Major MacNeese proves uninteresting, we'll quickly move on to Major Pullham, time being an element in our urgency."

"Very good. If there's any 'promising' behavior, we'll mark it and make a determination then."

"Yes, remember that Jack, by my theory, is a scout first and foremost. If he has a plot running, he'll reconnoiter first. That should be behavior easy to recognize and give us ample preparation time. He never improvises; he's got it all well thought out in advance."

Excellent plan. However, in practice it was not nearly so neat. What we hadn't figured on was the utter boredom of detective work, and for highly cognitive men with playful imaginations always on the lookout for spontaneous wit, unusual images, irrational occurrences of moment, the odd cloud formation, a beautiful face, a well-cut suit, a particular shade of color on the hubcap of a cabriolet, a tone in the air that reminded one of a particularly thrilling passage in Wagner, all the little irrelevancies that life regularly throws up to the overbusy of mind, the ordeal was degrading, exhausting, and excruciating. Detectives we might be playing at, but detectives we were not. We were either too intelligent or too silly.

Major MacNeese was married with two small children. His wife was a beauty but of a class that probably would have prevented a further rise in the army or society even had he not gone off on s/ID. He had secured, through connections, a fine job as assistant supervisor of the shipping department of the East India Company and therefore worked in their extensive rooms located immediate to Canary Wharf. It was such a fine job, surely a thousand a year, and it came to him so quickly that we quickly concluded it was part of some larger arrangement. We believed that his true employer, using his contacts, was an intelligence department attached to some governmental concern, army, foreign office, some tiny room in a Whitehall cellar, and he was possibly in charge of shipping men of low repute or criminal intent, purloined military documents, currency for payroll of spies, perhaps guns and powder, even dynamite, into or out of Britain under the guise of his civilian career. That made sense but was not terribly interesting, for a shipping executive of secret dynamite is still first and foremost a shipping executive. Ho-hum, and pardon me for nap time.

Major Pullham was more interesting. His employment, again gotten no doubt through contacts, was with the manufacturing concern of Jacoby, Meyers & Devlin, which specialized in selling various metal accoutrements to the army, such as mess-kit items, lanyards, belt buckles, and water bottles. Since he was the cavalryman of high renown—8th Irish Hussar, recall, with all those initials scattered in his name's wake—he knew all the generals of horse and all the procurement processes and was able to maintain his firm's contracts for horse-related metal implements, such as bits, spurs, cinch buckles, and so forth, that kept the British hussar and light or heavy horseman firmly in saddle as he galloped through waves of Pathan, whisking them down with the sharp edge of his Wilkinson. Pullham had married above station to a wealthy and connected woman and was a sort of smooth charmer, being a handsome man with good manners, a courtly fashion, a ready wit, and a comfort that eased his way among the betters of society with whom he mingled on a daily basis.

The third fellow, Colonel Woodruff, was probably the bravest but also evidently the most severe. He lived alone, a dull little man in black, mainly, and had no true employ except his own intellectual curiosity. He spent his days in the British Library reading rooms (I had never noticed him, nor he me), where he was quite happily compiling the first English-Pashto dictionary and grammar, a document that was needed desperately by at least four other human beings on the planet. As I say, drab, with a clerk's mien.

However, he was an old hand, having been east since 1856, survived the siege of Lucknow during the Great Mutiny, and commanded a battalion of foot of the 66th at Maiwand, which stood off several separate horse charges; when our positions were broken, he was able, by shrewd land navigation and language skills, to get all his survivors back to Kandahar. Not satisfied with that accomplishment, he went back into the field in mufti and, for a week after the battle, brought stragglers back in. Then he and he alone made the desperately dangerous journey to Kabul, where he became Fred Roberts's head scout and led the Roberts relief column back to raise the siege at Kandahar. It was he, on the night before the battle, who scouted the Khan's positions and made Roberts understand how to attack. After the rout, he was awarded the VC for that, although he could have been awarded it for any of the actions of the previous week. After all of that, he went s/ID for the next full five years, doing God knows what in the high Khyber Mountain passes. To look at him, you'd have thought he owned a teashop or was a third-grade railway clerk.

So we rotated among them over the week before the approach of the first November occurrence of the proper moon phase, I doing more of the digging through files, Dare more of the on-scene reportage. I must say, he had a talent for it and seemed to enjoy it rather more than I would have thought. "It's so nice to be among actual human beings in actual society for a change," he said enthusiastically, "instead of locked amid books, no matter how stimulating they might be."

We learned, first of all, that if no man is a hero to his valet, neither is he one to his detective. MacNeese, for example, while the exemplary servant to his employers, both nominal and subrosa, and to his family, occasionally bought a French postcard or two on his way home, for private titillation and release, we presumed. We weren't sure what to make of it; perhaps, though there were no indications, were he Jack, the pictures would render him tumescent, and he needed that impetus to do the murders. Admittedly, it was far-fetched; more probably, the occasional secret release calmed him and turned him away from the temptations he might succumb to otherwise on his daily to-and-fro through the lascivious streets of Whitechapel.

As for Pullham, it was sex as well. (How much of human activity is infiltrated by desire! That was a lesson well learned!) However, it was sex after the fashion of an adventurer, which was clearly his personality type. He had two mistresses, one of whom his wife had no knowledge of and one of whom she did. He saw them regularly over lunchtimes, skipping the midday repast and thereby keeping his figure lean and dashing. Once he saw both of them on the same day, taking a late dinner with Lady Meachum. He was insatiable. It was observed that at any chance encounter with an attractive woman, he immediately went into full seducer's mien, came alight, as it were, attentive, his hands seeming to accidentally touch and caress his prey, an invitation whispered into her ear, this to servant girls, clerks, shopkeeps, and high ladies as they came across his prow. The man was a satyr. Again, that might be a Jack indicator, on the theory that for a woman hunter, slaying the rude street girls was a refined pleasure to be enjoyed after having grown tired of endeavors involving mere sex conquest in the field. But again, it was kind of silly, wasn't it? This man had everything, and if material values were important to him (marrying Lady Meachum seemed to indicate they were), why would he risk it all by knifing the odd tart during the crescent moon? I could make no sense of that issue. The other aspect that made him unlikely was energy. The fellow was engaged at all waking hours, in mandates of career, mandates of society via Lady Meachum's importuning, or mandates of his perpetually engorged chuz, which seemed to guide him whenever his schedule would allow it.

That left Colonel Woodruff. His flaw was hardly a flaw. The man worked relentlessly and seemed completely isolated from society in his mad urge to decipher Pashto grammar and verb tense. Perhaps it kept the devils of memory and regret at bay. Equally, he did not mix with old military colleagues and recount the good old days; possibly, to him, they were not so much good as merely old, and he was content to leave them lie. In fact, he would go weeks without speaking to another soul. He was a priest, not only a priest but a damned Black Jesuit, of sublime discipline and isolation and absolutism. But once every ten days or so, he would allow himself a night off and indulge his solitary vice.

So odd. It must have been a habit picked up in the east, and one wondered what it did for him, except perhaps still the voices he must have heard, the visions he must have seen. Whatever the case, he left his rooms and walked—a great walker he was, his short little figure never slowing, his progress much more severe and less patient than that of other walkers and went to the dock area, and then went to one of three dens, unmarked on the outside, and spent the night.

At first we had no idea what the places were, and thought they might be brothels, but he stayed way too long for a brothel visit. Professor Dare volunteered to wait him out while I went back home to catch up on sleep.

The next day the professor reported that after the colonel had left, he himself entered to ascertain the nature of the vice and discovered it to be an opium den, where men of all races paid to lie on divans and a Chinaman would bring them long-stemmed clay pipes; they would imbibe (is that the term?) and pass into a trancelike stage, not quite sleep but more a tranquil semiconsciousness with their eyes locked on infinity, their bodies still, their breathing imperceptible, their minds voyaging to wherever. Since the drug was more of the sort that stilled the body than animated it, it would never act as an enabler of the kind of vigorous action that Jack demonstrated.

As the end of the first week of November approached, we had nothing except a load of information on three heroic officers guilty of only the petty sins of human yearning for various denominations of comfort. But if Professor Dare had lost faith in the veracity of his thesis, he never admitted it to me. Quite the opposite, he was adamant that it had to be one of these three, and as he pressed his case, perhaps I saw a hint of the violent zealotry of the kind that Harry Dam had reported. I do not mean there was threat in his behavior, just dogma. He knew, he knew, he knew. He could not be wrong. That was the bedrock of his conviction.

CHAPTER THIRTY-ONE
The Diary

November 3, 1888

———

I write this one quite drunk, ha ha. I felt I needed to real relacks relax. The pressure is building, I am crushed between lives, I am so close, but yet there is much to do. I will allow myself some diversion.

One place, ha ha ha, I knew to be safe was the Tailor's Thimble, in Marylebone, far from the slough of despond called Whitechapel. It is uncharacteristic of me to let go, as I subject myself from long habit, long, long, long habit, to the utmost of disi discipline and letting go is is not a thing I do easily.

But the Thimble, in the afternoon, is largely empty, and so I sat and had three glasses, then a fourth, of champagne.

"Celebrating then, are we, sir?" a feller asks.

"Indubitably, friend. Feeling generous. Care for a glass?"

"Wouldn't mind if I did, and thanking the gentleman kindly."

So he scootched up on a stool and I nodded to the barkeep and soon enough my new friend was having a quaff of bubbly as well.

"Never had it before," he said. "It tickles the nose."

"It tickles more than that after time," I said.

"What business is yours, sir?" he asked.

"I handle rearrangements," I said. "Business is good. There's a lot of rearranging to do. And you, sir, what would yours be?"

"I was a rigger. That is, sir, I rigged the ropework on the construction cranes we used in the digging of the tunnels of the Underground. Not just tunnels, sir, but buildings, too, bridges, anything requiring heavy weights moved and placed. Raised in the trade, trained by my father, who was trained by his before him. People take it for granted, but it's a tricky business and, done wrong, can spell all sorts of mischief."

"So when I sail blithely from the City to Marylebone or cross over a river wide and deep enough to drown a battalion, you're the lad who made it happen?"

"A tiny part of it's my work, sir. It was good work. I raised three kiddies and now all are in trade or honest labor."

"Well, by God, sir, you've provided civilization with a long ton and a half more than I have. Here, porter, the bottle. This man drinks to his fill on my tab!"

The bartender scurried over, made a bottle ready with ceremony, and Mr. Hoyt, for such was the name, and I had a merry time together. He was quite a decent man and laughed at my bad jokes and puns, never grew intemperate even though the company had jettisoned him at sixty-five without so much as a farthing or a fare-thee-well. We both wept a tear for his wife, and agreed that liquor eased the pain.

"And you, sir? If you do not wish to speak, I understand. But somehow the burden is less when you share it, even for a bit, even with a stranger."

"There was a woman, I lost her. There was a friend, I lost him. I hate them for the pain they caused, I miss them for the love they provided. It's a banal story. Commonplace, pitiful. I try not to get all weepy, because in other respects, I was so lucky."

"But it's love that's most important, now, isn't it. When all is said and done, love is what lasts, or the pain of it missing, that lasts as well."

"It's surely so," I said, turning to more bubbly.

CHAPTER THIRTY-TWO

Jeb's Memoir

Suddenly, it was November 6, which was just in advance of the high-water mark of the quarter-moon and the run of days most likely for Jack to express himself once again. We had to make a choice on which man to follow if indeed he went one of those nights.

"Tell me," Dare said, "which of our three boys we should pick for our game, given that either he's cleverly disguised his intentions or none of the three has a thing to do with this."

"I would say we could abandon Major MacNeese. With his job's long hours, his children underfoot, his wife's love and engagement, he's the least likely candidate. Leaving out of it how his brain works, the chap is too busy for Jack's kind of all-night action."

"I had hoped you would reach that conclusion. So of the others, Major Pullham and the heroic Colonel Woodruff, VC, which do you prefer?"

"The case for Woodruff is strongest." I said. "He is alone all nights or in an opium den. His life is Spartan, dedicated to a duty that, it seems to me, is of dubious usage to the world, and therefore has more discipline for controlling himself for as long as he can. He comes and goes and reports to nobody. He does not drink with friends or hang about with other old soldiers. It's as if he's in mourning. So he, of the three, has by far the most ample opportunity, and given his battle experience and his long service s/ID, the most exposure to the sort of violence and carnage of which Jack is so happily author. He would be by far the most auspicious choice."

"I have reached the same conclusion," he said.

"As for the adventurous rake Major Pullham, he is clearly a kind of sex maniac, but not our kind of sex maniac. He lives to have intercourse."

"He does indeed."

"So he engineers such a thing at each opportunity, plus keeping up a busy professional life and being a willing partner in Lady Meachum's ambitious social plans, which means he must be all ritzied up for suppers, brunches, weekends in the country, even the odd ball or masquerade, as those of that class are so idiotically inclined to do. So the question must be asked: How would he have time? He'd have to plan like a genius, and though he's clearly a gallant sport, there's no indication he's a genius."

"It would not seem so."

"However . . ." I said.

"Yes."

"The rings. We are forgetting that Jack took Annie's wedding rings."

"Your point?"

"Rings are treasure. Goods. Material things. Clearly, Major Pullham needs to prosper. Though he is not primarily a thief, he could not help but snatch something there that he thought had value. For Woodruff, there seems to be little of the material world in his mind. He does not have, he does not acquire, he has no interest in things. They insult him. His acts are pure."

Dare considered. "The point is well constructed. I would not have thought of it."

"So. Does hunger for treasure trump abundance of opportunity?"

"A believer in capital—that is, treasure—would argue that it did."

"It is indeed human motive, well verified in history, literature, myth, and folklore since ancient times."

"I must say, I do agree."

"We are in accord?"

"Indeed. To Major Pullham, then, boulevardier, dasher, swordsman, cavalryman, ace salesman of horsey gimcracks and gewgaws, and Jack the Ripper," said the professor.

CHAPTER THIRTY-THREE

The Diary

November 6, 1888

It is almost over. I have but once more piece of butcher's theater to provide the horrified, titillated busybodies of London. And the great city demands that it be a corker. I have to surpass all previous efforts and stamp my legend on the face of the town as permanently as Big Ben or St. Paul's Cathedral or the stone intricacy fronting the Houses of Parliament. Those three plus Jack: London, linked in memory forever.

What does one need for a masterpiece? Clearly, I needed time and space and privacy. The street had done well in the early going, if somewhat insecure. Moving to sealed-off squares and yards was an improvement. But none had light, room, and security, and I'd had too many by-the-whiskers escapes with blue bottles just missing me or me just missing them, with cart drivers and night watchmen and all the riffraff that coagulates in the rotting East End good nights and bad, fair and foul, morning, noon, or night.

Thus I took my most monstrous risk today. I tried to make it as safe as possible, minimize the play of fate, discipline myself severely for the part I need play, not give in to temptation to show off my wit or learning or eloquence, but keep hard and steady on course, wheel locked or tied in.

I chose my wardrobe with some patience, acquiring a dingy, stained frock and a bowler that looked as if it had been dragged behind the omnibus, escaping none of the shit the team of beasts normally left on our city streets. White shirt, though tending toward gray, frayed at the collar; black four-in-hand, utterly unremarkable; my dingiest boots, no spats, no knife hidden away in belt beneath frock.

Garbed several levels below my station, I got to the Ten Bells at the busy hour of eleven P.M. It's not a big place, with the bar in a square island at the center eating up more floor space, so it was crowded, smoke hung in the air, gambling games were in full drama, yells and shouts and curses filled the air, most of the inhabitants being men either preparing for a night's friction in the alleyways all 'round or recovering from same, and so it was a diverse group united only by sex impulse: bankers, stock traders, beer wagon teamsters, sailors, soldiers perhaps, hod carriers, maybe a construction laborer or two. Many looked like something out of Mr. Dickens's sugar-glazed ingot of Christmas treacle, perhaps the low clerk Bob Cratchit, drinking to oblivion after whoring away the money that should have been saved against Tiny Tim's operation, ha ha.

Exactly as I desired. I sat at the bar, sipping stout, enjoying it, I smoked a cigar, I laughed and seemed as animated as any of them, and after I felt comfortable and had assured myself that none of Abberline's plainclothesmen lurked about, I enjoyed the rhapsody of Jack. You heard it everywhere.

"Think he's gone? Been a bit."

"Not Jack. That boy'll ride his horse hard to the end."

"Sooner or later, he'll jigsaw a dolly and a copper will round the corner. Copper goes to whistle, gives chase, and soon enough the revolver squad arrives. One shot, and that's the end of Jack."

"One shot? More like fifty, and they'll knock off a parson, two choir members, and a wee lassie in the volley!"

In time, I entered a conversation with one of the barmen, a burly chap with reddish muttonchops and hands and forearms that you might find on a dock worker. Tattoos, too, signifying naval or army service or to the East for John Company. He had the beady eyes of a man who noticed.

As for entrée into a conversational encounter, the universal welcome mat to chat was conjecture about Jack, every man's obsession.

"I say, friend, I heard a rumor they got Jack already."

"No such bloomin' luck," he said. "My wife's brother's a copper for Warren, and he's telling us the boys in blue don't have nothing, not a clue, not a direction, not even a scrap of evidence. Most of the witnesses is liars, and Jack's by far a cleverer boy than anybody knows. It ain't luck getting him by, it's brains, it is."

"I agree," I said. "From what I hear, he's been a hair away from apprehension four or five times, and the coppers just missed it together."

"He's clever and he's got guts," the barman said. "Bloke is mad as a hatter, but you've got to admire the cheek on the bugger."

We lapsed into silence, he drifted off to fill glasses with gin or stout or beer, exchange cheer, josh a gal or two, and eventually return to my area for a lounge. But I knew the man, like all the men, wanted to talk Jack. I waited for him to think of something to say, and finally he did.

"Quarter-moon's coming up. He'll do it again, you watch. He's got a thirst now, bad, likes the blood, but most of all likes the way the town is all rattled. Him, one lad, bringing five million people to a dead halt. Must be a feeling."

"I'll never know," I said. "I'm too busy adding sums by gaslight to squash a fly."

"That's me, too, brother, slinging suds twelve long hours a day," he said.

"Let me ask you something."

At this point, another round of professional activity ensued as he tended to his customers, a rowdy lot, and when I caught an eye, I pointed to my empty glass, and he nodded and brought me another, almost black it was, with a cusp of foam like frosting on a Christmas cake. I took a mellow gulp, enjoyed, and then leaned a little closer. "I'm betting a feller like you, works in here, knows a thing or two. Pays attention-like. Hears a lot, forgets nothing."

"Perhaps it's so."

"Yes, well, here's the point. I'm a married man, see, but I likes the plea-sure when it's safe. I come down here once every two or three months off money I've cribbed up the wife don't see. It don't harm no one, is how I see it."

"It sure don't," he said.

"Exactly," I said. "Now, here's my little issue. I can't help think of what happens if I'm with Judy in the alley, all steamed up, boiler set to pop, and Jack comes along and decides to do two tonight instead of one."

He laughed. That is, larfed. "Old son, Jack's down on birds. He ain't picking out men yet, is he now?"

"He ain't till he is. I'd hate to be first. You don't stand much chance against a fellow so right with a knife."

"Not without the Royal Artillery, you don't."

"So here's my play, friend. Worth a shilling. Would you know of a gal who's got a room? You could visit her there, be all safe and tidy and away from Jack's ways with the blade. I'd pay the tariff, knowing it's more than the thruppence standard. The safety would be worth it."

"Hmm," he said, scrunching up an eye.

Then business called, and he tended some others, paused for a time to josh two men who looked like barristers slumming, poured three gins for a gal in the trade who wound her way back to a table where she sat with two friends, lit a fellow's cheroot, then drifted back. The shilling was on the bar, under my hand.

He came close, I released, he snatched and pocketed. "All right, chum, you didn't hear this from Brian Murphy, now."

"Got it."

"Fellow named Joe Barnett, lives with a gal off and on. Now I hear it's off. She lets her friends double up when it's cold out and they can't make doss. He don't like that, as the room is small. So off he goes, all the girls is talking about the poor thing. She's a pretty thing, too, though somewhat gone to flab. Says she worked in a high-class house once. She ain't in here now, but she's on the streets most nights; believe me, she ain't at choir practice."

I laughed.

"Little heavyset, blond, though, like an angel you'd see in some old painting. Rosy-cheeked, bosom all aquiver, you'd enjoy a romp with her. Name's Mary Jane Kelly, any of the girls knows Mary Jane, they does, and she lives just down the avenue in McCarthy's Rents."

"McCarthy's Rents?"

"Fellow named McCarthy owns it. It's really called Miller's Court. Rank little place, one of them hole-in-the-walls, you go in a passageway, it's all little rooms back there. She's in thirteen, if I recall."

"Mary Jane Kelly."

"She was in earlier tonight. She's in a lot. Or at the Britannia, drinking it up as fast as she earns it. Got the gin bug bad, poor thing, and when she's all hooched up, she likes to sing. I cuts her a break now and then, slipping her a free one. But she'd be the one for you, friend."

CHAPTER THIRTY-FOUR

Jeb's Memoir

Major Pullham lived in a smart house on Hoxton Square in Hackney, perhaps a mile and a half north of Whitechapel. It was all gentry, the best sort of tidy, prosperous, upper-bourgeois London, the ideal toward which all Englishmen were instructed to strive. His—actually, Lady Meachum's—house stood on a street of grace in a state of grace, happily a peer of its cohort, stately, refined, well kept, an ample recompense for a dashing cavalryman shot at ten thousand times in his career for the crown. Too bad he wasn't satisfied with it alone, but then that's the nature of the beast.

I arrived at eleven P.M. Indeed, the quarter-moon now and then shone through the rushing clouds and a brisk wind sent the branches of the abundant trees clackity-clacking. It was really late autumn, and they had changed color and wore scarlet and russet threaded through their crowns, and the leaves, upon achieving the perfection of dry death, fell in swirls to earth and clotted gutters and lawns. The suggestion of rain was heavy in the air, and I felt it would fall before dawn. I had accordingly worn an ancient, used-to-be-father's mackintosh over my brown suit, and a plaid scarf around my neck and my crumpled felt hat, pulled low over my ears. I wasn't going to let rain stand between myself and Jack.

I found Professor Dare exactly where we'd planned, at a bench in Hoxton Square a good hundred meters from the major's dwelling, but with a plain view of it. The major could not leave without our knowledge, as the back-of-yards formed a nice parkground but held no exit, being buttressed on all sides by houses such as his.

"Is he there?" I asked.

"Indeed. He and Lady Meachum returned at ten from some sort of social gathering. They were all topped up in silks and diamonds, so perhaps it involved the Mayfair set or some other golden collection. The hansom dropped them off, they let the last servant return to quarter, and now they are in the bedroom. Perhaps he's atop her now, shouting 'Onward, old girl, let me into the breech!' and that's that for the evening."

"I believe we'd hear her scream in bliss," I said. "It would overcome even the rush of the wind."

We both laughed. Over our adventure, an enjoyable comradery had sprung up, which was perhaps why I reacted so angrily to Harry Dam's calumny. Dare was every bit as ironical as I, every bit as radical, every bit as aware of the pomp and circumstance of empire and the core of rot it concealed, but a little bit more cold-blooded. He never grew angry at the ugliness of what hid in plain sight before much of London's sleepy eyes; he only enjoyed a dark chuckle now and then. He was truly the Holmesian ideal.

"Here," he said, "you may as well take this now. It's quite cumbersome."

With that, he opened his cape, did some dipping and unbuckling, and passed something over to me. It was quite heavy, an object in a leather pouch, the leather pouch in a nest of strapping. I felt it deposited on my lap and was astounded that its weight appeared far more than its size indicated. I bent, peeled through the leather strapping, got to the object concealed in the pouch, and while at first it made no sense to me in the low light of a far-off gas lamp, it gradually resolved itself into more or less known forms.

"Good heavens," I said, genuinely shocked, "a gun."

"Yes, it is. Damned big one, too, I'm told."

I saw that it had a kind of curved wooden hand grip, and by that, I pulled it partly out of its sheathing and realized it had double hammers over double barrels. It was only a foot long or so, and thus its messages were contradictory. The part I'd pulled had a rifle quality, or perhaps shotgun, as there was a hinge and latch by means of which one could break it and insert shells; but there was no stock, only the thick, curled wooden grip. It had no barrel length, either, which disqualified it further from the rifle or shotgun category.

"Howdah . . . you do?" the professor said merrily.

"Er, I don't—"

"It's called a Howdah pistol," he said. "Evidently I had an uncle who spent his life and fortune accumulating heads to hang in a hall in his home. Pointless, if you ask me, unless the heads were human, but alas, none was. He died, perhaps under wildebeest hooves, and it came to my father, and when he died, it came to me along with other knickknacks of dubious usefulness. I've had it in an upstairs room for years."

"Is it a hunting gun?"

"After a fashion. It's not for when you are hunting them, however, but when they are hunting you."

I said nothing, not following.

"In India, they hunt tiger from little compartments cinched about an elephant's back. Sahib need not walk in brushy, punishing jungle as he draws near his quarry. He rides in comfort, as befits the raj. But the tiger is smart. Sometimes he climbs a tree and, knowing he's hunted, will wait concealed in the branches until the elephant passes by. He's not stupid. He knows he has no quarrel with the elephant. He knows who his enemy is, so he leaps into the compartment up top and readies for lunch. In those closed circumstances, the rifle is too clumsy to maneuver. Sahib pulls his Howdah pistol from its scabbard, cocks both hammers, and, as the tiger lunges, fires two immense bullets down its throat. Sahib and Memsahib live to eat mango chutney another night and have many tales to tell."

"It's a last-ditch sort of thing," I said, finally grasping the concept through the irony.

"Indeed. And what better to have along if, by chance, we jump Jack and he jumps back. I doubt we can argue him into dropping his knife, brilliant though we may be, so it's on you to cock and fire. The caliber is something called 5-7-7 Kynoch, whatever that means, but the size of it will certainly dissuade Jack from further fuss."

"It's loaded?"

"Half the weight is the ammunition, my friend."

"I don't know if I could shoot a man," I said.

"The knife in his hand and the smile on his face will convince you otherwise. Furthermore, it's much better to have it and not need it than the opposite."

Strapping the belt together, I realized it was meant to be slung over one shoulder so that it dangled under the other. Affecting this process, after accommodating my jacket and mac to it, I found it nested comfortably enough there, although its weight was not borne by any part of my body but rested on the bench.

Then we settled back. We were nestled in a copse of trees at the center of the square, near the statue of Hoxton, whoever in hell's name he happened to be; no Bobby could see us unless he came through the square itself, and Professor Dare assured me they never did.

"The rich," he said, "need no extra patrol. They are quite safe behind their walls of rectitude."

And so we sat, and so the time passed, the clouds grew thicker, and the occasional beams of wan moonlight ceased to pop through the clouds; perhaps the wind increased, although perhaps it was merely that I grew cold in the waiting, with my nether side resting on the cold stone of ceremonial bench. A hansom now and then passed, and occasionally a party of pedestrians, usually loud under sway of drink, came by, but no one entered the square, and there was no business from the house.

Finally, when I could stand it no longer, I pulled my pocket watch and made out that it was well past one. Over two hours of sitting.

"It's begun to look like nothing," I said.

"I agree. He's at least an hour's walk from Whitechapel's loins, which would move his action to two, then he's got to find a bird, engage her, move her toward privacy, rip her, and head back. Quite an agenda to finish before—Hello, what's this?"

Hello, indeed.

A figure emerged from the major's house, definitely male, well prepared against the coldness and oncoming rain, dashed across the street, where there were fewer gaslights, and began a hunched though purposeful stride in the direction of Whitechapel.

"By God, sir, it's him," said the professor. "I've seen the walk from afar many times in the past week. He's a strider, of no patience nor elegance, hungry for the advance, and so is that one."

"Let's—"

"No," he said, "he'll turn at the corner, but not before issuing a looksee. Military training. We stay still until the turn, and then we're off."

We watched as he receded, and as the professor had prophesied, he stopped at the corner and had a good look around. It being deserted in this happy little nook of London, two blokes as weird as the professor and I would have stood out like clowns had we been upright and mobile. But even at that distance, it was clear his eyes picked out nothing in the trees in the center of the square, or anywhere, and in a second, he was off. And so were we.

We rose—oof, suddenly taking the full weight of the Howdah against my shoulder, I realized how heavy the blasted thing was!—and were after the fox. We pushed ourselves, our strides determined, and reached the corner he'd negotiated a little before he reached his own next corner, and saw him again.

The professor produced opera glasses, gave them a look, and confirmed that he was no longer cautious but was bounding ahead, his destination presumably Kingsland Road, which led to Commercial and thence to the guts of Whitechapel's flesh trade.

"All right," he said, "let's ourselves straight to Kingsland. He's cutting diagonals to save time. At Kingsland, we'll hail a hansom and take it toward Whitechapel, looking for him. If we see him, we pass him and set up on either side of the street ahead of him, and one watches from across, signaling the other, who never looks around."

"Have you done this before?"

"Hardly. If you've better, please inform."

"I'm the total novice."

"Then let's hither."

And we did, cutting hard three blocks to Kingsland. Damn the luck, no hansoms in sight, the traffic sparse, the thoroughfare largely empty, as this was no dolly land. We gamely thrust ahead, down the street, aware that our vertical to his diagonal had probably put us six blocks behind him by now, and we cursed our luck, and our curses had effect.

The hansom seemed to arrive from nowhere, and the fellow behind said he was going off duty, but I told him I'd pay a premium and he said yes to that, and in we went as the vehicle trembled ahead. It was a relief to get the weight of Dr. Howdah off my shoulder and keep it from banging hard against my hip, where it surely would bring bruises. It was also a relief to catch up on oxygen, produce some saliva to wet my dry lips, and sip air at leisure instead of desperation.

We rumbled along, clippity-clop, clippity-clop, keeping a sharp lookout on either side. Guessing the major would be on the right, I yielded that position to the professor and set myself to examine all the pedestrians along the left side of the street. As it became Shoreditch, by that enraging and confounding London tradition the population on foot grew thicker, then thicker still when it took its angled right on Commercial and headed down that long stretch of well-lit and quite busy thoroughfare, darting in and out between the delivery wagons that plowed the road twenty-four hours a day, even as the pedestrians were darting in and out of the now mostly closed costers' stalls. The gaslights did their duty, the pubs and beer shops and odd retail cast their light as well, but it had the kind of crazed affect of chiaroscuro, expressing an emotional value but no specific imagery. Jangle-jangle was how it felt, the whole thing with a mad carnival flash to it, made more urgent by the stress I felt and the fear I also felt that I might miss something and have the blood of a victim on my hands the next—

"Dr. Ripper, I presume," proclaimed the professor.

"You have him?"

"Walking as bold as Cecil Rhodes across Africa with a pocketful of diamonds," he said. He looked up, poked open the spy hole that allowed contact with the hansom driver, and said, "Two more blocks, then drop us on the left."

"Aye," said the driver, "but mind your bloomin' 'eads, sir, as she's started to rain."

What impact would that have on things? Jack had never worked in the rain. Perhaps it would drive him back. Or perhaps he'd try to work indoors or make some other arrangement, I thought, and realized that if so, we'd never catch up, and this one would go down as a miss. The professor paid the driver.

We pulled away, took up a kind of boys'-spy position behind a shuttered coster stall—we would have looked quite mad to passersby, had they noticed, but of course they didn't—and waited, and yes, here came, recognizable by his powerful gait and lack of patience, Major Pullham of the Royal Irish Hussars, now wrapped up like Private Pullham of the Royal Irish Horse Shitscoopers. He was, by the rules of his class, in mufti.

He appoached, drew even with us, and then forwarded his way along.

"I will go on the advance," said the professor. "You stay on this side of the street. I will look back at you, but never at him, for your signals. Understood?"

"Excellent," I said, and that is just what we did. The professor dashed across Commercial, set himself up, and walked briskly a hundred feet ahead of the major. He never looked back at the major but looked across to me, as I had positioned myself fifty feet behind the man, though on the opposite side of the street. Block after block I signaled straight ahead. Passing Fashion Street, then Wentworth, the professor gambled that the major would go right on Whitechapel, and plunged around the corner without hesitation. The major cooperated and we continued our little game of tag down the avenue.

Another pause as he went into the Ten Bells, right on the corner of Commercial and Fournier, across from Spitalfields Market, and had a draft of beer while we twiddled thumbs outside in the lightly falling rain.

"I'm guessing he was checking for Peelers," said the professor. "He goes around, checks for knots of them, for the direction of their foot patrols; he looks for plainclothesmen in the crowds. I'm also guessing he has a spot already picked out, one he's not used before, and after he quaffs his fill, he'll ease out, taking his time, and at a certain spot slide up to Judy and ask for her company. Agreeing, she'll lead him into a dark alley or down a dark street. Having scouted, he's anticipated her choice."

"I follow," I said.

"I think we should abandon our magic following trick. We might have to move faster. If he takes her into the alley, we have to be on the couple instantly. He never hesitates. He'll go to knife, but before he can hurt her, we have to call him out and secure him. The gun will control the transaction."

"Shouldn't we alert a Bobby?"

"Do you think it wise?"

"Ah—" I considered, seeing as many pitfalls as possibilities. "I'm agnostic at this point."

"Perhaps it's too much to control. Following, interceding, capturing, restraining, *and* calling a Peeler? Too many tasks, easy to mix up or forget or execute without confidence. We're on him now, exactly as we thought; we'll play it out and take the prize."

I swallowed involuntarily. I made a secret promise to myself not to get too close. The man was fast with the blade, and in a blinding second, before I had time to react, he'd have my heart in his hand, munching it like an apple. No, no, I told myself, Jeb, old boy, you think too highly of yourself to end up that way. Keep your distance, remember to cock the damned gun, and if he steps toward you, send him to hell. Be the hero. Welcome the endless love. *Just remember to cock the damned gun!*

We stood there, across from the pub and could see him hunched at the bar. In a bit, more people within moved about, obscuring him, but he couldn't have come out, as there was only one exit.

"He's coming," said the professor. "Oh my God, he's got one, he's got a Judy!"

Indeed it was so. He emerged, dawdled, and in another few seconds a young woman came out, by her demeanor and wardrobe of the whore sub-set and the smaller still prey subset. She moseyed ahead until out of view of the patrons in the bar through the broad windows and, once in shadow, paused to look back. He leaped to her side with mock gallantry, which made her smile.

"Here we go," said the professor.

We rushed crazily across Commercial, hearing the shouts of drivers as we interrupted their rights to passage through the muddy concourse. Meanwhile, the rain pelted down, stinging our faces and forcing us to squint, but somehow we made it with no incident other than additional mud to our boots from the glop that had become the road surface. We arrived on that side of Commercial about fifty feet behind the happy twosome as they walked down the street, arm in arm. They had elected not to try Fournier but ambled down Commercial, past Christchurch and its towering steeple, and down another block. I got a good view, and I must say, if this were Jack, the public would be shocked.

Far from the creepy, anonymous skulker, his face cadaverous, his eyes haunted, his teeth pointed, this Jack was a merry seducer. We could see how totally engaged he was in charming her. Perhaps that was the plan, to gull her toward defenseless love with wit and then cut her down. Perhaps he enjoyed the moment when she saw the knife and knew the cad was her killer and the shock stunned her face.

But he was laying it on with a trowel. I could see him whispering in her ear intimately; evidently he was a wit and quite experienced in the art of making women comfortable (an attribute I sadly lacked): Her face, turned admiringly toward him, radiated rapture at his performance and affection for the man behind it. I watched as she seemed to gradually melt in to him, until they were not two walking side by side but one, of four-legged persuasion, in perfect unison and of one heart, easing their way down the sidewalk, too close to worry about costers' stalls, too close to note the others passing them by at a far faster pace, and too intent on each's response to the other to notice the two hooded gentlemen fifty feet behind them, matching perfectly their pace.

At last they came to a side street on the left, and I saw them put their heads together as they came to a halt, and then she giggled and he guffawed and they turned left.

"All right," said the professor. "Now it gets dicey. Get that gun out so you don't have to pull it while he's cutting off your ears."

I obeyed, sliding it out by one hand and easing it more or less under my mac, and we nodded, each took a deep breath, and steeled self against the upcoming. The rain was really falling now, cutting horizontally, propelled by angry wind, and a chill lay upon all and every. Perhaps hoarfrost in the morning? Who knew what morning would bring? At that moment, we took the corner hard and stepped into the blackness of an alley and saw in a second the figures of two people, enmeshed.

"Remember to cock the gun," the professor whispered.

CHAPTER THIRTY-FIVE

The Diary

November 7, 1888

This was quite new. Before, they were apparitions in the night. I didn't see their faces clearly until I'd killed them, hardly to their advantage. The slack of death did a great deal to undercut beauty, if any beauty there had been to begin with.

But Mary Jane, in full bloom, was a lively, roundish specimen who generated goodwill and happiness wherever she went. She was a full-bodied thing, just a bit beyond the age at which you could call her a girl, and it was hard not to desire her, with her blond hair and her buxom figure and her happy smile for each and all.

After the barman's description, I simply observed and was surprised that I hadn't noticed her before. I didn't bother asking anyone to point her out, since it was unnecessary. She was clearly visible from the window of the Ten Bells, so I didn't have to reenter and risk the barman fixing my face in his memory, as I was sure he had not previously. I could see her sitting at a table with a gaggle of "the girls." For all their forlorn history, they were a gay, larky lot who enjoyed each other's presence, enjoyed the hospitality that the Ten Bells offered, and most of all enjoyed the glass of gin set before them. Like women of all sorts, from the Hindu Kush to the Amazon and the Danube to the Yellow and the Mississippi to the Colorado, they spoke a private language of gesture and enthusiasm, loved the thrill of gossip and slander, were united in their contempt for the men who had ruined so many of their lives, and brought out absolutely the best in each other. I could tell all that from their animated postures around the table.

She was the lively one. One could hear her laughter through the glass, perhaps even feel it in the reverberations in the air. Her eyes were blue and her skin pink and firm. She seemed far from The Life, as it was called, even if she was famous within The Life. I knew tragedy haunted her, as it did so many of the girls. They all seemed to come from broken homes, were runaways or had been kicked out of hearth and home, some to turn to the streets, some already drawn to the streets. Her current torment came from the abandonment by the man in her life, a fellow named Joe Barnett, whom I watched visit her every evening. He was a shaggy brute by my standards but maybe a good-hearted man in the end, not too judgmental, willing to accept Mary Jane for what and who she was. His visits suggested some possibility of reengagement, as neither could quite let the other go. At the same time, it wasn't as if she were making amends to Joe, for she still took tups for pay, let others of her trade sleep in her tiny room on cold fall nights, still hit the gin three, four, sometimes five times a day. She couldn't say no to it, to her eternal damnation. I don't know if she turned to drink for escape or she escaped to turn to drink, but it was the core of her existence, as I have observed her over the past few days.

The Ten Bells and the Horn of Plenty were her main spots. She'd wander outside and, sooner or later, find her beau for the next hour. Then the happy couple took a turn down Dorset. This was a dark scut of street that ran a few blocks until it came to an end, and its reality was elemental "English poverty," if such a style were to be named, meaning brick tenements looming inward on each side, undistinguished by any wit or cleverness, just brick boxes laid end on end one after another, under low chimneys that spewed out coke fume, to combine with London fog into a yellow soup that sometimes smeared the streets. The housefronts were identical but for futile attempts at individuality, such as a flower pot here, a flag there, a yellow door, a rug hanging from a window, otherwise just the dullness of warehouses for forgotten people.

Mary Jane would take her beau a bit down Dorset, and thence—you had to know where to look for it, for it was easy to miss—she'd lead him into a passage wide enough for but one person. That was the entryway to Miller's Court, and it cut between buildings for fifty feet of enclosed brick closeness, where it opened into the space that earned it the comic designation "court": This was an interruption between the continuity of the buildings that offered yet more frontage for dwellings, apartments, or really rooms, chockablock, two stories in height, tiny in dimension, in which yet more desperate souls could be stockpiled until they died and were buried in nameless paupers' fields. Someone owned it, someone collected rent, someone profited, but you wouldn't house pigs in such shabby circumstances.

Mary Jane was in No. 13. I know because entry into the court was by no means guarded, and because so many of the inhabitants were prostitutes, men came and went without notice at all hours of the day, except perhaps those right before dawn, when even the most wicked seem to need their sleep. So I had, more than a few times at odd hours when I had no pressing business, ventured into it, poked about, nodded at the occasional neighbor who paid me no attention. I had my heart's fill of preparation on this one. It goes to show that in England today, a fellow in a four-in-hand, coat, and bowler can go anywhere and remain unseen, for so universal is the uniform of Victoria's tight little island that it confers instant invisibility.

Moreover, despite the hue and cry of the newspapers, I noted nothing in the way of Jack the Ripper fear or panic among even the denizens of Whitechapel, to say nothing of the city itself and the larger nation that encompassed it. There were more coppers about, of course, but they were worthless. They had been guided by that General Idiot himself, Warren, who proclaimed that they must be on the lookout for the "suspicious." In that regard, I saw an amusing scene. Two constables had waylaid a bloke who indeed looked suspicious, as he wore an old shooting coat and a slouch hat; he looked like the very embodiment of seedy danger on the lurk. They had him buttressed against a wall and their billies out for a good cosh if he gave them business. One had already gone to whistle for more Bobbies, and through it all he was yelling, "But I am George Compton Archibald Arthur, Third Baronet of Arthur of Upper Canada and a lieutenant of the Second Life Guards," while the bigger of the two bruisers was saying, "Sure you are, sir, now you just hold steady while we get to the bottom of all this," all as I, Jack actually, perambulated by, looking as normal and unsuspicious as Mr. Jackson, traveling representative of Cooke's Bone, Joint, and Teeth Elixir. That was the point: The beast himself would be unsuspicious, never suspicious.

The lack of general fear had a sound basis in human nature: Each person was secretly wedded to the fantasy of his own immortality and, as consequence, completely given over to the delusion that it couldn't happen here, it couldn't happen now, it couldn't happen to him. I was aware that I was the malevolent god of *here, now, you.*

At first it appeared there'd be trouble with Mary Jane's door. How was I to enter it? The door was eternally locked, I guessed by the mechanical magic of a spring-driven mechanism, and I was no lock picker and it was late in life to pick up new skills, especially those as recondite as slipping a betty into the tumblers and turning them. Besides, no one in my circle would know such a thing, and how would I find a teacher?

Since the construction was rather flimsy, I judged a good shove might cause it to give way, but you could never predict how wood split; it might crack like a rifle shot as I broke through it, and wake up all of Miller's Court, so I'd find myself at the end of an ad hoc vigilante committee rope, dangling off the chimney and making the area by far more famous than it deserved. I assumed that Mary Jane had the key, and I wondered about hiring a fellow to pick her pocket, a trade that was not uncommon in London. Yet that possibility came fraught with difficulties, as in where would I find one of those fellows, why would he not suspect me (I could tell him I was a spurned lover meaning to give her a thump when she got home, but once my atrocity had been delivered, he would be smart enough, would he not, to add two plus two and point me out to the coppers, or at least furnish them with a description that didn't involved a mysterious Jew man with a gold chain and a beak nose!).

No, no, that would never work. But by nightfall—my third foray into Miller's Court—I solved the case, verily like Sherlock Holmes. Since the court was empty—it was ten, most of the girls were out on the street but hadn't brought John home yet; most of the poor folk who were forced to endure the squalor out of lack of other opportunities were well abed—I felt free enough to examine more carefully. Mary Jane's room was first on the right as you passed out of the entry passageway, but beyond it was a nook or gap where the privy, dustbin, water pump, and trough were set. If you dipped into the nook, you encountered two windows in the wall of Mary Jane's room, one located in close proximity to the door on the ajoining wall. It occurred to me that through the window, one could easily reach the inside latch of the door and spring it.

I drifted close, made as if to drop a thing and bent to pick it up so as to justify my coming to a halt at that particular spot to unseen watchers, and as I arose, I made the astonishing discovery that the window was absent a pane. I put a quick hand through the opening, moved the curtain, and though it was dark, I could see within easy reach the latch, with its pull button for withdrawing the bolt, a common feature on perhaps 3.9 million of London's 4 million doors.

I let the curtain fall and, without a haste denoting bad intentions, meandered toward the passageway, checked to see it was clear of incomers, and exited to Dorset Street. I knew I had found my way into Mary Jane's place for the privacy I so urgently required.

Upon reaching the street, I turned right and continued down Dorset, now and then pausing to scan behind me, not out of worry but out of general principle. Nothing untoward obtained. And so I crossed Dorset, reversed direction and returned to Commercial, and ambled slowly back to the Ten Bells, in hopes that I might see my darling again.

She was not there. It was odd. Not at the Bells, not on the street, not on her back in her room, doing her duty. Where had the angel gone? I puzzled, worried that she had reunited with Joe Barnett and they'd gone off to get married or something. I found it a rather crushing possibility. And then I saw her. She was with a fellow, not unlike me, dowdier perhaps, but clearly of the largely anonymous middle class, a clerk or tradesman or mechanic, out for his night of purloined bliss on the power of coin he'd not turned over to the missus. The two of them chatted amiably as they wended toward paradise, passing me without noting me, and were on to their tryst and I to my thoughts.

Suppose, then, I worried, on the night hence when all was set for, I penetrated and she was not there? She and Joe were at the pier in Brighton or walking a country lane outside Dublin, as I had heard the Irish trill in her voice. Or some bully had coshed her and run off with her purse and she was nursing a lump in some charity ward. All could happen as easily as not, and that was the problem of orienting to a particular place and time. You could not control the comings and goings of others. The possibility simmered in my stomach like an undigested lump of beef, turning sour in the bile. Agh, the frustration in it jabbed me immensely, and the prospect of losing all the careful planning and reconnoitering I had invested in the effort irritated me considerably. It occurred to me that instead of my careful plan, I might have to improvise another. I determined to put one together now so that I didn't have to, come the night in question, on the fly.

I reasoned that, were I in this neighborhood on the hunt for Mary Jane and I encountered her absence, the next place to go was the Bells, as it seemed to represent a coagulation of girls. The barman might recognize me, as unlikely as that might seem, for he was a man who daily encountered three hundred faces, but the place was so widely windowed, I could pass by on the outside and determine if the Judys at rest inside for refreshment might soon exit. Noting one, I could wait until she moved, and I saw in my mind's eye a play like the others: I approach, utter a banal "how do ye do?", receive an invitation to accompany, and begin a mosey down this part of Commercial, which, though closest to 29 Hanbury, was still virgin territory for Jack. Where would I take her, where was my goal? As I wandered back down Commercial after parsing it for signs of ladies of the trade—they were there, as usual, in abundance—and after passing the lofty and majestic Christchurch, which was the Bells' next-door neighbor across Fournier, I passed another block and came across a nice little alley. I examined it. Ah, excellent. It was obscure, another brick passageway that almost certainly went undocumented on all but the most precise maps. Peeking into it, I saw how easily I could lure my theoretical Judy into it to do her job, and there do my job. It might be better, even, for so close to Commercial—it would be the closest yet to a throbbing concourse—it could have the impact I so desired and needed. It wasn't quite what I had in mind for Mary Jane, but it would do, and it served the purpose of calming my apprehension.

Well satisfied with the day's labor, I headed back to other duties. Whatever happened, I believed, I was well prepared.

CHAPTER THIRTY-SIX

Jeb's Memoir

I had my thumb splayed across the twin hammers of the Howdah, which I gripped by the wooden forearm under the double barrels. I could easily crank them back, and that momentum would drive my hand to grip and triggers, and I could dispatch Jack in under a second if it came to that.

Dare and I approached, and I felt my heart hammering against my chest, my breath hot and dry in my nostrils, the bitter cold of the rain having vanished in the urgency of the action unfolding in which I was a key player.

He stood over her, leaning against the brick wall, while she seemed to have fallen to her knees. Were we too late? Had he already unleashed the death strokes, and had she in turn tumbled to earth to spurt dry of blood in the falling rain while he looked down, watching her die? That was what the scene suggested to me, and it filled me with rage.

Here at last was the beast.

Here at last was Jack, in flagrante.

We were too late for this poor pretty bird, yes, but by God, there'd be no more gutted women in London, as we had tracked and felled the brute.

Without consciousness, I drew back the hammers and felt each lock in its place as my hand slid down, acquired the checkered curve of the wooden grip, grabbed it stoutly, felt my trigger finger extend to lay across the twin levers with just an ounce of preshot pressure, and braced myself for the explosions but an ounce or two away.

We moved on the oblique to see more clearly and . . . no, she was not dead. In fact, on her knees, facing him, she was quite active. My rage transmuted to befuddlement as I tried to make sense of the posture. Her face was close in on his waist, perhaps a bit below it, her hands were gripping tightly against his flanks, and her head seemed to be somehow pumping in a certain rhythm that was primitive, even elemental, in its need.

"Yes," I head him cry, "my God, yes, oh yes, oh yes, so close," and then a guttural shudder arose from deep in his being as he seemed to endure a spasm and undulated in one powerful thrust and his cry became "Ahhhh-hhhhhhhhhh."

"Come on, then," said the professor in my ear. "This is not what we thought. Quick, turn and out."

With that, we abandoned the alley. By now the rain fell in thunderous quantity, quite soaking us. It cut visibility. We got back to street, I with dangerously cocked and loaded Howdah pistol in my hand, now a veritable ticking bomb whose explosion could kill or maim, and would embarrass if we were spared those outcomes.

"Put that bloody thing away," the professor said.

I dipped next to the building, under some sort of commercial overhang, and using both hands, I decocked gently, tripping one trigger with hammer secured, then easing that liberated arm down and repeating the ordeal for the other barrel. The weapon was appropriately rendered safe for holstering, which I did, and pulled my mac tight around it. The drama over, I could now feel the treachery of the rain. I shuddered even as, ahead of us, Major Pullham, just as jaunty and perhaps even jauntier than before, bounded out of the alley. His face was split by a large, happy grin, he seemed impervious to discomfort, and he passed us by without noticing our strangeness as he called, "Cab! Oh, say, cab!"

A hansom pulled up, and the driver leaned to pop the door. In leaped the major and was away in a trice, disappearing down Commercial in a glaze of rain. Meanwhile, his poor employee—or, I suppose I should say, his ex-employee—emerged and turned the other way, heading back to the Bells for a rest after her exertions and possibly to spend her thruppence on a nice gin.

"Look," said the professor, "it's late, it's raining, we're soaked, we almost killed a man innocently whoring along with his tart, and I suspect with the weather, Jack has awarded himself surcease. Let's return to quarter, begin again tomorrow night, and this time focus on Colonel Woodruff."

"Since he never goes out, that should be a boring sit," I said.

"He will surprise you, I feel it. Cab?"

"Yes."

He hailed a hansom and in we climbed. Since mine was the farthest out, the cabman took me home first, and I climbed out, a miserable wet rat, longing for tea, biscuits, and bed.

"Then tomorrow, eleven P.M., outside the colonel's rooms, well dressed for night action in November."

"Indeed."

"And wipe down the Howdah before you retire. Drops of water can rust the finish."

"I will," I said.

With that, he tapped the roof of the cab, the driver's whip snapped, and the vehicle lurched off. I turned up the walk to the dark house, entered, trudged up the stairs, and stripped my clothes off. The mac would be all right if I had need of it tomorrow; the wool suit might be damp. To hasten its return to norm, I hung it off a chair near the fireplace and lit a small log via some kindling, knowing that it would glow all night. I toweled off the Howdah and did not return it to holster, discerning that leather might attract moisture, but instead let it sit on the desk while the leather cured next to the suit on the chair. I trudged barefoot and naked to the bed, threw myself in it—it was close to five, according to my pocket watch—and pulled up the covers. I was asleep in seconds, though not without a return to the moment when I almost pulled the twin triggers and sent poor Major Pullham and his Judy to the next world, not that there was a next world.

If there were dreams or nightmares, I have no memory of them. Instead, it seemed that not ten seconds later, Mother was shaking me hard, pulling me from sleep. I uttered unintelligible sounds as I emerged from unconsciousness and found her over me, the usual look of contempt and dismissal on her severe and formerly beautiful face.

"Get up, get up," she said. "There's a cabman here. Dress and be gone. I cannot have strange cabmen standing around in my foyer."

It took a few seconds as cobwebs full of butterfly wings, fly legs, dustballs, and the odd dead leprechaun cleared themselves from my mind. Finally I achieved a version of clarity. "What's he want?" I said.

"He says he's from O'Connor, and he's here to take you somewhere you're needed. I must say, this whole newspaper business you've got yourself in is very annoying to me. Now I find you have a Goliathan pistol over there, capable of blowing down a wall."

"I'd be happy to loan it to dear sister Lucy, Mother. Perhaps she can play with it in the garden. Do tell her to look down the barrels and pull the triggers to see if it's loaded."

"You are too loathsome for words," she said. "Now hurry. I am giving the cabman your tea this morning because he is working and you are lazing about like a dog. Hurry, hurry."

She left in high snoot, as if that were different from any other form of being for her, and I pulled on my clothes, locked the Howdah in the desk drawer on the general principle that anything so dangerous should be locked away, and headed downstairs.

"Now, then, what's all this about?" I demanded of the cabman.

"Sir," he said, "Mr. O'Connor has requested that you be conveyed swift as possible to 13 Miller Court, Whitechapel."

"God in heaven, man, why?"

"Sir, there's been another one, that's what Mr. O'Connor told me to tell you. This one beyond imagination, so the early reports suggest. You're to get to it and get details fast for the next edition."

November 8, 1888

_____

Dear Mum,

I ain't sent you the other letters but now my plan is to wrap them up with this one and send 'em all along, so you and Da can have a good laugh.

It's a happy time down here. It's been such a while since Jack has been about, we girls are sure he's gone. They say he favors a quarter-moon, coming or going, but he's missed a couple now.

Maybe he's gone to try his luck in America! Maybe Sir Charles's Peelers have done scared him off, as they're everywhere these days. Maybe he fell in a hole and got eaten by rats, the cheesy bugger.

Joe says we are quit of him, and that he's a lucky lad, because if Joe had gotten ahold of him, he'd of hammered and chopped him so bad, wouldn't be enough to put on sale at the fish market.

Anyhow, thought you'd want to know.

I did get a little rowdy tonight after my gins, but didn't have no customers, as it's raining. I sang too loud and Liz upstairs pounded on the floor to get me quiet. Sorry, Liz! Hope I didn't wake Diddles the cat! Sorry, Diddles!

Anyhow, I'm feeling right safe and good now. It's pouring out and not even the Ripper would go out in that cold soaking. I'm locked in my little room, I've had my gin, the fire's burned low and tomorrow's a new day and I am full of hope.

Best and love, Mum.

Your loving daughter,
Mairsian

CHAPTER THIRTY-SEVEN
The Diary

November 9, 1888

———

I got there around five A.M. If the world was expecting dawn, that was not yet evident. A gloom had clapped itself across the city and scored the night with bitter rain. A wind blew nails through the air, to chill the skin and the soul. The streets, even in the hustle-bustle of Whitechapel, where the ever rotating wheel of sex walk dominated, were quiet. Only now and then could a pedestrian be sighted in the shrouded element; all the Bobbies had retreated to warmer climes. Only a madman would be walking about with impunity.

Equally, Miller's Court, a city in its own way, was empty of humanity. All the bad little girls, their thighs smeared with goo, their mouths slack and distended by cocks, were abed for a little peace and dreams of prosperity. Working families, of whom there were a few so unfortunate as to share whoretown with the Judys, had yet to arise for their twelve to sixteen hours of routine exploitation in whatever form of hired slavery it was their fate to endure. I went swiftly to the window of No. 13, reached in, feeling as my fingers found the lock button. I pulled it and heard the click that indicated the spring had sprung.

That easily I was in. Her little cave was dark, though embers glowed in the fireplace. It was no more than twelve by twelve, and whoever would consign a human being to so small a space was himself criminal, though since it was Mary Jane's own fondness for the laudanum of gin that brought her there, it was she herself who was largely guilty of the crime against Mary Jane. Character, as much as system, was in play in this case. I was soon to add my meager share of woe upon the lady, but it was she herself and the society in which she existed that had engineered such colossal cruelty. I was merely the last in a long line of criminals who feasted on their victim's weakness.

I slid off my overcoat as I stood there, then slid off my frock coat. I rolled up my sleeves, letting my eyes adjust to the dark. In time, they accommodated and I saw her, her flesh translucent and delicious as she lay in slumber, breathing gently in the wan light, slightly tilted to her left, pinning that arm beneath her, her nubbin nose and pouty fount of lip oriented likewise to left. She was, however brief it would last, a picture of beauty. I could see her clothes neatly folded on the table next to her bed, along with a few folded pieces of paper, letters, evidently. She had been reading them prior to slumber.

She was not naked. She guarded her sweets against the curiosity of strangers with a flimsy chemise that fell in soft, tantalizing disarray to reveal as much of Mary as any would need to want to see more of her. I could identify the hollow of her throat, the smoothness of her shoulders, the alabaster glow of her skin, the mild flattening effect that gravity had on her two voluptuous, ripened breasts, which lay toward me, constructions so gelid of flesh and so perfect in distribution that it was all one could do not to approach and demand suckle, anything that would draw a lad close to those eternal udders and their awesome whisper of the bounty and pleasure of life.

I pulled on my gloves and snapped them tight so that the leather glowed. They had been through much, and I had one more ordeal for them to protect me from. I reached back and slipped the butcher from the belt that had secured it against the flat of my back, under my jackets. I stood there for who knew how long, lost in computation. Which angle, which hand, a cut or a stab, a hand to mouth, or would the first wound be powerful enough to buy silence through the few seconds of the dying? Would she thrash, kick, buck, twist? She looked so formidable that I doubted she'd take her passage easily.

Decisions made, I stepped to the side of the bed.

I stood over her, heard the soft murmur of her lungs as, beneath her breasts, they processed oxygen into life fuel for her, watched her occasional twitches or shudders as, unknowing, her body evinced its aliveness in its incapacity to achieve the perfection of stillness, heard a swallow, a gulp, a sniffle, perhaps some of the other ablative sounds of a body functioning properly in sleep, stretching, bending, unwinding in tiny degrees here and there. I felt the radiation of her warmth, I smelled the sweetness of her body.

I cut her throat.

I pressed her face with my right hand down deep into the mattress, and with my left—though not as strong and educated as my right, which I had so come to rely on, I found it clever enough to do the job—I began low and cut hard and high, feeling the sharpness of the blade as it bit and sliced through the layers of muscle and cartilage, the skin being nothing of an obstruction. I had grown sensitive to the feel of the blade as it engaged and vanquished tissue and felt the subtle textures of each structure of the throat as the blade intercepted them.

She struggled, and with my stronger right, I forced her facedown into the mattress and could see it distended and distorted by its friction against the yielding cotton sheets and whatever underlay to render the mattress soft. Her right hand, unregimented by her body weight, clawed a bit, grasping for life, but ever more feebly. I cut again, nearly in the same track, and her muscles fought me, she bucked and died harder by far than any of the first four, that arm whipping out in final spasm, her leg straightening, then reloading to straighten again. She was a strong girl, no doubt about it, full of life and dreams but no match for the prim efficiency of Sheffield's best steel as it glided through the ensheathed arteries and veins. Again, curiously, more blood by far than before, and I felt her struggle against the pinioning leverage of my strength, and desperate if muted noises issued from her crushed mouth. Her heart pumped her empty before it quit.

And then she was gone. It took nearly a minute. The blood soaked the mattress, and it looked as if she lay in the midst of a strawberry pastry, melted and collapsed and turned squalid by the passage of hours since the party broke up.

Now to work. Now to give London and the world what I felt those two corrupt entities demanded in their despicable way, and who was I but their humble servant? I would give the shopgirls much to natter about for a few days.

Where there was flesh, softness, ripeness, the quiver, the undulation beneath the skin, the sense of heaviness and softness, I cut. I cannot re-member much about it, only that once started, the temple once desecrated, all restraints were magically removed, and whatever darkness has wormed its way to the center of my brain had full vent and expression. I was in a delirium of destruction, as if the body were an insult to the philosophy of my life, and only in destroying it could I reclaim my sanity.

I cut her guts out. I had done so before, but in the dark alleys, in the out-of-doors, worried terribly about the arrival of the odd Peeler or stroller to give the shout, but that fear removed, I emptied her, pulling out sacks of glistening coils and flinging them about the room, where they struck the wall with the sound of a wet sock slapping hard.

I got in among the sweetbreads and cut out various shapeless dark ob-jects, pulling them when they stuck, amusing myself by placing them in odd spots by sheer whimsy, and thus built an altar of the sundered, kidney under her head, liver between her feet, spleen by the left side of the body. The flesh I sliced off her thighs and abdomen went to the table, where it lay like long shreds of cheese drying in the sun. Her thighs, whose embrace would have meant the arrival to paradise of any who found himself so en-meshed, I cut to bare bone. The same to the curve of abdomen, the well of life, removing three giant slabs to lay upon the table. I turned her a bit to breach her right buttock, and my knife savaged it as if it were the family porker on Easter Sunday, with God above looking down and smiling. I went to the neck and jabbed, using the point of my knife, since for some reason the neck's wholeness offended me, and I hacked and chopped at it, scoring it of flesh, reaching spine. I laid bare her upper chest and took her heart. It did not struggle but came readily to my hands after a cut here and there, a gross lump of muscle gray in the light, heavier than one would have thought, still bathed in the slipperiness of the blood it sent crashing through the body. I took it to my frock coat and dumped it in the right pocket, knowing that it would be well hidden by my outer coat.

My gloves were heavy with blood and smeared with near-liquid fat, my wrists and forearm speckled, and I knew spatter had arrived to my face and shirtfront; if seen, I would be the Jack all feared, Jack the Demon, unfazed by his entry into the world of viscera and carnage where so few men are comfortable. Iron Age soldiers who fought intimately with sword and spear would know what I knew, as would today a few doctors and perhaps morticians, but for most the body's integrity was a philosophical given in their perception of the world. To breach it was to turn things upside down, and that was part of the magic of my oversize impact upon the tidier world.

At last, only the beautiful face lay unmutilated. It was even composed, untouched by the horror of the body to which it belonged. That could not stand, and what followed was the lowest depravity to which I had sunk, as even I, a connoisseur of depravities, understood. Like a drunken butcher attacking a carcass, I attacked the face. I had no system, no thought, no plan, only an objective, which was to inflict as much cruelty on the beauty as possible, to offend all the poets in heaven and all the painters in hell, and all of humanity that worshipped beauty, which is to say, all of humanity. I hacked. I twisted and pulled. I sawed. I jabbed. I cut off her nose, cheeks, eyebrows, and ears. I cut her lips down to chin. I gashed her whimsically, to no design, simply looking for a new patch of skin to desecrate. Each foray left its own record of gore, and cumulatively they became a thing no longer human, so ripped and torn and shredded that to look upon was to know that there were some among us who knew no limits. It was, I thought, a good message for the coming modern age. No atrocity is beyond man, as I have proved here tonight.

At last I was done. I left her eyes intact, because I wanted all to know she had at one recent point been human. That moored the abstraction of my work in reality. It happened, furthermore, that my last burst of energy left her face tilted left, so that her stare from beyond greeted any copper or reporter who entered her queendom. It was an artistic touch, I thought, if inadvertent.

My handiwork, in the dim light, was a landscape of ruin, as grotesque as Carthage after the Romans or Troy after the Greeks, but all worked in the compass of a single woman's body. I stood back, breathing hard, bathed in sweat, perhaps awobble in my knees and aflutter in my stomach. It was time to leave reverie behind and reenter the quotidian. I knew I had to move swiftly, for soon the world would be up and about. I went to the window and peeked out, seeing that a full third of the sky was blurred by light, as the sun was beating itself upward, though behind a shelter of cloud. I could see spatters where the rain still fell, and the strong wind pushed it like gunsmoke across the narrow little court that bore the name Miller's and was soon to become famous.

I went quickly, unrolling my sleeves, sliding into my coats, replacing my steel. Fastening my scarf, pulling the coat tight to button, restoring my hat and pulling it low over eyes that showed nothing. At that point a perversity yet beyond afflicted me. I went to, pulled up, and stuffed in my pocket the letters I had noted on the table. Now I had to read them, having shattered the vault of her body so as to shatter the vault of her privacy. It gave me a shiver of extra pleasure. I, Ripper, I, Evil, I, Tomorrow, I, Forever. Then I took my exit. When the door shut behind me, I heard Mary Jane's efficient lock clicking obediently as it bolted itself closed and the world out.

The rain still fell. I thought of an old verse and appropriated it to my usage: "Western wind, when wilt thou blow, the small rain down can rain." I thought, "Christ, that I were in my bed and my love in my arms again," knowing bitterly that my love would never be in my arms again, and that the world would be—had been—made to pay for that folly.

CHAPTER THIRTY-EIGHT
Jeb's Memoir

It was the usual muck-up, only worse. At least the rain had ceased to fall, though its moisture hung in the gray air, and it left puddles and sloughs of congealed mud everywhere it could, mischievous devil that it was. In this miasma, the crowds intensified on Commercial, and the hansom driver had to whip his horse to drive it among them down Dorset. Meanwhile, newsboys with placards and clumps of papers were already selling the news, EAST END FIEND SLAYS AGAIN, that sort of thing. You had to look carefully to see the day's other big news, which is that by that insane coincidence which the God who does not exist seems to enjoy so heartily, just before Jack started hacking, Sir Charles Warren had resigned. So I supposed it could be said that on the night of November 8/9, 1888, Saucy Jacky sent off two, not just one. He was a busy lad, he was.

I pushed my way to the narrow passage by yelling, "Make way, Jeb of the *Star*," and, though grudgingly, the Whitechapelians drawn to slaughter admitted my passage. Forcing my way through the narrow passage, I entered the court, which was jammed with coppers and plainclothesmen and the usual newsrag riffraff of the Jack beat who had been accorded a close-up perch to the little room that I presumed held the body, and would perhaps be allowed a quick and tasty glimpse of what Our Boy had wrought this time out. I saw Cavanagh of the *Times* and Renssalaer of the *Daily Mail* and several others, plus the motley assortment of penny-a-liners, as well as a boy from the Central News Agency, who looked a bit shaky. If this was his first Jack experience, the buzz in the crowd ("I 'eared 'e done 'er right good this time. Ain't nothin' left but guts 'n' 'air!") suggested he'd be losing his breakfast soon.

I didn't deign to join them, and they hadn't spotted me, so I peeled off and spied my friend Constable Ross standing quiet sentry to the left and edged to him. I didn't want to confer in public, so as to embarrass him, so worked my way not to him but near him, and shielded in the crowd, whispered, "Ross, it's me, Jeb. Don't turn around, but get me up to date."

He didn't react, but I knew he'd hear and figure out a way to make the exchange easier. He turned, held out his broad arms, and began to chant, "'Ere now, back it up, then, people, let us do our work." Nobody backed up, but it brought him to whisper distance.

"Hello, Mr. Jeb," he said. "Oh, this one's a dandy, it is."

He gave me the rest. At ten-forty-five A.M. Thomas Bowyer, an agent from Mr. McCarthy, the owner of the court, knocked on Mary Jane's door to make another attempt to get her to pay rent, which was several weeks in arrears. No answer. Knowing the property, he moved around the corner, where, owing to the odd angles of the court's haphazard design, two windows permitted vision into her room. He reached in one with a broken pane, pushed the curtain aside, and saw her remains on the bed about ten feet away. Horrified, he ran back to his office, and he and McCarthy went to get the blue bottles, and the circus commenced. Now, nearly three hours later, all the stars were in accord: I noted Arnold, chief of H Division; Dr. Phillips, the examiner; and a chap who seemed to have stopped off on his way to his bank or brokerage. That had to be the famous Inspector Abberline from downtown. Abberline a hero in some accounts but not in this one, was of standoffish mien, his thinnish hair creamed over his pate, his mustaches drooping, his suit—not a frock-coat fellow, I'll say that for him—immaculately pressed.

Any mysteries that the court may have contained were by now obliter-

ated by the wanderings to and fro of coppers, reporters, citizens, the curious, maybe even, for all we knew, Jack himself. Yet for all the activity, there
was no activity.

"Why is no one doing anything?" I asked Ross.

"They're all waiting for Commissioner Warren to arrive. He will have
bloodhounds with him, and that's thought to be the latest in scientific de-
tection."

"Good Christ," I said. These idiots didn't know Warren was gone.

At that moment, Abberline's frosty gaze struck me, and he came over.
"Mr. Jeb, is it not? Here to find more avenues of criticism for our hard-
working policemen, are you, and to make the apprehension of this brute
more difficult?"

"Inspector, love me or not, allow me to give you some helpful information. I'm told you're waiting on Sir Charles. I've just arrived and have not
been sealed up here for two hours, so I know what you do not: That is, Sir
Charles will *never* show up. At least not in official capacity, because he has
no official capacity. He resigned late last night."

If Abberline had a reaction, he kept it to himself, though I thought I saw
a shade of gray pass across or beneath his otherwise grimly controlled face.

I watched as he went to Arnold, the two conferred, and an order was
given. McCarthy was called up and, armed with an ax handle, began to
pummel the door heroically. It yielded to his thunder, the door was sprung,
and the official party entered. In seconds McCarthy emerged, went to his
knees, and vomited.

"Oh, my," I said.

Abberline came out, face blank as per normal, and signaled a fellow
with some photographic equipment to enter. More science. For the first
time the crime scene would be recorded by means other than memory.
Then he came to me. "All right, Jeb," he said, "you have helped, now I will
help you. Constable, let the man pass, and we'll show him what Jack has
brought to London today."

To the jeers and catcalls of the other press boys, I was led in. It soon
became evident that this was no favor; Abberline meant to get me puking

in the yard, too, so all the fellows could enjoy a good hard laugh at my destruction.

My first reaction was not horror so much as confusion. What I saw fit no pattern. "Dissonant" was a term that came to mind: It had no melody, structure, harmony, undertone, contrapuntal melody; it was just a random pile of notes, lines, and staffs. As my eyes adjusted to the darker palette of the room, I forgot musicality and moved next to the idea of a butcher shop in which the anarchists had detonated a small bomb, for heaps and piles of meat seemed to be laying about, and the walls had been spattered crimson.

I looked upon it—it was no she but only an it—as it lay at bed's edge, and in a few seconds my mind was nimble enough to pick out the form that lay beneath the desecration.

"Holy Jesus," I said.

"Not Jesus at all," said the sanguine Abberline, "but Jack."

Had she been a pretty girl? Had she a bonnie smile, a sparkle to the eye, a pert button nose, lips of cushion and comfort? I hope memory had the answer, because as of now, no one would ever know. It was not a face at all but a kind of mask of red death, after Poe's helpful presentation of the apt phrase, all grisly and chopped, with chasms where features had been, all the more hideous for the fact that the more you looked at it, the less abstract it became, until it resolved itself into something precise and quite beyond metaphor, beyond literature, beyond even the great Poe. It took one's breath and breakfast away, but fortunately, owing to Mother's war on me, I had no breakfast to contribute to a festival of vomit; however, if nothing in my stomach raised itself up, I felt a shudder down to my knees and had a moment of wooze as I rocked back and forth. The cold of November, especially as admitted by the open window and now shattered door, kept well in control the odors that would have been choking, and that was a great aid in control of intestinal reactions, but I broke out in sweat and felt it roll down inside my suit.

"Who was she?" I uttered.

"Neighbors say a tart named Mary Jane Kelly, among other aliases. A nice enough girl, they say, no need whatsoever to do her up like this."

"Can she be identified in such condition?"

"We're looking for a Joe Barnett, paramour, who knew her best. He'll have to make the identification official. That is, if he's not the fellow himself."

"I thought it was a Jack job."

"Certainly seems as much, but the death cuts are on the right, not the left. Perhaps that's how he found her and cut her lying down, finding it the easiest way."

There was a sudden pop! and flare of illumination, as the photographer had finally gotten his kit assembled and in action. The flash device admitted the vapor of burned chemicals, whatever they were, strong enough to make me wince. He set about to take more pictures, snapping plates in and out of the box, adding flash powder to his device and the like.

I bent close and looked into the one undestroyed aspect of her visage, her eyes.

"If you're looking for the image of her killer, save your effort," said Abberline rather snippily. "Old wives' tale. Seen a hundred in my time, no image on any of 'em."

I stood, shaking my head. The great Jeb, at last with nothing to say.

"All right," said Abberline, "you've had your peek. Now be a good boy and share your findings with your peers and keep them out of my hair while we set about to learn all that can be learned until Dr. Phillips makes his own determinations."

I was escorted out and set free. I went to the press boys and told them what I had learned, and they appreciated my generosity. Though our papers were at war, we were friends and colleagues at ground level, and I shared what I had, then joined the general scramble to find a phone cabinet and get it off.

CHAPTER THIRTY-NINE
The Diary

November 11, 1888

—————

I read poor Mary Jane's letters. Perhaps as an homage to her youth in a reasonably happy family in Wales, she signed them in her Welsh baby name, Mairsian, as Mary Jane translates into that language. They seemed to be to an ideal mother, as her own had abjured contact with her whore daughter, which again seems to me a tragedy. Is not the passion between mother and daughter one of the most intense in human life? It should never be sundered, for the damage it does to both parties is incalculable. It says something for the hideous sanctimony of our age that Mary Jane's mother cared more for the pressure of society than for any loyalty to the produce of her own loins. A whore daughter was a disgrace, and the poor mum probably sat up nights haunted by ghosts of sexual imagery, which she tried to banish but could not, of what was being done to her daughter by various blackguards and rogues. And yet what is done by them is really, as Mary Jane knew, nothing. It swiftly becomes so routine as to be utterly meaningless.

The Mary Jane revealed is not without interest. She seems bright, though hardly brilliant, at least in her powers of observation and her knowledge of her own self. When I read of her weakness for the taste and blur of gin and how it drove her to destruction, I am not so moralistic (Jack? moralistic?) as to see it as a "weakness," a flaw that only discipline and punishment can overcome, if one were to make the effort, and since Mary Jane was one of eleven children, no parent could spare the time to make the effort.

Her symptoms seem to me more of a sickness than a weakness. For some reason she needs the drink, it completes her, it fills her with confidence and self-value. Thus it can be treated only with medicine, not moral posture.

Why, in our modern age, has not science created something to relieve the symptoms of alcohol longing? If we can create substances that enslave people—gin, opium, tobacco, laudanum—why can we not create substances to unslave them?

I suppose, now knowing Mary Jane, I wish to construct a dream world in which she was retrieved from her descent, and thus it was not her under the blade of my butcher. She'd had her six kids and was happily married to a mill foreman in Manchester and her brightest boy would go to university, the next would take up a trade, the third would go to service, and the three girls would marry solid men and repeat the cycle. However true that may be, some other unfortunate would have been the subject of my enterprise on November 9, and who's to say she was more or less deserving of what mad Jack served up that night.

It should come as no surprise that I am by now tired of Jack. His use is at an end. I hope to kill him soon and go on about my life, that is to say, the life I deserve, the life I am destined to have, the life I have so brilliantly contrived and boldly acted to obtain. It's fine that I feel a little down now. It's to be expected.

CHAPTER FORTY

Jeb's Memoir

My prime regret was that I had been so wrong about Major Pullham, and even as we were set to prevent him from getting what he so desired, the actual Jack was stalking Mary Jane. I cursed myself for imposing my prejudice upon Dare's superior, Holmesian deducting process. I had been a fool to open my mouth.

And all the time I was preening, feeling so brilliant, clever Jack was engineering a carefully wrought scheme: He had to make sure she was alone and asleep, which, it seemed to me, would have involved a careful observation of the site. It's true she helped him considerably, according to neighbors, by singing until she passed out, alerting any watcher that she was in her dreams and alerting Jack that he had free passage, but again, that information was available only to a careful watcher. It showed all the attributes of the well-planned military mission. Then there was the fact that a few nights before the crime, a barkeep at the Ten Bells named Brian Murphy had been coshed to death on his way home late. Most of the coppers dismissed it as just another robbery crime, maybe pulled off by the High Rips or the Bessarabians, who may have been in cahoots with Murphy, but it was odd that he was known to be conversant with the girls. Could that have had anything at all to . . . Well, it mucked up considerations and clarity, so I tended to dismiss it, so as to concentrate on the play we had before us still.

The truth is, we should have gone with Colonel Woodruff. He was, after all, the better possibility, assuming the professor's analysis to be correct (I still believed in it and him). I could not but think of a scene in which we smashed out the window as the colonel was about to strike and, seeing the Howdah, knowing the jig to be up, he threw himself toward us and, without thinking, I double-blasted him to hell. Yes, Mary Jane would be alive, yes, Professor Dare's genius would be proclaimed, but more to the selfish point, I would be the hero and have whatever it was I desired and be the success I believed myself, having achieved my destiny. No, no, all gone, and as I thought about our choice, I realized it was I who had pressed for the major instead of the colonel, on grounds that the theft of Annie Chapman's rings suggested a material aspect the colonel lacked.

I saw that I was wrong! The truth was, I didn't want it to be the colonel. No one did or could. The long years of service, the VC, the blood spilled by him and from him, all spoke to a kind of nobility, and that such a man could commit such crimes seemed not merely grotesque but in some way an indictment of humanity. It was too dark a message to be acknowledged.

Yet it had to be the colonel!

It just had to!

But how could we know?

It was here that a little bug began to whisper in my ear. Louder, louder, little bug, I need to know more. Well, sayeth yon bug, if it is indeed the colonel, and he is indeed "dyslexic," as the spelling on the Goulston Street wall suggested under the auspices of Professor Dare's learned eye, then would his condition not be obvious in his official reports or his own private writings?

If the latter, insisted the bug, the only way to obtain such was to secretly enter his rooms and make a search. But the consequences of such a foray going to disaster were so ominous and humiliating that I knew it to be a gambit I could never bring off. I began to quake even in thinking about it.

The bug had an excellent idea: Contact Penny again and see if it were possible for him to talk the colonel in the War Office into filching for just a bit of something written by the colonel in his own hand. Anything, actually. I needed a few minutes with it to see if there was some weird spelling event where letters drifted this way and that or vowels dropped in unexpectedly, as if for tea, and such and such and such.

I will spare the reader and myself the efforts it took to facilitate such an occurrence. No need to dramatize what is essentially a bureaucratic process that involved two or three meetings, much energetic flattery on my part, some shunting around and dipping up and down. We'll pass on the details, and the truth is, I'm not sure I'd remember them even if pressed.

Needless to say, it all came about, though not without considerable ramification. I found myself in a pub on the far side of the Thames, trying not to attract suspicion as I awaited my visitor while consuming a ploughman's lunch and pretending to drink (I actually only gargled) a glass of ale.

He was late, slipped in, seemed nervous and hardly military. Tall, slim fellow, rather handsome, no names involved, he was dressed in civilian finery of the higher aristocratic caste, while I chose to wear the brown suit.

"All right," he said, "Penny vouches for you and I owe Penny much, even if I don't care for the *Star*, particularly its pacifist politics and love of Irish mischief."

"Sir, I have nothing to do with politics. I'm merely a fellow working out possibilities on this horrid Jack thing."

"I would hate to believe a man such as Colonel Woodruff were involved. He served the crown with fidelity and courage for thirty-five years."

"I mean him no disrespect. I do not suspect him." How easily I had come to the lie, which was another reason to get quit of journalism before it debased me too much. "I hope by this means to exclude him from any suspicion."

"All right," he said. "I have purloined two handwritten pages from his report on events at Maiwand on July 27, 1880. I will give you ten minutes with them. You will understand immediately why he never made brigadier. He writes too well. He lacks that turgid coroner's sensibility and always takes responsibility. The brilliant staff officers who rise have the gift of evading consequences and covering themselves not in glory but in a fog of innocence. They are never responsible for any balls-up. With pen in hand, they produce a cold porridge of bromide, vagueness, flattery, and evasion. Thus Burrows, with experience at nothing but boot licking and arse caressing, is the top boy, and a hero like the then-captain is off on a flank, stuck in the muck of battle. This is why we just barely win our wars."

"I see."

"As you join the colonel, you will understand immediately that you could not have come at a worse moment. His regiment was located as anchor at the bottom of a loop the idiot Burrows had put out, against which Ayub Khan was supposed to dash his advance units and be scattered. Alas, the Khan had arrived with his main force, twenty-five thousand strong, many of them mounted, and they had the advantage of numbers as well as ammunition, rations, water, artillery, and familiarity with the territory. As for Burrows, it was his first battle, and it was enough to get him permanent placement in the British army hall of dunces, along with Cardigan at Balaclava and Chelmsford at Isandlwana."

When the snatch of report that the colonel had removed for me begins, Colonel—then Captain—Woodruff has noted with alarm that the "loop" is collapsing and that men, both British and Indian, are fleeing, many having dropped their arms. He realizes his company, E of the 66th Foot, must stand strong to cover the retreaters, else they'll be slashed down by the Khan's cavalry before they make it a fiftieth of the way back to Kandahar. This he does until in danger of being overrun, and when no more retreaters can be seen, he orders a fighting withdrawal to the village of Khig, where better cover may be found. His surviving troops take up position to repel the charging Afghans, and although I can't quote an extended passage from memory all these years later, I remember the extreme vividness with which the then-captain expressed himself, mostly its coolly precise language, so perfect for evoking a desolate and brutal day of death and slaughter in the baking sun and swirling dust of a far-off place not worth a tuppence and a crust of bread on any street corner in London. I think it went something like this, only much better:

I noted that Khig was overlooked by a hill immediately to its southern extreme, flanking our lines. Fearing the enemy in such placement would have angle advantage to bring fire, I determined to send a small unit to secure and then defend the hill until out of ammunition. I chose Color Sergeant Matthews to lead, not merely because he was sound and salty but because among my senior noncommissioned officers, he alone was ambulatory. He had only been wounded twice. He was also one of those hearty lads who enjoys a good brawl, and the more desperate the circumstances the more fun it is for him. He took twelve equally hearty lads and made his way to the top of what I privately christened "Little Round Top," to make his stand, exactly as Chamberlain had done at Gettysburg, though I doubt the pious Chamberlain could fathom Mattuwes's exquisite gift for expressive profanity, so common among the better class of our magnificent cockney warriors.

While we on the low ground turned back multiple direct charges until our Martini-Henrys were near to glow with the heat of the firing, and at one point were firing at ghosts so shrouded in dust you could only know a hit when you heard the slap of lead on meat, I noted much churn and drama atop Little Round Top. Fearing the loss of so many men and realizing that were they left up there as we retreated, they were doomed, I decided to withdraw them. I looked for an orderly to bear the message, but all were either dead or absorbed in bayonet work. I assigned myself to the task.

I had a brisk run up the slope. It is exhilarating to be shot at and missed, and it does provide energy where none had seemed available. I recognize that in the British army, officers in charge normally do not fight but merely lead, but alas, this noble tradition was not acknowledged by the Pathans. I felled four with my revolver, the last so close I could smell his stinky breath. Then, the gun being empty and my belt devoid of cartridges, I tossed

it away and devolved huenceforth to Wilkinson. Again I was set
upon by dervishes, each more colorful than the last, all armed
with scimitars of great curve, sweep, and gleam. They slashed,
I parried, attempting to rotate such that they were never able to
put a front together and attack simueltaneously. In this way, one
after another, I prevailed. Wilkinson should be commended for
its excellent craftsmanship, as even when my grip grew slippery
in the blood that close combat inevitably produces, at no time did
the weapon loosen or turn in my hand or did its edge dull in all
the cutting I was required to perform.

Making the crest, I saw that the situation was desperate. Of
the twelve, but five remained alive, all wounded. Color Sergeant
Mattuwes had taken many cuts and lost much blood. Another
charge was brewing. Picking up a rifle, I organized the survivors
into a ragged line, waited until the hordes were upon us, and
commenced a volley, followed by rapid fire. I myself, again in violation of order and tradition, fired my rifle as quickly as I could,
until it appeared the wooden forearm had been set afire by the
heat of the barrel, and a tendril of smoke rose and drifted from my
piece. I looked and it was the same for all the boys, their weapons
leaking vapor into the dusty air. Oh, for a Gatling; it would have
made such a difference. In any event, our sustained fire broke the
charge, and it appeared we held once again.

In the lull, I ordered the survivors down the hill and off they
went, spryly, happy to be sprung from Little Round Top's death
trap. I must say that however much our arms failed on the bat-
tleground that day, no man of Company E, 66th Foot, retreated
before being ordered to do so, and when ordered, did so in good
order, keeping fire discipline throughout the whole process and
applying bayonet where necessary. What superb soldiers they
were, and how privileged I was to command them!

As for me, I could not leave Mattuwes to the fate of the
Afghan women and their cruel knives. Lord Jesus, how I hated

what those vicious harpies did to our wounded boys, as I had seen far too much of it. I managed to get Mattuwes up and, with him leaning on me, the two of us made it down the hill. At one point, three more Pathans joined the scrap and I was forced to send them to their happy warrior's paradise, although I took a bad cut on my arm. The last fighter was on me with his dagger when I managed to get the bayonet, grabbed off the desert floor where a retreating fellow had dropped it, thank heavens, into him. I saw no other place to enter but his neck, cutting arteries and veins and producing torrents of a blood as red as my own. To see a man die at such close range, nose to nose as it were, is a terrible thing, no matter how fiercely one hates the enemy. Somehow I got the sergeant back to our redoubt and immediately issued orders for a retreat under fire.

Game little bastard, our Huw, eh? He charges up the bloody hill, kills three men with pistol and three more with sword, commands a last volley to drive the beggars back, sends the other men off the hill in the lull, and then drags his wounded sergeant down the slope to safety. Halfway there, three brigands jump him, but he's swift enough to cut them all down—I'll bet that was, as we say in Ireland, one hell of a donnybrook—while nearly getting his arm chopped off. Having sent the enthusiasts with the scimitars straight to hell, he continues to drag the sergeant, who, though I don't know because further adventures were contained on pages I did not have, I dearly hope survived. You may hate the soldier's cause, but it is hard to hate the soldier.

Yet that is not why I was there, not to admire the guts of one Huw Pickering Woodruff, but instead to check his spelling. And so I looked carefully, hoping there would be no anomalies, and for a time, so it seemed. But then: for henceforth, "huenceforth." And for Matthews "Mattuwes." And "simueltaneously" from simultaneously. Under certain circumstances, perhaps fear, fatigue, confusion, or other battle pressures, he insisted upon inserting a "u" for "e" and moving the "e" into the next available vowel position, or if none was available, sticking it in or forgetting it altogether. What would make such a thing happen? He couldn't even see it. It was some bizarre crick in the mind, brought on by who knew what, meaningless except as an identifier.

And the rest: the hatred of the Afghan woman, easily generalized. The calmness in the face of the close-by cut to throat and the gush of crimson it produced. It was all there.

"And what have we learned?" asked the colonel.

"Nothing of note," I lied. "He is indeed a brave man. Do you know much of his background, may I inquire?"

"Welsh-born, Sandhurst grad, third son of a Methodist minister, not much money in the family but a strain, clearly visible in the colonel, of brilliance. Now doing nothing but dictionary work, whereas in a sane world he'd be a cabinet minister."

I nodded, though tried to hide how disturbed I was by the unassailable logic I had uncovered that the bravest of the brave was indeed Jack the Ripper.

"Now I shall be off, Mr. Jeb. Jeb, what kind of name is that, by the way? It seems I've given up some confidential information to a man whose name I do not even know. Come now, sir, at least explain yourself."

"It's a journalistic trope," I said. "I was called as a youth various things, sometimes even Sonny. But I was in the register as a junior, even if my father was a drunkard and I cared not to be known by his name, so to some I went forth by his initials, which were G.B. My sister, a wonderful girl, could not keep the two letters apart, and in her mouth they elided into Jeb. So that is me, and for the record, sir, since you have asked, the moniker would be Shaw, George Bernard Shaw."

CHAPTER FORTY-ONE
The Diary

Undated

———————

Egress

I slipped out of the court, down the narrow passageway

and took my right to whatever street it was.

I cannot remember

though it was but hours ago. Had a plague come

as I was to work, and had it taken the rest of humanity?

It seemed I walked for days through the gray drift of the inclement,

my eyes squinted against the sting of the dagger-like drops,

a shiver running through my body as it tried to adjust to the cold.

Emptiness and echo everywhere, bits of paper blowing loose and tattered,

a dog with slattern ribs and no hope in its rheumy eyes, the smell

of garbage, shit, piss, and of course blood riding the cold breeze.

But in time, I saw them. One, then two, then three or four,

humans, that is, gradually assembling to face the day and whatever hell that meant.

I saw a teamster drive six mighty steeds down the street to deliver barrels of whatever,

I saw a copper standing vigilant, on duty however ineffectual, I saw a scatter of children,

full of energy and long and fast of leg, perhaps off to school or mischief,

I saw a mum or two, in a hansom carriage I saw a gentleman, maybe that was a Judy off the next block, maybe the small hunched gentleman a barrister or a barrister's clerk,

a butcher, a baker, a candlestick maker, a tinker, a tailor, a beggarman, a thief.

None of them so much as acknowledged me.

And why should they? After all, I was one of them.

CHAPTER FORTY-TWO

Jeb's Memoir

I told Professor Dare about my confirmation that the colonel had shown signs of the dyslexia condition that was the primal clue in his quest and that, as predicted, he had emerged from a morally nourishing humanitarian background.

"For my part," I said, "I was not checking on you. I just had to know. It is unsettling to put such suspicion against so heroic a man. Something in me finds it unsavory."

"Would you adjudge that physical bravery trumps deep moral evil? Is that your position?"

"No, of course. That not being so, however, does not make it anything to celebrate."

"All right. I concur. Let us be sure, then. Have you another mechanism by which he may be tested?"

"No, of course not. It's just that—" Then I said, "You would not say that unless you did."

"Something has occurred to me. It's somewhat dangerous, I suppose, and neither of us is particularly heroic."

"Enter his rooms and search when he is absent?"

"I haven't the spice for that, and I doubt you do, either. We are not cracksmen but amateurs, particularly in the action department."

"True enough. So have you come up with something Sherlock Holmes might have conjured?"

"That damned fellow again. I must read that book you seem to think so highly of. As for this trick, it's rather too basic for this Holmes's elegant genius. You must merely ask yourself. It's there, if you ponder rigorously. When is he vulnerable? When might his guard be down? When would he be unlikely to pull knife and cut his way out of an issue?"

I thought. I thought. I thought.

"His opium habit," I finally said. "The drug puts him in a dream state. He may babble or confess or scream in guilt or cry in remorse. We do not force it upon him, he welcomes it and sees it as routine. But I could be there."

"Is it in you to do so?"

I knew nothing of opium, its element, its practices, its dangers. But at the same time, I could not proceed with leverage against a man who had a VC without more proof that I believed in.

"I will find it in myself," I said.

I was not without resources. I tutored with Constable Ross, assuming correctly that in his experience on the streets and within London's lowest dives, rookeries, brothels, beer shops, gambling halls, and dogfighting arenas would be an acquaintanceship with opium dens. I was right, and thus armed, I waited outside and down the street on a bleak block on the margins of the Dockland for the colonel to show up, as the professor had insisted he would. Indeed he did, his banty stride giving him away, his energy in contrapuntal rhythm to the grimness of the spot somewhat amazing.

It was so West End melodramatic that I felt I was viewing something lit for the boards. He slid against a wood door in an otherwise blank brick wall and knocked, and just like onstage, a slot opened in the door, his identity was confirmed, a code was exchanged, and he was admitted.

"All right," said Ross, who'd accompanied me on this trip to the demimonde as a buttress against my own terror, "now wait for him to get his pipe going, for the first calming effects to take hold, and then approach."

"Indeed," I said. "Damn, it's cold."

"It is, but soon you'll forget the outer world. Now repeat to me what I have said."

"I must partake of the first and even the second draw. The Chinaman will be watching. If I don't, thugs will beat me and toss me out. From that point on, I can choose to not inhale but merely hold and release the vapor into the air and cut my consumption remarkably and only half descend into madness. I will feel effects, no doubt, dizziness, mild hallucinations, color exchanges, shape-changing, but nothing a man with a strong mind can't handle."

"What else?"

"Ahh"—drawing a blank, and then—"oh yes, the drug will hit me like a rugby tackle. I cannot avoid that, as I have no tolerance. It's not Mother Bailey's Quieting Syrup. I must not panic and instead let it take me. The stuff liquefies under heat, so one must be careful not to spill the pipe, as it will be a giveaway."

"Very good, sir," said Ross.

"And you're sure I'll write 'Kubla Khan' when I emerge?" I said.

Ross didn't get my little witticism and only said, "I don't know about that, sir."

We waited another twenty minutes and no more customers arrived.

"All right, sir, now's the time, there's the good chap."

"See you in a bit, or so I hope," I said.

"You'll be fine."

I drew my mac tight, my hat low, and headed across the cobblestones to the doorway, pushing my way through low drifts of fog that had blown in from seaward. It was getting more West End by the moment. Excellent job on the dry ice for fog, Mr. Jones!

I slid in the doorway and rapped three, then two, then waited. The police intelligence was good, and in a few seconds the slot opened and I saw a pair of slanted eyes.

"*Bawang hua,*" I said, which means, I believe, "flower king."

More good intelligence. The slot snapped shut, the door opened. I slid in, hammered immediately by the drifting pall of fume in the red air, as all the lanterns were tinted in that hellish shade.

"A pipe, old man, and none of that for-shite Turkish sludge. Your finest Persian silk, if you please." It was gibberish to me, but again Ross had advised well. The Chinaman looked me up and down, but I'm guessing to him occidental faces were as formulaic as Oriental faces are to Englishmen, and at any rate he could not classify me as miscreant, so had only the density of my brown tweed to go on, which he found acceptable. Then he led me down the hall where a Laskar brute who looked as if he chopped heads for a hobby sat grimly under a sign that said PIPES AND LAMPS ALWAYS CONVENIENT. A beaded curtain hung in a doorway to the left, and he led me through it.

I beheld the glare of red lanterns, and in that illumination I saw supine men and heard the shift and sigh and squirm of their presence, and my eyes adjusted. The reddened vapor drifted in the air; the place seemed squalid and damp and dry and hot at once; groans, low moans, giggles, and coughs rose softly. The smell, oddly, of toasted nuts was present, though it had disturbing undertones. Glow worms burned against the dark, reddening with the draw, diminishing as put down. My eyes found better focus, and what I beheld was a hall of profound stupor, men beyond movement or care, spilled across wicker divans, their bodies lackadaisical as rag dolls, all pretense of rank and show completely abandoned, all jaws flaccid, all eyes fixated on eternity or infinity or the place where the two somehow met. I could not make out the colonel, but I could not make out anyone.

The Chinaman poked me and jibber-jabbered, small paw out. When I placed in it the standard three and six for a thimbleful, he looked disappointed, so I passed over another tuppence to show goodwill. He led me, I shed myself of hat and coat, and he bade me go supine on my own divan. There were four of them placed about a red lantern glowing in the center on a brass-plated table. I lay for a few minutes, letting my eyes further refine, not daring to peer about, as it wasn't the sort of place where friendly eye contact was encouraged.

In time, my host returned with a long clay stem, slightly curved, which at its end held a small cup. Ross had provided me with a veteran's retinue of tricks, so I drew the cup close to eye for a check, scraped the brown paste inside, drew off a little under my thumbnail, and brought it to nostril for sniff and to tongue for taste, as if I were capable of discerning the difference between Turkish and Persian. It had neither odor nor taste, as far as I could tell, but I nodded and winked at the deliverer and he sped away.

I placed the pipe cup atop the lantern and waited for it to absorb enough concentrated energy to begin to smolder. I had been instructed that it was impervious to live flame; only the application of pure heat, as passed through the conduit of soft metals, ignited it and began its alchemical magic. Obviously I was being watched, so when I saw tendrils of vapor, I put it to mouth and applied suction.

Nothing happened. Odd, Coleridge had seen far-off lands, his imagination liberated by the stuff's mythical ability to provoke, but I saw nothing. I blinked again, thinking, Opium: overrated.

And then . . . My, my, isn't *this* interesting. It was a sense of pleasure that can only be called acute. My skin felt soft, my body warmed pleasantly. In a few seconds the acute metamorphisized to the chronic. Pleasure was general. I seemed to forget who I was and why I was there. I lay back and for a second believed I had found paradise. Drat! Too early to make such a claim, for the next second completed my journey through the upper levels of poppyland and brought me to the destination the opiate had selected for me.

I was in a concert hall, alone, though well dressed. Upon the stage was my sister. The applause was tumultuous, although again I was by myself in the ranks of red-plush seats, and I was not clapping. Lucy, the adored one, accepted the enthusiasm of the invisible crowd with grace. She was quite lovely, in a rather low silk gown, a small but firm bust with a string of pearls about her swan's neck. There was serene confidence on her beautiful face.

She sang. An aria from Wagner, I think, though one of his gentler, more romantic ones, nothing with dark clouds and northern war gods bashing each other with sword and hammer. Her voice was exquisite, but the odd thing was that each note emerged shimmering from her throat and found a place in midair above her, moreover then transfiguring into a bird of bright plumage. I saw nightingales, peacocks, blue parrots, proud ocher hawks and falcons, even some prehistoric saurian birds festooned in the colors of the rainbow. In time an aviary of dazzling brilliance had taken grip on roosts above her beautiful head, and the radiance of the color had a kind of translucent sparkle to it, so that it caught, refracted, redirected, and amplified the lights of the hall.

She stood, crowned. The glory of the music was enshrined in the pigment of feathers above her, the whole thing rather awesome. It seemed to be a scene from some sort of devotional. It was whoever God may be, adoring her formally.

I had always hated her. Where I struggled, she soared. Where I bumbled, she triumphed. Where I was unloved, she was worshipped. She had been sent here, I was convinced, to make mockery of my many failings, my lack of talent and industry, my crude ways, my slithery mendacity, my awareness that the music that was the river of life in our family would not be my destiny, while it would be hers in diamonds.

The astonishment was how proud I felt. Shorn of my fury at her position of supremacy in the family, I felt the cascade of love. That was my sister, my flesh, my family, my blood up there, and it reflected so well upon me that I could not but take immense contentment from it.

Yet into this demi-paradise—my true expression of love for Lucy, which I have heretofore hidden from all, most especially myself, the depth of her talent, the perfection of her beauty unsnarled by jealousy and fear— came at last the snake, except it wasn't a snake, it was a large brutish boar (an opium pun? bore? boor? brother?), horned and snuffling, grunting, leaking filth and offal, his unorganized ways suggestive of violence.

He wandered, sniffing, munching, probing his way across the stage. Lucy did not panic nor race to safety. Her love abideth. She reached to his hideous head and stroked it, knelt to it and switched to Brahms, something delicate and soothing. She tamed the savage heart of the beast, which happily went to knees and then full supine, placed its great snout upon the floor, and began to snore rapturously, lost, perhaps, in its own opium dreams. These images, I might add, were as vivid to me as any in reality. What they symbolized, I have no idea, if anything at all. Yet they have stayed with me and will, I believe, forever.

I blinked and found myself back in the den, in the drifting pall of red haze, watching as now and then someone drifted this way or that. I was sure my trip had lasted but a second or two. However, once reality more or less returned, I became bored. If one does not smoke opium in an opium den, what is there to do? There is otherwise no entertainment, so the answer is nothing, and I did nothing for an hour or so, pretending to draw a lungful of the gas into my system now and then. Generally, however, I was quiet, and after more than a bit of time, I felt secure enough to look about in the low light.

I could not see him, but I could not see anyone or anything except the seething red vapors. At a certain point, a fellow across from me decided he'd been voyaging through the universe enough for one evening, and rose and stumbled out. That opened a vantage, and across the room, at another grouping of four divans, I made out the silhouette of the colonel's derby, read the shortness of his form, and by that method identified him. His face was still, somewhat blocked from view by a large bat that hung off his nose. He seemed oblivious, as oblivious as all of them, and I wondered if he were dead. But now and then I'd detect motion, see a pipe rise, its stem put to mouth, and the glow suffusing the air above the cup signifying a deep inward draw. He must have had big lungs, as his ingestions were heroic in their length and depth. He also must have had terrible dragons in his brain, if it took that much to soothe them.

More eons passed. In other words, ten minutes went by, even if those ten had no place in real time, and two of the smokers from the colonel's little collection of four got up to stumble out. As they shambled toward the door, the Chinaman attended them, and in this brief little circus of activity, I slipped off my divan and took up one next to the colonel.

Finally I got a good look at him. His face was rather dour, as if gravity had a special grudge against him and pulled his flesh downward at twice the going rate. Morever, the large bat that dominated his lower half turned out to be a spectacularly droopy mustache. It must have weighed a stone three. His eyes were lightless, he stared at nothing, he looked at nothing, he said nothing. He was utterly still.

I lay next to him. He was in a very deep place. I did notice one hand was closed into a tight fist, suggesting it gripped something, proof of tension unusual for this place, since the point seemed to be languor as an expression of collapse and escape.

By now it must have been close to dawn. I hoped poor Ross hadn't frozen himself stiff. It was getting to seem rather pointless, as one learns nothing from a man so far gone as the colonel. But at a certain moment, he stirred.

I turned upward to his face and saw what might be called a just-after-battle stare, the stare of a commanding officer who sees his men slain and gutted in the sun.

He sensed my attention; our eyes met. I could seen pain in his. The drug, which offered such merciful surcease, had at last worn off. He was naked to memory in that moment, perhaps not yet hunkered down behind the Spartan war shields of self-discipline and willed stoicism that kept him sane. It was a rare moment.

"The blood," he said. "There was so much of it. Blood everywhere, the poor girl. You see, it's on me. I was the one. Her guts, her face, all butchered up, all cut to ribbons. Me, see, I was the one who done it."

"Sir," I said, "are you all right?"

"I killed her, you know. No one else, me alone. God help me, it was a terrible thing, but I could not help myself."

Though this confession should have stirred horror in me, it inspired compassion. He was so in pain.

"Sir, would you like me to get you some water? Perhaps you have a fever and need a doctor?"

He wasn't listening. He opened his hand to examine what he gripped so hard in his fist, and I nearly fell out of my own divan. He held Annie's rings! I had to make certain I wasn't the one hallucinating, so I closed my eyes hard and long, then opened them and made certain I saw what I saw, which was indeed two rings in his large palm.

"She wore them both, you know," he said. "It fell to me to take them from those still, bloody fingers. I am beyond damnation. Hellfire awaits, and rightly so."

With that he arose, turned, and walked out.

CHAPTER FORTY-THREE
The Diary

November 19, 1888

———

The funeral. It seemed that once the papers recounted the thoroughness with which I had hashed poor Mary Jane, she became London's favorite martyr. It was not to me to point out that, alive, she was invisible to the gentry who would not so much as spit in her direction, unless of a dark night they were tupping her sweet loins for a few pennies' worth of ejaculate deposit, after which it was back to nothingness for her. In death she became magnificent, a star, however briefly, more so than any actress or opera singer. They had not read her letters to her phantom mum, they had not wondered at her addiction to demon gin, they had not missed her brothers and sisters.

When it turned out no money was available to send her on, a churchman named Wilson, the sexton of St. Leonard's Church in Shoreditch, put up the sum. I'm guessing he thought it would get him to heaven, and I'm guessing that it will, assuming heaven exists, which it doesn't. According to the *Times*, Mary Jane was laid into polished oak and elm, a box, that is, with metal fittings. A brass plate would accompany her into the dirt: "Marie

Jeanette Kelly, died 9 November 1888," so that He above would not get her mixed up with another Marie Jeanette Kelly, unless that one, too, had died on the ninth.

Sexton Wilson's crown and pounds and guineas went rather far: They obtained two wreaths of artificial flowers and a cross made up of heart seed, which went upon the coffin, which was put into an open two-horse hearse to be drawn all the way from the mortuary to St. Leonard's.

The crowds—I was one of the thousands, in a dowdy bowler, lumpy dark suit, and black overcoat, looking like the clerk of a clerk who clerked for a clerk, but a really important clerk—were quite hysterical with grief. A crowd is a fearsome thing. If you are in it, you cannot fight it, and I did not. It frothed and flashed and rolled and rumbled, filling all the streets around the mortuary and the path from that grim little house of the dead to the slightly more prominent St. Leonard's, whose steeple, though a piercing construction, was no match for the Christchurch missile that soared Godward. But it was, as the shopkeeps say, nice.

Absorbed in the bosom of the crowd, I did note something of interest and must mark it down. In this case it was the women who were the driving force of that mass of flesh and sadness called The People, and you could feel them yearning to be close with Mary in her box, to touch it somehow. What possible motive did they have? To assure themselves that they were alive and that she was not? Or to remind themselves that as long as Jack was about, their own grip on life was fragile? No, I think it was something vaster, more universal: They invested in her, poor Welsh-Irish whore given to song when drunk and knowing no way of saying no when a thruppence was offered by a cad who wanted to have a spasm of jizz with someone other than his dour old lady; they invested in Mary Jane, shredded and splayed in her box, as Woman Universal. Somehow, I don't know how, it would link up with the suffragette movement and other uniquely feminine power dynamos who are only now finding the voice and the means to express themselves. Mary Jane was the eternal woman, I, Ripper, was the eternal man, even though sex had been quite far from my mind as I ripped.

I watched from afar as the coffin was removed from its transportation and borne by four men into the church, where presumably Sexton Wilson and the St. Leonard's parish priest said the proper wording in our tongue and the ancient papal one, sufficient to consecrate the poor bird and send her on the next step.

In and out of the hearse, her journey was lubricated by gestures of universal pain and respect, as hats came off (including my own, for however unholy that may seem, I could not stand against the will of the mass without inviting severe repercussion), and from the women came such a wailing as had never been heard. "God forgive her," they insisted, as if their words could so convince Him, whereas I believed that though He did not exist, had He, He never would have had need to forgive, for unlike our social lords, he understands that one does what one must to get through the lonely, dark night.

In a short time, it was over. She was transported by the same four back to the hearse and her intimates—the paramour, Joe Barnett, her landlord, McCarthy, and a batch of soiled doves who claimed to know her well—traversed the churchyard to clamber into the mourning carriages the sexton had acquired for their use, and the whole parade began the second part of its journey, to the St. Patrick's Catholic cemetery in Leytonstone, six miles hence. At this point, the crowd began to fall away, I among them, though I stuck with the procession longer than most. But there seemed no point in watching the final act, as Mary Jane was slipped beneath our planet's surface, there to begin her sure return to the elements of chemistry we all share.

Besides, I had more important work ahead. My campaign was almost complete. It had but one trick left to be brought off, and it was essential that it be done quickly, that is, within the mourning period, as again, a quarter-moon approached.

CHAPTER FORTY-FOUR

Jeb's Memoir

How much more settled could it be? That discovery lifted tonnage from my shoulders. It was clear at last. Now to action.

At exactly ten P.M. on the night of the full quarter-moon, the colonel emerged from his building, an immense pile of brick and morticed stone called Fenster Mansions, on Finsbury Street, and began that instantly recognizable walk. I was on one side of Finsbury, the professor on the other, and at first it was easy to keep up and keep in contact with the banty little chap. You would know him in an instant; one wondered how he could pass anonymously on his missions. That walk was the walk of a fellow in full command of all faculties, a stout-hearted, unquenchable fellow, born heroic and determined to beat all schedules to his destinations, actual or metaphorical. I couldn't get a good look at his face, for he wore his bowler jammed seriously low, almost to the brow line, and he hunched as he proceeded. But it was familiar, I suppose, from a hundred odd nightmares: the man in black, dowdy and anonymous, yet with purpose, the knife concealed, swift of hand and sure of cut. Many a time it had jerked me from sleep. And now: no dawdler he, no meandering fool, no drifting sprig on the current. He plowed ahead, our colonel, cock of the walk.

It was on Bishopsgate that the trouble began, for he had a shrewd way of disappearing into crowds, and being of limited stature, he went invisible or at least under flag of camouflage rather adroitly. At least three times I lost sight, had a cold spasm of fear icicle its way into my colon, cursed myself for stupidity, but then caught sight of him and hastened to reacquire enough proximity to observe and trail but not to give myself away.

As for being followed, he gave no sign of notice. It was not in him to go cautious and look about nervously. At the same time, he didn't walk directly anywhere. At Bishopsgate, as he coursed through the City, he took a hard turn down Houndsditch, then down another crossing street, evading Mitre Square, where poor Cate had taken the knife, and headed straight to the guts of Whitechapel. It was as if he had a course already set; he knew where he was going, and it was something well prepared for. I thought of the professor's profile of the man: As a scout and raider, he would be aided by familiarity with terrain, knowledge of police pattern, drift of crowd, density of horse traffic, availability of midnight thrush for the plucking, and having settled those details far in advance, now had no doubt as to destination, approach, and execution.

But if he had a plan—and he must have—it was not evident from his journey through and about Whitechapel on that frosty night, a clear one, with the silver arc of lunar glow above and the soft coal-gas-fired lamps below, and the bright spears into the street and awash the sidewalks from the pubs and beer shops, and the forest of shadows created by the locked-down costers' stalls and the herds of anonymous citizens, Judys, Johns, walkers, the banal, the afraid, and the drear, who gathered and meandered thickly everywhere. It seemed he was driven to set foot on the pavement of all streets. The names flew by as he rushed along, and I could tell that my physical hardness was eroding, as a rock to wind and sea, and my breath came hard, and yet still they flashed by, it just went on and on. Underneath my layers, the heavy Howdah pistol was flopping against my ribs, bringing bruise, while its strap, around the other shoulder at the neck, weighed into the flesh unpleasantly. I was a disaster in brown suit!

The streets were crowded, the costers' stalls on the big ones impeded vision and progress, a dip across the lane put a stream of horse traffic as further impediment, I felt the bump and jostle of others on the pavement, it was all too much. I first gave up on Professor Dare, as I could not keep track of both him and the colonel, and the times when I was merely guessing at the colonel's direction and progress became longer and longer. At least twice, as I sank into despair at my failure, I happened to catch a glimpse of him a block farther along or farther back, and so I was off again. I was huffing, sweating, my knees trembling, most of the world gone to fizz and spark in my vision, and I knew it was only a matter of time before I lost him. Another girl would die, nothing could be done. I guessed he did this on all his forays, against the remote possibility that he had been found out. It was a professional's edge: Assume you are known and act accordingly, that's the safe track. Never assume you are unknown and expect success without effort or caution.

The break finally came sometime after eleven. It was the fourth time I had lost contact with him, and when I made a rush across New Road just above Commercial, almost getting trampled in the process, I looked at where I expected him to be and he was not there. I guessed where he'd gone, and when I got there, he was not there. I looked up, down, east, west, south, and north, I changed vantage points, I achieved some height by climbing steps to a stoop, I dashed down a little street, but still: He was gone. I looked for the professor. I could not see him, either.

I cannot tell you what a fool, a failure, I felt. The whole slough of despond emptied its contents upon my head, soaking me in woe. I sat there, feeling the chill as my body temperature dropped in the lack of effort, I sucked for oxygen, having gone without, I yeaned for a sip of water to quench the Arabia that lay behind my lips, I heard the drumming of my heart, I felt the jostle and thud of other passengers in the night as they voyaged by me on the sidewalk, and I faced the reality that he was gone and I had nothing.

I felt the heaviness of the Howdah gun under my left shoulder and felt the strap cutting into my right shoulder. I pulled my slouch hat lower, as if to protect the sweaty nape of my neck from a breeze that evinced itself with aggression, and of all things, I could hear Mother saying, "George, I told you you'd never amount to a thing. Now, be a good fellow, put this London business behind you and return to the export-import business in Dublin, marry a nice Protestant girl, and settle down. Leave the glory to Lucy." Perhaps I had a moment of Jack madness then, because I realized what pleasure it would be to smash the woman in the face with a balled fist.

However, I quickly put down that reverie and resolved to action. I pulled myself ahead through the crowd and against the aches, pains, agonies of doubt, and self-disparagement, and in time, came to Whitechapel where it intersected with New, turned up it, and headed toward the Aldgate East Station, where Professor Dare and I had agreed to meet at eleven-thirty P.M. if we lost contact with each other or the colonel.

Along the route, there was no sign of either man. I found a pub, seeing that I had more time to kill, and ordered a bottle of ginger beer to break up the ick that had coagulated in my throat. My plan, such as it was, was to reconstitute on the fuel of the ginger concoction, then return to the streets and circle on the hope that I might encounter one or the other. My secret dread was that poor Dare would interrupt the colonel carving, attempt to intercede, and for his trouble be carved himself. He hadn't the gun that was so necessary to control the transaction.

Circle I did without incident, becoming random watcher as opposed to aggressive follower. I dipped into many black alleys and passageways, hoping to encounter Jack on the job, but instead came across banal business relations between the odd John and Judy and, feeling as if I had breached another's privacy, departed forthwith. None of the rutters ever noticed me, thank heavens.

At last it was nearly eleven-thirty P.M., and the traffic had somewhat lessened. Though Judys could be seen about, and Johns as well, it was clear that even the randiest of the randy had either had his jizz festival or given up for the night. The chill had to do with this, for no man wants his backside exposed to the cruelties of the north wind; besides, it does much to convince a chuzz to remain at attention. So there I was, ambling disconsolately toward Aldgate East Station, set for rendezvous and redeployment elsewhere, when I saw him.

It was the walk, that bounding, leaping strut, still going full blast as if his internal engine were full of blazing coal, and looking neither left or right, not bothering to check behind, he took a turn into Aldgate East Station, that low structure with mansard roof and the affected symmetry to the architecture of an elegant country house. It took itself all too seriously; after all, it was merely a shed for boarding carts, not the royal court of the Sun King. But more Versailles than shed, it wore its sign, METROPOLITAN RAILWAY, rather proudly above the portico, which was overdecorated in the French Empire way, because it could be done, not because it had to be done.

I paused. I grabbed my pocket watch and saw that it was on to eleven by twenty-eight after and the night's last train was due in two minutes. Was he dipping in to meet someone? It made no sense. No Judy would be arriving for duty by that last train, the station platform would be deserted, what could the man want except, perchance, to use the loo? I hesitated, and then my eyes lit on a moving figure as it dashed across Whitechapel Road, unimpeded because the horsedrawn traffic had become so light, and recognized by lope, style, fashion, grace, and intent Professor Dare, his tweed cloak afurl on the breeze, his slouch hat low and tight against that same breeze. He had triumphed! He had stayed on the job while poor Jeb had not been up to task! Now, that, I thought, was a hero.

He dipped into the station, unarmed, and I knew that I must get there fast to provide support and use the gun if necessary.

It took me under a minute to get to the station, and it was deserted. I raced to the bank of ticket windows and found them all closed, because there were no outgoing trains requiring tickets, and the man at the turnstile had departed, for there were, of the same reasons, no tickets to be punched. I negotiated the blockage, climbing gamely over with far less grace than ragged hurry, got to the other side, and plunged down some stairs.

Around me, gigantic steel beams buttressed the complexities of the best brick craft in the history of mankind, challenging the ages to destroy them and aware that they would win that challenge. I felt absorbed by the hush of the place and its jags of light and shadow where electrification, rare in the East End, sent a latticework of illumination across my view.

The stairs yielded to the ironwork bridge that spanned the tracks beneath, and I raced down it, amid the intricacy of strut work held stout by fist-sized rivets and baked under bright black paint. It was like being swallowed by the Industrial Revolution itself, and I could hear my footsteps echoing against the iron grid of the flooring. Echoes were everywhere, for I had entered a cavernous space, more cathedral than station, overtopped with a vault of pane glass now dark for lack of sun to penetrate it from above, sustained by yet more latticed girders, all of it heavy with the smell of combustion, for the engines ate coal like hungry monsters, belched smoke and soot and grit, which had already turned the shining structure ancient in effect, with smears of carbon accumulating on glass and polished tile far faster than the architects had calculated. I came to a vast stairway and raced down the glowing marble, to be deposited on an endless platform two feet above the tracks. It was a vast and empty space, unpopulated except by the wild disarray of shadow, and far away, at the end of the platform at the exact entrance to the tunnel through which fled or raced the mighty trains, were the two men.

It was as if they were in primitive combat, like two ancient priests set to battle for control of the cult and policy for the future: the man of science and rationality and the man of pure rage and gift for action, until he was nothing but action. Man of future, man of past. From whence we came against whence we were going. Were they about to fight? Good Christ, what would such an outcome be, the colonel's skill and evident muscularity matched against the larger size of the other man? The colonel would have tricks, the professor size and weight. The colonel would be fast and mean, but the professor would have righteousness on his side, and although God clearly did not exist, I felt that if He did, He would step in on the side of the professor. If He did not, I would come to the professor's aid with my trusty double-barrel, which I withdrew from its holster and positioned in my hands so that my thumb abutted both hammers and could quickly adjust them to active condition. I would in my small way speak for civilization, justice, the powerless and truly unmourned unfortunates, and all the high moral noble causes that man has fought for. That is, assuming I remembered to cock the damned thing!

I raced toward the combatants, who, I could see, were circling each other, wily antagonists caught up in the drama of whether it was best to spring or counter-spring. At that point the colonel chose a policy. It was the policy of the spring.

Like a ram, he built off the power of his thighs a lunge that carried him hard against the professor, finding that man ill prepared to meet such a charge. The professor yielded, falling backward and almost immediately setting himself, though not with much in the way of confidence, and they butted together, came apart on impact, closed again, grappled, arms flailing, feet shuffling, leverage sought, strength avoided, both at full strength bent hellaciously against the other. It was not boxing, which I had seen and admired for its science. There was no science, only strength pitted against strength, wit against wit, and in a second, the colonel used some trick to go under and around the larger man and bring him with a thud to earth. The professor took the fall with grace, rolled, and came up to face his antagonist, who had not found footing enough to pursue advantage, and the two crashed together again, all limbs flailing, hands snapping, gouging, each trying to grab something. They were too close, I saw, to unlimber classic punches, so it was all about strength of grip and the clever slipperiness of escape.

It was also horrible. Each face was gnashed in fury, and each had bared fangs, and each set of eyes was clenched into slits behind which each gauged the other, looking for weakness. I got there and heard "You insane bastard, you monster!" from the professor as he leaped and closed on the smaller man, while the colonel shimmied loose and found freedom to throw a hard punch in the midriff, which straightened the professor but did not stop him from landing his own blow flush on the man's ear, banging the head backward.

They were so caught in their crazed intensity that they had not even recognized my presence. I flew at them, turning at the last second to deliver a cross-body impact with my shoulder and knock them both back and apart. The colonel slipped but was nimble enough to regain his footing.

I leveled the pistol at him. "Hold, sir, by God, or I'll dispatch."

"He has an ally!" screamed the colonel to God. "Mad but with an ally."

"Thank God, Jeb," said the professor.

"Sir, draw away so that you are not covered by the gun," I said, and then the colonel moved against me so fast it was a blur, and in a second I felt the gun yanked hard from my hands. He pivoted to thrust me between himself and the professor, who lurched at me, and for just a second the three of us were in some insane Laocoön of struggle and tangle, the gun the serpent with which and for which we all struggled, and there was then a moment when the colonel managed his trick and stepped back, leveling it, screaming, "Now, by God, you madmen, back and desist or I shall unleash the volley!" and as he turned to rotate the gun to cover the professor, he was the fraction of a second late, and the professor gave him a mighty two-handed shove, and back he went to precipice and over, where he hit with a thud on the tracks, the gun flying away.

I meant to regain it, but in that exact second the colonel, not three feet from and two feet beneath me, was illuminated in the glare of a locomotive's lamp, and in the next fraction of a second—no watch existed fine enough to measure the speed at which all this transpired—he was gone and the raging engine whizzed by us in its own penumbra of blurred speed, a great burgundy and bronze beast, gleaming and glowing, all parts grinding, syncopating pistons, spraying contrails of steam and spark and sulfurous fume from several sources. It was still a hundred yards of platform from full halt.

If the colonel screamed as fate took him, I do not know; I heard nothing, so loud was the roar of the engine.

And that fast, it was over.

I stood, mind slow to calculate or react, rooted in abject paralysis, gibbering for air and words, finding neither, aware I had the trembles bad, and felt the sweat literally gushing from my body. When I returned to sentience, it was as if nothing had happened. I was standing next to the professor on the platform, the train was at full halt, bringing a sense of light and civilization to the emptiness, a few last passengers were ambling off, hurrying to get to bread, bed, or drink. No alarm had been raised, no crisis seemed to have been unleashed, no whistles, no Bobbies, no rush of witnesses, no panicked crowds.

"He's gone," the professor said.

I had no words.

"He went down too close to the engine for the engineer to see him, and it's too much machine for a tremor to be felt. They'll find him in the morning. Come on, now, let's depart."

"Should we—"

"No," said the professor. "If it becomes known now, it's out of our control, and then it's anybody's story. Besides, let the little bastard have his half-column in the *Times*, and everybody will read it as a suicide, and there'll be a week of 'Poor old Woodruff, VC and all.' Then we can do the right proper job of telling the city the story of Jack and what we wrought and why no more gals will be sliced apart, and we will get what is coming to us."

It made sense then. It makes sense even now. Holmes always gets his man.

"Let's hence," he said, bending to secure the butcher knife that lay afoot.

And we went out of the station into the cool December air.

CHAPTER FORTY-FIVE

Jeb's Memoir

After the turmoil of the night, I didn't think I'd ever sleep again. But I did, dreamless and dark, if anything with the feeling of simple gliding through the night sky. Still, my mind was so provoked, it awoke me within a few hours, so I took a bath, gobbled something of breakfast, happily ignored Mother who happily ignored me, and took a hansom by ten A.M. for the professor's.

We had said nothing on the way back from the station, as if the ordeal had drained us of all cogency. At that point, I felt too worn down to attempt to make sense of plans or consider ramifications. I considered the same of the professor. He himself answered his door and led me to his study, where he'd been having morning coffee. He offered me the same, but I was too agitated to settle down to civilized ritual. My poor mind was aflutter with doubt. "I turn to you for insight. It would help me so much in the construction of the story. What was driving him? How did his mind work, that it could be so heroic in the one quarter and so malevolent in the other? What was his motive?"

"I have puzzled myself. It was something Beneath, I think. Remember how I believe that there's always a Beneath to a written piece? Clearly such a phenomenon springs from the fact that the mind itself has a Beneath, which we may not feel, acknowledge, understand, but which guides us."

The colonel, the professor said, never really left Afghanistan. He was forever in the war. "Give the man credit. He understood that he was damaged, he understood that he was dangerous, and perhaps more heroic than the action that earned him his VC was his struggle against the demons that had infiltrated his Beneath. He tried to adjust, he tried to discipline himself from his impulses by concentrating on his Pashto dictionary, or if his dreams, anguish, memories, physical pain got really bad, by smoking the opium. But it was no use. He lost in the end."

I was astonished how empathetic Professor Dare was in regard to a man who had within the past twelve hours come within a hair of murdering him. But such, I felt, was the greatness of the man. Under his sarcastic exterior, his own Beneath was compassionate and humane.

"He was haunted by the screams of young soldiers gutted in the night by Afghan women in the retreat from Maiwand, and he had to bring surcease to it. He had to make the screaming stop. Vengeance, even symbolic, was his final recourse. He could not deny it. So he went out on his own missions and did to them what they had done to his men. It was a narcotic. It took more and more violence to satisfy him. We cannot really blame him; he is, after all, us. He is the consequence of empire."

"Yes," I said, "that I understand."

"Thus, *motive* is not a meaningful term here: *impulse, undeniable desire, total and compelling need*, those terms are more realistic."

"He was, then, Jekyll and Hyde?"

"I think Louis Stevenson simplified by making each unaware of the other's presence. No, no, it's a matter of integration, merger, that somehow the Beneath takes over and manipulates the sentient. The Beneath, I believe, is like the iceberg, the seven tenths that lurks beneath the water. It is therefore the more powerful, the more masterful, the more brilliant."

"I suppose I see," I said. "I hope I can make the world see."

"I'm sure you will."

"Then I'm off to the Sholes machine, and I will—"

"Now hold for a second," he said. "I do have, since you have convinced me that this is the course you mean to pursue, a suggestion."

"Yes, of course," I said.

"This is a precipitous time for your enterprise, and I wonder if you are aware of that fact."

"I am aware that the public is desperate for an end to the menace and terror of Jack," I said.

"Not exactly. As of December of last year and more so since June of this year, a great many members of the public, particularly people of our sort, who matter and determine the course of our nation's mental drift, have come to believe in the moral and intellectual authority of the amateur detective. As a figure, he is enlarging in the public imagination, even while that of the professional police detective has diminished. You yourself, to judge by your comments, are in his thrall. The horror of Jack and the utter failure of Warren's coppers to halt or solve it has perhaps multiplied this condition. The people want a heroic detective to solve it. In their bosom, they yearn for a man to emerge who has insights, understandings, analytical and deductive powers, forensic attributes, a knowledge of darkness and its methods, and the will and righteous energy to project such on the malefactor while protecting the public. The public yearns for Sherlock Holmes."

"Of course," I said. "I had admired the creation. I see him and Watson in us, I must admit."

"I have at last read *A Study in Scarlet*, in the Ward Lock edition. It seems to have entered that zone of private but vast awareness. Because Conan Doyle, an opthalmalogist, as I understand it, created the ideal detective. Sherlock Holmes: a man of science, a man of deduction paramount and refined, a man of calm, overall a man of complete rationality who sees what others have missed and is able to put facts in their proper order and context."

"Exactly," I said, quite pleased that the living Sherlock Holmes had validated my insight.

"The structure is also interesting. He himself does not narrate. He is, rather, observed by a junior partner, a fellow of keen observation as well as astute literary powers. This would be Watson, an MD actually, recently retired from military service. Holmes solves the case, Watson tells the tale."

"You are suggesting—"

"What I am suggesting is that before you write your story, you reread Conan Doyle's. In that way you will learn how someone has done it masterfully, the rhythms between the narrator and the hero, the careful placement of clues, the cycle of interpretation and revelation, all reported in oak-solid, dead-lucid English prose. That is, read *A Study in Scarlet* again and then write your story in the penumbra of its influence. Thus will you prosper. Thus will you do justice not only to Dare and Jeb but to Polly, Annie, Long Liz, Cate, and poor Mary Jane, and in a way, even to poor Colonel Woodruff, God rest his tormented soul."

"Excellent advice," I said. "I shall forthwith. We must publish the day after the funeral, even if they have not found the body. It is imperative that we name the colonel, so that the police may open his rooms and there, no doubt, find Annie's rings, perhaps a knife, perhaps some pickled bits of Judy, some bloody rags, all signs of his perfidy, making our case air-tight."

I stopped at Mudie's on New Oxford and bought the Ward Lock & Company edition of *A Study in Scarlet*.

And so it was that afternoon that I reintroduced Mr. Holmes and his amanuensis, Dr. Watson, to my life. It was a cracking good read. Conan Doyle wrote clearly and directly, without affectation or ruse. Moreover, he had a gift for vigorous narrative that perhaps approached Louis Stevenson's or Dickens's even at this early stage of his career. I roared through the thing a second time, transfigured and pleased to be in the company of two such interesting gentlemen. While I saw a lot of Holmes in Dare, however, I saw very little of Watson in myself, except by structure of the story. Where Watson was wise and well salted, I was impetuous, ambitious, perhaps too brilliant to do anybody any good as an assistant, having a need for my own way and the prime spotlight. Knowing that, I told myself, would be very fine guidance for the long article I was about to write, for I would be able to control my love of self enough to let the true hero, Professor Dare, have center stage. It would benefit not only him but me as well.

When I was finished, I found myself exulted. I saw exactly how the professor thought the book would excite me to my best effort, as it was sure to do—I was so filled with energy, I was ready to buckle down right then and there!—but I had to admit there was more to Holmes than met the eye. Conan Doyle, as seen through the behavior of Mr. Holmes, was clearly a wise man and had thought at length about darknesses of the heart and the tricks to which so constructed people will go to achieve their own ends, and the responsibility of he who investigates to see the truth and not the illusion created. "There's the scarlet thread of murder running through the colorless skein of life, and our duty is to unravel it, and isolate it, and expose every inch of it." That was indeed what our real-life Holmes and Watson had done in re: Jack, was it not? That was what Professor Dare and Reporter Shaw had done, was it not? We had skillfully understood what Jack's acts inferred of him as to experience, type of mind, and skills available, and using them as our guideline, we had uncovered a pool of such men and tested our thesis to the point where we had found the man with knife in hand—and stopped him by the intervention of good fortune. Subsequent information would only prove our point. It was a triumph of cool rationality over clumsy attempts at mantrapping, the only thing the police departments could manage.

I was most furiously proud of one thing. It was Holmes's own description of method, and I saw how brilliantly we—the professor, that is—had put it to work. "Before turning to those moral and mental aspects which present the greatest difficulties, let the inquirer begin by mastering the more elemental problems."

And what would the most elementary aspect of the case be?

What made Jack Jack?

It was not that he killed, as many have, and will, kill. That is the sad part of human nature. That was the scarlet thread. No, it was that he did so silently, efficiently, and then *got away*.

That was the elemental essence. He got away. How did he get away? Well, the professor had many ideas, all pertinent: He planned well, he had superb night vision, he had experience in night work and knew just how much moon he needed to give him advantage, he reconnoitered his sites, he was slight, so he could get out of tight spots as in Dutfield's Yard, he was—

That was it. His slightness was key to the whole thing, and the professor had foreseen that, applied it to the case, and unlocked it. It was clear how Colonel Woodruff had used his slightness.

One thing lay ahead. I had to go to Dutfield's Yard. I had not seen it, having spent that night first in Mitre Square, for the second of the "double events," being the end of poor Cate Eddowes, and then on Goulston Street, where the dyslexic "Juwes" clue had been left. I must get to Dutfield's, I thought, and have a look around and understand this aspect of the elemental.

I awoke merrily, had a nice breakfast and even a half-decent chat with Mother, who was all alight—knowing nothing of my triumph—because Lucy would sing a small role in *La Traviata* at the great Paris Opera House. She was beginning to make her way in the professional world.

I think that breakfast was the peak of glory for me. I remember thinking, Oh, but Mother, if you only know what your dim son, the failure, the disappointment, the bearer and inheritor of his drunken father's dreams, has been up to and what glories await him.

It was brisk out, and I decided to walk. I had not gotten far when I came upon a crippled old gent by the wayside, his mangled leg affecting his whole progress, sending tremors through him, and suddenly he seemed to stumble, and I reached magnanimously to help him. He pivoted not to accept aid but to ram a Webley revolver into my guts.

"Ought to blow a big, bloody hole in you, sir," he said, "and dance a jig as you empty out."

It was Lieutenant Colonel H. P. Woodruff (Ret.) (VC, KCB).

III

IN THE FORESTS OF THE NIGHT

CHAPTER FORTY-SIX
Jeb's Memoir

"You are dead," I gasped.

"It'll take more than a locomotive to kill this old buzzard. I still have a cat's reflexes. I went flat, and the beast lumbered over me. I crawled to safety."

"Then, sir, you are Jack the Ripper."

"I am no more Jack the Ripper than you are Queen Victoria. What madness has Dare infected you with, you bottlehead? Convince me you're his dupe and not his partner, and maybe I won't plug you before I plug him." He rammed the hard barrel of the revolver deeper into my flesh.

My mind, as it so often does when confronted with naked aggression, simply collapsed into shards. I was worthless.

"Bunny brain! Cat ate your tongue, the whole thing? Now, you walk with me over to Russell Square all nice and happy-like, and we'll sit under a tree and have a little chitchat. Move to get away, and I'll finish you here."

The gun—and the limp—disappeared under his cape; he straightened and pushed me gently across the street. I could see the vaulted arches of the elms ahead. We entered the park and found a quiet bench. The cheek on the fellow. He held me at gunpoint in the middle of the most civilized square in the world, and all about me, ladies and gentlemen, boys and girls of the British empire, wandered to and fro, oblivious to the mortal drama in which we were locked.

We arranged ourselves, though I could make out the shape of the big revolver under his topcoat, easily at hand. He could draw and shoot in a second.

"What is Dare to you?"

"We have been looking into the Ripper. Our investigations have indicated that he is you and that you are mad. You have Annie Chapman's rings, I saw them in your hand in the opium parlor. You confessed to killing her. 'The blood,' you said, 'her guts were pulled out.' More, you share a spelling impediment with him in the form of the rogue vowel U you dropped into the Goulston graffito."

"You are a buffoon," he said, "a tweedy twit with aspirations of grandeur and the sense of a frog in a hot pan. The rings were brought to me by my betrothed, Emily Standwick, God bless her gentle soul, who was murdered and butchered by Sepoy on the road to Lucknow on the first night of the Great Mutiny of 1857, thirty-one years ago. I have carried them with me ever since, as I have carried the image of what was done to her. Yes, I smoke a pipe, because sometimes the memories are too savage and I long to end them with a large piece of lead from the revolver. "

"A convenient story."

"Easily verified."

"Dare is—"

"A madman."

"Sir, he has a profound moral vision of the world, which he hides behind witty cynicism. But he believes in the possibility of world peace and the equal sharing of material goods. He believes that differences in language keep us apart."

"I've read his book," he said.

"He believes in universal language, universal culture, no national disciplines, no reason for war or poverty, no hate, no jealousy. It's utopian, I admit, but it shows a profound moral sense."

"Ask the girl chained in his cellar how profound his moral sense is."

I let this ominous declaration hang in the air a bit. No need to prompt him. The pause was theatrical, and when, with his superb sense of timing, he'd milked all the drama out of it, he proceeded. "Allow me to tell you a thing or two about the moral Professor Dare. About five years ago he was done with the theorizing. He decided on an experiment. The idea was to take an unfortunate off the streets who swallowed her H's, washed when she could, and perhaps even once in a while said yes to a thruppence offered by a fine English gentleman for a lean-to in a dark alley."

I said nothing.

"So he finds a cockney waif. And he works on her. And I do mean works. It wasn't easy. It wasn't just a few voice lessons. He had to tear her down and build her up again new. It was a battle almost to the death: screams, threats, hysterics, sleepless nights, even those chains in that cellar."

As he spoke, I could see it. Behind Dare's languor and sarcasm, a crazed zealot could have existed. The sarcasm, the wit, the grace—maybe that was all camouflage for the elemental Thomas Dare.

"Where is this going?"

"After six months of grinding, he reintroduced her to H. 'In Hertford, Hereford, and Hampshire, hurricanes hardly ever happen,' over and over again, night after night, until the poor child was in hysterics. He brought her to the miracle of the vowel A. 'The rain in Spain stays mainly in the plain.' Over, over, over yet again. Mad to begin with, he made her half mad, the poor child, with no defenses, no place to run, no inner strength. And yes, he did it. I must say, near-on destroying her, he beat her until she spoke like a true lady of means. Not only that, cleaned up, put in fashionable gowns, she turned out to be, God in heaven, beautiful. He squired her about town for a bit, showing her off, showing off his triumph. Was he using her for immoral purposes? You're a man. You tell me."

I let this sit where it was. I had no comment. It disappointed me how right it felt, as ascribed to Thomas Dare.

"I hope you're not waiting for the happy ending," said the colonel.

"Please continue."

"It seems another man was involved."

"She met someone?"

"Someone was living with Dare. Nobody got a good look at him, but he was gone every day, then up every night late, writing in his attic room. Anyhow, it seems that even as Dare fell in love with his creation—"

"Pygmalion," I said.

"This isn't literature, you bloody fool. This is what's real and dark in the world. This is what bites. The core of the situation is that Dare's in love with this girl, but in the end the other man cannot stand what Dare's doing to her. Maybe she reminded him of someone he knew and loved thirty-one years earlier. So one night, the other man gives her a pile of money and urges her to run away, to get away from Dare because she is too much Dare's toy; he will crush her to nothingness. Dare wants a statue, not a wife. She knew that, she saw that in him. So just before Dare is about to announce his betrothal to Miss Elizabeth Little, she disappears."

I tried to justify it. If true, it meant merely that Dare was a bastard, but he had tendencies toward being a bastard anyhow, as that is so often the penalty of greatness. "I'm trying to think how this fits in. It speaks to character, not action."

"Character *is* action," said the colonel.

It was here that it finally occurred to the idiot inside my head to ask about the mysterious "roommate" who seemed to be the servomechanism for all the turmoil.

"I say, even for having spent so much time reading, you are thick," said the colonel. "*I* was the other fellow."

I must have gulped or swallowed or blinked, for I could not have encountered this without an appalled reaction. The colonel, however, kept his disinterested duty face square to me, betraying nothing.

"If you"—I struggled—"if he, if . . ." and then I was out of ifs and left with only one. "If he knew you, the profile preceded the murders," I blurted. "He knew it all, your skills, your career, your spelling deficiency, your strong vision, your courage. He knew of your rings, your memories of a young woman butchered. The murders were informed, shaped, sculpted to fit the profile. Then . . . who committed the murders?"

There could be but one answer.

CHAPTER FORTY-SEVEN
Jeb's Memoir

Three days later, I invited Professor Dare to meet me at Dutfield's Yard, the murder site of Elizabeth Stride. I chose four P.M. It was a brisk December afternoon, though I was impevious to a lot of treacly Christmas nonsense.

The professor seemed chipper enough. He was the jovial ghost of murders past, I supposed, and I made an effort to match his easy glee. He was in tweed, as usual, with a warm slouch hat of wool keeping his magnificent head of blond hair warm. He smoked a jaunty pipe, his cheeks were pink, and he radiated happiness and satisfaction. I don't believe I'd ever seen him so at peace and content with the world.

"Yes, Jeb. Please tell me what you need. I am at your disposal."

"Sir," I said, feeling the chill as we stood next to the wooden slats of the door in the gate that led into the yard where poor Liz had been killed what seemed so long ago, "I was not here that night, so I need some guidance if I'm to put this one together in a story. It's my weakest account."

"Yes, yes," he said. "But do recall, I have not been here, either. Perhaps the two of us can work it out."

With that, we opened the gate and confronted Liz's falling place, which was now bare and prosaic, a simple joinery of brick wall to the pavement of the yard. Looking inward, we saw not much space, hardly justifying the name "yard," hardly bigger than Miller's Court, just an opening between the crazed and unplanned construction that marked the East End where the bricklayers designed the city on the fly. We could see a couple of small shops and, deeper in, a stairway running to the balcony of a small cottage. Nothing at all remarkable.

"I make it here," I said, pointing to the spot where it seemed certain Liz had been discovered, just beyond the rotational arc of the open right-hand door.

"So it is."

"Jack has killed but not desecrated. He is caught by an interloper who has just opened the gate. He freezes. The driver of the cart, sensing his pony's sudden reluctance, jumps off his wagon and strikes a match. He sees the body in the cone of light. He goes racing off to alert colleagues, and Jack slides out in the narrow gap between the pony cart and the gateway."

"That, I believe, is how the papers had it," he said. " Do you have another idea?"

"Hmm," I said. "I'm just astounded how he was not spotted as witnesses and coppers arrived. The driver did not hold on his alert. He returned with three colleagues from the club almost immediately"—I pointed to the two-story building that formed the northern boundry of Dutfield's Yard beyond the gateway, and its doorway just twenty feet beyond where we stood—"by way of its main entrance, which fronts on Berner. It was quite full, as some sort of anarchistic meeting was taking place, and in under a minute more of those men poured into Berner Street and were very soon swarming thickly on the area. Meanwhile, the coppers were quick to arrive—street constables, that is—plus many people from Berner, and farther up, from the well-traveled Commercial. It was hardly an obscure spot."

"I cannot answer for what the newspapers say. Perhaps you should discuss this with your friend Harry Dam, when he is not busy constructing an auto-da-fé for the Jews. But what you are describing does not seem to me impossible. Remember, he's slight, and thus the pony won't shy at him, thinking him a child and fearing no whip from him. He's slight enough to squeeze between the cart and the gateway and be gone quickly."

"I suppose," I said, "but the pony is already alerted, already skittish, by smell. It seems just as likely that the sudden appearance of a figure from the dark, child-sized or not, would have caused the nervous beast to create a disturbance."

"Who knows the minds of ponies?" said the professor.

"Fair enough," I said. "But does it not strike you odd, Professor, that we are hard upon the single building in London that is regularly trafficked by revolutionaries, secret policemen, spies, the whole monkey house of Mittleuropean battle between autocratic governments and the men who would overthrow them. This building would be, would it not, full of intrigue, plot, plan, various stratagems and deceits, to say nothing of talents for escape and evasion?"

"Have you been talking with someone?" he asked. "That does not seem like your sort of intuition."

"Not at all," I said. "It just came to me in the writing."

"Ah. In any event, what difference does it make, ultimately? They're all politicals. Such men would have no interest in a fellow cutting up whores, because it advances no revolutionary cause. They are a hard breed."

"Indeed. However, all those men, no matter of what faction, have one thing in common, which I would term 'fear of raid.' They are haunted by raids, have memory of raids, have themselves escaped raids. The raid spells their apprehension, execution, imprisonment, or exile. It means that all they stand for is destroyed. Theirs is a dangerous universe and a fragile one. So does it not stand that they would have an escape from such a place? They are not the sort to be caught like rats in a trap. Come, let's examine."

We walked into the unlocked building, entering by way of that side door onto Dutfield's Yard, finding ourselves in a dingy corridor, which in one direction, back, seemed to lead to a printing shop from the mechanistic sounds, and in other direction, toward the street, where a kind of foyer must have offered a stairway that presumably led to the large meeting hall upstairs. There the workers were bellowing out a hymn to worker solidarity much sung in radical nests across Europe. It was so loud its vibrations seemed to be banging hard off walls and wood. Instead of joining the chorus of heroes, I took Dare to a door just a bit down the corridor toward the foyer. It, too, was unlocked, after the anarchists' happy assumption that property is theft and no hindrance should be placed in the way of those in need. I was certainly in need. This in turn took us down a few steps into a cellar, which contained what cellars contain: crates, rusted tools, refuse, scrap, rat holes, spiderwebs, dust, the smell of dankness.

"Hardly a highlight of one's London tour," said the professor.

"Let's see, however, if it contains treasure, which may be found in the most unlikely of spots."

We poked about, undisturbed. It was rather dark, so the going was somewhat difficult as we bumped and bumbled about until I said, "Hello, what's this?"

I pointed to the cement floor, where squibs of candlewax had accumulated, as if much illumination had been required on this one spot.

"Very Sherlock Holmes of you, sir," he said. In a second I pushed aside the nearest crate and found it easy enough going. It slid three feet to the right and, when moved, revealed a ragged but ample hole chopped into the cement, though all its excavation debris had been carefully swept away. The two nubs of a ladder stuck beyond the edge of the hole.

"I would say tunnel. Isn't this interesting? Built, I'm sure, to save the anarchists from goons hired by the tsarist secret police or foreign agents being hunted by our own Special Branch. Wouldn't you think that a brilliant tactical mind like the colonel's would have understood the high theoretical possibility of such a structure existing and looked for it? Perhaps that is why he chose this spot, knowing a secret escape was possible."

"Capital thinking," said the professor. "It existed theoretically, now it exists actually. By God, this is a wonderful discovery."

"Shall we see where it leads?"

"We have a moral obligation to do so."

I went first. It was not a long descent, perhaps ten feet, and it led to no vast underground chamber but into what appeared to be a kind of abandoned sewage containment, though of ample height and width for a man to nearly stand. One would expect a lantern at the base of the ladder to assist the escapees, and there it was, a primitive candle-powered implement whose contribution to illumination would be more helpful to morale than practicality. As the professor eased his way down, I found matches carefully wrapped against moisture, unwrapped them, ignited one, wincing at the flare, set the wick aflame, then closed the glass front of the piece, which magnified its vividness somewhat. Lifting it in my left hand, I exposed the gap in the ancient terra cotta through which the anarchists had battered their way to gain access; sweeping the lantern about, we saw that the length of space ran about ninety feet or so. At the same time, the miasma of abomination rose to our noses, for at one time this was a privy, to Romans, to medieval Londoners, who knew? Perhaps it contained Samuel Pepys's shit or Messrs. Johnson and Boswell's. It was said London was undergirded by abandoned tunnels and chambers; the anarchists had simply encountered one and put it to use against emergency. We were not alone, however, for then we heard the skittering or chittering or scrabbling or whatever word may be used to describe the sound of large numbers of rats. We had entered their kingdom, though the firelight drove them away from us, not from fear, I'm guessing, for what would five hundred such creatures fear from us, but because the blaze of light disturbed their delicate darkness-adjusted eyes.

I pointed to the end of the vault. "It's a big crapper," I said. "Romans and Normans must have shat here. I'm guessing that comes out in some abandoned building in Fairclough Street."

"Yes, yes," said the Professor, who had fully entered the place. "The colonel dips in the side door while the pony cart driver runs for aid on the street, and first a few, then a lot of, anarchists spill from the main door. He's vanished in seconds, makes his way to the exit, and is out unseen very quickly. From here it's but a ten-minute walk to Mitre Square, where he has ample time to track and do his horrors to Cate Eddowes. Yes, this is a brilliant discovery, Jeb, and it will do well to enhance the accuracy and drama of your piece."

"Yes," I said, "but here is my problem. This is the only secret passage in any of the murder sites. I have examined them exhaustively. Neither Buck's

Row nor Hanbury Street, certainly not Mitre Square with its several passageways out, and nothing in Miller's Court could be construed as a secret passage. Only here. What is interesting is that, as you and I have just proved, there is no limiting provision for size in achieving passage. Full-grown men fit quite nicely. So the most elementary and the only empirical point of your profile—Jack's slightness—is thereby disproved. That, furthermore, is the only empirical index to his identity. All the rest are cognitive, based upon inference of what he knew, what he learned, what his skills would be. But the whole theorem rests upon the conviction that his size was essential to the commission of the crimes. Yes, he was slight, but it had nothing to do with anything. A man my size or even yours could have escaped after killing all five without difficulty."

"Possibly, then, I was wrong. I seem to have been right in all other interpretations, if I recall correctly."

"Indeed. It comes to nothing, does it? Oh, unless one *knew* that the colonel was slight, and inserted that condition into the profile as a means of specifying him among the others."

"I must say, this seems an odd direction."

"I have learned some things since last we spoke, which will perhaps explain the oddness of my tangent. I have learned, for example, that under your commanding personality and capability to light up a room, you are an angry man. You have been exiled from the polite society of academics and intellectuals on account of unsavory rumors concerning your behavior. They now shun you and pay you no attention."

"I bear them no animosity, I assure you. Our ideas diverged. They're too reformist, and they find me too cynical. It was always an uneasy fit."

"Not as I hear it. The precipitating event of your exile was a bizarre 'experiment' that you undertook several years back, rumor of which left many uneasy. You invited a London street girl—a whore, certainly, like Annie and Long Liz and the others—into your home. You and a colleague labored with her night and day for well over six months, and it was desperately hard work for both you and the girl, a Miss Elizabeth Little, I believe. It brought you to the point of madness and violent anger. Assumptions include beatings, sexual improprieties, various profligacies. As for your colleague, you attacked him at one point. That, too, frightened off all your friends. They abhor physical violence. He now seems to have vanished."

"So he has," said the professor.

"So, too, has the girl. Did she flee to the country, go to America, commit suicide? No one knows, but it seems like the old Greek tale of Pygmalion, where the sculptor fell in love with his sculpture. Except in your version, you had much congress with the poor child."

"This is beginning to disturb me. Are you making accusations?"

"Another question might well be: Who was your colleague? I believe it was Colonel Woodruff, who had come to you upon mustering out from mutual fascination with the mechanisms of language. He lived with you while you were working with Elizabeth. When he saw how you were abusing Elizabeth, he objected, and under his advice—and I'm betting with his money—she fled."

"I loved them both. They betrayed me. That is all. Not much of a tale."

"It never occurred to you that she might fear you rather than love you. It never occurred to you that Colonel Woodruff would—selflessly, as was his style—send her away because he feared what you might do to her. That is why you attacked him at the university."

"So dear Jeb isn't as simple as I thought. Not simple but slow, too slow."

"You see how it follows. You devise a 'profile' for the crimes that indicates no one but Woodruff, down as far as the two rings he carried with him since 1857. So detailed were your plans that you approached me even before you had unleashed the J-U-W-E-S clue, which you used to snag me. And how snaggable I was. But in order for the proof to hold, there must be murders. What good is the profile without the murders? It follows that the murders were informed by the profile, not the other way around. That being the case, there can be only one killer."

He said nothing.

"Dr. Ripper, I presume," I said.

"At your service," he said.

"Your madness and your brilliance are in perfect syncopation. Your madness kills to express your rage at her betrayal, and your brilliance finds use for it by constructing a 'Ripper' who terrifies the city and whom you track and vanquish. You get everything. You take everything from the weakest of all women on earth, the most powerless and degraded. You have your revenge on the colonel, who besides being murdered is then to be eternally damned in history. You want credit as the man who discovered and killed the Ripper, and it is my job to hand it to you. You get everything in return and make yourself in a society that has exiled you."

"It's too bad you're so late to understanding," said the professor. "Elizabeth was, too. She never quite apprehended me. My score isn't five, it's six. She was the first. She will not step out of the shadows to reveal my friendship with Colonel Woodruff. Nor will you. A few others got in the way. The colonel, of course, a bully here, a bartender there. All done in a good cause, I assure you."

I saw his hand disappear under his coat and reappear with a butcher knife.

"I will find another newspaper fool," he said rather calmly, as with the weapon he was controlling the action. "I will get what I deserve, as I have paid back those who betrayed me."

"You, sir, are despicable."

"Who are you to judge me, you tiny man? You offer the world nothing. I offer everything, from my genius to my higher morality to my designs of utopia. But to employ them I must rise, and rise I will and rise I have."

I beheld him then: creature of nightmare, avatar of destruction, murderer from the dark hole of the Beneath, radiant in self-love and madness. Jack flagrante, Jack in excelsis, Jack *gloria mundi*, Jack rampant, Jack *fortissimo*. He was all that and more. It was Jack the Ripper, fully bloomed and unleashed, the butcher knife in his right fist, held high as he meant to step forward and drive it deep into me, knowing his strength was so much greater than mine, knowing how and where to place the blade, knowing that he had the physical skill to make the thrust and cut a hundred times out of a hundred.

"Look on me, you fool. Know who I am. It is worth your life to enjoy the privilege of a meeting with Jack. You are nothing before him. I, Ripper, now take your meaningless life and go on and on and on. Jack is forever."

He had never been Sherlock Holmes. He had always been Mr. Hyde.

He stepped toward me, cocking his arm for the killing blow.

The bullet struck him in the shoulder, exploding a mist of wool fiber and atomized flesh, destroying it. He spun, dropping the knife as his beautiful tweed sleeve went limp, began to pulse and leak as it absorbed a tide of crimson, while the echo bounced and died along the bricks, dust fell from vibration and the rats, their tiny eardrums dashed by the sound, began to chitter and frisk.

The colonel stepped from the darkness, his Webley smoking in his hand. "You are arrested, sir," he said.

Jack the Ripper looked upon us, the blood running through the fingers that tried to stanch its flow. "A trap, then," he said. "Artfully done, between writer and soldier who engineered another miraculous escape. My compliments, Huw, but then you always were the hero. And I loved you, Huw, as I loved her, but the two of you hurt me and thwarted me to the full extent of that love."

"Thomas, I loved you as well, but your genius turned to madness and evil. I could not save you. Now, sir, you must pay."

"Not at your hand. I believe the dark prince already sends his minions to fetch me."

He was right. The skittering turned to a scrabbling and then a clamor as five hundred clawed sets of feet advanced in their regiments and battalions, engorged by the smell of fresh blood. The vermin army hit him hard and began to scale his legs.

Squirming, seething, raging, Jack-mad in their own bloodlust, the vermin surrounded him and began to mount his legs, to crawl up his coat, to slip under his jacket and into his shirt. They crawled upon each other's backs in their greed of flesh, becoming a new beast, featureless like a surge of animate pelt heaped at his legs, alive with squirm and slither and scrabble and squeak and chitter. It was as if he were being swallowed in the maw of some inchoate predator, in ravenous action so malleable and supple that its form was liquid. And though he beat at them, his blows were useless against the blood-mad truth of nature, raw, cruel, indifferent. The rats swarmed to and overwhelmed his face and began to eat it. He screamed, and such a cry it was, containing encyclopedias, whole languages, of pain and horror.

Colonel Woodruff shot him in the head and down he went, still.

I blew out the candle and we made straightaway to the ladder and in seconds were back to the surface of the known world, where December had declared its early darkness. We exited the club, where the chorus of song had drowned out what traces of gunshot might have made surface, went from Dutfield's gates, and made our way toward Commercial, where, among the bright lights of the costers' stalls of apples and cheeses and bright cloth, the hubbub of the beer shops, the jostle of the ladies and their suitors, made even more vivid by Christmas excitations, we reentered what was called civilization.

"All right, then," said Colonel Woodruff, "it is done and you have your story."

"I am not sure I will write it," I said.

"It's a free country, sir. Write or not, as you choose. But let me push an argument against you. It's one thing if Jack is a foreign monster, a mad Russian or Jew, one of the *them* we seek to educate and civilize, charging only everything they've got. It is quite another when he's one of *us*, of fine family, produced by our best universities, born on high and lived on high in a fine house on a fine street, published, respected, influential. For that man to have been raving evil might provoke some to sense corruption in the system. And I am wise enough, it may surprise you, to understand the system is indeed corrupt. But it is also necessary, at least for now, while our species is in its infancy. So if a smart lad like you and an old buzzard like me know it, no harm is done. If the ignorant, thus far obedient, but ever volatile masses know it, mischief is loosed. And who knows where mischief leads?"

"I will consider," I said.

Twenty-four years have passed, and I have finally made up my mind.

I got to the professor's house well after midnight. I had no keys, for who would have checked what was left of him? But the door gave to my shove, and I paused in the foyer, listening. If his Scots housekeeper were there, she was sleeping. Gingerly, I climbed the steps and turned in to his study.

I did not dare light a candle or turn up the gas jet. In time, however, my eyes adjusted to the dark, and what I did not see in detail, I saw in memory. I recalled all the gizmos he'd designed to help overcome his fellow man's speech pathologies, whether a terrible accent that anchored one forever to the bottom of society, or a stutter that made a man gobble like a turkey in getting a simple declarative statement into the ether. Such a noble calling, so perversely betrayed.

I made my way to his desk. All the drawers slid open save one, and with a screwdriver picked up for that reason, I pried and poked, felt wood splinter, and it popped open. Inside was nothing but a single volume.

I picked it up, made my way to the window, and by the wan light of gas lamp from Wimpole outside, made out that it was a journal, perhaps a diary, with dates setting off each entry. It took no genius to comprehend that the dates aligned with the murders.

"When I cut the woman's throat, her eyes betrayed not pain, not fear, not but utter confusion. Truly, no creature can understand its own obliteration."

That was how it began.

I paged through, seeing accounts of them all, Polly, Annie, Long Liz, Cate, and finally and most horribly Mary Jane. Even a poem! Four letters were folded into its pages; they seemed to be from some poor girl to her mum. Later I would learn who she was.

I rolled them up, slid them into my jacket, and quickly exited.

The night was fresh and clear. I didn't look for a hansom but walked the mile and a half to my mother's house, considering what to do next. I had the world at my fingers with the diary. I could reveal and publish and become rich, famous, powerful, godlike, whatever.

Yet the colonel's words weighed heavily on my mind. Thus my decision: I leave the volume to my estate, and if it sees the light of day, it is on my descendants.

On the other hand, I give myself this gift. Having wrung it out in my own mind, I have decided I will proceed with my project. Art is made from life or it is no good, and all this happened to me, so it's mine to use, even if I must force it into comedy to escape its darker implications. I will use the characters, the root situation, and avoid the slaughter: Distilled toward purity, it will be a tale of ambition, intellectual vanity, even relentless will, but also courage, the dignity of unfortunates, the wisdom of soldiers. It will end long before the murders begin, and to me at least, it will explain how such a thing could have happened. No one else will so understand. I will call it *Pygmalion*.

As for Dare, he lies undisturbed in the tunnel, if the tunnel lies undisturbed under the Anarchists' Club and hasn't been ruptured by the constant reconstruction of London. That I do not know. The fuss over his disappearance ended swiftly, and it seems he is forgotten, even if Jack, his creation, will never die. But that is a fraud, cake for the masses, so what difference does it make?

Indeed, only in one quarter does the memory of Thomas Dare persist, and it is not he that is remembered but the flavor of his flesh. For he can be commemorated only by his brethren, the other creatures of the dark Londontown Beneath, the black rats.

BIBLIOGRAPHY

Books, Journals, eBooks, and Web Articles

Ackroyd, Peter. (2011) *London Under: The Secret History Beneath the Streets.* London: Chatto and Windus.

Beadle, Bill. *Reinvestigating Murder: The Kelly Enigma. Journal of the Whitechapel Society.* http://www.casebook.org/dissertations/ws-reinvestigating-murder-kelly.html.

Begg, Paul; Fido, Martin; and Skinner, Keith. (2010) *The Complete Jack the Ripper A to Z.* London: John Blake Publishing, Ltd.

Begg, Paul and Bennett, John. (2012) *Jack the Ripper. CSI Whitechapel.* London: Andre Deutsch.

Bradshaw & Blacklock. (1888) Bradshaw's Continental Rail Guide. Bradshaw and Blacklock. Manchester. https://archive.org/details/BradshawsContinentalRailGuideSeptember1888.

Burns, Michelle. *Rippermania: Fear and Fascination in Victorian London.* http://www.casebook.org/dissertations/dst-rippermania.html.

Cornwell, Patricia. (2002) *Portrait of a Killer; Jack The Ripper Case Closed.* New York: G. P. Putnam's Sons.

Cullen, Tom. (1965) *Autumn of Terror: Jack the Ripper, His Crimes and His Times.* London: The Bodley Head, Ltd.

Dew, Walter. (1938) *The Hunt for Jack the Ripper. I Caught Crippen.* http://www.casebook.org/ripper_media/.

De Quincey, Thomas. (2013) *Confessions of an English Opium Eater and Other Writings.* Oxford: Oxford University Press.

Dickens, Charles. (1870) *The Mystery of Edwin Drood.* http://archive.org/stream /mysteryofedwindr00dickrich#page/n9/mode/2up.

Doyle, Arthur Conan. (2014) *The Man with the Twisted Lip.* Lexington: Kartindo Publishing House.

Eddleston, John J. (2010) *Jack the Ripper: An Encyclopedia.* London: Metro Publishing.

Emmerson, Andrew. (2000) *The Underground Pioneers: Victorian London and Its First Underground Railways.* Harold Weald, Middlesex: Capital Transport Publishing.

Evans, Richard J. *The Victorians: Art and Culture.* Gresham College, April 10, 2010. http://www.gresham.ac.uk/print/2611.

Evans, Stewart P., and Skinner, Keith. (2001) *Jack the Ripper: Letters from Hell.* Gloucestershire: Sutton Publishing Limited.

Evans, Stewart P. "Suspect and Witness—The Police Viewpoint." *Ripper Notes.* http://www.casebook.org/dissertations/rn-witness.html.

Gray, D. (2011) "Contextualizing the Ripper Murders: Poverty, Crime and Unrest in the East End of London, 1888." Invited Keynote presented to: Jack the Ripper Through a Wider Lens: An Interdisciplinary Conference, Bossone Research Enterprise Center, Drexel University, October 28–29, 2011.

Haggard, Robert F. "Jack the Ripper as the Threat of Outcast London." *The Annual Journal Produced by the Corcoran.* Department of History at the University of Virginia. http://www.essaysinhistory.com/articles/2012/90.

Harrison, Shirley. (1993) *The Diary of Jack the Ripper.* London: Smith Gryphon Limited.

Lambert, Tim. "Daily Life in 19th Century Britain." http://www.localhistories .org/19thcent.html.

Laurence, Dan H., ed. (1981) *Shaw's Music: The Complete Musical Criticism of Bernard Shaw.* London: The Bodley Head, Ltd.

London, Jack. *People of the Abyss.* 1903. The Project Gutenberg eBook. 2005. http:// www.gutenberg.org/ebooks/1688?msg=welcome_stranger.

Magellan, Karyo. "The Victorian Medico-Legal Autopsy Part I: Dissection in Pursuit of the Cause of Death." *Ripperologist.* http://www.casebook.org/dissertations /rip-victorian-autopsy.html.

———. "The Victorian Medico-Legal Autopsy Part II: The Whitechapel Murders— Autopsies and Surgeons." *Ripperologist.* http://www.casebook.org/dissertations /rip-victorian-autopsy-2.html.

———. "Cutthroat: A Detailed Examination of the Neck Wounds Sustained by the Whitechapel Murder Victims." *Ripperologist.* 61, September 2005, pp. 21–24.

———. Jack the Ripper: The Whitechapel Murders and Jack the Ripper. 2001–2006. http://www.karyom.com/index.htm.

McClain, Cherise; Dodd, Carl; and Rosenthal, Julian. Estimating Mary Kelly's Time of Death. *Ripperoo.* http://www.casebook.org/dissertations/ripperoo -todeath.html.

Moore, Alan, and Campbell, Eddie. (1999) *From Hell.* Paddington, Australia: Eddie Campbell Comics.

Morley, Christopher J. (2005) *Jack the Ripper: A Suspect Guide.* EBook. http://www .casebook.org/ripper_media/book_reviews/non-fiction/cjmorley/.

Osborne, Derek F. "A Curious Find in Goulston Street." *Ripper Notes.* http://www .casebook.org/dissertations/rn-curious.html.

Parris, Leslie, ed. (1994) *The Pre-Raphaelites.* London: Tate Gallery Publications.

Rosenthal, Julian. "Double Trouble: Elizabeth Stride and Catherine Eddowes." *Ripperoo.* http://www.casebook.org/dissertations/ripperoo-double.html.

Rumbelow, Donald. (1975) *The Complete Jack the Ripper.* Boston: New York Graphic Society, Ltd.

———. (1988) *Jack the Ripper: The Complete Casebook.* Chicago: Contemporary Books.

Sala, George Augustus. (1859) Victorian London—Publications—Social Investigation/ Journalism—Twice Round the Clock, or The Hours of the Day and Night in London. http://www.victorianlondon.org/publications/times.htm.

Segerdal, Alistair. Jack the Radical: How Gruesome Murders Activated the Strangest Left-Wing Campaign of All Time. http://www.fee.org/the_freeman/detail /jack-the-radical.

Shpayer-Makov, Haia. "Journalists and Police Detectives in Victorian and Edwardian England: An Uneasy Reciprocal Relationship." *Journal of Social History.* Vol. 42, No. 4, Summer 2009. http://www.thefreelibrary.com/Journalists + and + Police + Detectives + in + Victorian + and + Edwardian + England %3A . . . -a0202479941.

Smith, Robert W. "Predicting the Weather: Victorians and the Science of Meteorology." *Victorian Studies.* Vol. 48, No. 1, Autumn 2005.

Smithkey III, John. The Pubs of Whitechapel. http://www.casebook.org/victorian _london/dst-pubs.html.

Smyth, Jon. "A Piece of Apron, Some Chalk Graffiti and a Lost Hour." http://www.casebook.org/dissertations/dst-graffito.html.

Sugden, Philip. (2002 rev. ed.) *The Complete History of Jack the Ripper*. London: Constable and Robinson, Ltd.

The Whitechapel Society. (2011) *Jack the Ripper: The Suspects*. Stroud, Gloucestershire: The History Press.

Typewriters in the Early Office. Early Office Museum. http://www.officemuseum.com/typewriters.htm.

Vanderlinden, Wolf. Considerable Doubt and the Death of Annie Chapman. *Ripper Notes*. http://www.casebook.org/dissertations/rn-doubt.html.

Weather Conditions for the Nights of the Whitechapel Murders. Courtesy of Casebook Productions. http://casebook.org/victorian_london/weather.html.

Wilde, Oscar. (1891) *The Picture of Dorian Grey*. https://archive.org/stream/pictureofdoriang00wildiala#page/n5/mode/2up.

Journals and Newspapers

Daily News, London, 1888

Echo, London, 1888

Evening News, London, 1888

Ripperologist, Wood, Adam, exec. ed.

Ripper Notes, Norder, Dan, ed., and Vanderlinden, Wolf, assoc. ed.

Ripperoo, Rosenthal, Julian, ed.

Times, London, 1888

Daily Telegraph, London, 1888

Pall Mall Gazette, London, 1888

Star, London, 1888

Essential Web Sites

Casebook: Jack the Ripper. http://www.casebook.org

Jack the Ripper Forums. http://jtrforums.com/

The Victorian Dictionary. http://victorianlondon.org/

The Victorian Web. http://www.victorianweb.org/

Victorian Era England. http://www.victorian-era.org/

Jack the Ripper 1888. http://www.jack-the-ripper.org/

Wikipedia: Jack the Ripper. http://en.wikipedia.org/wiki/Jack_the_Ripper

LearningVictorians.http://www.bl.uk/learning/histcitizen/victorians/victorianhome
.html

CrimeLibrary:JacktheRipper.http://www.crimelibrary.com/serial_killers/notorious
/ripper/index_1.html

Whitechapel Jack: The Legend of Jack the Ripper. http://whitechapeljack.com/

Wiki: Jack the Ripper. http://wiki.casebook.org/

Metropolitan Police: Jack the Ripper. http://content.met.police.uk/Site/jacktheripper

BBC History: The Victorians. http://www.bbc.co.uk/history/british/victorians/

Historical Documents

Inquest: Mary Kelly. *Daily Telegraph*, Tuesday, November 13, 1888. Casebook:
Jack the Ripper. http://casebook.org/official_documents/inquests/inquest_kelly
.html.

Inquest: Mary Ann "Polly" Nichols, *Daily Telegraph*, Monday, September 3, 1888,
Page 3. http://www.casebook.org/official_documents/inquests/inquest_nichols
.html.

Inquest: Annie Chapman. *Daily Telegraph*, Tuesday, September 11, 1888, Page 3.
http://www.casebook.org/official_documents/inquests/inquest_chapman.html.

Inquest: Catherine Eddowes. *Daily Telegraph*, Friday, October 5, 1888, Page 3.
http://www.casebook.org/official_documents/inquests/inquest_eddowes
.html.

Inquest: Elizabeth Stride. *Daily Telegraph*, Tuesday, October 2, 1888, Page 3. http://
www.casebook.org/official_documents/inquests/inquest_stride.html.

Dr. Thomas Bond's Postmortem on Mary Kelly. http://www.casebook.org/official
_documents/pm-kelly.html.

Letter from Thomas Bond comparing the murder of Marie Jeanette Kelly (Mary
Jane Kelly) with four of the previous murders, and an assessment of the murderer (copy of same in MEPO 3/140, ff 220—223) http://discovery.national
archives.gov.uk/details/r/C6222011.

Web Articles and Pages Accessed

The "Jack the Ripper" Autopsy Reports. http://www.pathguy.com/jack.htm

Casebook: Jack the Ripper. Dr. Thomas Bond. http://www.casebook.org/witnesses /thomas-bond.html

History of the *Star*. http://thestarfictionindex.atwebpages.com/the.htm

History of England. London History. http://www.historyofengland.net/london -history

Learning Victorians. Victorians 1837–1901. Overview of Victorian Age. http:// www.bl.uk/learning/histcitizen/victorians/victorianhome.html

Learning Victorians. Victorians 1837–1901.The Working Classes and the Poor. http://www.bl.uk/learning/histcitizen/victorians/poor/workingclass.html

Learning Victorians. Victorians 1837–1901. The Rise of Technology and Industry. http://www.bl.uk/learning/histcitizen/victorians/technology/industry.html

Learning Victorians. Victorians 1837–1901. Health. http://www.bl.uk/learning/hist citizen/victorians/health/victorianhealth.html

Learning Victorians. Victorians 1837–1901. The Built Environment. http://www .bl.uk/learning/histcitizen/victorians/environment/builtenvironment.html

Learning Victorians. Victorians 1837–1901. Crime and Punishment. http://www .bl.uk/learning/histcitizen/victorians/crime/crimepunishment.html

Learning Victorians. Victorians 1837–1901. Transport and Communications. http:// www.bl.uk/learning/histcitizen/victorians/transport/communication.html

Learning Victorians. Victorians 1837–1901. The Middle Class. http://www.bl.uk /learning/histcitizen/victorians/middleclass/themiddleclass.html

Learning Victorians. Victorians 1837–1901. Popular Culture. http://www.bl.uk /learning/histcitizen/victorians/popculture/culture.html

The British Newspaper Archive. Newspaper Titles. http://www.britishnewspaper archive.co.uk/home/newspapertitles

Wiki: Jack the Ripper. September 1888. Elizabeth Stride. http://wiki.casebook.org /index.php/September_1888_Elizabeth_Stride

Casebook: Jack the Ripper. Press Reports. http://www.casebook.org/press_reports/

Jack the Ripper 1888. The Jewish East End—Immigration. http://www.jack-the -ripper.org/jewish-east-end.htm

The Public Domain and Review. A Dictionary of Victorian Slang 1909. http://public domainreview.org/collections/a-dictionary-of-victorian-slang-1909/

Victoria and Albert Museum. Victorians. http://www.vam.ac.uk/page/v/victorian/

Wikipedia: Victorian Poets. http://en.wikipedia.org/wiki/Category:Victorian_poets

The Samuel and Mary R. Bancroft Collection of Pre-Raphaelite Art. http://www.preraph.org/searchresults.php?rp=11&

Wikipedia. List of Nineteenth-Century British Periodicals. http://en.wikipedia.org/wiki/List_of_19th-century_British_periodicals

Jack the Ripper. Bruce Paley. A Bit About Myself and a Jack the Ripper Mystery. http://jacktheripper-brucepaley.blogspot.com/

The National Archives. Image Library. Crime. https://images.nationalarchives.gov.uk/assetbank-nationalarchives/

Crime Library. Jack the Ripper. http://www.crimelibrary.com/serial_killers/notorious/ripper/html

Demographia. England Largest Cities. http://www.demographia.com/db-ukcities.htm http://www.english.uwosh.edu/roth/VictorianEngland.htm

Victorian England. An Introduction. https://www.wwnorton.com/college/english/nael/victorian/welcome.htm

Poet Seers. Victorian Poets. http://www.poetseers.org/the-great-poets/victorian-poets/

The Proceedings of the Old Bailey. London, 1800–1913. http://www.oldbaileyonline.org/static/London-life19th.jsp

The Steampunk Forum. Telephones in the Victorian Era. http://brassgoggles.co.uk/forum/index.php?topic=37221.0

Saucy Jacky. A Ripper of a Site. http://saucyjacky.wordpress.com/victims-canonical-five/

Gian J. Quasar. Scarlet Autumn. Jack the Ripper and the Whitechapel Murders. http://www.bermuda-triangle.org/html/jack_the_ripper.html

Jack the Ripper. http://ripperthesis.wordpress.com

Stanford Encyclopedia of Philosophy. Karl Marx. http://plato.stanford.edu/entries/marx/

The Basics of Philosophy. Socialism. http://philosophybasics.com/branch_socialism.html

Darwin's Theory of Evolution and the Victorian Crisis of Faith. A Critical Reading of Dover Beach. http://hamiltoninstitute.com/darwins-theory-of-evolution-and-the-victorian-crisis-of-faith/

Victoria and Albert Museum. Victorian Circus. http://www.vam.ac.uk/content /articles/v/victorian-circus/

Music in the Victorian Era. http://shsaplit.wikispaces.com/Music_In_The_Victorian _Era

Early Office Museum. The Earliest Writing Machines. http://www.officemuseum .com/typewriters.htm

Hemyock Castle. Glossary of Money Terms. Official and Slang. http://www .hemyockcastle.co.uk/money.htm

ACKNOWLEDGMENTS

Ripperologists will note, I hope, that in most cases I have stayed well within consensus regarding the Autumn of the Knife. There are a few "willed" inaccuracies that I had to insert to sustain a dramatic structure. In acknowledging them, I hope to stave off penny-ante criticisms.

—Mr. Diemschutz said in testimony that he went in the side door of the Anarchists' Club, not the front door on Berner Street, as I have it. I had to move him out of the yard so that Jack could do what Jack did.

—The journey of the missing half of Mrs. Eddowes's apron was more complicated (and more tedious) than the streamlined version I have provided, but it came to the same thing. Readers should thank me.

—No evidence was ever encountered suggesting a tunnel from the Anarchists' Club.

—Contra my account, the newspapers paid no particular attention to Annie's missing "wedding rings." Also, all the headlines and news copy are of my own invention.

In one area I am apostate. That is the method of Jack's attack on his first four victims. Consensus has decided that he knocked them to the ground first, muffled their screams with his left hand, and cut their throats, beginning under the left ear, with his right.

I believe, as I have dramatized here, his angle was directly frontal; he faced his victim as if to purchase service and attacked suddenly with a sideward snap of arm and wrist and essentially drove the blade into the throat under the ear in a vicious chop, then rotated about the stricken woman to draw it around as he eased her to the ground. I hope to find a forum to say more on this issue at a later time.

Now on to thanks. Lenne P. Miller was instrumental in the composition of *I, Ripper*. He researched it to breadth and depth, as the bibliography should make clear, and he read, reread, and rereread the manuscript, hunting for the errors someone as notoriously sloppy as I am is prone to make. It took at least three drafts for me to figure out how to spell "teetote." If the book is as remarkably accurate as I believe it to be and as accurate as any fictional account, that's because of Lenne. If there are mistakes, that's because of me.

I should also mention the remarkable website Casebook: Jack the Ripper. Scrupulously maintained and scrupulously fair, it provided quick answers to basic questions and deeper answers to deeper questions, and gave me the sense that someone was watching over me. Hope the boys enjoy what I've done with their labors.

Besides his research, Lenne also came up with a great idea for the plot, which helped me keep it ticking along. Mike Hill, another good friend, pitched in with a keen idea, very helpful. I am notoriously prone to ignoring other people's ideas, if I can even summon the patience to listen to them, but in these two cases, the ideas were so good, and so much better than anything I had or would come up with, I had to acquiesce. Guys, the check is in the mail.

One of the early champions of my take on Jack was James Grady, the thriller writer and a good friend; his enthusiasm actually carried me for years while I tried to work out a way to tell the story as it had occurred to me in a flash one night. Bill Smart was another early and vociferous backer, and his enthusiasm was such a help. Any writer stuck in a plot hole or a character swamp or an editor jam knows how much it helps to have a guy who'll back you up, pull you out, tell you you're the best (even if it's not true!), and send you on your way. Bill was that guy for me.

Others include usual suspects Jeff Weber and Barrett Tillman. Newcomers (but old friends) were Frank Feldinger, Dan Thanh Dang, who supplied me with a crucial woman's view of the proceedings, and Otto Penzler. Walt Kuleck, author of the *Owner's Guide* and *Complete Assembly Guide* series of firearms books, provided invaluable expertise on a host of non-firearms issues. David Fowler, M.D., the Maryland Medical Examiner and a friend, advised on technical issues. My great friend Gary Goldberg kept the technical aspect of the operation going brilliantly. Someday he'll have to explain to me exactly what "digital" means. My wife, Jean Marbella, brewed 240 pots of coffee, which got me up and got me upstairs. My thanks to them all. I am a fortunate man to have such folks in my circle.

One question you might have: Steve, since you've done all this research for a novel on Jack the Ripper, do you know who he really was?

My answer: Of course I do. Watch for it. It's going to be fun.

ABOUT THE AUTHOR

Stephen Hunter has written twenty novels. The retired chief film critic for *The Washington Post*, where he won the 2003 Pulitzer Prize for Distinguished Criticism, he has also published two collections of film criticism and a nonfiction work, *American Gunfight*. He lives in Baltimore, Maryland.